DEVIL'S DOMINION

A MEDIEVAL ROMANCE

BY KATHRYN LE VEQUE

KATHRYN LE VEQUE NOVELS

Medieval Romance:

The de Russe Legacy:
The White Lord of Wellesbourne
The Dark One: Dark Knight
Beast
Lord of War: Black Angel
The Falls of Erith

The de Lohr Dynasty:
While Angels Slept (Lords of East Anglia)
Rise of the Defender
Spectre of the Sword
Unending Love
Archangel
Steelheart

Great Lords of le Bec:
Great Protector
To the Lady Born (House of de Royans)

Lords of Eire:
The Darkland (Master Knights of Connaught)
Black Sword
Echoes of Ancient Dreams (time travel)

De Wolfe Pack Series:
The Wolfe
Serpent
Scorpion (Saxon Lords of Hage – Also related to The Questing)
Walls of Babylon
The Lion of the North
Dark Destroyer

Ancient Kings of Anglecynn:
The Whispering Night
Netherworld

Battle Lords of de Velt:
The Dark Lord

Devil's Dominion

Reign of the House of de Winter:
Lespada
Swords and Shields (also related to The Questing, While Angels Slept)

De Reyne Domination:
Guardian of Darkness
The Fallen One (part of Dragonblade Series)

Unrelated characters or family groups:
The Gorgon (Also related to Lords of Thunder)
The Warrior Poet (St. John and de Gare)
Tender is the Knight (House of d'Vant)
Lord of Light
The Questing (related to The Dark Lord, Scorpion)
The Legend (House of Summerlin)

The Dragonblade Series: (Great Marcher Lords of de Lara)
Dragonblade
Island of Glass (House of St. Hever)
The Savage Curtain (Lords of Pembury)
The Fallen One (De Reyne Domination)
Fragments of Grace (House of St. Hever)
Lord of the Shadows
Queen of Lost Stars (House of St. Hever)

Lords of Thunder: The de Shera Brotherhood Trilogy
The Thunder Lord
The Thunder Warrior
The Thunder Knight

Time Travel Romance: (Saxon Lords of Hage)
The Crusader
Kingdom Come

Contemporary Romance:

Kathlyn Trent/Marcus Burton Series:
Valley of the Shadow
The Eden Factor
Canyon of the Sphinx

The American Heroes Series:
Resurrection
Fires of Autumn
Evenshade

Sea of Dreams
Purgatory

Other Contemporary Romance:
Lady of Heaven
Darkling, I Listen

Multi-author Collections/Anthologies:
With Dreams Only of You (USA Today bestseller)
Sirens of the Northern Seas (Viking romance)

Note: All Kathryn's novels are designed to be read as stand-alones, although many have cross-over characters or cross-over family groups. Novels that are grouped together have related characters or family groups.

Series are clearly marked. All series contain the same characters or family groups except the American Heroes Series, which is an anthology with unrelated characters.

There is NO particular chronological order for any of the novels because they can all be read as stand-alones, even the series.

For more information, find it in **A Reader's Guide to the Medieval World of Le Veque**.

This novel is dedicated to my wonderful husband, Rob, who puts up with me when I go into the writing cave for weeks on end. It's also dedicated to my wonderful friends who do the same thing – watch me go into the writing cave and wait patiently for me to come out again and interact with the normal world.

Lastly, it's dedicated to my fabulous editor, Scott Moreland, who goes above and beyond every time.

And to my readers… it's dedicated to you, too! Without you, none of this is possible!

Hugs,
Kathryn

TABLE OF CONTENTS

PROLOGUE

1179 A.D., Late Fall
Four Crosses Castle
Welsh Marches

"THE GATEHOUSE HAS been breached!"

The small lad heard his mother issue the words, such panic pouring out of her mouth that it was difficult to understand her. Terror vomited out of every pore in her body. But the small lad understood little of what was causing her such fear. All he knew was that he and his sister and mother had been locked up in the keep of Four Crosses Castle, a castle that had belonged to his family for generations, for two straight days. Food was running in short supply and he had been hungry all day because of it. A little bread and cheese was all his mother had been able to give him and his sister that morning and they'd had nothing else since.

He also knew that there was a great siege going on, great projectiles and war machines trying to break down the walls of Four Crosses, and they couldn't chance opening the keep in any fashion, not even to accept the wounded that had been shoved into the stables, stables that were now burning. The wounded were burning even as men struggled to move them out of the stables, filling the air with the heavy, greasy smell of burning human flesh.

But the young lad didn't know what the smell was; he just knew it made his nose wrinkle up. It also made his belly ache, like he wanted to vomit forth but couldn't. After two days of little food, there wasn't much to come up anyway.

"Come, Bretton," Lady Brethwyn de Llion grasped her five year old son by the arm, pulling the boy along as she ran for the chamber door. Her daughter, two years older than Bretton, delayed them slightly by going to grab her poppet, causing her mother to scream. "Ceri, *come*! Come now!"

The little girl scrambled after her mother and brother, following them out of the chamber and down the dark, narrow stairs that spiraled to the next level. There were servants on that level, waiting for them in the darkness, men and women who were weeping and whispering fearfully. Once Lady de Llion reached the group, she gestured frantically to the small hall off to the left.

"Down into the kitchens below and out through the postern gate," she hissed. "Hurry! There is no time to waste!"

She dashed off, dragging her children along behind her as the servants followed in a panic. It was a great rush into the small hall with its tall hearth and hungry dogs, and on to the trap door cut into the floor that led by ladder to the kitchens below. The trap door had been propped up, tied off with a piece of rope to hold it firm. Lady de Llion put her children on the ladder first, helping them down, as the servants hovered around them and pushed their way onto the ladder once Lady de Llion followed the children.

Even though they had been frenzied, the group had been orderly until a great banging was suddenly heard upon the keep entry door. Like terrified animals, everyone froze for a moment, listening, realizing quickly that it was the enemy army attempting to break their way into the keep. Order dissolved and the servants began shoving each other out of the way, making their way down the ladder, pushing and falling through the hole into the kitchens below. One of the servants, an old man who tended Lord de Llion, fell on top of Ceri.

The little girl was nearly crushed beneath him and Lady de Llion screamed, kicking the man off her daughter and gathering the child into her arms. Ceri was nearly unconscious, badly injured, and cried out when she tried to breathe because it hurt. Lady de Llion was beside herself as she kneeled on the dirt floor, clutching her child against her.

"You fool!" she screeched at the servant, who had broken his arm in the fall. "You have killed her! Damn you!"

The old servant was weeping at what he had done, holding his broken arm against his body in a painful gesture. Bretton stood next to his mother, watching the situation with big eyes, having no real idea what had happened but knowing now that the ordeal was becoming increasingly frightening. They were running, running from something terrible. It was something terrible that they had feared for two days and the terror was tangible now, worse than ever. He could nearly taste it. He wanted his father, a man upon whom all things calmed and comforted. He missed him. He tugged on his mother's arm.

"Mama?" he asked. "Where is Papa?"

Lady de Llion wept, clutching her daughter in one arm and reaching for her son with the other. She thrust the boy towards an older woman.

"Rosalie, take him," she begged. "Take him and run. Take him far, far away from here and do not return, no matter what. Do you understand me?"

The older woman with the missing teeth grasped the boy, who was more intent on staying with his mother. In fact, he fought against the older woman for the privilege.

"Aye, my lady," the older woman said, finally picking the boy up, who was kicking and screaming. "But you must come. Stand up and carry the lass! We will all help you!"

Lady de Llion held her little girl tightly, who now had bright red blood about her lips that were turning shades of blue. She was gasping for every breath, growing weaker by the moment.

"Nay," Lady de Llion sobbed. "She is… my sweet Ceri is dying. And my husband! He is dead, too!"

One servant broke away from the group and threw open the bolt of the heavy iron door leading out into the kitchen yard beyond as the others hovered around Lady de Llion.

"My lady, *please*," the woman holding Bretton begged. "Come with us!"

Lady de Llion had already given up the fight. She wasn't a strong woman in the best of times and now, with the great jaws of defeat snapping at her, she was more inclined to surrender than to resist. She shook her head violently, her wimple coming loose and spilling forth dark hair.

"There is no hope," she muttered. "De Velt has won. He has put my husband to the stake and soon he will put me to the stake. But I cannot allow it, do you hear? I will not!"

With that, she stood up, carrying her daughter with her, and moved to the butcher block that stood big and heavy in the center of the kitchen. All manner of butcher knives hung from an iron frame overhead and she grabbed a long, slender, and wicked-looking knife that was used to filet meat from the bone. Without hope, without any comfort or sanity whatsoever, Lady de Llion plunged the knife into Ceri's small chest, stilling the little girl forever. As the servants screamed and moved to stop her, she turned the knife on herself.

Bretton saw the entire incident. It was surreal, beyond the comprehension of the small child, and he was too shocked to utter a sound. He just stared at his sister as her blood ran bright red upon the dirt of the kitchen, mingling with his mother's blood from a slit throat. It was a horrific scene, but one not unknown in the annals of a de Velt attack. Whenever the man took the offensive, he left no living body in his wake.

Bretton only had a few moments of seeing his mother and sister in their blood bath before Rosalie was stealing him from the kitchen, racing through the dark and bloody night to the postern gate that led down the eastern slope of Four Crosses, down a narrow and treacherous path, through thickets of trees, to a stream below that fed into the castle's water supply. Others followed in her wake.

It was dark down there, shielded from the castle above by a thick canopy of branches overhead. Bretton, the shock of his mother and sister's death sinking deep, had begun to weep but Rosalie put her hand over his mouth to still the sound. They could hear men behind them, de Velt's men, and they were desperate to quiet the boy. The group of refugees plopped into the stream, following its path as it ran through the vale, hiding their tracks from those who would follow. Rosalie carried Bretton until the boy grew heavy and then she passed him to another man, the castle smithy, who carried the sniffling lad for another hour until they felt safe enough to clamor out of the stream.

It was a desperate flight in the dead of night, feeling de Velt's death-grip that had come upon them all. The land was hilly and rough here and the small group struggled through it with only a sliver moon above to light their way. The smithy, in the lead, ended up on a goat path that wound its way up a small mountain to a relatively flat summit. They had to gain their bearings in this dark land, to determine where to go to safety, but a sight on the eastern horizon caught their attention.

They could see flames in the distance, atop a mountain, and they knew that it was Four Crosses Castle. De Velt didn't normally burn the castles he confiscated so the refugees of Four Crosses could only imagine that someone, mayhap Lord de Llion himself, had set the castle ablaze. There was no way of knowing who had actually caused the blaze, but one thing was certain: Four Crosses Castle, as they knew it, was gone forever, destroyed by a man whose bloodlust was second only to his evil. Satan himself trembled in fear of Jax de Velt and his apocalyptic destruction. No man survived it. Those who stood on the mountaintop, watching the flames in the distance, knew they were among a very select few. God had been with them this night because they, in fact, had survived.

Gentle tears filled the cold night air, tears from the few women who now realized they were alive, now realized they were homeless. It was much to bear. As the servants began to discuss what they should do now, where they should go, Bretton stood and watched his castle burn.

His papa was there, his mother and sister, too. All he loved was burning before him. He was sad, terrified, and overwhelmed with the course the night had taken. He wasn't sure what to feel any longer. He was simply numb, as numb as a child could be. All he knew was that a man had caused all of this horror and destruction, a terrible man of terrible reputation, and that man's name was de Velt. *Ajax de Velt.* It was a name seared into his brain, never to be forgotten.

It was a name he learned to hate. Hatred would breed revenge. Even at his young age, he could feel an unalterable sense of vengeance.

CHAPTER ONE

The month of May, 1205 A.D.
Alberbury Priory
Shropshire, England (the Welsh Marches)

THE ALARM HAD come after Vespers when everyone was settling down for the evening and soft prayers were being uttered throughout the cloister. The flames from a few lit tapers danced in the darkness, casting shadows upon the wall, tapers that were quickly doused by nuns who were in a panic. Women in coarse woolen garments had raced through the priory, spreading fear along with them like a great, vast blanket of doom. Something terrible had come to their door, something that did not recognize the sanctity of the church, and the only thing left for them to do was flee. Their only defense, the shield of religion, had been destroyed. Death had come to Alberbury.

In the novice's dormitory that smelled of lye and smoke, a palpable sense of terror filled the long and cavernous room as the Mother Prioress and several senior nuns flooded in, rousing the neophytes from their beds. These women were in training to become the brides of Christ, living spartan lives and being taught that discipline and suffering were the only true paths to God. Clad only in a rough woolen sleeping shift that they had made with their own hands from wool that had come from the priory's herd of sheep, the young women struggled out of their beds.

"What is the matter, Mother?" a young woman gasped. "What has happened?"

The Mother Prioress, a very old woman who was, in fact, a distant member of the royal family, grabbed the girl by the arm and very nearly yanked the limb out of its socket.

"No questions," she hissed. "Thou must do as thou art told. We must leave this place now."

The reply only bred more fear and confusion. "Please, Mother," another girl said as she gathered a worn cloak from the stool next to her. "Will you please tell us what has happened? Why must we leave?"

The old prioress didn't look at her charge. In fact, she didn't look at any of them. There were eleven altogether, young women from the finest families throughout England, and it was her duty to keep them safe. But it was a duty that she could quite possibly fail at and the thought scared her to death. The proud old woman had never failed at anything. As she opened her mouth to chastise yet another question, a massive crash could be heard back in the abbey, as if the very walls were coming down. The young novices looked terrified while the older nuns simply appeared sick; sick because their world, their lovely and pious world, was about to come crumbling down around them.

"God's Beard," the girl who had asked the initial question gasped. Her eyes were wide with fright. "What on earth was that?"

The prioress eyed her associates a moment before answering. "A plague has come to Alberbury," she whispered, grabbing two of the girls closest to her. "We must flee now or we will not survive. Doest thou understand?"

The girls could feel the woman's terror, mingling with their own, and it was enough to get their legs moving. It was so dark, however, that one girl tripped over the nearest bed, falling to her knees before being pulled up by her friends. Together, the group of four nuns and eleven novices headed for the rear entrance to the dormitory. It was a chaotic and hectic flight, and as one of the older nuns brought up the rear, hanging on to a small young woman with golden hair, she began to mutter.

"The Devil has come to our door," she hissed. "Satan himself has emerged from the darkness and now he intends to feed upon us. We will become fodder for his demons."

The novice nuns looked to the old woman, fear and confusion on their faces, but the Mother Prioress scolded her.

"Sister Mary Josepha, silence!" she breathed. "Thou speaketh nonsense. Keep thy lips closed for if thou must murmur, be it a prayer to God."

The older nuns' squabbling was nothing new. It happened constantly and the novice nuns were unmoved by it. As they ran, however, one young woman kept glancing over her shoulder, seemingly above the panic for the moment. She seemed to be calculating the situation, pondering it more than the others. She was afraid, that was true, but she was also trying to figure a way out of it, if such a thing were possible.

"But where will we go?" the young woman with dark hair and bright green eyes wanted to know. She was a pale, delicious beauty with a sharp and inquisitive mind that often saw her knuckles rapped as a result of that outspoken intelligence. "If men are trying to burn down the priory, it would stand to reason that they have more than likely compromised the village down the hill. We cannot go there and there is no safe haven left for miles around."

The Mother Prioress hissed at the woman. "Silence, Allaston Eugenia," she demanded. "We will head to the creek and hide amongst the grass and trees. Remember thy Bible; let the rocks and the trees be my army. They will protect us."

Lady Allaston Eugenia Coleby de Velt wasn't entirely sure the old prioress was correct but she kept her mouth shut. It seemed to her that they needed to do more than simply hide in the bushes. They needed to get far, far away, but not knowing the area particularly well, for she grew up in Northumberland, she wasn't at all sure where they should go. Still, it seemed as if the old prioress was being foolish. There had to be more they could do than shield themselves in the bushes and pray they were not discovered. But she was at a loss to know exactly what that "more" should be.

So she followed the group of women, stumbling through the dormitory door that led into the cloister and out across the well-kept dirt of the gardens. The prioress' accommodations were directly in front of them, a dark and loveless building, and they skirted the one-storied structure, heading for the rear of the priory and the open fields beyond. The moon, a silver sliver in the blackness of the sky, provided little light. Everyone was tripping and scuffling as they went.

The smell of smoke was heavy as they moved and they could hear the shouts of men and the bray of animals coming from the east and south sides of the priory, the areas that were mostly exposed to the road and the world beyond. Although there were fifteen in their small group, there were at least thirty more nuns who were still unaccounted for, women who had either already fled or were foolishly hiding in the priory. At the moment, there was no way to hunt for all of them, so the Mother Prioress had gathered who she could. Fifteen out of a total of forty-five nuns was a dismal statistic but it was the best they could do under the frightening circumstances.

Allaston was towards the rear of their group as they made their way around the prioress' lodgings. She was helping Sister Mary Josepha with a young woman, not a particularly healthy young woman, who was having trouble running. The girl was wheezing and coughing with the exertion.

"Please, Annie," Allaston begged softly. "You must be brave. You must hurry. We must run!"

Annie was having a great deal of difficulty. "I am trying!" she gasped, tears in her eyes. "But I am so frightened, Allie. Who would attack a priory? It is a house of God and meant to be safe from all!"

Allaston shushed her because she knew the Mother Prioress would only yell at poor Annie for sounding so weak. The Mother Prioress did not like weak women. "Evil men have attacked us," she said simply. "In the end, it does not matter who it is. All that matters is that we must get away from them."

Annie was bordering on sobs, made difficult by her heavy breathing. "What will become of us?" she wept. "Where will we be safe?"

Allaston didn't have an immediate answer for her friend, trying to think of something positive as the group came around the corner of the prioress' lodgings. All that lay before them now was dark, open fields and the creek beyond with its copse of trees and heavy foliage. Before Allaston could speak a word, however, those in the front of the group came to an abrupt halt, causing those in the rear to crash into them. Allaston ended up on her behind as the group of hysterical women came to sudden stop.

Allaston had very narrowly avoided hitting the wall of the structure with her head as she went down. Grunting, she picked herself up and her gaze happened to fall on the Mother Prioress and the fields beyond. She was looking to see what had caused everyone to come to a dead stop and as her eyes adjusted to the dark night, she realized that the fields normally filled with sheep were now filled with men. Hundreds of them.

Terror filled her as she realized there would be no safety in the trees and rocks tonight. That which they had been attempting to flee was now surrounding them, like something dark and evil and smothering. Men with torches had been waiting for them, waiting for their quarry without effort, and if Allaston had been any wiser about warfare she would have realized that the commotion at the front of the priory had been designed to drive the inhabitants out of the back and right into a trap. The tactic had worked. They were all snared.

Some of the young women broke into tears at the sight of all those soldiers. Allaston stood up, a big mud stain on her rump, holding on to Annie as more men on horseback began to surround them. They could hear crying and pleading in the distance as several other nuns were brought around from the front of the priory, now joining the group of fifteen. It was more terror than any of them could bear and they huddled together in a frightened mass.

Behind them, there was a good deal of commotion going on as the big priory began to go up in flames. Men were purposely throwing torches through windows to ignite the interior of the structure and great rolling flames could be seen billowing out of the windows near the chapel, lighting up the night. But at the rear of the priory, an army was gathered around the group of frightened nuns, waiting and hovering over the women like vultures waiting for the kill. As everyone seemed to stand around in tense and terrible silence, the Mother Prioress stepped forward.

"Who art thou?" she asked loudly, though her voice was trembling. "Who wouldst sully our sanctuary with fire and terror this night?"

No one replied right away, but one warrior on a beast of a warhorse separated himself from the group. The horse was scarred and nicked, wearing mail across its neck and hindquarters. The warrior dismounted the horse and moved towards the tiny, bird-like prioress, like a hunter stalking prey. There was something heavy and terrible about the way he moved, his massive boots hitting the earth like great hammers against an anvil, reverberating through the dirt itself.

Even if the prioress hadn't been a small woman, any woman or man or child would have appeared small compared to the size of the warrior that faced them. Several inches over six feet, he had massive shoulders, arms, and enormous fists the size of a man's skull. Clad in well-used mail that grated wickedly when he walked, he wore a heavy leather tunic over the mail and a broadsword at his side that was almost as tall as the prioress herself. It probably weighed more than she did, too. His helmed head tilted slightly downward, the only indication he was looking at the prioress.

"Who are *you*?"

The voice that emerged from the closed helm sounded like Death; it was deep and raspy. If the Mother Prioress felt terror at the sound, she didn't show it. She bravely lifted her chin in response.

"I am the Mother Prioress of Alberbury," she said. "What is thy wish? Why hast thou done these terrible things?"

The helmed head didn't move. He was fixed on the Mother Prioress. "You have a de Velt here," he said. "Where is she?"

The Mother Prioress struggled not to look confused or intimidated by the fact that the man was asking for a woman in her charge, asking for her by name. It was enough to crack her composure.

"A de Velt?" she repeated, puzzled. "How wouldst thou know this?"

"It does not matter how I know," the enormous warrior replied. "I have come for her. Where is she?"

The Mother Prioress stared at him, shocked by the request. But it began to occur to her that this was not a random attack. This man wanted something and he wanted it badly enough to ransack a church to get to it. Apprehension clutched at her but she fought it off. She had never been one to give in to apprehension, anyway. It was an unfamiliar taste upon her tongue.

"What doest thou wish of her?" she asked. "The lady is under my care and we are protected by God. Thou cannot have her."

The helmed head tilted slightly. "In case you have not noticed, God did not save your priory from my army," he said. "I suspect he will not protect any of you if you do not provide me what I came for. I want the de Velt."

Fear began to spread through the women and a few of them turned to look at Allaston, although no one singled her out. Still, heads were moving about, including Allaston's. She was terrified that this man, a man who had shown no fear in burning a house of God, had asked for her. *You have a de Velt.* Dear God, how would he even know that? More importantly, *why* did he want her? She struggled not to let fear consume her as she watched the exchange between the warrior and the prioress with a good deal of dread. It was an effort not to shrink back into the shadows because she knew that any movement would single her out. It was imperative she remain still and unnoticed.

The Mother Prioress, however, held firm and did not reveal Allaston's presence. She might have been a proud woman who ridiculed the weak, but she was also inordinately strong. She wasn't about to permit this warrior, as bold and deadly as he seemed, to gain the upper hand. She didn't like to be told what to do.

"Rubbish," she snorted. "You shalt not have her and since thou hast burned our home, thou will permit us to leave and seek shelter elsewhere."

The helmed head didn't react at first. There was a long and tense pause, one filled with mounting terror as far as the women were concerned. Then, the warrior shifted on his enormous legs and the helmed head leaned forward as if to better peer at the stubborn old woman.

"Do you mean to actually *deny* me?" he asked, a hint of incredulousness in his tone.

The old prioress nodded firmly. "Thou shalt not have what thou hast come for," she said firmly. "I shalt not give thee any woman in my charge. Be gone with thee."

The helmed head didn't hesitate. One of his massive hands shot out and grabbed the prioress around the neck as the women behind her let up a collective scream. As the women wept and shrieked, the warrior pulled the old woman very close to his helm.

"If you do not give her to me, then I will kill you," he hissed. "When you are dead, I will move to the next woman and demand she give me the de Velt. If that woman denies me, then I will kill her and move to the next one until I am either given the de Velt woman or every one of your nuns is dead. Is this in any way unclear?"

The old prioress was struggling for air. Her vision was dimming but there was fight left in her. She would not be bullied even if it cost her everything. She was far too stubborn to submit and show fear.

"Then kill me," she rasped. "I will not give thee the woman."

The knight squeezed and an audible snap could be heard as he broke the prioress' neck. The nuns began to howl, tightening up their ranks in a fearful huddle as a few knights joined their leader and swarmed upon the nuns, grabbing women and pulling the group apart. It was clear that they intended to separate the women, perhaps to intimidate them in order to gain their wants. Surely one of them would break and tell them what they wished to know.

Allaston stood near the wall with Annie, watching the knights harass the weeping nuns. She was horrified that the leader had killed the Mother Prioress. It has been so quick that they had scarcely believed what he had done until the prioress was lying on the ground in a heap. Allaston had never seen anything so awful in her life.

But the sight of the woman's body jolted Allaston. She knew that she could not let these women protect her any longer. It would only get all of them killed. True, she was fearful for her own life but she was not so cowardly that she would let others die protecting her. But she simply couldn't turn herself over, nay. As stubborn and proud as the prioress had been, Allaston was equally stubborn. Sometimes she was foolish, too. She hoped this would not be one of those times. She had to help everyone, including herself. *She had to fight!*

"Stop!" she roared, pushing between the women that were standing in front of her. "Stop this instant! I am the de Velt!"

The knights, five of them including the one who had killed the prioress, came to a halt in the midst of their assaults. Seeing she had their attention made Allaston second-guess her bravery, but there was no turning back. She faced them with as much courage as she could muster.

"I am Lady Allaston de Velt," she said, her voice trembling. "What do you wish of me?"

The knight who had killed the prioress seemed to be looking at her. It was hard to tell with his visor down, but she was certain he was fixed on her. Before he could move, however, Annie, who had been standing next to Allaston, piped up.

"*I* am Lady Allaston de Velt," she said, breathing heavily and coughing. "I am the one you want."

Shocked, Allaston looked at her to shush the woman but suddenly, other women were shouting out that they were Allaston, too. Soon, the entire group was demanding that they were Lady Allaston de Velt and there was no stopping the onslaught. Shouts and cries filled the smoky night air.

Allaston was terrified of what the knights would do to them now that it was clear the women were intent on protecting her. She could see necks being broken by big, gloved hands and it filled her heart with fear for her loyal friends. Panic-stricken, she lifted her hands and began to cry out.

"Nay!" she called. "Nay, you will not do this! Please, cease! Do you not see that they will kill all of us? They will think us to be liars!"

Some women listened to her, some didn't. The ones who seemed most intent on disobeying her were the older nuns, crying out that they were, in fact, the de Velt that the knight was looking for. Allaston had never been so touched by anything in her life, all of these women prepared to sacrifice themselves for her, and the humbling experience drove her to tears. She simply couldn't let them do it. Frantically, she began waving her hands around.

"*Stop!*" she cried, moving away from the group as she did so. "Please stop! I am not afraid, do you hear? I am not afraid of him!"

She nearly screamed the last part and most of the nuns quieted down. Terrified, emotional, Allaston turned to the massive knight with the intimidating helm.

"I swear that I am Lady Allaston de Velt," she insisted, hear heart pounding and her breathing coming in frightened gasps. "These women are simply trying to protect me. Please… tell me what you wish of me, but do not harm them. I beg you."

The knight still hadn't said a word. His helm was turned in her direction and suddenly, he was moving towards her. He closed the gap rather swiftly, reaching out to grab her harshly by the arm. Allaston gasped in pain as the knight flipped up his visor, his shockingly bright blue eyes boring into her.

"You had better be the de Velt I seek or this situation will not go well for you," he hissed. "Convince me that you are who you say you are or I will kill everyone here, including you. Tell me now!"

He was growling and snarling, and Allaston was so frightened that she felt faint. But she took a deep breath, struggling to compose herself, as she looked into eyes that were the color of cornflowers. She'd never seen such a bright shade of blue. Her mind was so much mush, overwhelmed with fear, but she fought to clear it. She had to.

"My… my father is Ajax de Velt," she said, her voice quaking. "My mother is Lady Kellington. I have three brothers and two sisters, and we live at Pelinom Castle in Northumberland."

The knight's grip tightened, nearly breaking her arm. "Name your siblings," he growled. "Quickly!"

She jolted because he shook her to emphasize the speed at which he expected her to deliver the answer. "My eldest brother is Coleby," she said, verging on tears but fighting against them with every breath. "I have two more brothers, Julian and Cassian. My sisters are Effington and Addington. They are younger than I am."

The knight's eyes were blazing, but that blaze was as cold as ice. It was a deadly glare, something Allaston had never seen before, but she began to suspect that she must have given him the right answer because his grip hadn't tightened. Nor had he otherwise displayed displeasure. In fact, his expression seemed to ease. His features, as much as she could see them through the helm opening, had relaxed. After several anxious moments, the eyes flickered in a calculating gesture.

"How old is your father now?" he asked.

Allaston swallowed hard. "I… I am not exactly sure," she said. "I believe he has seen fifty-eight or fifty-nine years."

"Does he still go to war?"

She shook her head unsteadily. "Nay," she replied. "He has not gone to war since I have been alive. I have never known my father to fight."

That seemed to surprise the knight, for his eyes flickered and she thought she saw confusion in the mysterious depths. There was puzzlement at the very least.

"How old are you?" he asked.

"I have seen nineteen years."

The knight's sense of confusion seemed to increase. "Your father has not gone to war in nineteen years?" he asked as if astounded by the mere thought. "But he is a warlord. How is that possible?"

Allaston wasn't sure what all of these questions were about, but as long as she continued answering him, the knight seemed to remain calm. She was determined to keep him calm.

"I do not know," she said. "He... he did do some warring before I was born. I know because my mother told me, but I have never known the man to fight, even when his liege called for aid. My father sent his men but he did not go."

"Who is his liege?"

"Yves de Vesci, Earl of Northumberland."

The knight just stared at her. His grip seemed to lessen as he pondered her words, but the confusion in his expression was soon replaced by suspicion.

"Your father is the most wicked warlord ever to walk the earth," he finally said. "His atrocities are legend. Surely you know this."

Allaston was perplexed by the path of the conversation but she was afraid to say the wrong thing. His grip on her arm had lessened, that was true, but she was positive it would grow brutal again the moment she said something he didn't like. She could see it in his eyes, an edginess that bordered on madness.

"I have heard of my father's past," she said honestly. "My mother has told us... things. But he has not done that in over twenty years."

The knight just stared at her. It was apparent that the entire conversation with her had him seriously mystified. Allaston gazed back at him, waiting for the next barrage of questions and fearful that she would say something to displease him. He'd already proven he would kill with the slightest provocation. She didn't want to become his next victim. After several long seconds of staring at her, of perhaps mulling over his next move, his grip on her tightened once again and he dragged her over to one of the knights standing nearby. He thrust her at the man.

"Take her," he ordered. "No harm will come to her. Is that clear?"

The knight reached out and grabbed Allaston by the arm. "Aye, my lord."

He began to walk away with her in his grip but Allaston dug her heels in. "Wait," she said anxiously, craning her neck over her shoulder to look at the big knight. "Where are you taking me?"

The knight with the bright blue eyes didn't answer. He simply flicked his hand at the knight holding Allaston and the man yanked on her, pulling her away and back towards the bulk of the army. The knight with the bright blue eyes watched her go, watching her as she disappeared into the darkness and contemplating his next move. It wasn't long in coming. He crooked a finger and motioned to the nearest knight.

"Find me one woman and one woman only," he said. "Make sure she is sane and speaks clearly. I have a message for her to deliver."

The knight with the big scar across his lip nodded. "Aye, my lord," he said. "And the others?"

The big knight's gaze moved to the priory behind them, now burning solidly. Heavy, dense smoke spit into the night sky and the fire was spreading. Soon, it would hit the dormitory where the women had come from. He didn't want to leave an entire herd of witnesses, witnesses who could come back to haunt him in more ways than he could comprehend. He was a man who tended to eliminate anything, or anyone, who could contest or oppose him. He was a man who had learned a long time ago the value of a human life; there was none.

"Take them back into the church and lock them in," he said, his voice low. "Make sure the doors are secured so they cannot get out. The fire will do the rest."

The knight with the scar nodded smartly and went on his way, muttering the orders to the other knights and a few soldiers standing nearby and, together, the group of them began herding the women back towards the burning priory. The women, realizing that they were being corralled to their doom, began to wail and plead for their lives. Before the big knight turned back for his charger, he saw a couple of his soldiers grab two or three of the women and pull them away from the pack. As he mounted his horse, he could hear the screams of those women being raped.

It made no impression on him. Nothing in life ever did. He had a mission and he had since he'd been five years of age. Nothing was going to stop him in his quest to see his mission completed and now he had what he had come for. After years of planning, of suffering, and of hard work, his scheme was about to come to fruition as he'd hoped. He finally had a de Velt.

Now, he would set the trap.

CHAPTER TWO

Lioncross Abbey Castle
Hereford, Welsh Marches
Three weeks later, the month of June

T HE EARL OF Hereford and Worcester was a man known through-out England. Much like William Marshal or Hubert de Burgh, Christopher de Lohr had the reputation of power, wisdom, and connections to the crown but, unlike the other two, when it came to the de Lohr dynasty, there was much more fear and admiration in the mix. The man, and his brother, David, had seen much service in the name of Richard, much of it in The Levant and in France, and that made them more experienced warriors than most. The de Lohr war machine was legendary.

It was a legendary status that came with responsibility, however. The de Lohrs had held the Marches for years, and quite ably, so when there was trouble along any stretch of the Welsh Marches, all roads seemed to point to de Lohr as a source of aid. However, the most recent trouble experienced along the northern stretch the Marches in Shropshire was something different from the usual raiding or isolated skirmishes. This had the earmark of conquest, much as a similar surge several years ago had. As Christopher had read the missives from the north, from the Earl of Shropshire no less, he couldn't help the sense of foreboding that had swept him. He didn't want to think about the potential for another devastating surge against the borders, but that's exactly what this seemed to be. What's more, Shropshire seemed to put a name to all of the chaos – de Llion. Christopher had recognized the name and immediately sent for someone he suspected might have more information on it.

Christopher sat on Shropshire's missive for eight days, the time it took for him to send a missive to Whitebrook, in Wales, and for the man he sent for to make his way to Lioncross. But once that man appeared, Christopher had convened all of his knights with the exception of his brother, who was in Kent, to discuss the missive from Shropshire.

It was a bright afternoon in late May when de Lohr assembled his men in his richly appointed solar in the bowels of Lioncross. The old castle had stood on that location longer than any other structure on the border. It had once been a Roman outpost and a church before it had been incorporated into a castle. Therefore, the walls around them held more of a sense of experience and doom than most.

All of them men could feel it, particularly the man that had ridden from his home in Wales just due west of Gloucester. Sir Rod de Titouan, a handsome man with black hair and lively blue eyes, wasn't exactly sure why he had been summoned by the great de Lohr, but he knew it couldn't be good. Something was brewing and Christopher evidently wanted him to be a part of it. Having arrived from Wales only an hour before, he was seated in the solar with a cup of good wine and a platter of food at his fingertips. The knights who wandered in to join him in their wait for de Lohr were all men he had fought with. He liked seeing his old friends again.

"De Titouan," Edward de Wolfe, Christopher's right-hand man, smiled warmly at Rod as he entered the room. A tall man with golden-hazel eyes, he was brilliant and politically savvy, and it was rare that Christopher made a move without him. He reached out to clap Rod on the shoulder. "It has been a long time since I last lay eyes upon your ugly face."

Rod grinned. "A year, at least," he said. "It was last February, I believe. I have been fifteen months without your hideous hide and I have considered myself blessed."

Edward laughed loudly and moved to take a second cup of wine from the pitcher on the table next to Rod. "Blessed, indeed," he scoffed. "You have missed me terribly. Admit it."

Rod, still grinning, took a long drink of wine. "Never," he said staunchly. "But, because I do not wish to see you weep like a woman, I will say that I *am* somewhat pleased to see you."

Edward clinked his earthenware cup against Rod's, in a toasting gesture. "As am I," he said quietly, taking a long drink. "How is it at Bronllys Castle these days?"

Rod shrugged. "I spend my time between Bronllys with my grandfather and Whitebrook with my mother," he said. Then, he sobered dramatically as sad memories came to the forefront. "She is not the same since Rhys' death, you know. Nothing brings her comfort except for Rhys' son. Maddoc seems to be the only one she will warm to these days. My father is very worried for her."

Edward's expression softened. "Your brother was a great man," he said, deep sorrow in his tone. "I still cannot believe… that is to say, I keep expecting him to walk through the door at any moment. The man was so big and powerful and vital. I cannot accept that he is gone. I cannot accept that Lawrence is gone, either. That raid on Ludlow last February was a particularly devastating one. We lost two of the best knights I have ever known."

Rod nodded faintly, thinking on his older brother, Rhys du Bois. He was his half-brother, actually, a massive man of uncanny strength and skill. Last year, Rhys had been entrusted with a mission of vital importance and ended up falling in love with the woman he had been sworn to protect. He has lost his life trying to keep her safe. At least, that was the story everyone knew. The accepted truth was that Rhys and his lady-love had died after being captured by opposing forces, but the reality was something much different. The only people in the entire world who knew the real story were David de Lohr and Rod, and they would take that secret to the grave with them. The secret was that Rhys, in fact, had not died on that misty morning. He had escaped, as had the lady, and were now living in anonymity in France. But, in a sense, Rhys du Bois had died that day, at least, the man they remembered had.

But Rod shook himself from that secret, fearful that he might say something to inadvertently suggest he knew something more to the story. Instead, he sought to change the subject and tried not to be too obvious about it.

"I miss Lawrence," he said, pouring himself more wine. "As frightening as the man was, I still miss him."

Edward was back to smiling, a lopsided gesture. "He was as gentle as a kitten," he said, "provided one did not anger him."

Rod was back to smiling also as he drank his wine, glad to be off the subject of his brother. "True enough," he said. "Now, tell me, why am I here? What has happened that the great and mighty de Lohr has sent for me?"

It was a given fact that whatever Christopher knew, Edward knew, so Edward didn't try to brush off the question. In fact, he thought to give Rod a bit of a warning so that he wouldn't be blindsided by Christopher's interrogation. Setting his wine cup down, he drew up the nearest chair.

"Trouble in Shropshire," he said quietly. "We received word from Robert de Boulers, Earl of Shropshire, that there is a mighty army sweeping through his lands, conquering or destroying everything in their path. They laid siege to Clun Castle and Knighton, badly damaging the castles and stripping them of nearly everything of value before moving to the Marches and taking Cloryn Castle. Then, they moved north where they raided Dolforwyn Castle, moved north into Shropshire, and burned Alberbury Priory to the ground."

Rod was looking at him with great concern. "*Burned* Alberbury?" he repeated, incredulous. "God's Teeth, what army *is* this?"

Edward was grim. "Mercenaries from what we are told," he said.

"The army has literally come out of nowhere, although there is rumor that they came by cog from Ireland and landed in Liverpool. They went south from there and ended up on the Marches."

Rod's eyebrows lifted. "*Irish* mercenaries on the Welsh Marches?" he spoke in disbelief. "Are we certain of this?"

"Nay, not entirely certain. It is only rumor."

It was startling information. Rod grunted. His astonishment was evident. "We have heard of the siege of Cloryn Castle," he said. "It is north of Bronllys Castle, about a two days' ride, and we heard from a passing merchant that the castle had been taken but he did not know by whom. This is the first I have heard of a mercenary raiding party moving along the Marches and it is definitely the first I have heard of a priory being burned."

Edward was shaking his head. "This is no ordinary raiding party," he said softly. "There is a pattern to this madness, evidently. De Boulers has been watching it closely because most of the activity has been along his borders, but Cloryn is not that far from where we sit. Therefore, Chris is watching the activity closely as well. This not only affects Shropshire but it affects Hereford as well. Think about it, Rod; Cloryn Castle taken? Clun and Knighton raided? Sweeping onward towards Montgomery and Powis? Think on your history, man. We have seen this before. What does this say to you?"

Rod thought very hard on the question but before he could answer, the solar door opened and a massive man stepped into the room.

Christopher de Lohr, Lord Warden of the Marches, Earl of Hereford and Worcester, looked directly at Rod as he entered. A massive man with a crown of thick blond hair and a neatly trimmed blond beard, he indeed resembled a lion. His nickname during the time of Richard had been the Lion's Claw because he had been Richard's champion. Much of the politics of England during Richard's reign had been directly attributed to de Lohr and his ability to hold the throne for a king who had spent very little time in England. Even now, as the man stood in the room, it was as if he had sucked all of the air out of it. One was left to gasp in awe. Men such as de Lohr were living legends.

"Rod," Christopher said, greeting the man with an outstretched hand, which Rod rose to take in friendship. "The last time I saw you, it was in battle in the snow. You are looking considerably warmer."

Rod shook his hand firmly before releasing it. "Thank you, my lord," he said, eyeing Edward. "Mayhap I am warmer, but de Wolfe thinks I have only grown uglier. I will grant you that I am not as handsome as my brother was, but I suffer not when it comes to feminine attention."

Christopher grinned, revealing straight, white teeth. "Edward has always been jealous of your beauty, so pay him no attention," he teased. "The sons of Orlaith de Llion are beauteous lads, indeed."

Rod laughed softly. "My mother is a beautiful woman, so that would stand to reason," he said. "Although I believe my father might claim some credit, at least for me and my younger brother. We are de Titouan, after all. De Llion is only on my mother's side and they tend to be a motley bunch."

Christopher nodded, a grin on his lips, but he soon sobered. There was no more time for pleasantries as far as he was concerned. "I heard Powis and Montgomery mentioned as I came in the door," he said, shifting the focus to the subject of Rod's visit. "I would assume that Edward has told you about the missive from de Boulers?"

Rod sobered as well, reclaiming his seat as Christopher confiscated a chair near the hearth. "He has," Rod said. "I have not heard of most of this, except we did hear about Cloryn Castle."

Christopher eyed Edward. "Did you tell him everything?"

Edward shook his head. "Only of the pattern of destruction," he said. "We did not discuss anything beyond that."

Christopher grunted, collecting his thoughts for a moment. When he spoke, it was with the intrinsic seriousness of a man who had seen much death and destruction in life.

"Since Edward has told you the gist of what has gone on, I will come to the crux of it," he said. "There is a mercenary army raiding through the mid-Marches following the pattern that Ajax de Velt set out twenty-five years ago when he blew through the Marches and confiscated six castles and burned countless others. I was not at Lioncross Abbey during that time and my wife, who grew up here, does not remember the fear of that time because she was too young, but I have spoken with local lords who well recall that terror. De Velt, as you know, was like nothing England or Wales had ever seen. The man was from the depths of Hell itself in both tactics and ferocity."

Rod's expression was very serious. "I know," he said. "I remember it, too, simply because my mother's brother was the garrison commander of Four Crosses Castle at the time. That is up north, towards Powis Castle, if you recall. I remember my grandfather, my mother's father, speaking of de Velt impaling his son on a spike for all to see and leaving the man's body at the entrance to the castle for about six months before they finally took him down and buried him. My uncle had a family as well, a wife and two children, but they were lost in the destruction. The entire family was killed and my grandfather still harbors the hatred and fear of that time. I have heard him speak of it."

Christopher's gaze lingered on the man, thoughts rolling through his sky-blue eyes as he looked steadily at Rod. He chose his next words carefully.

"There is now another army doing the same thing de Velt did," he muttered. "Only this army has done something de Velt did not do – burn Alberbury Priory. But they did not burn it at random. They went there with a goal in mind."

Rod was puzzled. "What goal?"

Christopher sighed heavily. "De Velt's oldest daughter was there, a novice nun," he said, his tone filled with dread. "This army took the girl and burned the priory, killing everyone inside. But they left one old nun alive to deliver a message, which was picked up by de Bouler's men."

Rod was completely shocked at the news. "God's Beard," he hissed. "What message could that be?"

Christopher glanced at Edward before continuing, as if the two of them held a great secret that was about to be unfurled.

"The army that took de Velt's daughter is essentially inviting de Velt to come and get her," he said. "It is a challenge, a summons, if you will. The army that took her has retreated to Cloryn Castle from what we are told and there they wait. Cloryn, as you recall, is an impenetrable fortress but they somehow managed to reclaim it and kill de Velt's garrison commander in the process."

Rod thought on that event, sighing heavily and scratching his dark head in thought. "De Velt's commander had to be a very old man," he said. "In fact, de Velt still controls five remaining castles along the northern Marches. All of de Velt's commanders, at least the ones that originally confiscated the castles, must be quite old by now."

Christopher nodded faintly. "Old indeed," he agreed softly. "De Boulers and I have discussed such things in the past. He believes the original commanders are no longer in control and that second generation de Velt men hold the castles."

"No one knows for sure?"

Christopher shook his head. "No one has approached those castles since they were originally taken," he said. "It is well understood to give them a wide berth. Even the Welsh will not go near them, fearful of bringing down de Velt's wrath."

Rod pondered that information. "But someone *has* approached them now, or at least has approached Cloryn," he said. "Whoever has done this obviously does not fear de Velt if he has taken the man's daughter and now uses her for bait."

Christopher had been mulling over just that fact for the past several days. He stroked his blond beard in thought. "This army… these men… are not from this land," he said. "Rumor says they are from Ireland, but de Boulers says they are mercenaries of the worst degree, men who feed on money and blood. Their commander, however, does not have an Irish name. He gave his name to the old nun as Bretton de Llion."

Rod stared at the man as his words sank deep. There was a very long and tense pause. But once realization dawned, Rod's eyes widened and his mouth flew open. Before he realized it, he was on his feet.

"Bretton *de Llion*?" he repeated, shocked.

"Aye."

"Are you *sure*?"

"Aye."

"But that… that is not possible!"

Christopher remained calm. "Why not?"

Rod was seized with disbelief. "Because Bretton de Llion is the name of the lad who perished when Jax de Velt destroyed Four Crosses Castle and killed my mother's brother," he nearly shouted. "He was my mother's brother's son – my cousin!"

Christopher watched Rod, who had a naturally passionate nature, work himself up into a lather. "I thought he might be related to you," he said evenly. "That is why I called you here – to see if you knew the name. I see that you do."

"Of course I do!" Rod exclaimed. "It is the name of my dead cousin!"

"Was his body ever found?"

Rod's mind was wild with the possibilities. "Nay," he said, dazed. "The castle was burned, the bodies burned. We only knew of my uncle because my grandfather never gave up hope that the man had survived and only found out well after the fact that he had not, nor had his family."

Christopher glanced at Edward, who took up the cause. "It is possible that the lad escaped, Rod," Edward said, taking the man's attention off Christopher. "If there was no body, then there is no confirmed death. It is quite possible he has survived and has now returned for revenge against de Velt."

Rod could hardly believe what he was hearing. He looked at Edward in utter and complete shock. "Are you suggesting that my cousin, whom we believed to have been murdered as a child by Ajax de Velt, has somehow come back to life?" Rod couldn't decide if he was more startled or outraged by that thought. "It is pure madness, de Wolfe!"

"Stranger things have happened," Christopher said softly. "You cannot discount anything. Certainly, the leader of this mercenary army could have assumed Bretton's name, but why? To what purpose? And what man other than someone who has spent his entire life stewing over the death of his family at the hands of de Velt would have the drive and hatred to go on a rampage like this and seek revenge against the very man who destroyed his loved ones? It makes perfect sense."

Rod was looking at Christopher with his mouth hanging open. Now that the initial shock and outrage had passed, he was clearly over-whelmed. In fact, he was weak with it. He plopped back into his chair and took his cup of wine, draining the entire thing.

"Oh, God," he breathed, pouring himself another measure. "This is madness, all of it. To say that Bretton has returned and is seeking vengeance against de Velt... dear God, is it even possible?"

Christopher sat forward, his razor-sharp gaze drilling into Rod. "Sometimes the dead aren't truly dead," he said softly. "They *can* return."

Rod returned the man's stare, realizing in that moment that Christopher was speaking of his brother, Rhys. Rod didn't know just how he knew that, but he did. He sensed it. Everyone believed Rhys to be dead even though he wasn't. Somehow, someway, Christopher knew the truth. It was in his tone, his expression, and his words. Perhaps David had told him. It was the only explanation and Rod knew the man was in on their secret as surely as he was living and breathing. *De Lohr knows!*

But this wasn't about Rhys. It was about Bretton, and with that awareness, Christopher's words came to make a great deal of sense. *Sometimes the dead aren't truly dead.* Aye, anything was possible. The more Rod thought about it, the more he realized that de Lohr was correct. Anything *was* possible.

Oddly, that mindset seemed to calm him. The wave of hysteria had rolled over him, leaving still waters in its wake. Not completely calm, but still nonetheless. Rod looked at Christopher, choosing his words cautiously.

"Possibly," he finally murmured. "But this is fantastic to say the least."

Christopher held Rod's gaze a moment longer before averting it as he rose from his chair. "Incredulous and amazing," he agreed. "But it is not impossible. There would be no other reason for the leader of the mercenary army to give the name of Bretton de Llion if he was, in fact, not Bretton. Why would he? It would serve no purpose. In my experience, the man gave his name because he wanted to be known. He wanted de Velt to know that one of his former victims was back to seek vengeance."

It made perfect sense. Rod, however, was still reeling. He drank the last of the wine in his cup, struggling to come to terms with what he had been told. He looked up at Christopher as the man moved to pour himself some wine.

"Then why am I here?" Rod asked. "What would you have of me?"

Christopher poured rich, red wine into an earthenware cup. "I wanted you to know the contents of Shropshire's missive," he said quietly, turning to face Rod with cup in hand. "I truly have no idea what is happening near my borders but it bears watching. My greatest concern at this point is that de Velt will respond to the challenge and if that occurs, we may once again be facing a horrendous bloodbath along the Marches greater than anything we have ever seen. De Velt is not dead. The man lives in Northumberland and he has, over the years, been quite generous in making restitution to those he wronged. He has donated heavily to several priories, Alberbury being one of them, and he holds a portion of the Scots border for King John. The Scots are not foolish enough to cross the border that de Velt defends. Bear in mind that, as I say this, de Velt still has a big army and I am quite sure this abduction of his daughter will not go unanswered. That is my greatest fear because if de Velt moves into Shropshire's lands, and consequently my lands, I will be forced to answer. I do not want to be sucked into a war against de Velt."

Rod knew that. He sighed heavily. "Bronllys Castle, my grandfather's castle, is only a few miles from Erwood Castle, which is a de Velt holding," he said. "It concerns me a great deal that this… this *mercenary* army would possibly try to reclaim all of de Velt's holdings. That would put us too close to the action and we'd suffer from the fall out."

It was evident that Rod couldn't bring himself to say Bretton de Llion's name, at least not now. It was still too new and shocking, all of it. Christopher could see how shaken the man was.

"That is why I wanted to tell you all of this personally," he said. "Not only because of the name of the commander of this army, but also because you must return to tell your grandfather what has transpired. It might be wise to vacate Bronllys and move south to Whitebrook until this matter has settled."

Rod shook his head. "My grandfather will not leave his post," he said what they all knew. "He is an old knight and has been there for over twenty years. He will never leave it."

Christopher watched the man's expression, seeing sadness and resignation there. "Then I would ask that once you inform your grandfather of what is happening, you return to me," he said. "Losing Lawrence and Rhys last year has left me low on trained knights. True, I have de Wolfe and Max Cornwallis, and I even have Jeffrey Kessler, who was my wife's family's captain of the guard before I married her, and I also have a stable full of young and strong knights, but I could use a seasoned commander like you."

Rod knew it was not a request. It was a kind way of saying de Lohr was demanding his services. "I understand, my lord," he said, "but my grandfather may have need of me, especially if I cannot convince him to leave Bronllys."

Christopher grew more impassioned. "That is exactly why I need you with me," he said. "I have the largest army on the Marches and if de Velt moves, *if* this mercenary army moves, my army will be the first to engage them. Mayhap we can prevent them from getting to Bronllys. Do you see what we are facing, Rod? With de Velt provoked, this could be the resurgence of something more deadly and bloody than England has ever seen."

Rod was coming to see that and the truth was that it scared him. Not much in this life scared him, but this did. Perhaps the only way to help his grandfather, or even his family, was to remain with de Lohr. After a moment, he nodded his head.

"Very well," he said. "I will remain with you until this crisis is over. But let me return to Bronllys to tell my grandfather. He must be on his guard."

Christopher couldn't disagree. In fact, he was in full support of it. "When you tell your grandfather, will you speak of Bretton de Llion's apparent return?" he asked. "I am not entirely sure how much good that will do your grandfather to know that. There is nothing he can do about it in any case."

Rod shrugged, thinking of how his grandfather might react to such news. "I am not sure what to tell him," he said. "Knowing my grandfather, he would ride to Cloryn Castle to see if the commander really is Bretton and more than likely get himself killed in the process. But, on the other hand, he lost a grandson last year and he has not recovered from it. Mayhap... mayhap it will do him some good to know that it is possible another grandson has returned from the dead."

"A returned grandson who is tearing up the Marches and murdering nuns?"

Rod merely shrugged again. He didn't have an answer. Christopher drank his wine, mulling over the situation in general, as he turned for his seat near the hearth. Somewhere outside of the solar door he could hear a baby crying, reminding him of his family safe within these old walls. Walls that could face a beating if the Marches were consumed by the flames of warfare. He didn't like the thought.

"Let us hope we all live through this," he muttered, lowering his bulk into the chair. There was gentle fire in the hearth and he gazed at it a moment, deep in thought. "There was something else that de Llion told the old nun, something interesting."

Rod looked at him. "What was that?"

Christopher was still staring at the flames. "He told her to tell de Velt that the Devil was coming for him."

Edward grunted at the arrogance of the statement. "There is a very old proverb that says it is better to be the right hand of the Devil than in his path," he muttered, interjecting his opinion into the conversation. "In this case, however, I have no desire to side with Satan. I do not even wish to side with de Velt."

Christopher looked up. "There is another saying, from the Bible, and it is all I can think of at the moment," he said. "Somehow, it seems very prophetic for this situation."

Edward glanced at him over the top of his cup. "What is it?"

Christopher's attention returned to the flame, seeing death and destruction within the flickering embers. He simply couldn't help the feeling of doom in his heart. "Behold a pale horse," he murmured, "and his name that sat on him was Death. And Hell followed with him."

They sat in silence after that until the wine was gone and the fire died out. Even then, they continued to remain, each man lost to his own particular thoughts of disaster. No matter which side of the Marches one was sitting, the Devil seemed to be approaching from all sides.

And Hell would undoubtedly come with him.

CHAPTER THREE

Cloryn Castle
Welsh Marches
Three long weeks.

WELL, AT LEAST she thought it had been three weeks because she had scratched off every passing day on the wall with a small rock. It had been three weeks since she had been abducted from Alberbury Priory and taken to an unknown castle and put into a vault that was dank, dark, and dirty. Moss grew on the stone like green slime and there was a constant water drip against one of the walls, puddling up on the floor and giving everything a terribly moldy smell. It also made Allaston sneeze and she had been doing little else since being locked up in this dismal hole. It was a horrible, depressing place.

She had a bed of old straw to sleep on and a few rough blankets that smelled like horses, so she assumed they were for the livestock. Normally, she would have shunned such things, for she grew up in a house where she wanted for nothing. Her parents had spoiled her, just as they had spoiled all of their children, but the past year had seen her attitude for finery change dramatically. The nuns of Alberbury had pushed thoughts of material pleasures right out of her mind, which had been difficult considering how overindulged she had been. Her pride, and tastes, had been a difficult thing to contain, but now, sitting on her bed of straw and covered with horse blankets, she found she had no pride at all in material things. If she hadn't the blankets, she would have frozen to death so she was grateful for what she had, however raw.

Three weeks. Those words kept rolling around her head because she was fearful that she was going to spend the rest of her life down here in the darkness. Since the cell had no window, she really only knew the number of days from the meals she had been brought. She was given food to break her fast and then a small supper every night, usually consisting of terrible leavings from what looked to be bigger feasts. She was given the scraps. Hungry as she was, she ate them.

Allaston hadn't seen the blue-eyed knight since the day she had been brought to this place and locked away. The only people she saw were soldiers as they brought her food, and those soldiers spoke with Irish accents. Two of them did, anyway, which confused her but she didn't dare strike up a conversation with them to ask them where they were from. They didn't seem to be the conversational type.

So she sat and waited, but waited for what, she didn't know. She had no idea why she was even here and she had long since gotten over being terrified for her plight. No one had hurt her or had even tried to in spite of the face that she was a prisoner. She was cast into the vault and left alone, forgotten. She was positive she was forgotten.

Until the morning of the nineteenth day of captivity. She had slept a miserable night, cold and hungry, and the sneezing she'd suffered from since her arrival had turned into a cough. Her head was stuffy as was her chest, and her throat felt as if it was on fire. As she lay on the straw, shivering, she heard the iron grate at the top of the stairs open. The stairs led down from the gatehouse into the vault and she could hear heavy bootfalls on the stone as someone descended. She assumed it was a soldier bringing her some food but she was too weary and ill to sit up. Besides, there was no reason to eat if she was going to spend the rest of her life in a dank cell. The quicker she hastens her death, the better. She didn't want to live like an animal for the rest of her life and from her perspective, she couldn't see any way out. She was trapped.

So she lay there, unmoving, as someone came to her cell door. She heard the bolt being thrown and the door as it was jerked open. Because of the moisture in the vault, the oak door tended to swell and stick. Big, heavy footsteps entered the cell.

"Get up, woman."

It was a deep, raspy voice. Allaston had heard it before. Startled, her head popped up and she struggled to sit up as her eyes fixed on a man of enormous proportions. He was clad in a leather tunic, woolen breeches, and massive boots, and she would have had no idea who the man was except that she recognized the vibrant blue eyes. They were the eyes of the knight who had burned Alberbury.

Stunned, Allaston managed to sit up enough so that she was on her arse, but the entire time her focus was riveted on the man before her. He had black hair, cropped short, and a square jaw beneath a sprouting beard. His neck was thick and muscular, just like his shoulders, and his arms were easily as big around as her torso. She'd never seen such size. True enough, he'd been covered with tunics and mail the night they had met and she had attributed that to his colossal size. She was coming to see, however, that the man was simply big in general. The mail and other protection didn't make a significant difference in his overall bulk. He was, simply put, built for the raw brutalities of warfare.

The knight stood in the cell, filling it up with his fearsome presence. His gaze was steady upon Allaston as she stared back apprehensively.

"We must speak on a few things," he said in that rumbling, hoarse voice. "I am assuming that three weeks in this hole has not dulled your sense of reasoning. I am assuming we may carry on an intelligent conversation or has the mold gone to your head?"

Allaston shook her head, her fear turning into disgust at his callous attitude towards her current situation. It was in his tone, in everything about him. He couldn't have cared less for her state of being. She should have known that from the three weeks he had left her in the vault, but hearing him speak was the ultimate confirmation. In fact, the more she looked at him, the more disgusted she became. He was heartless, cold, and evil, and biting her tongue had never been one of her strong points. She spoke before she could stop herself.

"What kind of man would keep a woman locked up in this... this beastly place?" she asked. "I have committed no crime yet you treat me as a criminal. Why have you done this to me?"

The knight's gaze remained even. Slowly, he cocked his head. "I suppose it is natural that you want to know who I am and why you are here," he said. "That is a fair expectation."

"Fair?" she repeated, her tone bordering on incredulous. "What would you understand about fair? Fair is not locking an innocent woman away in a horrible, moldering cell when she has done nothing to warrant it. How have I wronged you that you would abduct me from Alberbury and lock me away?"

It was a snappish tone she used, one of rebuke. Her abhorrence toward him was evident, but the knight's expression didn't change.

"I would suggest you not speak to me in such a fashion," he said evenly. "You might not like my reaction."

Frustrated, furious, Allaston sighed harshly and turned away. She couldn't stomach looking at the man any longer. She started coughing, struggling with the illness that was sweeping her, and trying not to succumb to the depression that grasped at her like cold, knowing fingers. Those fingers knew she could be easily snared given her circumstances. As Allaston grappled with her emotions, she could hear the knight's joints popping as he shifted on his big legs.

"My name is Bretton de Llion," he said, his raspy voice low. "I was born in Wales at a castle called Four Crosses. It is north of our location, near Powis Castle. When I was five, a great plague swept through the Marches, destroying everything in its path. Castles were burned, men put to the stake and murdered, and babies crushed. The plague soon came to Four Crosses and killed my father, my mother, and my sister. That plague had a name – Ajax de Velt."

Allaston, who had been facing away from him, remained still as his words sank in. Even when the full impact hit her, she didn't look at the man because, suddenly, everything was coming clear. Now, she understood why he had taken her from Alberbury without benefit of further explanation. Aye, she understood a great deal now.

As she'd know on that bloody, terrible night when Alberbury burned, the knight, now given the name of Bretton de Llion, had come to the priory with a purpose. He had been seeking a de Velt, but the mystery had been his purpose. Now, he had revealed it. Allaston was no fool. She could smell vengeance upon the still air of the cell. She knew what her father had done those years ago. Her parents had never hid the fact, although the man Jax de Velt was today was quite different than the man he was years ago. The man back then had been an animal. This knight, this big and horrible knight, was out for vengeance against that animal. Allaston's depression deepened.

"Just kill me now and be done with it, then," she muttered. "That is why you took me from Alberbury, is it not? To kill me? Then do it and let us be done with this madness."

Bretton continued to stare at her. He was very good at remaining impassive. "Who said anything about killing you?" he asked. "I do not intend to kill you, at least not at the moment."

Allaston sighed heavily. "Is that so?" she asked, turning to look at him with dark-circled eyes. "If you do not intend to kill me, then you must intend to punish me somehow for what my father did to your family. That is the only reason I am here, is it not? I will say again that if you intend to torture me, get on with it. Your hesitation and your mind games do not impress me. If you are going to make me suffer, then do it."

Bretton met her gaze without flinching. It was difficult to tell if she had angered him with her slander against his behavior because he hadn't reacted one way or another. The man had a good deal of self-control. That much was clear. After a moment, he folded his big arms across his chest.

"I am not intending to impress you or tease you," he said. "But you wanted to know why you are here. Now you know."

Allaston shook her head, her dark hair stringy and dirty along her cheeks. "You have told me that my father killed your family," she said, "but you have not told me *why* I am here. What do you intend to do with me?"

She had a point. Bretton cocked an eyebrow. "That should be obvious," he said. "I intend to use you to get to your father."

Allaston stared at him then she burst out in weak, taunting laughter. Illness and fatigue had weakened her manner and she found she had little control over what she said. She felt so terrible that it didn't matter any longer. She'd spent three weeks in this hellish hole. The only way out was death and she was coming to welcome it. She was so very, very tired.

"Is that it?" she asked. "You intend to use me as bait? Lure my father to his doom? He is too smart for that and too smart for you. You have wasted your time, knight, and now you would waste my life with your foolish plan. He will never come. You will have to think of something else if you plan to engage my father."

Bretton didn't react for a moment and Allaston didn't particularly care one way or the other. She coughed heavily after the laughter faded and averted her gaze once more, too sick to give in to the fear that had clutched at her these many weeks. Now that she knew why she was here, it all seemed so foolish and wasteful. As she lost herself in a powerful coughing fit, Bretton broke from his stance.

One minute he was standing near the cell door and in the next, he was unsheathing a sharp dirk that was strapped to his left forearm. Allaston saw the flash of the knife as he descended on her, flinching away from him just as he grabbed her hair. He snatched the entire bunch of her dark hair, which hung loose to her knees and, looping the mass in his fist, he used the dagger to cut through the loop and therefore cut off about two feet of her hair.

Allaston gasped as she watched the man come away with a big fistful of her hair. She grabbed at her remaining strands to see how much he had cut off and was met by blunt-cut ends that were about the length of her buttocks. Her hair had been very long before and was now just simply long, glorious strands of liquid silk. Her eyes flew to Bretton accusingly and he met her gaze, as impassionate as always.

"We shall see how foolish my plan is when your father receives your hair as proof that I hold his daughter captive," he said, sounding rather confident. "We shall see if that brings him to my doorstep."

Allaston was furious that he had cut her hair. "It will *not*."

"We shall see."

"And if it does not?"

Bretton cocked a dark eyebrow. "Then mayhap I shall use you as a concubine," he said, watching her pale cheeks flush red. "What could be worse to the almighty de Velt than to have his daughter a slave of an enemy? I shall impregnate you, again and again, and teach my sons to hate their grandfather. I shall breed an army of warriors against Jax de Velt from the loins of his own daughter."

Allaston was overwhelmed with the horror of his suggestion. "You cannot," she hissed. "I am destined for the Church. I am to be a Bride of Christ!"

Bretton cocked his head, a thoughtful gesture. "A bride, aye," he said slowly. "But not of Christ. Mayhap I will wed you myself, a further insult to de Velt. I will send the bloody bed linens from our wedding night to him to show him that I have taken his flesh and blood as my own, to do with as I will. And you still do not think that will bring the man to my doorstep? Think again."

Allaston gazed at him with more hatred than she had ever experienced. In fact, she was wild with it.

"I will kill myself before I let you touch me," she snarled. "You will lose your bait, your captive… you will lose everything!"

Bretton had little doubt that she meant what she said. "Mayhap," he said quietly, eyeing the woman. "But I would not worry about taking your own life. Whatever illness you have will more than likely kill you before you can take a dagger to your throat."

Allaston nodded with great flourish. "One can only hope," she said. "As long as I am dead before I have to feel your filthy hand against my flesh, that is all I am concerned with."

Bretton actually cracked a smile, thin and without humor. "Then I will have to take you before you rot away from whatever is killing you," he said. "I prefer my women pliable. The only way you will be pliable is if you are too ill to fight back."

Allaston's hatred was turning to rage. "Touch me and you will regret it," she hissed, "for I will fight you to my dying breath."

He didn't doubt her for a minute.

È

IN THE GREAT hall of Cloryn Castle, men were settling down for the evening. The hall was older, with a great fire pit in the center of the room rather than a hearth in the Norman fashion, and smoke billowed up to the ceiling and hung about in great clouds before escaping through several roof vents in the thatching. It was long and skinny, with a dirt floor and four massive feasting tables in various positions around the room. It was a big enough room for de Llion's entire army of twelve hundred men. Rough, crude, brutal mercenary soldiers that lived life moment by moment rather than day by day. Such were the uncertainties of their world.

Soldiers that were currently celebrating another victory in a campaign that had been full of them. After the destruction of Alberbury Priory, Bretton and his army of Irish and Germanic mercenaries had moved south to Ithon Castle, a rather small but important outpost and they had succeeded in breaching it. The garrison commander, a son of one of Jax de Velt's greatest generals, had been killed along with his wife and three daughters. Bretton hadn't shed a tear throughout the event and, when everyone was dead, he had decapitated the dead commander and had sent the head with one of his soldiers to Jax de Velt's residence in Northumberland. By his estimation, ten days after Ithon's destruction, de Velt should have the head. De Velt should already be concerned with what was happening to his Welsh properties.

That was how de Llion wanted it. The nun left alive to deliver a message, the daughter of his greatest enemy kidnapped and languishing in the vault… aye, that was how Bretton wanted it. All of this was quite calculated and, so far, had gone according to plan. Bretton, as well as his hired men, were pleased. But Bretton couldn't take the time to savor the victories. He had a schedule to keep and it was that schedule that occupied his thoughts as he made his way into the loud, smoky great hall. As he approached one of the big tables where his commanders were gathered, one of them, a big man with a bald head and big teeth, lifted a cup to him.

"Another castle is ours, Bretton," the man had a heavy Irish accent. "That is cause for much celebration."

Bretton sat down on the bench opposite the man. There was a pitcher of cheap red wine and a few cups within his reach and he took a vessel, filling it to the rim.

"Aye," he agreed, almost modestly. "Ithon is indeed ours and now staffed with my men. My messenger should have reached Northumberland by now and I suspect de Velt is looking at the head of his garrison commander and wondering what in the Hell has happened."

There were three other commanders at the table in addition to the big, bald one. One commander, with a shock of wild blond hair and big arms, pounded the table with his fist in agreement.

"He will want to know," he declared. "De Velt's curiosity will get the better of him, bringing him right to our doorstep."

Bretton eyed the man. "What will bring him to our doorstep is the daughter," he said. "I have just sent a rider off with a second token for de Velt, one he should be receiving in a few days."

The commanders were curious. "What token?" the big blond asked.

Bretton drank deeply from his cup before answering. "Hair belonging to his daughter," he replied. "I have just sent him a mass of silken dark hair."

The blond commander looked at the others, surprised by de Llion's statement. "Did you kill the woman?" he asked, rather hesitantly. "You did not mention that you would kill her."

Bretton shook his head. "Nay, d'Avignon, I did not kill her," he replied. "She is still safely tucked away in the vault, although she seems to have become ill during her stay. She is not well."

A big commander with curly auburn hair reached for the pitcher and began refilling his cup. "What do you intend to do about it?" he asked. "If she dies before we can lure de Velt, then our efforts will have been for naught. We were lucky to find her as it was. Who knows how much trouble it would take to find another de Velt offspring."

The man had a point. Bretton turned to look at his second in command, a friend for many years. Grayton du Reims was related to the Earl of East Anglia and was a wise and powerful man. He was a warrior with impeccable bloodlines, a younger son of a father who would not inherit lands or titles. Therefore, Grayton had to make his own way and, at the tender age of eleven, had run away from home to earn his fortune. He had worked for a mercenary knight who had taught him his trade, a vocation that Grayton eagerly took to. He was not a consecrated knight but should have been. He was skilled and powerful, and Bretton relied on him a great deal. His wisdom was paramount in all things.

"Then what would you suggest?" Bretton asked. "Send for a physic? Purchase expensive medicines? She is a prisoner and nothing more."

Grayton frowned. "She is a valuable bargaining tool," he countered. "Take your emotion out of the situation, Bretton. What you have is a very valuable commodity. I have been against you putting her in the vault since the beginning, you know this. I have made no secret of it. You must take care of this prize if you are truly going to use her to lure her father. It seems to me that you have turned your hatred of de Velt onto the daughter. She is the embodiment of all you loathe. If she dies, she will do us no good, and I did not burn a priory and kill nuns in vain."

Bretton didn't want to admit that Grayton was correct. He was stubborn. "You are mad," he muttered, noting that the servants were starting to bring forth the evening meal. "She is an object and nothing more. I do not hate her nor do I love her. She means little more to me than this table."

Grayton shook his head. "You would repair this table if it was broken because it serves a purpose," he said. "So does the woman serve a purpose. Get her out of the vault, make her comfortable, and hope she recovers."

Bretton made a face. "*You* get her out of the vault and make her comfortable," he said, too prideful to admit Grayton was right. "I put her in your care if you are so concerned about her."

"Then you agree with me?"

"I agree that you worry like an old woman. And if she escapes from you, I will have your head."

Grayton grinned. Bretton was as stubborn as they came. Slapping the man on the shoulder, he stood up and made his way from the hall. The other commanders watched him go, including Bretton, who eventually turned back to his wine.

"D'Avignon," he said, turning the focus away from Grayton and his correct assessment of their prized prisoner because he was starting to feel foolish about it. "Now that we have been returned to Cloryn for a few hours, how do the men fare? Well enough so that we should be prepared to move to our next target by the coming week?"

Sir Olivier d'Avignon, the burly blond knight, paid great attention to his liege's question. After a moment, he nodded. "They seem well enough," he said. "Since we landed in Liverpool, we've done nothing but march from one place to another, so if we could remain at Cloryn for a few days, it would serve the men well. They need to rest after the warfare we have conducted. It has been rather taxing."

That was putting it mildly. Sieges, death, destruction, men impaled on poles and decapitations were only part of the havoc they had wreaked. But that was their way, the manner in which Bretton's army functioned, having taken their clues from Ajax de Velt and his reign of terror those years ago. Bretton thought back to the path that had brought him to this moment in time, thinking over all of the work and sacrifice he had to make in order to see his desires fulfilled. Lost in reflection, he sipped pensively at his wine.

"From Liverpool, we laid siege to Clun, Knighton and Dolforwyn. We weren't trying to take those castles, only harass them. Then it was straight to Cloryn Castle," he muttered. "Once our base was established at Cloryn, it was on to Alberbury for the de Velt daughter. The man we paid to locate the de Velt children took three years to find one we could get to and, in the end, we found de Velt's daughter just where he said she would be. Once we confiscated her, we brought her back to Cloryn and locked her in the vault while we moved on to Ithon Castle, another of de Velt's holdings. Now, it belongs to me as well. After Ithon, we will take Rhayder Castle and then we will have an unbreakable link of three castles, all bordering one another. Once we have that stretch of the border secured and under my control, we will move to Comen Castle, Erwood Castle, and finally Four Crosses Castle. By that time, I will have taken every castle along the Marches that de Velt ever held and, hopefully, he will be moving his army to engage me."

The commanders listened to the plan that had been drilled into their heads ever since they had known Bretton. Much like the rest of them, Bretton had a background as a mercenary but, unlike them, he had lived the life of a mercenary with an end goal in mind. The man had plans. Mercenaries didn't come any meaner or deadlier than Bretton de Llion. Since having lost his parents at a young age, his younger years were rather blurred but it was rumored that he had been sold to a merchant who had taken him to Ireland and subsequently abused him until he had been old enough to fight back.

After that, it had been established that Bretton had become a squire for an Irish mercenary who had taught the lad his trade. Powerful and skilled at only seventeen years of age, Bretton left his Irish master and began to sell his sword to anyone who would pay a high price, earning himself a great deal of money in the process. Then, it was his turn to hire men on, and with his army for hire, he had made even more money because Ireland was full of lords willing to pay to destroy their neighbor. But there came a point where de Llion had his own plans for his army, and that was to take six castles along the Welsh border, castles that belonged to the feared English warlord, Jax de Velt. Bretton's men came to understand that there was a vendetta in these plans, a vengeance that sang of bitterness and sorrow, something de Llion wouldn't easily discuss.

But he did discuss it, every so often when he was drunk, and the reasons behind his vendetta would make brief appearances, enough so that his commanders understood that de Velt had murdered his family and stolen his father's castle. Men with vendettas were often the fiercest and the most isolated of men. Fierce because there was emotion in their cause and isolated because their pain was their own. Bretton de Llion was one of these men. He kept his emotions bottled up, yet wore his pain on his sleeve in the guise of blood-letting brutality, an odd combination. He was lonely, as he had been his entire life, and that was the way he wanted it.

"It is difficult to believe that we are finally here," the commander with the heavy Irish accent spoke in response to Bretton's statement. Sir Dallan de Birmingham was from a fine Irish family and had indeed been knighted, but he discovered early in his career that he liked being paid for his services. His loyalty could be bought and de Llion paid handsomely for the privilege. "All of the years we have been planning this – how long has it been? At least six years that we have been planning to take de Velt's castles in Wales. The plan has become a part of my very foundation and I am eager to establish myself along the Marches."

Bretton eyed Dallan. The man was in it for the money and power, purely. He was greedy and he could be shifty, so Dallan was a commander that bore watching. As long as things were going his way, he was loyal to the core, but the moment he was displeased, he could very easily show that displeasure in dangerous ways.

"Your time will come," Bretton said steadily. "I promised you a castle and you shall have it, but it will be a castle of *my* choosing.

Rhayder is rumored to be a large castle with two villages paying tribute, so mayhap that will be the one I grant you. Mayhap not. Either way, you will never forget that your loyalty is to me above all else."

Dallan's easy manner hardened somewhat as he gazed at Bretton. "You need not remind me," he said. "My loyalty is yours for always. I swore fealty to you and that is not in question."

Bretton's gaze was deadly. "See that it is not," he said, lingering on Dallan a moment just to make sure the man understood his message clearly. After a long pause, he turned his attention to the fourth commander at the table, sitting silently as the others conversed. "Teague, you have mentioned that Rhayder sits on an outcropping of jagged rocks and incorporates those into its defenses. When was the last time you visited Rhayder?"

Sir Teague de Lara was the last of the four commanders, the youngest at twenty years and four, and also the biggest. He was a big, silent, brooding man, long-limbed, with light brown hair and a granite-square jaw. Another knight from a fine family, the House of de Lara was one of the most powerful families on the Welsh Marches. Teague had fostered at Godric's Castle on the Marches and had an intimate knowledge of the area, which is why Bretton had recruited him. He knew the families and the locations of much along the border, if not much in England, and had proven himself a valuable resource. Because of it, Bretton paid the man better than the others and treated him with more respect than most.

Teague was aware of his value but never made a show of it. Like the other men, he was in it for the money. The fifth son of a brother to the Lord of Trelystan, he would be inheriting little upon the death of his father. He saw his time with Bretton as a means to make his fortune and, so far, that had proven to be the case. At his young age, he was quite wealthy, and he listened carefully to Bretton's question.

"Fifteen years ago, at least," he replied. "I went there for a tournament when I was fostering at Godric's. Because of the way Rhayder sits, the tournament was held on a field below while the castle sat up overhead like a great sentinel. I have told you that the rocks would be very difficult to scale and there is but one way in and out of the castle. Taking the gatehouse is the key."

Bretton listened again to what he already knew for the most part. "At some point over the next few days, I should like to see Rhayder for myself," he said. "Mayhap you and I can travel to the area and see the castle. In fact, I must see it in order to plan an effective assault."

Teague nodded. "Aye, my lord," he said, "but know that Rhayder will be one of the more difficult conquests. That castle and Four Crosses Castle are difficult simply because of the way they are built."

Bretton nodded faintly. "That is why I am leaving Four Crosses until the end," he said, his expression taking on a wistful hue before just as quickly vanishing. "I have not seen Four Crosses in twenty-five years but I still remember the manner in which she is perched atop a mountain. I also remember a postern gate and a secret path, which may work to our advantage."

Teague, Dallan, and Olivier were watching him, listening to the man's words reflect on a subject he very rarely spoke of. Teague was the first one to reply.

"I have never seen Four Crosses although I know where it is located," he said. "What do you know of her gatehouse and defenses?"

Bretton thought back to the years of his childhood, inevitably remembering the last day he spent there without worry, remembering his father as the man had put him on a pony and allowed him to ride about in the stable yard. He could still hear the voice of Morgan de Llion telling him to sit up straight and keep his heels down. But he shook himself from further reflection, mostly because it still upset him after all these years. He focused on Teague's question instead.

"Four Crosses has no gatehouse," he told them. "The walls are circular, fifteen feet high in places, so the matter will be destroying the gate to gain access. If de Velt could do it those years ago, then I certainly can. It should not be an issue although the general siege on the castle will be more difficult than some of the others because of its location. Still, I do not anticipate failure. Just the opposite, in fact. We will prevail."

Olivier and Dallan appeared confident, passing assured glances between them, but Teague kept his focus on Bretton.

"Mayhap we should do a reconnaissance of Four Crosses as well," Teague said. "Things could have changed in twenty-five years."

Bretton nodded thoughtfully. "It would mayhap be wise to see it again," he said. "We still have Comen and Erwood Castle as well. You had better send scouts out to survey them and report back. Now that we are here, and established, it is time to educate ourselves on the future of our undertakings."

Teague agreed. Pouring himself and Bretton more wine, they eventually turned the focus of the conversation to other things, things that were well away from the horrors of battle. It was rare when they spoke of anything other than business, but in this case, after three major sieges, they took the liberty to relax, just a little, although each man did not relax completely. They were due to move to Rhayder Castle in a few days and the conversation inevitably turned in that direction.

For Teague, Dallan, and Olivier, war was never far from their thoughts and the riches it would bring them. For Bretton, war was his only thought and the vengeance it would provide him.

It was all he lived for.

CHAPTER FOUR

S OMEONE WAS NUDGING her foot.

At least, she thought so. She could have very well been dreaming because the fever she had been sporting for the past few hours had given her very odd dreams. She dreamt that she had bird wings at one point, and yet still another dream had her being able to breathe underwater. And then there was the foot-nudging, which she thought was all part of her bizarre dreams until she opened her eyes and realized she was no longer dreaming. She was awake and someone was still nudging her foot.

Coughing, she turned her head slightly, bringing it off the stale straw to see a big warrior standing at her feet. He was tall, with wavy auburn hair that flowed to his shoulders. When the warrior realized she was lucid and looking at him, he cleared his throat softly.

"Demoiselle," he said quietly. "You will come with me."

Allaston wasn't clear on his words. In fact, she didn't particularly understand him. "Where will I go?" she asked, her voice scratchy.

The big knight didn't say anything, he simply held out a hand. Allaston stared at it before eventually realizing that he wanted her to stand up. Feeling as poorly as she did, that was no simple feat, and it was a laborious process before she was able to get to her knees. Coughing had overcome her and she had to pause in order to let a coughing spell run its course. On her knees as the sputtering died down, she was in the process of trying to get to her feet when the knight reached out and grasped her arm.

It wasn't a rough grasp, nor was it gentle. He was simply taking hold of her. The next thing Allaston realized, the knight was putting a hand on her forehead to feel for her temperature. As she shivered in his grip, she heard him hiss.

"God's Bones, woman," he exclaimed. "You are on fire."

Allaston didn't respond. She was too sick to care much about anything at the moment. Therefore, she followed like a dumb animal as the knight led her from the cell and up the slippery stone steps that led to the gatehouse. The knight could have been leading her to her doom for all she knew but, with a feverish mind, it never occurred to her to be fearful or suspicious. She was simply doing as she was told.

It was sunset as he took her out of the gatehouse and into the bailey beyond, but even the weak light from the setting sun hurt her eyes after three weeks in the vault and she squinted, going so far as to put her hand over her eyes. That stopped her forward momentum and she teetered a bit, disoriented and dizzy. The next thing she realized, the big knight had swept her into his arms and was carrying her across the bailey.

Having no point of reference with any part of the castle other than the vault she had been in, the scenery passed by her in a blur; a big, darkened bailey, some small individual structures she didn't recognize, and finally great stone steps that led up into a towering keep. She only knew it was tall because she had removed the hand from her eyes briefly. She saw stone towering into the sky and closed her eyes again because it hurt to keep them open.

From the cold openness of the bailey to the dark, cool innards of the keep, she could feel the dampness of the structure as the knight carried her up some stairs. By this time, her face was on his shoulder because she was too exhausted to lift her head and her eyes were throbbing with the introduction of light after three weeks of darkness. He walked and walked, and then she heard a door slam. Soon, she was being set down.

"You will remain on this bed until I return," he said, his tone grim. "If you move off this bed, I will put you back in the vault. Is that clear?"

Allaston simply nodded, eyes closed. She heard him move across the floor and then a door open and close. She could hear his footfalls fade away.

Sleep claimed her once more. She had no idea how long she had been asleep because when she awoke, it was to soft voices in the chamber. She could hear people moving around, taking. She heard the splash of water as it was poured. In a dream-like haze, she heard all of these things. Then, someone was shaking her awake.

"Woman," came a soft voice. "Get up, now. I've had a bath brought for you. Get into it and clean up. You will feel better."

A bath. Allaston swore she had never heard more beautiful words in her entire life. She struggled to sit up with the thought of lovely water. God, it had been so long since she'd had a bath. It had been so long since she had been clean or warm. Was it possible such things still existed?

"A bath?" she repeated weakly. "But… but I have nothing to bathe with."

"What do you mean?"

Allaston could see the big iron tub near the hearth, steam rising out of it, and it was like the lure of food to a starving man. It was calling to her. The hearth, too, had been stoked and a soft blaze was glowing. *Warmth!* Male servants had filled the tub and were finishing with the hearth, quickly leaving when their task was finished. Water was leaking out on the floor and puddling, but it didn't matter. She saw the almighty bath as her cure and salvation, all in one.

"I do not have any soap," she said, her eyes riveted to the steaming water. "Nor any clean clothing."

The knight's gaze lingered on her. "I will see what is in the other chambers," he said. "There was a lady here, once. Mayhap she left behind items that are serviceable."

Had Allaston been sharper and not wracked with fever, she might have thought on his words. *There was a lady here, once.* But she didn't think on them. She really didn't know what the knight meant by it. There was no way she could have known that the lady of Cloryn had been rounded up with her husband and killed by the very men who held her prisoner. All Allaston cared about was climbing into that tub and being warm for the first time in weeks.

As the knight went about hunting down something for her to wear that wasn't soaked with dirt and filth, Allaston struggled to remove her clothing. Since she was not yet a fully consecrated nun, her clothing was simpler than those who had taken their final vows. She wore undyed woolen undergarments, a shift and rudimentary breeches that tied at the waist, and over that she wore a simple gown of unbleached wool that was a dirty white shade, dark and stained now with weeks of wear upon it. It didn't fit her very well and was secured around her waist with a rope made from woolen strands.

Since she wasn't fully consecrated, her hair was still long and usually worn in a tight braid. That braid had come out long ago and the loose hair had given Bretton the opportunity to grab it and cut it. Pushing her heavy hair out of the way, she struggled to remove her simple leather shoes and proceeded to untie the knotted belt around her waist.

The belt fell to the floor. She tried to remove her shoes standing up, but her balance was terrible so she ended up sitting down on the bed to do it. When the shoes came off, she struggled to her feet to remove the breeches, untying them and letting them fall to the ground. By the time she stepped out of them, the knight returned with a bundle in his arms.

Allaston watched with as much curiosity as she could muster as the knight tossed the bundle onto the bed. He began pulling it apart, setting things aside that he had wrapped up in the fabric.

"Here," he said, pointing to a few items he had set aside on the mattress. "I found soap and oil and something for your face, I think. It smells like mint. And here are a few shifts and surcoats. The lady that was here before you was bigger than you are so these might not fit properly but at least they are clean. I would suggest you bathe, dress in these clean clothes, and go to bed. I will send a physic in to tend to you."

Allaston simply stood there, watching him as he picked up one of the items he brought, a small alabaster pot, and sniff it. "Where is the lady of the house so that I may thank her?" she asked weakly.

The knight turned to look at her, realizing her fever-muddled mind was perhaps not very sharp based on her question. "She is no longer here," he said. "Hurry, now. Take your bath and get to bed."

He turned to leave but Allaston stopped him. "What is this place called?" she asked.

He paused at the door, hand on the latch. "You are at Cloryn Castle."

Allaston thought hard. She believed she had heard the name before. "Cloryn?" she repeated. "And who are you?"

"I am Grayton."

Allaston's fogged mind emerged for a brief, lucid moment. "Thank you for your kindness, Grayton."

He didn't acknowledge her. He simply left the room and shut the door, leaving Allaston alone in the chamber that was growing progressively warmer with the heat from the fire.

The lure of the bath proved too great for her to delay any longer. Allaston took the soap off the bed and pulled the coarse gown over her head. Then she proceeded to peel off the rest. She left a trail of clothing to the tub, tossing her garments off as she went. By the time she reached the old iron tub, she was completely nude and she climbed in, slipping and landing heavily on her bottom in the tub and sending water sloshing everywhere. But she hardly cared. She dunked her head beneath the waterline and lingered there for a few seconds before emerging. Already, she felt better.

The cake of white lumpy soap in her hand smelled of lavender and she proceeded to soap every inch of her body from her head to her toes. The hair was washed, her face washed, and everything else on down the line. She didn't have a scrub brush so she simply used her fingers, scrubbing until she could scrub no more. Everything was washed, rinsed, scrubbed, and smoothed.

Not only did the bath clean her body but it seemed to clean her mind as well. She was still fogged with fever but not nearly as bad as she had been. She was thinking much more clearly, so much so that she perked up and began to really look at her surroundings. The chamber was very well appointed with a comfortable bed, a big wardrobe, a small table with two chairs, and a big tapestry near the bed that seemed to depict a knight and lady in a romantic setting. In truth, it was a wealthy room, much like the rooms at her home, Pelinom Castle.

Cloryn Castle. She had heard of it before. In fact, she'd heard her father mention the name but little else. Her father wasn't one to discuss his business with his children, although he did discuss it with her older brothers, Coleby and Julian. They were being prepared to take over her father's empire one day so it was natural that her father spoke to them about such things.

As she sat in the cooling water, she began to think on her siblings, sisters and brothers she missed very much. There was Coleby, her eldest brother who was big like their father but blond like their mother, and then Julian, who was the spitting image of her father. She was next, as the eldest daughter, and she tended to favor her father more than her mother also. Then came Effington and Addington, or Effie and Addie as they were called, two blond sisters that were born thirteen months apart and resembled twins more than single-birth siblings. She missed them the most. Effie had a loud mouth and loved jokes while Addie was very sweet and sickly a good deal of the time. Then, there was baby Cassian, who wasn't so much a baby as he was an active toddler. He was as smart as a whip and a joy to the family.

Aye, she missed her family very much. She hadn't seen them in over a year and she could only imagine how her father was going to react to a gift of her hair delivered to his doorstep. Even though she had never known her father to go to war since she'd been born, there was always a first time. He was fiercely protective over his family and she knew he wouldn't take her abduction lightly. But she would not tell de Llion that, not when the man was so eager for Jax to respond to him.

So she sat in the tub and pondered her fears for the future as the water cooled. Eventually, she was forced to climb out, drying off her prune-like skin with one of the shifts that Grayton had brought her. She didn't have anything else. The oil he'd brought her was still on the bed and she picked up the phial, smelling the contents. It, too, smelled of lavender and she smoothed it sparingly over her parched skin before donning a second shift of very soft wool. It was very fine and, she was sure, very expensive.

Much as Grayton had warned her, however, it was too big for her but she didn't care. She put it on, and gladly, and also put on a dark blue brocaded robe over the top of it. The robe was very heavy, lined with rabbit fur, and sleeveless so the long, belled sleeves of the shift were revealed. Digging around in the pile of garments, she came across a pair of mismatched woolen hose with no ribbons to secure them, so she simply put them on and folded them down so they would stay on her feet.

Dressed warmly for the first time in weeks, she sat by the fire to dry her dark hair, running her fingers through it because she had no comb. She kept inspecting the ends, ends that de Llion had so brutally cut, lamenting the fact that he had cut her hair by at least two feet. But in the same breath, she thought it rather foolish to lament cut hair when she would be cutting it anyway when she took her ecclesiastical vows. Still, it was her last claim to vanity.

On the floor next to the hearth, Allaston continued to dry her hair and reflect on thoughts of her family and future. The fever still lingered and she would cough every so often, but overall, she felt much better than she had in a very long while. She was lost in thought, basking in the warmth of the fire, when the chamber door opened. Startled, she turned to see a most unwelcome sight.

৪৪

BRETTON WAS STILL in the great hall, still at the feasting table lingering over a sixth cup of murky red wine when Grayton entered. Around them, the men had finished feasting and were now playing games of chance or telling loud stories over the buzz of conversation. The hall itself had grown smokier from the fire that had been stoked into mammoth proportions as Grayton crossed the floor, kicking the wandering dogs aside and refusing to get sucked into any gambling games. He managed to reach Bretton without getting pulled into a dice game, which was difficult for him. He usually didn't have much self-control when it came to games of chance.

"It seems that the men do not intend to sleep tonight no matter how weary they are," he commented as he sat down on the bench next to Bretton. "We may end up breaking up fights from all of the money changing hands in these games."

Bretton was exhausted and the wine was making him half-lidded and somewhat drunk, a rare state for him. But he had worked harder than any of them as of late and, for once, was letting his guard down. He glanced at Grayton as he took another deep drink from his cup.

"Mayhap," he said, somewhat neutrally. "How is the prisoner, Mother?"

Grayton grinned. "She is in the keep and bathing three weeks of cold and filth from her body," he said. "I will send our surgeon to tend her. There may be something he can do for her fever."

Bretton scratched his head. "Is she going to die?"

Grayton shrugged. "It is hard to say," he muttered, reaching to collect a cup of wine from the center of the table where it lingered with a full pitcher nearby. "I do not think so, but I suppose time will tell."

Bretton grunted. He thought on his prisoner, a spawn of de Velt. He hated her purely based on her father in contradiction to the lie he told earlier. He had said that he neither hated nor loved her, which was far from the truth. He hated her because she bore the name de Velt. He hated her because the man's blood ran through her veins, and he hated her because it was her father who had ruined his life. He had abducted her because he knew what it was like to lose those he loved and he wanted de Velt to feel the same pain. Aye, he wanted to hurt Jax, a man he didn't even know, because Jax had hurt him in the course of his conquest. Twenty-five years of a simmering hatred had matured into a horrible vengeance.

The wine flowing through his veins was dissolving his self-control. It was causing him to have wild thoughts. So the prisoner was bathing, was she? Although he had given Grayton permission to tend the woman, he wasn't particularly keen on the fact that his prisoner had some freedom. He wasn't too keen on a de Velt moving freely about the keep. She was a prisoner, wasn't she? She deserved no more consideration than she'd had before, languishing in a vault. No de Velt deserved more than that, in his view.

The more he thought about it, the more agitated he became until he slammed the cup down and rose abruptly from the table. His destination was the keep but he didn't mention that to Grayton. He didn't want the man to come with him. Therefore, he kept silent as he quit the hall, even when Grayton and Dallan called after him. He ignored them. He had a prisoner to see.

The keep of Cloryn Castle was tall and built like a big, square box. It even had stone steps leading to the second floor entrance which was a rare feature. Most stairs that led into keeps were wooden so they could be burned and keep access cut off in the event of a siege. But Cloryn's keep had an enormous entry door that was made of iron, impossible to burn and nearly impossible to breach, so it was this door that Bretton moved through. By the time he reached the steps that led to the upper floors of the keep, he was working on a righteous rage. *Damn de Velts!*

He hit the second floor landing and was preparing to take the stairs to the third floor when he heard coughing. Lured by the sounds, he ended up at the second of two large chambers on that floor. He could feel the warmth from the room escaping through the gaps between the door and the door frame. Hand on the latch, he shoved the door open.

Very warm air hit him in the face. The first thing he saw was Allaston on the floor next to the hearth, her eyes wide on him and her fingers frozen in her hair as she had been raking the digits through it, trying to dry it in the warm air. Bretton took several big, angry steps into the room, his gaze fixed on the prisoner, but as he drew close it occurred to him that she was an extremely beautiful woman. Cleaned up, with some color in her cheeks, she was utterly spectacular.

The realization set his anger back a few notches, inviting an extreme amount of bewilderment into his drunken mind. *Beautiful?* Was it possible a de Velt could actually be beautiful? Momentarily stumped by his conflicting thoughts, he just stood there and stared at her as if he wasn't entirely sure which direction to take. Should he bellow and be angry and drag her back to the vault? That was his original intention. But now, at this moment, he couldn't seem to do it. He just stared.

Allaston stared back. His appearance was startling and unwelcome. The last time she had seen the man, he had threatened to impregnate her. She had threatened to kill herself if he tried to touch her. She wondered if they were about to see these events come to pass. Taking a deep breath for courage, for strength, she removed her fingers from her hair.

"Your man, Grayton, brought me here," she said steadily. "I am most appreciative of the consideration. My thanks to you."

His anger was knocked back another notch. He'd never noticed before, but she had a rather sweet voice. Was it the wine making him notice such alluring traits about her, he wondered? The wine was doing bizarre things to his thought processes.

"Have you eaten?" he asked. *God's Beard, man, why should you care?*

Allaston shook her head. "I have not," she said. Then, she pointed to the bath. "But I have bathed. Your man was very kind to provide me with clean clothes."

Bretton looked at the bath, now full of cool water. He could smell the lavender. Then his eyes returned to her, noting the glistening dark hair, reflecting red highlights in the firelight, and her bright green eyes were spectacular against the backdrop of her alabaster skin and dark brows. Rather appalled at his lustful thoughts, he moved away from her, aimlessly, noting the garments on the bed and then her dirty clothing on the floor. He pointed at the collection on the floor.

"Burn these," he said. "You will no longer need them."

Allaston watched him as he moved near the bed, which put her on edge. Beds were where marriages were consummated. She wasn't quite sure how she could fight the man off if he was intending to force her into bed so she remained by the fire, nervously looking about for a weapon should he try. There was a large fire poker a few feet away. It made her feel a bit better knowing she was closer to the poker than he was. She could get to it first should he try anything. At least, that was her hope.

"They can be washed," she replied evenly to his statement about her clothes. "I see no need to burn serviceable clothing."

Bretton looked up from the bed, staring steadily at her. He just stood there and looked at her but it was clear there was something on his mind. His entire manner held something odd, something of curiosity and angst and bewilderment. After a moment, he tore his gaze away from her and resumed his aimless wandering.

"Tell me something," he said.

Allaston watched him pace. "If I can."

His wandering eyes found the great tapestry near the bed, the one with the lord and lady on it courting in romantic love. He fingered the expensive piece.

"Explain this to me," he said. "Explain to me what kind of man your father is."

Allaston wasn't sure this was a safe subject but she obliged. "I can only tell you from my experience," she said. "That is all I know."

"I realize that. Tell me."

Allaston paused a moment to collect her thoughts, hoping she wouldn't set him off with whatever she said.

"He is a generous man," she said. "He is strict, that is true, but he is a man of warmth and humor. He also has a head for mathematics and business."

Bretton turned to look at her, surprised. "Business?"

Allaston nodded. "My father has many holdings and between him and my mother, they manage them very well," she said. "Although I believe my mother is much smarter than my father is. She thinks so, too."

She was smiling faintly as she said it and Bretton realized it was the first time he had ever seen her smile. It was glorious. He could have very well been swept away with it upon his alcohol-hazed mind but he fought it. He fought it furiously. He mostly battled it by thinking of his hatred of de Velt and of the terrible things the man had done.

"And you are fond of him?" he asked as if bewildered by the entire concept. "Do you truly not have any idea the atrocities your father has committed? Do you truly not know what a monster he is?"

Allaston's smile faded. "I told you that all of that is in his past," she said. "I know he did some terrible things, but…."

"*Terrible*?" Bretton nearly bellowed. He came away from the tapestry and headed in her direction. "Terrible is to burn a house down, or loot a village. Terrible is to kill a man who was only defending what was his. What your father did went beyond terrible! Do you know that he would take all of the knights and soldiers he conquered and run big stakes through their anus, up through their intestines, until the sharp part of the stake emerged from the man's neck or chest or shoulder? Then, he would drive the end of the pole into the ground and leave the man to die as if he was no more than a mindless animal. If the loss of blood or the destruction of his entire body didn't kill him quickly, the elements surely would. Your father, this man you speak so fondly of, did that to my father. My father was a good man, a man with great love for his family, and your father put him to the stake as if he was less than human. Jax de Velt treated my father as if he was no more than a side of beef and not a man with a heart and soul. That is what *your* loving father did to my father."

By the time he was finished, Allaston was looking at him with tears in her eyes. In that rather drunken tirade, she understood a great deal, more than she ever had. She was both terrified by it and touched by it. Sympathy and fear played hand and hand in her mind. Aye, she had known that her father had done atrocious things, but it wasn't something she ever thought about or dwelt upon. She didn't like to think her father capable of such things, but now, she was forced to face it.

"Every man has a past," she whispered. "Many men have killed."

Bretton's eyes narrowed. "Aye, many men have killed, but what your father did was beyond killing," he said. "He took what was most valuable to a five year old boy. He took away my entire life in a single, dark night. Memories are all I have of a wonderful life that was. My life since then has been focused on one thing – the destruction of the man who took everything away from me. Destruction of the man who nearly destroyed *me*."

Allaston could see, in those few short sentences, that there was pain somewhere in that anger. There was a flicker of grief there that drove de Llion. It was what fed his spirit. At that point, she did the only thing she could do; she begged forgiveness.

"I am so sorry," she whispered. "I am so terribly sorry your happiness with life ended that way, but the man that did that... I do not know him. That is not the father I know."

Bretton stared at her, feeling very strange as he did so. He wanted to give in to her sympathy, he truly did, but then he would remind himself that this was the daughter of the man he had sworn to hate. His inner struggle was great.

"Mayhap you do not know that man, but he still exists," he assured her. "Your father still exists. Therefore, his evil still exists. Do you know what I plan to do?"

Allaston shook her head fearfully. "Nay."

Bretton drew close to her, going down on one knee so he could see her better. He could smell the lavender on her, assaulting his senses, and he struggled to ignore it. His heart was nearly bursting with emotion, brought on by the wine, and he was unable to stop the words spilling out of his mouth.

"I intend to take back every castle your father conquered on the Welsh Marches," he said. "I have two already, Cloryn and Ithon. Then, I will proceed to take Rhayder, Comen, Erwood, and finally, Four Crosses. Your father's men man these outposts and those I have captured, I have put to the stake in the same fashion your father did. Jax de Velt is getting a taste of his own tactics and once I am finished confiscating his castles, I will meet the man on the field of battle. It is inevitable that he will come to me, for I have several things that belong to him. But I have something that means more to him than all of the material possessions combined. I have you, and you will bring your father to my doorstep whereupon I will best the man in battle and put him on a stake just like he put my father on a stake. I will watch Jax de Velt die a slow and agonizing death and call it justice. *That* is what I intend to do."

Allaston looked up at him with baleful eyes, tears spilling down her cheeks. "You cannot do that," she whispered. "My father is not the man you knew. He has changed. You *must* allow that men see the error of their ways and proceed to live a good life."

Bretton's eyes were riveted to her, seeing such haunting beauty the more he scrutinized her. He struggled not to let himself be distracted by it.

"Mayhap," he agreed, his raspy voice low. "But your father did not see the error in his ways before he killed my family. We all have to pay for our sins one way or the other."

Allaston couldn't help but notice he was leaning rather close to her and instinctively, she pulled away. "Are you God, then?" she asked, wiping at her cheeks. "Only God can punish sinners. That is not your right."

Bretton stared at her a moment before breaking down into a grin. The man had a devastating smile of big, white teeth.

"Nay, I am not God," he said, "but I have been called the Devil, and these castles I take back from your father are now part of my dominion. There has never been another warlord like me nor shall there ever been another one like me. I am unique unto myself, with more power than Jax de Velt could ever hope to have."

Allaston sighed heavily at his boast, which turned into a coughing spell. She ended up coughing into her hand, struggling to breathe. She was starting to feel ill again, from his words more than from actual illness. It was frustrating to hear him speak of such hatred for the man she loved.

"Then I am sorry for you," she said. "Look at you. You are obviously a powerful and well-spoken man, and men like you are a premium commodity. You could do so many things with your life, swear fealty to any number of wealthy lords or even to the king himself, but instead, you focus all of your power and intelligence on vengeance. Your father is dead and killing my father will not bring him back. In fact, I would suspect that even if you are able to murder my father, all you will feel is a hollow sense of accomplishment. What will my father's death bring you? Happiness? I doubt it. You are an embittered and unhappy man and no amount of killing is going to satisfy that hole in your heart you are trying so desperately to heal."

Instead of flare, Bretton actually found himself listening to her. She spoke rationally, not with fear or emotion, and he found that her manner intrigued him. She was a calm and collected lady in the face of death and, in spite of everything, a small seed of respect sprouted for her. Nothing she said was untrue. In fact, it made a good deal of sense. After a moment of digesting her words, he actually smiled.

"Mayhap that is true," he said, watching her as she tried not to look at him. He could tell that she didn't like what she saw. "But I intend to find out. In any case, this is what I have planned for most of my life and no one will convince me otherwise. It is something I must do."

Allaston was looking at her hands, the floor, anything not to look the man in the eye. "These men that fight with you," she said. "Do they feel the same sense of vengeance that you do? Did my father wrong them as well?"

Bretton shook his head as he sat back, ending up on his bum a few feet away from her. "Nay," he said. "They are in it for the money and properties I can provide them. We are a mercenary army, my lady. Did you not realize that?"

She glanced at him, sidelong. "All of them?"

"All of them."

"But where did you find all of these men?"

He cocked his head thoughtfully, his gaze moving between her and the snapping fire. "In Ireland," he said. "After I escaped your father's carnage, I was sold to a merchant and ended up in Ireland. That is where I grew up, where I learned my craft, and where I compiled an army big enough to take on Jax de Velt. My men are well paid, my lady."

Allaston's head came up and she looked at him. In the soft light of the fire, he actually looked quite handsome with his square jaw and dark hair. He looked almost… normal. But he wasn't normal. The man was a killer.

"Who sold you to a merchant?" she asked. "You were a mere child. Who did this?"

His rather pleasant expression faded. "Servants that used to work for my family," he said. "I escaped with a few of them and, in the end, they simply didn't know what to do with me. An old woman had been taking care of me and when she died, her husband sold me. He did not want a young boy about the house and opted for the money I could bring him."

Allaston was listening intently to a rather sad story. "The merchant used you as a slave?"

Bretton's features tightened as he stared into the flame of the hearth. "Among other things," he muttered softly. "When I became older, I ran away and found an Irish mercenary who agreed to take me as an apprentice in exchange for work. It was a difficult life but I learned a great deal. I am not afraid of hardship."

Allaston was rather surprised he was opening up so much about his personal life, but she knew it was the drink. He was still exhibiting some signs of having imbibed too much. Still, his tale was a sad one. It began to occur to her that if perhaps she played to that sad tale by showing sympathy, perhaps she could gain his trust somewhat. Perhaps if he stopped viewing her as the flesh and blood of his hated enemy, things might be different. One could hardly kill someone they liked or at least felt a connection to. Perhaps if she was nice to him, it would pay off in the end. She had to try.

"I do not imagine that you are," she said. "It sounds as if you have had a very difficult life. I suppose, in a sense, that I do not blame you for what you feel. I cannot say I would feel any differently if a warlord had killed my father."

His bright blue eyes were intense on her. "A warlord will," he said. "Make no mistake, my lady. A warlord *will* kill your father."

She held his gaze steadily. "So you would do to me what my father did to you?" she asked. "You would take away my father, too?"

"At least you had your father for a good deal of your life. That is more than I can say for myself."

He was making it difficult for her to be nice to him but she continued to try. "And you think that killing my father will somehow replace those missing years with your father?"

He shook his head. "Not replace," he said. "I am not looking to replace anything. I am looking to right a wrong."

"By creating another wrong?"

"Call it a reckoning, if you will. An eye for an eye."

Allaston believed him. The more she spoke with him, the more she realized he meant every word he said. It was a sad and sickening realization. "You have thought this way for so long that it has become a part of you," she muttered. "What happens after you kill my father? Do you go on with your life, marry well, and raise a family on the blood of vengeance? Will killing my father make all things possible for you? I wonder."

He cocked an eyebrow. "Don't," he said, his gaze lingering on her. "There is no reason to discuss this any longer because you will not convince me otherwise. I must do as I must, and you will have to accept it."

I must do as I must. He sounded rather final. She realized that she had to do what she must as well. Her attempt to be sympathetic to him hadn't worked, so she had to try another tactic. She wasn't sure what that was yet, but she realized she couldn't wait around for the end of Jax de Velt to come. Perhaps it would be her end, too. She had to do something. She had to fight. She simply couldn't stand by and watch de Llion kill her father. Much as he had plans, she would have to have plans, also.

She would have to fight back.

CHAPTER FIVE

THE NEXT MORNING at Cloryn dawned foggy and cold. In the great hall, the soldiers who had slept in various positions all around the room were just beginning to stir. Bretton was up, having slept very little last night after his conversation with Allaston. She had planted things in his minds, things that made him think, and he had lay awake most of the night thinking on what she had said. So much of what she'd said made sense to him, but there was one particular question she had proposed that he couldn't seem to shake.

Will killing my father make all things possible for you?

He couldn't honestly answer that question. The truth was that he'd never given much thought to his life after killing Jax de Velt and damn the man's daughter for bringing the subject up. Of course he wanted to marry, if only to have heirs, but he had no chance of a good marriage from a good family, so he would have to take what he could get. He *could* get Allaston de Velt. She already belonged to him so he had been thinking on a marriage of convenience with her more and more. And even more than that after last night.

She was a beautiful woman. Aye, she was, even though it was difficult to think that way over a woman who carried de Velt's blood. That meant their children would also carry de Velt's blood. Did he really want to mix his blood with the blood of the man he hated most in the world? He had been wrestling with that very question. God forbid, what

KATHRYN LE VEQUE

if one of his sons ended up *looking* like Jax de Velt? Would he hate the lad every time he looked at him? He simply didn't have an answer for that.

Exhausted, frustrated, and in a foul mood, he entered the great hall in search of food and his commanders, in that order. The room was dark for the most part, the fire pit in the center having long gone cold, and it smelled badly of unwashed bodies and dogs. Over near one of the feasting tables, servants were starting to set out bread and drink. He made his way to the table and collected a mug of watered ale, stuffing some bread into his mouth as Grayton entered the hall well behind him. Bretton caught the movement out of the corner of his eye.

"A blessed morn to you, my lord," Grayton greeted him pleasantly. "I hope you rested well."

It was the wrong thing to say. Bretton looked at the man and scowled. "I did *not*," he said. "Where are the others? I intend to ride to Rhayder today to scout the location and I would take Teague and Dallan with me. I will leave Olivier here with you."

Grayton eyed the man. He knew he had spent a good deal of time with the prisoner the previous night but he'd not seen him after that. Bretton had evidently gone to bed after speaking with her, so this was the first that he'd seen the man. He was very curious to know what had gone on between him and the prisoner.

"As you wish," he said casually, eyeing the man as he reached for a lopsided cup of ale. "I've not yet seen your prisoner this morning. How is she faring?"

Bretton was back to his usual emotionless expression. "I would not know," he said. "I have not seen her this morning."

Grayton took a bite of his bread. "I did not send the physic to her last night," he said. "I had the odd feeling that you did not approve of my removing her from the vault, so I did not want to press the matter. If she dies, she dies. Her fate is consigned to God."

Bretton took great slabs of tart white cheese and put it on his bread, taking a big bite. "She was coughing last night when I spoke with her but she did not seem to be deathly ill," he replied, chewing. "In fact, she seemed quite well."

Grayton looked at him with surprise. "She did?" he said. "Most interesting. Mayhap she is healing, after all."

Bretton didn't say anything for a moment as he chewed his meal. Swallowing what was in his mouth, he spoke.

"Have you thought about what you shall do when we are finished with de Velt?" he asked.

Grayton shook his head. "I confess, I have not," he said. "I always thought we would move on to other targets."

Bretton glanced at him curiously. "Targets? What targets?"

Grayton shrugged. "We must continue to pay the men," he said. "I assumed we would continue doing what we are doing, even after we confiscate de Velt's holdings. Why? Did you have another idea about it?"

Bretton took another bite of bread, chewing thoughtfully. "I do not know," he said. "My goal has always been to reclaim de Velt's properties and kill the man to avenge my father. After that, I figured that I would live in one of these castles and administer my domain."

Grayton nodded, still not entirely sure why Bretton had asked the question about life after conquest. He'd only asked it after spending time with de Velt's daughter. Grayton was coming to wonder if the woman hadn't said something to Bretton to get the man's mind working. In any case, he picked up another piece of bread and shoved it in his mouth.

"We do not have to decide anything at this moment," he said, mouth full. "Complete conquest of de Velt's holdings is still a long way off. We have four more castles to claim and that will not prove easy. For now, I will go find Dallan and the other commanders and send them to you. Shall I send them here?"

Bretton nodded. "Aye," he said. "And make sure the grooms have the chargers prepared. Make sure the horses are well fed and watered."

Grayton nodded. "If you are agreeable, I will also make sure your prisoner is well fed and watered."

Bretton merely shrugged as if he didn't care one way or the other. With a quick glance at his liege, Grayton wandered out of the hall to complete his tasks as Bretton remained behind, eating the warmed mutton and gravy the servants brought around, watching the soldiers sleeping in the hall become lucid.

Men were stretching, groaning, and farting. A few were pissing in the fire pit. Bretton looked at his men, seeing brutal and seasoned soldiers, men who would probably continue as mercenaries long after Bretton decided to settle down and remain in one place. The more he thought on it, the more he realized he didn't want to continue conquest after he had confiscated all of de Velt's holdings.

At some point, he wanted to stop and enjoy the fruits of his labor and impeccable planning. He knew it was strange for a mercenary to think that way, but he couldn't help it. At some point in his life, he realized he wanted peace. He wasn't out for everyone's blood, only de Velt's. But until such time as he spilled it, he would continue to kill, maim, and burn until it got him what he wanted.

So he sat there and brooded over the future until the men began to crowd around the feasting table where he was sitting, grabbing at food and drink. When that happened, Bretton finished the remainder of ale in his cup and quit the smelly, cold hall. His intention was to go to the stable to see if his charger was prepared but as he quit the hall, he inevitably noticed the keep to his right. Dark and shadowed against the rising sun, his thoughts turned to the contents of the keep, to Lady Allaston de Velt sleeping peacefully on the second floor.

Damn that woman and her logic! He refused to admit that the woman was coming to intrigue him even though she was. He wasn't sure why but until he could figure it out, she would continue to weigh on his mind and he didn't like that at all. She could prove to be a deadly distraction.

He shifted course and headed for the keep.

❦

SHE WAS READY for him.

Allaston hadn't slept most of the night, either, even though she had been ill and exhausted. Every time she closed her eyes, visions of de Llion and his hatred of her father filled her mind. To her, Jax de Velt was a loving father and a strict task master. To de Llion, he was a killer. She could hardly believe that she and de Llion were speaking of the same person but she knew in her heart of hearts that there was no mistake. She had known of her father's past. But to her, it was just that – a past. That was not the man he was today. She wondered if de Llion believed he was doing the world a favor by eliminating the hated Jax de Velt, but that was a fleeting thought. After having spoken to the man in depth about it, she knew his motives were entirely self-serving. He was doing it for himself. For vengeance. It was vengeance she had to disrupt.

So she tried to sleep, and she did for a few hours, but well before dawn she awoke, her mind racing. She couldn't simply let de Llion lure her father to his death. She was determined to fight back, to stop him somehow, even if it meant her own life. She simply couldn't stand by and let de Llion complete his plans. Therefore, she rose very early with a plan in mind. It would mean de Llion's life or her own. Today, that would be decided.

The thought of violence terrified her. She had never really been around it until the night de Llion and his men came to Alberbury. She knew, however, that it would take violence to stop Bretton de Llion so she crafted an idea. The fire poker, the one she had noticed last night, was sitting near the hearth. It was the only thing in the room that could be construed as a weapon so it was what she intended to use. She fully intended to kill the man with it because she knew if she didn't kill him, he would kill her. It was his life or hers, and she would do all she could to ensure she would remain alive.

But it would be trickier after she killed him. She still had to escape the castle and that would be no easy task. But she presumed that if she could at least find the kitchens, then perhaps she could also find a postern gate. Most castles had them near the kitchens because of the commerce that was conducted with the cooks. Her hope was that she could get to the postern gate and flee before de Llion's body was discovered. She had to have that gift of time if she had a hope of escaping, and once she was free, she would run to the nearest church and ask for help.

Perhaps it wasn't a brilliant plan but it was the only one she had and, at the moment, she was desperate. She knew she had to strike first. De Llion had filled her head with frightening images and thoughts that were feeding her anxiety. All that waited for her here was doom and enslavement and she wasn't one to accept such a situation. She would fight for her life, for her father's life, or go down trying.

So she changed out of the heavy leather robe she had worn to bed, swapping it out for a few of the garments that Grayton had brought her. The first thing that went on was a shift of heavy linen the color of eggshells, as most linen was that color because it did not dye well. Wool was easily colored and she found a woolen surcoat of dark yellow that, once pulled over the sheath, fit her fairly well. It was well-made and expensive, she thought, simply by the way it was sewn.

Once her clothing was changed, she sought out her leather slippers. They were badly damaged from her time spent in the vault, shriveled and with some mold, but she put them on anyway over the hose she still wore from the previous night. Her hair, a rather unruly mass of black silk, was tamed by smoothing her hands over it and running her fingers through it, straightening it as much as she could, before braiding it tightly and securing the braid with a piece of cloth she tore from the hem of her dirty old clothing. She was dressed warmly and had shoes on her feet, so she was prepared when the time came to flee.

Her plans were briefly interrupted by a knock on the door. Nervously, she ran for the poker until she realized that it was a servant, so she went back over to the bed and sat as a small old man, dressed in ill-fitting clothing, brought her a meal to break her fast. Allaston eyed the food and noticed that it didn't look like scraps, which was surprising considering that was what she had been fed for the past three weeks. She was hungry, too, but she remained on the bed as the servant stoked the fire with some peat and wood he brought with him. When the fire was burning nicely, he quit the chamber and left her alone.

Once he was gone, she leapt up and ran to the food, shoving bread in her mouth and struggling to chew because it was so full. The bread was warm, freshly baked, and delicious. There was also cheese on the plate along with a cup of watered ale, and she drank deeply, thirsty. A little mound of warmed mutton didn't survive her hunger long and she chewed it up eagerly. In fact, she cleared the tray in little time, feeling much better after everything was gone. With her stomach, and manner, fortified she was better able to focus on what needed to be done. She had a feeling that de Llion would come around again today, this morning perhaps, and she would be ready for him.

So she resumed her seat on the bed as she waited uneasily and the room grew warm because of the snapping fire. It felt rather good. Growing restless and jittery, she fingered through the rest of the garments Grayton had brought her, a pile that she had kicked to the floor when she'd gone to sleep. There was part of a brocaded surcoat, just the bibbed portion without the skirt, another surcoat that was a very heavy blue wool, and then a cloak on the bottom of the pile that was dark green in color with a brown rabbit lining. It was quite nice and she pulled it out, inspecting it. She was in the process of fingering the fur when there was a single heavy rap at the door.

Startled, she dropped the cloak and ran to the hearth where the poker rested against the wall. Snatching the poker, she ran to the door, wedging herself against the wall so that when the door opened, she would be behind it. Trembling with both fear and anticipation, she didn't respond when someone knocked again. She remained still and silent. After a tense pause, the latch to the door lifted.

The door swung open, hitting her as it did, but she didn't utter a sound. She strained to catch a glimpse of someone entering, her heart beating loudly in her ears as Bretton came into view. He had his back to her as he stepped into the room and it was evident that he was looking for her.

Allaston took it as her moment to strike. The longer she delayed, the more chance there was of him discovering her in the shadows with a poker in her hands. Bringing the poker up, she stepped out from behind the door and aimed for his head, bringing it down as hard as she could right on the back of his skull.

There was a loud, sickening thud as Bretton pitched forward onto his face. He wasn't out cold, however. He was still moving around and Allaston whacked him again, as hard as she could. He fell still.

Allaston stood over Bretton with the poker still raised, preparing to hit him again when she realized that she had knocked him out. The man wasn't moving at all. Peering closer, she wasn't even sure that he was breathing and she could see blood on the back of his head, glistening off his dark hair. Poker still in hand, she bent over to see if she could tell if he was breathing, now having some indecision about her actions. What if she did kill him? That would make her no better than he was. It would make her a brute, capable of violence. She never had liked violence and now that she had committed a violent act, it only served to fuel her distaste.

But she couldn't back out of her plans now. She had already started the scheme in motion and there was no turning back. De Llion was knocked out cold and it was time for her to move. She had to flee, to somehow get out of this place. Tossing the poker aside, she bent down to make sure Bretton was still breathing before she left. A foolish gesture but she wasn't entirely cold-hearted about things. Even towards a man who was determined to kill her father. After last night's conversation with him, she had come to understand him a bit. He was a driven killer, but he'd also led a tragic life. As she looked down at him, she struggled not to feel sorry for the man.

But there wasn't time for sorrows or regrets now. She put her hand in front of de Llion's nose to see that he was indeed breathing, slow and steady. At least she knew he wasn't going to die as the result of her beating. Standing up, she turned hastily for the chamber door and ran headlong into a big, warm body.

Grayton had her around the neck before she could scream.

CHAPTER SIX

B RONLLYS CASTLE WAS a relatively small castle as far as fortresses went, but it was strategic. Originally held by Walter de Clifford, the High Sheriff of England, he had turned the castle over to Christopher de Lohr because the man had more manpower on the Marches and was less involved in London politics, in which Walter was entrenched. With the Marches as volatile as they were, it made sense to have the outpost manned by a lord who had an active interest in keeping the peace. Therefore, Bronllys Castle was an English-held castle, managed by de Lohr, in the midst of Welsh territory.

Sir Berwyn de Llion was the garrison commander for Bronllys, an old man who refused to give up his command. The man had grown grandsons but still he continued to remain active. His once-black hair was now mostly gray but he had a lot of it, and he was built like most of the de Llion men – muscular and big-chested. His teeth were still in good shape if not slightly yellowed, his heart gave him pain now and again, but those were the only signs of age on the man. He was still rugged and strong.

It was this man who greeted Rod as the knight entered the bailey of Bronllys. From high in the keep, which sat atop a massive motte, Berwyn had seen Rod approaching from the south. The fog that had blanketed the countryside for most of the day had finally lifted, affording brilliant views for miles. Situated at the junction of two rivers,

Bronllys guarded one of the main roads into Wales. One could not avoid the castle if one was traveling into Wales.

Excited by the view of his grandson returning, it took Berwyn some time to climb down from the keep, taking the narrow wooden steps down the motte and on into the bailey. By the time he reached the large, oddly shaped bailey, Rod had already been met by some soldiers and was dismounting his frothing steed. Berwyn was very happy to see the man.

"I am glad to see that the fortunes were with you," he said as he clapped Rod on the back. "And how is our illustrious liege? Did you give de Lohr my greetings?"

Rod was weary from his ride but he managed a smile at his grandfather. "I did," he said. "He sends his in return."

Berwyn began to pull Rod towards the great hall, which was built along the eastern wall of the bailey. "How was your journey?"

"Long."

"What did de Lohr want of you?"

Rod didn't say anything for the moment. He had been debating what to tell his grandfather about Bretton's return ever since he had learned of it. He and de Lohr had spent an evening debating about the positive and negative effects of telling the old man, but in the end, Rod knew he couldn't, in good conscience, withhold such information. It wasn't fair to Berwyn. Good or bad, the man had a right to know, especially if he had the potential of facing the man in battle.

"Come inside and we will discuss it," Rod said as they headed into the long, skinny great hall with its massive hearth and roaming packs of cats. No dogs at Bronllys, but feral cats everywhere. Rod even shoved one out of the way as he took a seat at the end of the big feasting table. "I have not eaten since before dawn, so feed me before I faint."

Berwyn grinned and sent a servant running to the kitchen for food and drink as he sat down opposite his grandson. He was inordinately attached to the man and had been for the past several years, ever since Rod came to serve with him. Missing his own son as he did, his only son who had been murdered those years ago, made him overly attached to Rod. He faced the man over the top of the well-scrubbed feasting table.

"Well?" he said expectantly. "What would de Lohr have of you?"

Rod eyed his grandfather. He was going to have to be very careful in how he brought about the subject of Bretton de Llion. As he'd told de Lohr, it was quite possible that his grandfather, in a fit of emotion, would ride straight to Cloryn to seek out the truth of the matter. Rod didn't want a big scene on his hands with his grandfather but braced himself for the possibility.

"It would seem that there is much activity happening on the Marches north of Bronllys and we must maintain vigilance," he began quietly. "De Lohr summoned me to warn us about it. It would seem there is a mercenary army raiding and confiscating castles along the Powis border."

Berwyn was grim. "It must be serious, indeed," he said. "Mercenary army, did you say?"

Rod nodded. "Remember when we were told of Cloryn's defeat by a passing merchant?" he asked, watching his grandfather nod. "Cloryn was just one tragedy in a long line of many. That same army moved on Alberbury Priory and burned it to the ground."

Berwyn's bushy eyebrows rose. "They *burned* a priory?" he repeated, aghast. "Why would they do this? The priory would have nothing of value, at least nothing that mercenaries would want."

Rod drew in a long, contemplative breath, pausing before replying as servants brought food to the table and set it down. He waited until the servants walked away before continuing.

"These are no ordinary mercenaries," he said, reaching for the pitcher of boiled fruit juice. He preferred that over watered ale in the morning. "De Lohr received a missive from Robert de Boulers not long ago. Most of the activity has been on de Bouler's borders and the man is understandably concerned. Evidently, the story is this – an army of Irish mercenaries landed in Liverpool several weeks ago and made its way to the Powis Marches, whereupon they wreaked a good deal of havoc. They badly damaged Clun Castle and Knighton Castle, and attacked Dolforwyn as well, although that castle held. But Cloryn didn't. They took it and then they moved on to burn Alberbury Priory. They went to Alberbury with a purpose, however. They were looking for someone."

Berwyn was frowning now. "I do not understand," he said. "Who were they looking for?"

Rod sighed faintly as he poured his drink. "Ajax de Velt's daughter," he said. "She was apparently a novice nun at the priory. They took the girl, burned the priory, but left one solitary old nun alive to deliver a message regarding their actions."

Berwyn was shocked. "What message is that?"

Rod took a long drink before answering. "The message is for Ajax de Velt," he said. "The mercenaries are following the same pattern de Velt did when he raided the borders twenty-five years ago. Every castle they have hit has been a castle de Velt hit, and Cloryn belonged to de Velt. They have taken it and they have taken his daughter. The message to de Velt is simple – if he wants his daughter, he must come and get her. This mercenary army is calling forth de Velt, Papa. They are summoning The Dark Lord himself."

Berwyn's initial shock faded and now he simply sat and mulled over the situation. He was an old man and didn't get too excited over things, no matter how bad they were. Calmer heads prevailed because panicked ones couldn't. After several moments of pondering the circumstances, he grunted and shook his head.

"I do not want to see de Velt on this border again," he said. "I remember when the man tore through here twenty-five years ago. It was as if Hell itself had opened up and Lucifer was marching upon us. The fear of that time was tangible. When he took Four Crosses Castle… well, that is a time I do not wish to relive. I cannot even stomach the thought."

The time had come for Rod to divulge what he knew. He tried to be gentle. "The commander of the mercenary army had a name," he said quietly. "He told the old nun to make sure she relayed it to de Velt. He gave his name as Bretton de Llion."

So much for not getting excited over things. Berwyn stared at Rod for a long, tense moment before his eyebrows lifted and his face went pale. He was having difficulty speaking, stammering and stuttering, until the words finally came forth.

"Bretton?" he repeated, aghast. "*Bretton* de Llion?"

Rod nodded, hoping his grandfather wasn't going to seize up right in front of him. "That is why de Lohr summoned me, in truth," he said steadily. "It was because of the name the mercenary commander gave. He knew that name was somehow related to us, to you. He thought it would be better if I told you."

Berwyn just stared at him. It was clear he was reeling. He began to shake his head, back and forth, almost wildly.

"Impossible," he gasped. "Bretton died twenty-five years ago."

Rod wasn't unsympathetic to the man's reaction. His, in fact, had been worse, comparatively speaking. At least Berwyn wasn't yelling about it.

"That is what I told de Lohr," Rod said. "But the man made some very good points. We never found Bretton's body. If there is no body, then there is no confirmation of death. It is quite possible that Bretton somehow escaped and has now returned to seek vengeance for what happened to Uncle Morgan. *Isn't* it possible, Papa?"

Berwyn was so off balance by the revelation that he literally reeled over backwards, catching himself on the table. Disoriented, he stood up unsteadily and Rod also stood up and went around the table to take hold of his grandfather. The man was all shades of incredulous and the grief, long buried these years, began to surface again.

"Nay," he hissed. "It is *not* possible. Bretton died along with Morgan and Ceri and Brethwyn. He has not come back from the dead."

Rod had hold of the man as he struggled. "Then why would this commander give that name?" he asked, trying to force the man to think.

"Why would he say he was Bretton if he was not? There is no reason for him to lie about his identity. All things are possible, Papa. Sometimes… sometimes the dead do return. Sometimes they are not really dead at all."

He was referring to his brother Rhys, of course, but he was not prepared to divulge that information, too. It would have been too much for Berwyn to take. As it was, the old man was struggling.

"Nay," Berwyn said again, more firmly. "It is *not* Bretton."

Rod wasn't surprised at the denial. In fact, he was oddly relieved by it. At least Berwyn wasn't demanding his horse so he could ride to Cloryn and see for himself if his grandson had indeed returned. Maybe he would, eventually, but for now, he was in utter denial. Not that Rod blamed him.

"Mayhap," he said softly, still holding fast to Berwyn. "In any case, there is a mercenary army running amuck on the Marches and we must be vigilant. De Lohr suggested we move south to Whitebrook until the threat has passed. He is very concerned should this mercenary move on Bronllys."

Berwyn was gripping his grandson as he stared at the ground. There were a million thoughts rolling through his mind but mostly, he was struggling against bone-numbing grief, the same grief he had experienced when his son had been killed. He was feeling it again, now for the grandson he had lost. Someone was playing a horrible trick on all of them. Along with that grief came rage.

"Nay," he said yet again, lifting his head to look at Rod. "I do not know who this… this *bastard* is who poses as my dead grandson, but I will find him and I will kill him, do you hear? He will pay for defiling the de Llion name. Are we now to be held in the same contempt as the name of de Velt because of the death and destruction he is committing along the Marches? I will not stand for it!"

Rod shook his head firmly. "You cannot do anything about it, at least not now," he said. "To ride to confront the man will only see you killed and I am not prepared to lose my grandfather so soon after losing my brother. Would you really do that to me? You will calm yourself, Papa. Go up to your chamber and remain there until you have calmed. I will send the physic up with a draught for your nerves."

Berwyn didn't want any part of Rod's mothering. "Nay, I will *not*," he said loudly. "I do not wish to rest. I wish to wrap my hands around the demon that falsely uses my name!"

Rod watched his grandfather pull away from him as he began to pace angrily. He had already said everything he could to calm the man so perhaps the only other alternative was to distract him. He was willing to try.

"What do you remember of de Velt's conquest on the Marches those years ago?" he asked, hoping Berwyn would follow his lead. "Whatever this mercenary commander is doing, it seems to emulate de Velt in every way. Did he come this far south?"

Berwyn was still raging about the imposter. "He took Comen Castle and Erwood Castle," he said angrily. "You know where those castles are, Rod. They are each about a half day's ride from here. He came very close to Bronllys but he did not try to take us. Let this imposter come now! I want to see his face!"

Berwyn went off on a rant about how he would tear the man limb from limb if he ever got ahold of him. Rod stood there and watched him, knowing the old man meant every word. Even at his advanced age, he was still formidable on the field of battle. Berwyn didn't get worked up very often but when he did, it was often unstoppable. Therefore, he simply stood back for a few moments and let the man work through his fury. All the while, Rod kept thinking about the mercenary army and their mimicry of Jax de Velt. As his grandfather raged, he began to recount some of the factors that he and de Lohr had discussed. They were factors that would interest Berwyn.

"If this mercenary army is indeed emulating Jax de Velt, then there is less of a chance they will come to Bronllys," he said. "However, they may very well move on Erwood and Comen. We will be able to smell the destruction from here."

Berwyn was muttering to himself, still pacing about, but he stopped when Rod's words sank in.

"That is true," he agreed. "We will have to make sure the castle is locked up. We will have to bring the villeins into the fold. It would not be safe to leave the villagers without protection."

Rod dared to move towards the old man who seemed to be calming somewhat. "Mayhap you should ride to the village and speak with them," he said, hoping it would deter the man from his outrage and focus him on something constructive. "We must tell them to be on their guard should the mercenaries make it this far south."

Berwyn nodded. "That would be wise."

"Would you like for me to go with you?"

Berwyn was weary now that the explosion of rage had eased from a roaring fire to a simmer. He was sweating and pale, but at least he was sufficiently calming. The storm had passed, for the moment.

"Nay," he shook his head. "You have traveled all day. You must rest. This is something I will do alone. I will go and speak with the priests so they can help spread the word."

Rod didn't push. He was glad that his grandfather was focused on something other than the imposter using the de Llion name. Now, the man was focused on the small village that was near the castle. There was a good working relationship between the two, something Berwyn had cultivated for many years.

"Very well," Rod said, watching his grandfather head for the exit of the great hall. "Are you sure you will be well?"

Berwyn nodded unsteadily, like a man who had too much on his mind. "Well enough," he said, pausing by the door to look at his grandson. "What you have told me… you have not told anyone else, have you?"

Rod shook his head. "Who else would I tell?"

"Orlaith."

Rod cocked his head, pursing his lips reproachfully. "I would tell my mother before I told you?" he asked in a tone that suggested it was a ridiculous question. "Of course I have not told her. I have not even seen her. She is at Whitebrook and it would have taken me at least four days to get there. Until we can confirm any of this, I see no reason to tell her that her nephew may be alive."

Berwyn wagged his head back and forth. "There is no reason for her to know in any case," he said. "Your mother was quite attached to her brother. His death saddened her greatly, as did the passing of his family. There is no need for her to know anything."

With that, Berwyn quit the hall to go about his business, leaving Rod behind to ponder that very statement. *There is no need for her to know anything.* But what if it was true and Bretton had returned as a hated mercenary? If that was truly the case, then he had to agree with his grandfather –it would be better for his mother to not know at all.

Still… he had to wonder if they would ever know the truth. Maybe Bretton *had* returned. If that was what had happened, then he had to wonder why the man hadn't contacted them. He had been asking himself that question since nearly the moment de Lohr revealed the name behind the mercenary army. Surely Bretton remembered his family. If he remembered Jax de Velt and the havoc the man wrought, then surely he would remember those who loved him from his childhood. Surely he remembered that he had family here on the Marches.

There was only one way to find out.

☙

IT WAS HER fault, really. She'd had the courage to attack the man but she hadn't been able to escape as she had hoped. Therefore, she was forced to face the punishment. She had taken a risk and it had come back in her face.

Allaston was back in the vault again. Grayton, upon discovering her over Bretton's unconscious body, had grabbed her by the neck and dragged her back down to the moldering depths of Cloryn's dark vault. He had quite literally thrown her back upon the dirty straw that had been her only bed for three weeks before slamming the grate and making sure it was bolted. The entire time, he'd never said a word, and neither did she. In truth, there was nothing for either of them to say.

That had been a few hours ago. Allaston huddled back against the wall, still in the fine clothing she had been wearing. She suspected that she was going to remain here forever, or at least until her father showed up. Mayhap then they would release her if only to dangle her before her father to show the man their prize. Truly, she only had herself to blame and was therefore resigned to her fate. Hysterics weren't going to change anything.

So she sat and waited, for what, she didn't know. She was confident enough that de Llion wouldn't kill her. He'd been clear that he needed her alive. So the only alternative was to keep her locked up because she had proven she couldn't be trusted. As she sat there and pondered the course of her dismal future, she heard bootfalls on the steps leading into the vault.

And so it comes, she thought to herself. Even if de Llion wasn't going to kill her, he had said nothing about not beating or abusing her. She deserved the punishment for what she had done and braced herself for that very real possibility. Resigned though she might be, it didn't stop tears of fear from stinging her eyes at the thought of what might lay ahead.

It was dark in the vault, as usual, with the only light coming from the stairwell that led to the gatehouse above. She could see a figure descending the steps, realizing it was de Llion simply by the sheer size of the man. He came off the stairs and turned in her direction but she couldn't see his face because the light was behind him. All she could see as he approached were shadowed features. It made it difficult to gauge his mood, which she could only imagine wasn't too good. When he came to the locked grate of the cell, he simply stood there. Even though Allaston was looking at him, she couldn't see his eyes.

"I was told to leave you down here to rot," he finally said in his raspy, deep voice. "I should, you know."

Allaston lowered her gaze from his shadowed face. "I would expect you to."

He paused before answering. "I would except for two good reasons," he said. "First of all, in spite of what you did, it was astonishingly brave. It showed cunning and resourcefulness. I did not expect a female to show such courage. Second of all, you could have easily killed me but you did not. I want to know why."

Allaston kept her gaze averted. "Because I am not a killer," she said. "In spite of what you think, in spite of the de Velt name, I am not a killer. I could not take your life. I could not take anyone's life."

"Then why did you knock me unconscious?"

"Because I wanted to escape. That was my only motive."

Bretton watched her lowered head from his position outside of the cell. After waking up with an excruciating headache almost two hours ago, lying on the floor of the chamber where Allaston had been, he truly had no idea what had happened. He remembered walking in the door and little else.

Pushing himself off the floor, he caught sight of the fire poker a few feet away. A perusal of the chamber showed that he was quite alone and that had been his first clue as to what had transpired. No prisoner and a suspiciously discarded poker. Only when he had left the room and gone in search of a soldier to sound the alarm that Allaston had escaped had he run into Grayton, who was returning from the gatehouse. Grayton had told him all he needed to know and Bretton had spent the last hour and a half listening to the man rant about Allaston and how Grayton had been mistaken to think the woman was worthy of being released form the vault. But Bretton, strangely enough, couldn't seem to agree.

So he sat and imbibed a couple of cups of wine to stave off his headache as Grayton fumed and the barber-surgeon put three stitches in the back of his scalp. When the wine was gone and the stitches were finished, Bretton chased Grayton away before making his way down to the vault where he now stood. Looking at Allaston's lowered head, he still couldn't bring himself to be angry about what she had done. One small woman had managed to do what no one else had ever accomplished – she had managed to disable him. Oddly, he found some humor in that as well as admiration.

"Where were you going to go if you escaped?" he asked quietly. "Do you even know where you are?"

Allaston's head came up and she looked at him. "Cloryn Castle," she said. "Your man Grayton told me."

Bretton nodded faintly. Then he reached out and threw the bolt on the cell, pulling open the old, creaking door with the rusted hinges. He just stood in the doorway, watching her.

"Where were you going to go?" he repeated.

Allaston shrugged. "I was going to find a church," she said. "I thought the priests would help me."

"Did you not stop to think that I would find you?" Bretton asked. "Alberbury Priory could not stop me. What makes you think another church would?"

Allaston shrugged. "I am sure that it would not," she said, some frustration in her tone. "I simply want to return to what I was doing before you came and tore me away from my friends and mentors. I want to return to the cloister. I do not want to be a part of your war games, de Llion."

His gaze lingered on her. "And yet, you are," he said, his voice soft. "What about your father? Did you plan on warning him about me?"

Her frustration grew. "Of course I did," she said. "I planned on sending him word that I was safe and not to engage you. Do you not understand? I want him to stay well away from Wales and well away from me because I love my father and I do not want you to kill him."

He was aware of her mounting agitation. "That is between me and your father."

Her eyebrows rose. "You just said I was a part of your war games," she said. "Therefore, this is between you, my father, and me. You have made me an unwilling participant in all of this."

He nodded, once, as if he understood her logic. "I will agree with you," he said. "But trying to escape me is futile. There is nowhere for you to go that I will not find you."

Allaston sighed heavily, exasperated. "That is probably true," she said. "But I will ask you this question, de Llion, and you will be truthful with me. Think back to that day when my father besieged Four Crosses. If you could have done anything at that time to save your father, wouldn't you have done it? That is what I was trying to do by making an escape attempt – I was trying to save my father."

Bretton pondered her words. As he did, he took a few steps into the cell, standing a mere few feet from where Allaston was huddled. He crouched down so that he could look her in the eye, seeing her ghostly pale face framed by the dark cloak over her head.

"I would have done anything to save my father that day," he said quietly, "but I was only five years of age and had not the strength, the knowledge, or the skill. Because I could not save him then, I have made it my mission in life to seek vengeance against the man who murdered him and you are a part of that plan. I am sorry if that if distasteful to you, but that is the way of things."

Allaston stared into his bright blue eyes. There was pain in her features. "But I love my father just as you loved yours," she admitted. "If you kill my father, you will be hurting me as deeply as you were hurt those years ago. Would you truly wish that pain upon me?"

Bretton found that he was having difficulty concentrating with her mesmerizing eyes fixed upon him pleadingly. It unbalanced him because he could feel something more than just a mere fixation. He could feel something warm spark. He'd never felt that kind of thing before and it startled him. He didn't understand his reaction. What he didn't understand, he didn't like.

"You are of no consequence," he said, his manner bordering on cold. "Whatever pain you feel is not my concern. I must do as I must and you will have to accept it."

Allaston sat back as if he had slapped her. Tears began to form in her eyes as the weight of his words settled. There was no changing his mind, she knew. She had tried to reason with him, to be kind to him, to fight him, and to submit to him. She had tried everything. Everything except one last final offering. She was at her lowest point, knowing what she had to do and dreading it. It took every last ounce of courage she had to speak the words.

"My father *is* my concern," she whispered. "I cannot talk you out of doing such a terrible deed, for your mind is set. But if it is a de Velt you want to kill, then instead of my father, mayhap you will consider me. If it is only de Velt blood you seek, I can give you mine."

Bretton's expression didn't change. "It is not your blood I want."

"But you want de Velt blood," she insisted. "Killing my father will bring you nothing, but if you kill me, then you are assured of hurting my father as badly as he has hurt you. Take my life, de Llion. It is worthless now anyway, for as your prisoner, all will assume you will have had your way with me. Everything I stand for is ruined. Take my life and send my body back to my father and I can assure you that he will be greatly hurt. I will willingly let you kill me if you will only cease your bloodlust against him. If you truly want to make the man suffer, then you must take my life to accomplish that."

She made sense, which concerned him. He didn't like the fact that she made utter and complete sense and, to a logical man, it was worth considering. Although he had always considered himself logical, he knew without a doubt that he could not kill her. Something about this woman intrigued him like no other human being ever had. She was fiercely loyal, intelligent, brave, and beautiful. He had trouble accepting a de Velt could be all of these things, but Lady Allaston was.

"Mayhap," he said after a moment because he didn't want her to suspect his reluctance to kill her. He thought the best way to control her was for her to never know what he was thinking, especially in matters like this. "I will think on your proposal. Meanwhile, you will come with me."

Allaston was emotionally edgy from her plea, now wary of his directive. "Why?" she asked. "Where are we going?"

"Back to the keep."

Allaston blinked, bewildered by the thought. "But why?"

Bretton stood up. "Because it is warmer there," he said. When she didn't move, he lifted his eyebrows at her. "Do you prefer it here?"

She didn't. Allaston shook her head unsteadily and struggled to stand. "Are you going to kill me there?"

Bretton reached down and pulled her to her feet. She didn't weigh much and he ended up nearly launching her because he pulled so hard. That being the case, he had to reach out to steady her and stop her momentum.

"I am not going to kill you at the moment," he said. "But I will punish you for trying to bash my brains in."

Allaston wasn't sure she liked the sound of that. "How am I to be punished?"

He was evasive. "I will tell you in time," he said. "But until then, you must promise me something."

Allaston was unsteady on her feet, trying not to step on the hem of her cloak as she walked off of the straw. "What can I promise you?" she asked, baffled. "Even if I did, would you believe me after what I did?"

He turned to look at her as he headed out of the cell. "Would you break a promise to me?"

Her brow furrowed. "It depends on the promise."

"Then you are not a lady of your word?"

She was growing frustrated again with his circular conversation. "God's Beard," she snapped softly. "Of course I am. What in the world do you want me to promise?"

Bretton fought off a grin at her irritation. "That you will never again crack me, or anyone, over the head with a poker or otherwise try to harm any of my men."

Her frown grew. "You make it sound as if I am a murderess."

His grin broke through then, he couldn't help it. "You did go after a man twice your size with a poker," he reminded her. "What if you *are* a murderess?"

"Then my promise will mean nothing for I will kill you in your sleep anyway."

He snorted, humorously. "I will make sure to sleep with one eye open, then," he said. "Will you promise me that you will never again be violent towards me or any of my men? If you cannot promise, then I will have to leave you down here and I do not think you want that."

He was right, she didn't. After a moment, she nodded. "Very well," she said reluctantly. "You have my oath that I will not try to harm anyone again."

"And you will not try to escape again."

She was more reluctant to promise him that. "But a prisoner is expected to escape," she argued weakly. "That is my right."

He snorted again as they reached the stairs leading up into the gatehouse. The light above was nearly blinding.

"If you try to escape again, I will chain you up and never let you go," he said. "If you want your freedom, then you must not give me a reason to take it away from you. Is that clear enough?"

He was being fair about the situation, a shocking attribute from a man who had, so far, shown nothing but rank brutality. He was actually showing her some mercy whether or not he realized it and Allaston knew this was more than likely a one-time offer. Should she betray him, then the situation would go very badly for her. Although she was prepared to die for her father, she wasn't prepared to be locked up like an animal for the rest of her life. Death would be preferable to that. Therefore, she did the only thing she could do. She nodded.

"It is," she said, slowly following him up the narrow stairs. "But if you are not going to keep me in the vault, where are you taking me?"

Bretton was taking the stairs slowly because she was. They were mossy and slippery, and she was unsteady on them. He watched her almost lose her footing on one before reaching out a hand to her.

"Here," he said.

Allaston looked up from the steps, noticing the outstretched hand but having no idea what it was for.

"What do you mean?" she asked.

He thrust the hand at her again to make his intention obvious. "Take my hand so you do not slip and break your neck."

Hesitantly, Allaston put her hand in his and he clamped down on her fingers, his heated grip against hers. But he was strong and steady, and she end up relying heavily on him to help her the rest of the way up the steps. Once they reached the ground floor of the gatehouse, he faced her and let her go.

"Since you will no longer be in the vault, I intend to put you to work," he said. "Tell me what you did at Alberbury. Surely you had assigned tasks."

Allaston frowned, this time with some outrage. "You intend to make me your slave?"

He cocked an eyebrow. "I intend to punish you," he said. "Tell me what tasks you had at Alberbury."

Allaston was still frowning but she complied. "My tasks were mostly kitchen related," she said. "I helped cook meals, tend the garden, and tend stock."

"Then your punishment will be kitchen-related," Bretton said, turning to head out of the gatehouse as Allaston followed. "There were only a few male servants left after I took Cloryn and it would be fair to say that our meals have suffered. That will now be your task."

She skipped after him, squinting her eyes in the bright light. "My punishment is to cook?"

"Your punishment is to be my chatelaine. I need one. You will run this keep to my satisfaction or I will take my hand to your backside. Is that clear?"

It was better than being in the vault. Even as she mulled over her new assignment, the first thing that popped to mind was how easy it would be to poison their food if she had access to the kitchen. A sick army could not march on her father. She hadn't promised not to poison them, after all. She had simply promised not to harm anyone or try to escape. She supposed that poison could fall under the vow not to harm anyone and, as she thought on it, the technicalities of it had her torn.

Being nice to the man hadn't worked. Reasoning with him hadn't worked. Mayhap her only recourse was to somehow prevent the army from moving at all. But she had a feeling if she did that, then again, the consequences against her could be horrific. De Llion had forgiven an attempt against him once but she doubted he'd forgive a second attempt. Perhaps she needed to contemplate the option of poison over a little more before doing anything. Now that he was placing her in a position of some trust, she would have to be careful and not betray that trust until she was absolutely sure she could get away with it. If that moment ever came.

She wondered if it would.

CHAPTER SEVEN

Two Weeks Later, Late June
Pelinom Castle, Northumberland
House of de Velt

THE DAY WAS mild and windy as a sea breeze blew in from the east, carrying seagulls upon it. The birds sometimes ventured this far inland, looking for food and scraps, their loud cries hanging upon the wind.

A very big man with dual-colored eyes and dark, graying hair pulled back into a tail at the nape of his neck was standing at the window of his solar on the second level of Pelinom's keep, watching the birds overhead against the blue sky. Ajax de Velt could remember when his older sons, Cole and Julian, would make slingshots when they were younger and try to knock the birds out of the sky. Once, they hit another bird, a beautiful bird with a red neck that had fallen out of the sky, wounded. The boys' younger sister, Allaston, had cried and carried on, and wanted to nurse the bird back to health. The boys had wanted to eat it. Jax remembered the battle that had ensued, which Allaston had eventually won because she was very clever and not afraid of a fight. God, he missed those days. He missed Allaston.

With a heavy sigh, Jax turned to glance at the package on his desk. It had been delivered a half-hour before by a messenger bearing colors that no one had recognized. The messenger had dumped the package at the main gate of Pelinom and fled. Once the package was retrieved, the messenger was well away and there was no point in pursuing.

The sergeant in charge of the gatehouse had delivered it to de Velt, seated in his solar conducting other business, but Jax had taken the package and opened it with some curiosity in front of the sergeant. What he had pulled forth had been unexpected and macabre. Reading the missive that had come with the contents of the package had nearly thrown him into a panic. He'd read the missive six times before the words sank in:

Your daughter from Alberbury is my prisoner. The hair contained herein belongs to her. I hold your daughter and will soon hold all of your castles upon the Welsh Marches. I have done to your men what you have done to others in the past. Your sins have finally found you and if you wish for your daughter to be returned in good health, you will come to me at Cloryn Castle. Time grows short.

The last sentence was a threat and Jax knew it. After having received a severed head a week ago, the head of a man who had been his commander at Ithon Castle in the Welsh Marches, Jax knew that something was afoot but he wasn't aware of how bad it was. Now, he knew. Someone was after him, his property and his family, and they wanted it badly enough to kill one of his commanders and abduct his eldest daughter. He'd kept the threat from his family, however. He'd never told them about the severed head, although his eldest son knew, but he wouldn't be able to keep the abduction of his daughter secret. Now the threat was becoming very real, and very grave, and they would all have to face it.

With slow, heavy steps, he crossed the floor back to the massive oak table that served as his desk. He stared at the contents of the package, in a wad on the tabletop, before reaching down to collect it. Strands of dark, silky hair lingered in his grasp as he inspected the nest of hair. It looked like Allaston's hair, soft and dark, but of course, he couldn't be entirely sure. He'd sent for the expert, and he was dreading the moment when he would have to tell his wife that their daughter was in danger. He still wasn't going to tell her about the severed head, for it was something she didn't need to know, but the delivery of the hair was another matter altogether. He knew she wouldn't take it well. Setting the hair back down on the table, he wandered over to the window again to contemplate his next move as he wait for his wife. She wasn't long in coming.

Lady Kellington Coleby de Velt slipped into her husband's solar, her hands full of something that she was either mending or making, he couldn't be sure. They had six children and four grandchildren, and she was always making or mending something. Petite, with blond hair gathered into a bun at the back of her head and big brown eyes, she was still a stunningly beautiful woman in her forty-fifth year. She easily looked much younger, this woman who had tamed The Dark Lord those years ago. She went straight to her husband, who was still standing near the lancet window, lifting her cheek for his kiss.

"One of your soldiers said that you wished to see me," she said, her attention on the bundle of material in her hands. She held it up, unfurling an infant's dressing gown in front of her husband. "Do you remember this? Cole was baptized in it. I am putting some flowers on it so he can use it for his daughter's baptism."

Jax looked at the unbleached linen with the delicate silk borders on the neck and on the sleeves. "What if he has a son someday and wants to use the same gown?" he asked. "Cole will not want his son to wear flowers."

Kellington shrugged, fussing with the stitching on the neck of the garment. "Then I will remove them," she said, glancing up at her husband as she made her way over to a chair near the hearth. "What did you wish to see me about, my love?"

Jax watched her for a moment, hating the fact that he was about to make her very, very upset. The thought was excruciatingly distressing and made him sick to his stomach, but he didn't have much choice.

Kellington had to know. As Kellington sat down and began to resume her sewing, Jax thought on what he was about to tell her. He wanted to be gentle about it.

"I received a missive today," he began, moving towards his desk where the wad of hair lay. Kellington had remained at a distance from the desk and hadn't noticed it yet. "There is something contained within it that you and I must discuss. It has to do with Allaston."

Kellington's head came up. "What's wrong?" she asked, her face immediately tense with concern. "Is she ill?"

Jax shook his head. "Nay, she is not ill."

His words did not ease her. "Then what message comes from Alberbury?" she demanded.

Jax put up a hand to quiet her. "The missive was not from Alberbury," he said calmly. "I will preface this by saying that Allaston is in good health for the moment, but it would seem we have a problem. According to this missive, someone has abducted her from Alberbury and is holding her for ransom."

Kellington stared at him and he could see the levels of shock rolling across her delicate features. Mild shock turned to moderate shock. Finally, her eyes widened and she set her sewing down, rising from her chair.

"How do you know this?" she asked with great apprehension. "What does the missive say?"

Jax picked up the mass of dark hair from the desk and silently extended it to his wife. Kellington stared at the hair a moment before taking it from him, her pallor going from a healthy pink to an ashen shade as she inspected the strands. Jax came around the desk, putting his hands on her shoulders comfortingly as he watched her examine the lonely mass of hair, beautiful strands without an owner.

"This hair came with the missive," he said quietly. "It looks like Allie's but I cannot be sure. Mayhap you can."

Kellington stared at the hair a moment longer before lifting it to her nose, smelling it deeply. Almost immediately, she broke down in tears.

"I can smell my babe," she whispered. "This is Allie's hair. I would know it anywhere."

"You are certain?"

Kellington nodded emphatically. "I would stake my life on it," she wept. "My God, what have they done to my child?"

Jax put his arms around her, holding her tightly. He felt so very sorrowful but in the same breath, he felt incredibly guilty. Whatever was brewing was directed at him with Allaston somehow caught in the middle of it. So many years of peace and now this. It was as unexpected as it was unwelcomed.

"I am assured she is in good health," he stated, directing her to sit back down in the chair. As they moved, he collected the parchment from the desktop. "Let me read the missive to you."

He did. Kellington wept softly as she listened, holding the dark mass of hair against her chest, over her heart. She was absolutely devastated with the turn of events. As he finished the last few words written before him, Kellington spoke.

"What does this mean?" she demanded, wiping at her nose. "Is there no ransom demand?"

Jax shook his head. "Nay," he replied. "As you heard, whoever has Allie wants me to go to Cloryn Castle."

"But why?" Kellington wanted to know. "I do not understand any of this. Why do they have her and why do they want you to come and get her?"

Jax sighed knowingly. "I believe the comment of my sins finding me is a clue," he said with regret. "Cloryn Castle, and five others, has been mine for twenty-five years, ever since I took a good portion of the Marches for my own in the years before I met you. Cloryn Castle was manned by one of my commanders, Orion d'Savignac, who left his eldest son in charge some years ago when he and his wife moved to the south of France for Orion's health. The man who wrote this missive states that he has done to my men what I did to men those years ago and has directed me to go to Cloryn Castle. I suspect that mayhap

Cloryn does not belong to me any longer. I further suspect my soldiers garrisoned there have met a violent end."

That was putting it mildly. As he'd told himself, he made no mention of the severed head from Ithon because it would only add more horror to an already horrific situation. As it was, Kellington was struggling to calm her tears.

"Do you think someone is trying to exact revenge on you somehow?" she asked. "Twenty-five years ago… you did some very bad things, Jax. Is it possible that someone is out for vengeance and is using Allie to get it?"

Jax was feeling guiltier by the moment. *My sweet Allie*, was all he could think. *Will she pay the price for my sins those years ago?* But he would not voice his thoughts. Kellington probably already knew them, anyway, and it would do no good to upset her more than she already was. After a moment, he sat back heavily on the top of his desk, gazing at the missive in his hand. He was a man of supreme control except when it pertained to his wife and family. They were the only ones who had ever seen the emotion he was capable of. And Kellington… his life, his love… she knew all of his dark secrets.

"That is exactly what I think," he said after a moment, feeling despondence creep upon him. "I did many things those years ago, things that were necessary in the course of conquest. Never did I apologize for my methods because they were my own. I remember you asking me once why I killed men, women, and children, and I told you that it was because every one of them was a threat to me. Mayhap whoever has Cloryn, and Allaston, is someone who had a relative who fell under my blade. Mayhap he has a blood debt to settle with me. I am frankly not surprised by it. In fact, I have expected something like this to happen at some point. It was only a matter of time."

Kellington was quieting since her initial outburst, wiping away the last of her tears. "If it is true that he seeks vengeance against you, then the missive seems to indicate he wishes to see you face to face," she said, looking up at him with her big brown eyes. "You are not going to do it, are you? You promised me twenty-five years ago that your days of battle were over. You have kept that promise for the most part except where the security of our castle or family was concerned."

Jax looked up at her, taking his eyes off the parchment. "If I do not go, I am sure it will not bode well for Allie," he said. "I have no choice. I must go and retrieve my daughter."

Kellington stood up, shaking her head. "So that is my choice?" she asked, agitation in her voice. "I must sacrifice my husband to regain my daughter? That is no choice at all, Jax."

"Do you want Allaston back?"

She threw up her hands. "Of course I do," she said. "But not at the expense of my husband!"

"Then what would you suggest?"

Kellington looked at her husband with some fear and he knew it was because she didn't have an answer. To her credit, she tried to make it seem as if she did.

"Mayhap… mayhap we could send a mediator instead," she said. "Someone who will bargain for Allie's release on your behalf. Mayhap the man who holds her will release her if we give him enough money."

Jax lifted his eyebrows thoughtfully. "That is possible," he said, "although if this really is a blood debt, or vengeance, a mediator may anger him. He abducted our daughter for a reason, Kelli, and it was not to gain money. Nay, the man who holds Allie wants to see me. It says so in this missive."

Kellington felt as if she was losing a fight. She didn't want to give up. She wanted her daughter returned but she wanted her husband whole, as well. "But surely there is someone well respected and powerful who can act as a mediator," she said. "At the very least, mayhap this man will stand with you and support you as you negotiate for Allie's release."

Jax shook his head. "You know better than to suggest I have allies all over England," he said. "Yves de Vesci is my only ally and that is because the man is my liege. Any opportunities for allies were destroyed many years ago, Kelli. No one will ally themselves with The Dark Lord and I do not want allies. They simply complicate things."

Kellington could feel her control of the situation slipping. "Then what of the men stationed at your other Welsh castles?" she asked. "You have six of them, five now if Cloryn is compromised. What of them? Surely you can gather your men from the Welsh outposts and converge on Cloryn to demand Allie's return? Mayhap he will release her by a pure show of force."

Jax shook his head. "That is doubtful," he said. "Moreover, if Cloryn is compromised, I have no way of knowing if the other castles are, too. I do not want to ride all the way to Wales, presuming my castles are still intact, only to discover those have been compromised. Nay, love, I will take most of the men from Pelinom and nearby White Crag with me. Those two castles of mine will provide almost one thousand men. That will be sufficient to march upon Cloryn and demand Allie's return, but if he does not return her, then I will have enough men to lay siege to Cloryn."

Kellington's expression suggested great displeasure at the entire scheme. "Then you are going?"

"I have little choice."

Kellington's gaze stayed on him a moment before hanging her head. "Then you are doing what this man who holds our daughter wishes," she said. "You are walking into his hands."

"I do not see any other way with Allie's life at stake."

Kellington was deeply torn. "But as long as you do not show your face, she will be safe because he will be expecting you to come," she said, trying to reason out her thoughts. "But once you arrive, I fear that his reasons for keeping her alive will end. She will no longer be of value to him once you appear if it is, in fact, you whom he truly wants."

Jax admitted the woman had a point but it didn't crush his resolve. "He wants me to come," he said, picking the parchment up from his desk and shaking at her. "I have no choice but to comply. If I do not, I risk Allie's life."

"And it is acceptable to risk your life, too?" Kellington fired back softly. She could feel the tears of heartache coming on. "I must risk you both? Jax, you are too old to be engaging in battle. You haven't fought a battle in years. Why can you not send someone to Cloryn to mediate or, at the very least, make sure Allaston is really there and still alive? Why must you simply march straight into the jaws of the lion simply because some man tells you to?"

Jax knew she was upset. He was upset, too, but he was also trying to do what he thought he needed to do. "The man who holds Allie has all of the power," he said, rather sternly in an attempt to make her understand. "I have no power at all. He has what I want, what I love, and he knows it. Therefore, I must do as he says. I must go to Cloryn to try and gain my daughter's freedom. All of your arguing will not change what needs to be done."

That was perhaps true, but Kellington was still trying to find another way that wouldn't see both her husband and child risking their lives. "What if you were to ask de Vesci to intercede on your behalf?" she asked, desperate. "He would do this for you."

Jax shook his head. "De Vesci is too old to travel these days. He cannot make the trip."

"What of Denedor, his captain of the guard?" she asked. "Denedor is very persuasive."

Again, Jax shook his head. "The last I heard, Denedor had taken his family to the Northlands because his grandfather had passed away and there was much turmoil as a result," Jax replied. "I do not believe the man has returned yet. Moreover, I doubt de Vesci would let him go. You know how he keeps the man close."

Kellington thought hard on more options. "What of William Marshal?"

"He hates me with a passion and you know it."

"Hubert de Berg?"

"I killed a nephew in battle years ago."

"The king?"

"John?" Jax snorted. "It would probably cost me everything I own. The less contact I have with the man, the better."

Kellington couldn't give up, not yet. She tried one last time. "Christopher de Lohr?"

Jax didn't immediately dismiss her suggestion. In fact, he actually seemed to consider it. "He is the most powerful marcher baron in England," he said. "I have never had any interaction with the man. I do not personally know him."

Kellington felt a stab of hope at that. "At least he does not hate you or want to kill you," she said. "I have heard talk of the man. They say he is fair and wise. He is liked a good deal. If such a man would intercede on your behalf, mayhap the man who holds Allie would respond to him."

Jax nodded cautiously, thinking of the Earl of Hereford and Worcester, a man he only knew by reputation alone. De Lohr had been one of the more powerful players in King Richard's court, a man known throughout the land for his fierce fighting and keen intellect. He had a brother, also, who was nearly as powerful. Christopher and David de Lohr were nearly legends in the annals of England's history, much as Jax was, but for two entirely different reasons. De Velt and de Lohr had purposely stayed out of each other's way, and for good reason; a battle between the two would more than likely lay half of England to waste. But times had changed. Jax was no longer a warmonger and de Lohr, from what he had heard, was enjoying peace along the Marches. The more Jax thought about it, the more he was coming to agree with his wife.

"De Lohr is well respected," he said. "The man is known for his keen politics and negotiating skills. As much as John hates him, he also respects him a great deal and regularly solicits his advice. At least, that is what de Vesci says. De Vesci has high praise for de Lohr."

Kellington nodded eagerly. "Mayhap you should send de Lohr a missive and explain the situation," she said. "Mayhap he will agree to help, especially with a young woman's life at stake."

Jax lifted his dark eyebrows thoughtfully. "It is more than that," he said. "The properties I hold are not far from Lioncross Abbey, his seat. If this man who holds my daughter begins to make trouble on the Marches, it will directly affect de Lohr. Mayhap he does not even know this is happening or, the more likely scenario is that he knows more than I do about it. Mayhap... mayhap I will visit de Lohr and seek counsel with him. Mayhap he can enlighten me as to what is truly going on along the Marches."

Kellington liked that idea a great deal. She felt as if help was on the horizon, someone who would aid Jax and aid Allaston. Although she was still in turmoil over the situation, realizing her husband would seek out Christopher de Lohr for advice eased her panic somewhat.

"Then go to de Lohr," she said. "Take your army and go to him. Solicit his counsel and his aid."

Jax looked at her. "There is a real possibility he will not accept my visit," he said quietly. "I am not exactly a man to be easily received. It is possible de Lohr will see me and my army and think I am there to lay siege to Lioncross and burn it to the ground. That is what a sane man would think, anyway."

Kellington shook her head. "For what purpose?" she asked. "You have no reason to attack de Lohr. Moreover, you stopped doing that twenty-five years ago."

"He may think I have decided to resume my conquest."

"Then you will have to assure him that you are not."

She made it sound simpler than it was but he didn't argue. He simply went to her again and wrapped his arms around her, hugging the woman tightly and struggling against the guilt that was trying very hard to consume him.

He knew this was his fault, all of it. Now, he had to face something he more or less had expected to face within his lifetime. The old hatred, the blood of the innocent, was coming back to haunt him. All of the murder and conquest he had conducted twenty-five years ago was returning to the forefront, but now he was on the other side of that battle line. Back in the dark days of his youth, he had been the one killing and maiming, confiscating property and people as if they were simply objects for the taking. He hadn't been human back then. He'd been a creature, a dark and terrible creature who fed off of human sorrow. All of England, Wales, and Scotland feared Jax de Velt because he was more ruthless than anything anyone had ever seen before. He had no soul. He had been darkness itself.

But that had changed when he had laid siege to Pelinom Castle and a young woman by the name of Kellington Coleby had made him understand things about life that he had never known. She had shown him love and happiness, humor and loyalty, and he had fallen in love with the woman. Twenty-five years later, he loved her more each day. They had a wonderful life together with a wonderful family, and The Dark Lord had changed into something unrecognizable, civilized and loving.

But The Dark Lord was still there, buried deep, now to be summoned forth by someone who was determined to threaten the safety of Jax's family. Woe to the man who summoned The Dark Lord again, for all of England would run red with blood if Jax de Velt went on a rampage. The more Jax thought on the bastard who had abducted Allaston, the angrier he became. He hadn't felt anger like this in years. Fire began to burn in the belly of the beast again, fire that had been dormant these long years. He understood vengeance, he understood it very well. Now, he had some vengeance of his own.

The man who abducted Allaston had called forth The Dark Lord and he was about to learn the truth behind de Velt's reputation.

Hell would follow with him.

CHAPTER EIGHT

Cloryn Castle, Late June

TWO WEEKS AFTER assuming the duties of chatelaine at Cloryn Castle, Allaston was starting to feel some connection to the place.

It was a strange connection, really, and she felt guilty for it, but two weeks of integrating herself into the inner workings of the castle inevitably left her feeling as if she knew the place. As if she somehow belonged here now. The fact that de Llion had virtually given her free reign over the keep gave her the strong feelings of connection. She'd never been a chatelaine before, nor had she ever really be in charge of anything, so it was natural for her to feel a bit proud over her domain, as twisted as that loyalty was.

But the truth was that she was still a hostage and a very valuable one, at least according to de Llion. She was only allowed in the keep, the kitchen yard, and the great hall. He told her if he ever saw her anywhere else that he would throw her in the vault and leave her to rot, so she was careful about staying to her allocated areas. It wasn't a difficult task because there was a good deal to do.

So she focused on running the keep and kitchens, involving herself in what she thought needed be done. She'd had a very good example set for her, her mother, and she tried to remember everything her mother had done, from the daily sweeping of chambers and hearths, to the daily menu for the kitchens. She buried herself in the tasks because it kept her mind off everything else, at least for the moment, and de Llion had given her a wide berth. In fact, she was sure he was purposely staying out of her way, as were his commanders, which was fine with her, all things considered. In fact, the only time she ever saw them was at mealtime.

But mealtimes were enlightening as to the function and plans of de Llion's army and Allaston learned very quickly to stay to the shadows and simply listen. She had discovered de Llion's plans to deploy his army, in fact, on the morning after she had tried to kill him with the fire poker when she had been helping serve the morning meal to Bretton and his commanders. They were speaking about future plans, ignoring the servants around them and not realizing that Allaston was listening to every word. Even if they had realized it, they obviously didn't care. She learned a great deal that morning about their plans to move on a castle called Rhayder that Bretton was planning to scout.

It wasn't as if she could do much with the information or warn Rhayder of the coming siege. De Llion had ridden from Cloryn later that day with a few of his men on his scouting mission and had returned after dark. The evening meal was uneventful but the next morning before dawn, the entire army had been assembled in the bailey and Allaston had helped in providing the departing army with provisions. Her first reaction in realizing that de Llion and most of his men were leaving was that it would be a perfect chance for her to make another escape attempt, but in the next breath, she knew how badly it would go for her if she was caught. De Llion was leaving soldiers behind and if they were to tell him she had tried to escape again, the consequences would be severe. Therefore, she decided it would be better for her if she didn't make the attempt. For now, she would wait. She felt as if she had little choice.

So she buried herself in her duties. She was coming to think that perhaps if she was obedient enough and helpful enough, de Llion might take pity on her and simply let her leave, although she knew it was a foolish hope. The man didn't have any concept of mercy. Therefore, on the morning fifteen days after having been awarded chatelaine duties, she awoke before sunrise and prepared once again to go about her tasks.

After bathing in some warmed water, she dressed in some of the garments Grayton had given her those weeks ago. The weather had been warming up as summer approached and they had experienced several days that were actually quite pleasant. Two days ago, she had been out in the kitchen yard and the warm sun had actually burned what flesh had been exposed around her neckline. It had even burned her nose, giving her a rather rosy and healthy countenance.

Because the morning had dawned mild, she knew the day would be warm again so she donned a light linen shift and, over that, she pulled on a fine woolen dress, not too heavy, that was the color of lavender. It was really quite becoming. It was simple, too, as it had a snug bodice, a rounded neckline, sleeves that were tight against her arms, and fastened up the side rather than the back so she didn't need help putting it on. Since there were no female servants about, whatever she wore had to be easy to manage herself.

She also had other things to dress with now. Several days ago, whilst going through the keep to organize supplies and inventory the contents, she had come across an entire room that had all manner of goods in it – more clothes, children's clothing, men's clothing, furniture, shoes, combs, belts, and even jewelry. The only people around these days were the soldiers de Llion had left behind when he'd departed from Cloryn and a few male servants who avoided her for the most part.

No one would talk to her except for the old cook, and he mostly spoke Welsh, which she didn't understand. Still, they somehow managed to communicate, but not enough so that she could ask him where all of the treasures in that room had come from. She remembered, once, that Grayton had told her a woman had left items behind. It looked to her as if an entire family had left items behind. Therefore, she left everything intact except for a comb and other hair items she had come across. She needed them and she hoped the lady, whenever she returned, wouldn't mind that she had borrowed them.

With her dark hair combed, braided, and pinned with a lovely comb in the shape of a butterfly, she left her comfortable chamber and headed down to the kitchens because the cook had butchered a pig the day before and she needed to determine how many meals they could get out of the meat.

Coming down from the second floor, she emerged from the stairwell onto the first floor of the keep, which contained a rather open room that was used sometimes by de Llion and his commanders to meet in, and then another smaller chamber with a door. In it, she had found a sewing kit and a carved wooden dog toy but little else. She still had no idea what the room had been used for but she rather liked it for her own private use, and she had even sat in it the day before and used the sewing kit to mend the hem of a shift she had torn.

Moving out of the keep, she was immediately greeted with warmer temperatures as the sun began to rise. In fact, it was quite moderate and she was enjoying the unseasonably warm weather, but as she moved to take the steps that would lead down to the bailey and, subsequently, the kitchens beyond, she caught a whiff of a horrible smell. Wrinkling up her nose, she looked around the bailey to see where the scent was coming from but all she could see was the big, triangular shaped bailey, the stables and trades off to the right, a big curtain wall with a gatehouse, but nothing else beyond that. It wasn't the smell of a latrine because she was well acquainted with that smell. It was a normal, everyday scent. This smell was something much different.

There was very little traffic in the bailey since de Llion had taken most of his army and she came down off the steps and headed towards the kitchens. The horrible smell hit her again as she crossed the bailey into the kitchen yards and she actually put her fingers to her nose. Whatever it was, it was quite nauseating. Once she entered the kitchen yard with its scattering of goats and implements used to prepare food with, she headed for the stone structure where the food was cooked but she was still looking around, attempting to determine where the terrible smell was coming from.

Everything in the kitchen yard seemed normal. There was a pair of servants standing over a massive, boiling pot near the wall of the yard, boiling a goat hide off some bones. Allaston has seen the servants nearly every day, men who were fixtures in the kitchen and keep. They would respond to any order she gave but they would never engage her in conversation. With the Welsh cook as her only conversational companion, she had to admit things were lonely sometimes.

As she watched the men work with the bones and hide, she thought perhaps to ask them where the smell was coming from. They couldn't avoid a direct question and would subsequently be forced to speak with her. Picking up her skirt so it didn't drag through a portion of mud, she made her way over to them.

"Good morn," she said pleasantly, watching two surprised pair of eyes turn to her. "Have either of you experienced that terrible smell around here? Would you know where it is coming from?"

The men stared back at her apprehensively, glancing at each other before shaking their heads and averting their gazes, looking back to the boiling bones.

"Nay, my lady," the older of the two said. "We… we do not know."

Allaston received the distinct impression they were lying to her. Two weeks of this pair avoiding her had pushed her patience to the end and she'd had enough of their evasiveness. She put her hands on her hips, struggling not to show her frustration.

"I think you do," she said quietly. "I am not sure why you two have ignored me all this time, but it will stop. My name is Lady Allaston and I am chatelaine. But I suspect you already know that. Why is it you ignore me so? You will tell me why you behave this way."

The men were looking at her fearfully by now. There was the older servant and then a younger, fatter servant who could have been the older man's son for as much as he looked like him. The round man looked to the older man, who seemed genuinely distressed. Hesitantly, the older man looked at Allaston.

"We are mere servants, my lady," he said. "We do our job and that is all. We do not wish… that is to say, we do nothing to anger the Lord of Cloryn."

Allaston wasn't clear on what he meant. "What do you mean anger him?" she asked. "Has he threatened you?"

The older man shook his head nervously. "Please, my lady," he pleaded. "Leave us be. We only want to live."

Allaston was further puzzled by his statement. "What do you mean by that?" she asked. "Why would you not live? I asked you why you have ignored me and you have given me answers I do not understand."

The younger of the two abruptly ran off, waddling away and disappearing around the side of the keep, but the older man remained. He carefully regarded Allaston, a soft morning breeze blowing about his thin gray hair so that it lashed him around the eyes. Still, his gaze did not move away from her. There was something in his expression that was both serious and grim.

"My lady," he said, his voice soft. "You must not ask questions you do not wish to know the answers to."

Her brow furrowed. "Like what?" she demanded. "See here, what is your name?"

"Blandings, my lady."

"Blandings, if you want to continue working in the kitchens, then you had better start making some sense," she said firmly. "I am in charge of the keep and kitchens, and if you want to keep your job, I will have answers. Is that clear?"

Blandings nodded, his features tightening with anxiety. "Aye, my lady."

She threw an arm in the direction the fat servant had gone. She pointed. "Who was that?"

"My son, Robert."

At least they were making a slight amount of progress. That was the most she'd gotten from the man in two weeks. "Very well," she said. "Does he speak?"

"He does."

"Then you will tell him to speak to me if he values his job."

"I will, my lady."

Her eyes watched him as she studied him curiously. "And you," she said. "What did you mean that I must not ask questions I do not wish to know the answers to? Of course I wish to know the answers, otherwise, I would not ask the questions."

"Aye, my lady."

"Do you know where that horrible stench is coming from?"

He hesitated. "Aye, my lady."

"God's Beard, then where?"

It was evident by Blandings' expression that he realized he had no choice but to answer her. He had been holding a big wooden spoon used for de-hiding the bones in the pot and he turned back to the simmering cauldron, stirring the boiling bones and hide.

"You have not been outside of the castle, my lady?" he asked quietly.

Allaston shook her head. "I have not," she said. "I have been told to stay to the keep and kitchens. Why do you ask?"

Blandings continued to stir, resigned that he was being forced to speak on something he could hardly bring himself to voice. His tone was so quiet when he began to speak that Allaston barely heard him.

"If you have not been outside the gates, then you do not know," he muttered.

Allaston was trying to follow what he was saying. "I was brought here almost six weeks ago," she said. "I was brought here in the dead of night, and bound in the back of a wagon, so the only time I was outside the gates was when I arrived. I've not been outside since. Why? What goes on out there? And what does that have to do with the terrible stench?"

The old servant swallowed hard, watching the boiling pot as he stirred it. He had come this far. He had to tell her the rest so that she knew everything.

"De Llion laid siege to Cloryn three months ago," he said softly. "The lord tried to fight him off. Lord Oreck was a very good knight and a fair lord. He fought valiantly for five days and four nights, but in the end, de Llion and his men managed to mount the walls. Once they were inside the bailey, it was only a matter of time before they breached the keep. They killed everything that moved, my lady. *Everything*."

Allaston was listening with some horror and sorrow. "I know," she said solemnly. "They came to Alberbury Priory and killed many nuns before abducting me. The last I saw of the priory, it was going up in flames. And then they brought me here. I spent three weeks in the vault before de Llion released me and made me his chatelaine, so I understand a bit of the workings of de Llion and his army. They are conquerors."

The old servant was looking at her, his wrinkled face pale and drawn. "They are much more than that," he said. "Do you know what he did to the people of Cloryn? To the lord and his wife and children?"

Allaston shook her head. "I do not know. I was not told."

The old servant was back to hanging his head again as he stirred. "The night they breached the keep, de Llion's men dragged the lady and her children from the keep. The lady was very kind and noble, and the two boys were brave and strong. They were so young, so very young. As de Llion's men had their way with the lady, right there in the dirt of the bailey, still other men took the two boys and... with the youngest boy, they took him by the ankles and swung his head against the wall, killing him. The other boy was taken outside the walls where Lord Oreck had already been impaled. As the man was dying, de Llion's men put the boy in front of him and slit his throat, right in front of his father. It was the last thing Lord Oreck saw before he died. Then, they tied the boy to Lord Oreck so the man could breathe his last against the cooling corpse of his son."

Allaston was beyond horrified. As she listened, her mouth hung agape and tears filled her eyes. It was the worst thing she had ever heard and bile rose in her throat. It was a struggle to swallow it, not to become ill.

"Impaled?" she whispered. "What... what do you mean?"

The old man labored through the physical description of what he meant, using the wooden spoon as an example of the impaling post. "They take a man and ram the post up through his anus," he said, using hand motions to describe the terrible deed. "The end of the spike comes up through the neck or the chest. Then they post the spike, out there beyond the walls, leaving the man to die for all to see."

Allaston seriously thought she might become ill but she fought it. The entire concept was far beyond what she had ever imagined the most horrible death to entail. She did not know her father had used the same techniques during his time at conquest. All she had been told was that he had killed many men during that time, a small mercy her mother had withheld from a young and impressionable girl. Therefore, the tactics used by de Llion were staggeringly shocking and gruesome. It was horrific beyond belief. Until she remembered what Bretton had told her of her father's savagery a few weeks ago.

"But... the wife?" she breathed. "What happened to her?"

The old man, seeing Allaston's brimming tears, began to tear up himself. He stopped stirring the boiling pot, closing his eyes tightly against the memories he was dredging up. Like a nightmare, they haunted him.

"They let every soldier who wanted a turn at her rape her," he murmured. "Several of them had her in the bailey and then they dragged her back inside the keep where even more soldiers had their way with her. She was abused until she was nearly dead, my lady. Then, they took her outside the walls where they impaled her on a post just as they had done to her husband, just as they had done to all of Lord Oreck's men. What you smell... it is the rotting corpses outside of the walls, my lady. It is the phantoms of Lord Oreck and the people who once used to live here."

Allaston clapped a hand over her mouth, stifling the moan of horror. The tears that had once been brimming were now running down her cheeks.

"Sweet Jesus," she wept softly. "All of them?"

The old man had tears on his face as well. "All of them," he confirmed quietly. "All of them but me, my son, and the cook. We were fortunate. De Llion and his men had killed most of the servants but when they came to us, it was reasoned that they might need some help with the meals, so we were spared. That is the *only* reason we were spared."

Allaston still had a hand over her mouth, trying not to sob aloud. "I... I was given clothing to wear," she whispered tightly. "I was told that the lady of the castle had left it behind so I did not think anything of wearing it. I had nothing else so I took it."

Blandings nodded, noting the lavender dress she was wearing. "That belonged to Lady Miette," he said. "She was a kind lady. She would not mind you having it, I am sure."

Allaston simply nodded, struggling against outright sobs. The hand was still over her mouth. "I will pray for her and for her family," she whispered. "I will pray for her soul and for her forgiveness."

Blandings watched her devastated reaction to the truth. He was touched, feeling somehow as if they both shared the same sorrow now. He'd been terrified to speak with her for two weeks. Now, he was no longer afraid. After hearing the circumstances behind her coming to Cloryn, he was a bit more understanding. She wasn't de Llion's whore, as he had feared. She didn't have the man's ear. She was a prisoner just like the rest of them. He began to feel guilty for having avoided her so much.

"If you need any assistance, my lady," he ventured. "Please call upon me or my son. We will help you."

Allaston simply nodded but her head inevitably turned in the direction of the gatehouse and thoughts of what lay beyond. "Sweet Jesus," she breathed. "All of those people out there, now rotting in the sun."

Blandings nodded sadly. "Aye, my lady."

"They must be buried."

Blandings sighed softly, turning back to his boiling pot. "Only the new lord of Cloryn can order that," he said. "If I could, I would bury every one of them with my own hands, but I cannot move beyond the kitchens. They will kill me and I have no desire to end up impaled."

Allaston looked at him, wiping the remainder of the tears off her face. The initial horror had passed, now she was left with a deep and abiding disgust. She was utterly revolted by all of it. "I do not fault you for that," she said. "But to leave them out there to rot… it is barbaric at the very least."

Blandings wanted to discourage her before she got herself in trouble. "I would not disturb the dead, my lady," he said. "They are dead, after all. Their souls are with God and the body is just an empty shell. Do not risk your life over empty shells. The new lord of Cloryn wants them there 'else he would have taken them down already."

It was wise advice coming from a servant. Allaston thought on it a moment, finally nodding her head reluctantly. "I am sure you are correct," she said, eyeing the old man. "Thank you for telling me all of this. I would not have known otherwise. You have been very helpful."

Blandings nodded, watching her as she once more turned her attention towards the gatehouse, closing her eyes for a brief moment before crossing herself.

"I will be done with these bones in a little while," he said, taking a stir at the pot again. "If you need anything done, you need only tell me. I will do it."

Allaston looked at the man, a grim smile on her lips. "My thanks," she said, taking a deep breath and squaring her shoulders. She was trying not to linger on the horror outside of the gates now that she knew about it, but she found it to be an impossible task. "I will be in the kitchen with the cook. We have a pig to prepare."

Blandings returned her smile before nodding and returning to his stirring. Allaston took a couple of steps in the direction of the kitchen before coming to a halt and returning her attention to the man.

"I intend to speak with de Llion about the dead outside the walls," she said. "Rest assured that I will not mention who has told me. I will go to my grave before I tell him what you and I have discussed."

Blandings nodded. "Thank you, my lady."

Allaston nodded her head, briefly, before resuming her walk towards the kitchen. All the while, however, her mind was filled with the army of dead outside the walls and a lovely lady named Miette. She couldn't get it out of her mind. Now, she was coming to realize the true scope of de Llion's brutality and the realization brought her great fear. He had told her once, back in those dark days when she was in Cloryn's vault, of the atrocities her father had committed, atrocities that were very much the same thing Bretton was committing. *Men impaled on spikes*. It made her shudder just to think about it. Whatever her father had done those years ago, Bretton was now doing, too.

Allaston recalled him saying something to her once, something that now made a good deal of sense.

I have been called the Devil.

Now, she knew why.

CHAPTER NINE

Late July

TWENTY-EIGHT DAYS AFTER leaving Cloryn for Rhayder Castle, Bretton was finally returning.

It was early morning on a clear day that already promised to be warm. The past few weeks had been unusually warm, something that he would have enjoyed had he not had to wear layers of wool and mail, which made him sweat and soaked everything. He was filthy, sweaty, and smelly, and he was eager to return to Cloryn to celebrate his latest victory. But that wasn't the only reason he was eager to return.

That de Velt daughter. He couldn't stop thinking of her. She'd been on his mind every day, mostly in the early morning or when he finally decided to get a few hours of sleep at night. The dark hair and pale green eyes reached out to him, enticing him until he could hardly think of anything else. In the midst of a battle campaign, it had been an annoying and unwelcome diversion, but it was one he was unable to stop. Even as they had secured Rhayder Castle, which had taken longer than expected, he found his attention turning to the trip back to Cloryn because Allaston was there.

So he'd spent sixteen days laying siege to Rhayder Castle before finally being able to mount the walls. It had been tricky due to the moat surrounding it. It had taken days to build platforms that extended across the narrow but deep moat, enough so that they could move in ladders to mount the walls. That was his main mode of operation, bypassing the gatehouse and going for the walls because they were often less protected than the gatehouse. If one could get up and over them, then it was much easier than trying to smash through a portcullis. He also made the best of postern gates, of which Rhayder had one. While some men used grappling hooks and ladders to mount the fifteen-foot-high walls, Dallan and Teague had managed to compromise the postern gate. Once the gate was open and his men flooded in, it was a short time before the drawbridge was lowered.

After sixteen days of besieging Rhayder Castle, when it fell, it fell quickly. Bretton had the entire castle secured within hours. Then he'd spent an additional eight days destroying the lord of Rhayder's army and establishing his own rule. There was a rather large village near Rhayder and he had made sure to convene a meeting of the town fathers to lay down his law and inform them of the penalty should he be disobeyed. The villagers had fearfully agreed, terrified of the macabre army of the dead and dying being impaled and posted outside of the walls. *The Devil is in our midst*, the whispers said.

Much as Ajax de Velt had done those years ago, Bretton de Llion did now – displaying the dead as a warning to all who would disobey or contest his authority. And with that, Bretton had three castles under his control. It was time to return to Cloryn, regroup, and strike out for Comen Castle in a few days. Comen's end was coming.

After traveling all the previous day, they had moved out before sunrise for their last few miles to Cloryn. The castle was sighted in the distance just as the sun began to rise and Bretton sent a rider on to the castle to inform the inhabitants of his approach. He also requested food and comfort for his men, a message that was directed at Allaston. As the army drew closer, Cloryn's gates opened to welcome them.

Approaching the castle from the east, they weren't hit with the stench of the dead until they were very close because of the path of prevailing winds. Riding at the head of his army with Dallan, Teague, and Grayton, the stench was stronger than usual because of the warm weather they had been having. Flies and insects were swarming as they approached the gatehouse. Near the gate itself, now open with the great fanged portcullis lifted, were the bodies of the lord and lady of Cloryn. But Bretton wasn't looking at the decaying corpses. He was looking straight ahead at the open gatehouse. But his commanders were looking at the bodies.

"Bretton," Grayton ventured. "Far be it from me to suggest how you conduct your campaign of terror, but this smell is not going to help anyone's appetite. It has been four months. Mayhap it is time to consider burying our enemies."

Bretton was still looking straight ahead as the gatehouse loomed overhead. "Six months," he said steadily. "Not a day less."

"Why?"

"Because that is how long de Velt left them up."

"And how would you know that?"

"Ask anyone who was alive during the time of de Velt's raids and they will tell you," he said. "He left the bodies of the dead up for six months."

Grayton looked at Dallan, who shrugged. There was no use trying to convince the man otherwise. He was obsessed with emulating, and punishing, de Velt, so it was not a subject open for debate. In fact, his obsession had been lucrative as of late, so they let the subject die and focused instead on what lay ahead. Food, comfort, and rest that they were all looking forward to.

Bretton entered the bailey of Cloryn and realized he was hoping to see Allaston right away, waiting to greet him, but all that met him was the vast, dusty bailey and several soldiers he had left behind to guard the fortress while he was away. Word of de Llion's victory was spreading among the men and Bretton could hear a cry of triumph ripple through the men as he dismounted. Men were shouting his name, rallying victory, as he pushed through them, heading for the keep. Behind him, they had brought three big wagons loaded with spoils back with them from Rhayder and he could hear his men happily claiming the treasures.

As Dallan, Teague, and Grayton began disbanding the men, Bretton entered the dark and cool keep. The first thing he noticed was that the floor was swept and dried rushes, tall grass that was harvested and dried especially to cover the floor, were spread about. It smelled like hay, which wasn't a bad smell at all. He liked it. The open room straight ahead that he sometimes used for conferring with his men was also swept and the tabletop scrubbed clean. There was even a fire in the hearth, inviting. He stepped into the room and ran his hand over the tabletop, noting it smelled of lye when he sniffed his fingertips. The lady had obviously been busy in his absence.

Taking the stairs to the second floor, he stuck his head into both chambers on this level but was met with silence. The top floor chambers, both of them, were the same. Curious that Allaston was not in the keep, he descended back to the entry level and headed out to the kitchens.

The kitchen yard was busy. There were two big pots boiling away over carefully stoked fires and he peered at both of them. One was a stew of some kind with beans and carrots, while the other seemed to be a big pot of chunks of meat and gravy. As he stuck his dirty finger into the gravy to taste it, he heard a woman's voice coming from the stone kitchen. Like a siren's call, the sound lured him.

Bretton came to a halt in the doorway of the kitchen, his gaze falling on Allaston as she faced away from him. Great smells assaulted his senses and heat slapped him in the face as the big bread oven was going full-bore, red-hot with crackling flames to bake with. As he watched, Allaston appeared to be kneading or beating something, he really couldn't tell. Whatever it was, she was working it heavily on the big, wooden tabletop in front of her.

"Uldward?" she called, looking over her shoulder towards the cook working on the other table. "Do you have the garlic chopped yet? I must add it to this dough. We must get it into the oven."

The big, burly cook hustled over to her, his hands full of something, and dumped everything he was carrying into the dough she was working.

"Salt!" Allaston commanded.

The cook grabbed a covered bowl that held their precious salt and liberally sprinkled it into the bread. He also put peppercorns in it, quite generously, and Allaston continued to knead it furiously. After flipping the dough over several times, as it was quite a bit of dough, she finally stood back from it, wiping at her sweaty forehead with the back of her hand.

"Now, form this into several smaller loaves of bread," she told the cook. "This should make at least fifty smaller loaves, two men to a loaf. Let me go see to the stew outside and then we will make more dough once all of this gets into the oven."

The cook moved forward to begin fashioning loaves of garlic-peppercorn bread as Allaston turned around to head out of the kitchen. But the moment she turned, she caught sight of Bretton in the doorway. Startled, she gasped.

"My... my lord," she stammered. "I did not hear... I thought some-one would tell me when you arrived. I did not know you had returned!"

Bretton could see that she was flustered, quite possibly frightened, that she hadn't been advised of his return. Perhaps she thought he had expected her to greet him. In any case, he held up a hand to calm her.

"We just now returned," he said, his eyes drinking in the sight of her. She was dressed in a light yellow surcoat and pale linen shift with her dark hair in a big, thick braid. He'd never seen anything more delightful and all of those days of dreaming about her were summarily satisfied by the sight. "My men are disbanding as we speak. I sent word ahead to have a meal prepared and I see that you have it well in hand."

Allaston had to admit that that she was startled by the sight of him as well as fearful. This warrior, this *Devil,* had finally returned. After all of the horrible things she had been told of him yesterday, she wasn't quite sure how she would feel upon seeing him again. At the moment, all she could feel was anxiety. But in the same breath, she felt something more, something very odd – something of warmth stirring within her chest, and the sight of his handsome, scruffy face was doing something very strange to her emotions. She thought her heart might have actually fluttered.

"Aye," she agreed, pointing out to the kitchen yard. "I have a bean and pork soup cooking and also the last of the mutton we had. It is cooking in a gravy that has peppercorns and onions."

His gaze remained on her, smoldering and weary, before turning to see what she was pointing at. "Have you done all of this by yourself?" he asked.

She shook her head. "I have had help," she said, thinking to perhaps emphasize the value of the servants he had not put to the stake. Perhaps emphasize her value, too, now that she knew what he was capable of. "Uldward and Blandings have been extremely helpful," she said. "Robert cut up the mutton to put in the pot. I could not have done it without them."

He turned to look at her again. "Who are they?"

"The cook and kitchen servants."

He lifted his eyebrows. "I see."

Allaston didn't have much more to say as the conversation waned. Nervously, she politely brushed past him through the doorway.

"There is already fresh bread and cheese in the great hall," she said as she moved by him. "Your men can start with that while I finish preparing the rest of the meal."

Bretton couldn't help but notice she seemed very nervous, not at all like the stubborn woman he had come to know. He followed her as she moved to the first big pot, which was bubbling with the beans and pork.

"It seems that you have done a great deal around here," he said. "I was in the keep. It is very tidy."

Allaston nodded as she took the big wooden spoon that was hanging on the tripod that was holding the pot. She stuck it into the soup.

"Aye," she replied. "In truth, there wasn't much to clean. The keep was fairly well kept."

He watched her stir. "I appreciate a tidy keep," he said. "You have done well."

His compliment made her feel rather warm in spite of everything. She started to say something but some of Bretton's men appeared near the entry to the kitchen yards, fighting over something. They had their arms full of what looked like goods of some kind. Suddenly, one man threw a punch at the other man and they went down, brawling in the dirt as other soldiers ran up and began shouting words of encouragement. Allaston stopped stirring the soup, looking on with concern and then horror as the man who had been punched first pulled a dirk and rammed it into the neck of his accoster. She gasped as Bretton moved away from her, quickly moving towards the men in a life or death battle.

He charged into the fray, yanking the bloodied dirk out of his soldier's hand and pulling him off the man he had mortally wounded. With the dirk still in his hand, he balled up his enormous right fist and plowed it into the killer's face, sending the man sailing backwards onto his arse. The man was knocked unconscious by Bretton's devastating blow and Bretton tossed the blooded dirk to the ground as he ordered the men who had gathered to clean up the mess. Dallan appeared, having been over at the gatehouse when the fight broke out, and he took charge of the situation.

With the mess being cleaned up, Bretton returned to the kitchen yard where Allaston was still standing over the soup, stirring it. He couldn't help but notice she wouldn't look at him. He also noticed that she seemed to be trembling, which piqued his curiosity. He'd never seen this woman nervous since he'd known her so it was natural to wonder what had her shaken. What could have happened since leaving Cloryn those weeks ago to have turned her into a nervous mess? He wondered.

"How has it been here since my departure?" he asked, hoping to discover the reasons behind her state.

Allaston stirred the pot gently. "Quiet, my lord," she said. "There has not been much to speak of, truly."

It was extremely rare that she addressed him as "my lord". Now, he was really curious. What could have happened to have changed her demeanor so?

"You have kept yourself busy?" he asked.

She nodded, tendrils of dark hair blowing in the breeze. "Aye," she replied. "Sewing, cleaning, and other things."

He lifted his eyebrows. "Speaking of sewing," he said, "I have several things that could use mending. I will bring them to you."

Allaston nodded. "Very well, my lord."

My lord again. His eyes narrowed at her, scrutinizing her, as he watched her stir. He was trying to figure out what in the world had her so nervous and obedient. Aye, obedient. The woman he knew before leaving Cloryn wasn't particularly obedient. But she certainly was now. Scratching his head, he simply turned away without another word and headed back to the bailey.

Bretton didn't see Allaston for the rest of the morning. He had been busy with his men and with a strategic planning session with Grayton, Teague, and Dallan. He had left Olivier at Rhayder Castle to organize and oversee the rebuilding of the damaged castle, so he only had his three commanders with him to charge on to Comen and Erwood Castles. But they would be enough. They were a loyal and hard-working bunch, and he considered himself extremely fortunate.

All the while in the planning session, however, thoughts of Allaston plagued him. He was curious to observe the woman's behavior again, to see if this morning had merely been a fluke, or a bad day for her. In fact, it concerned him so much that he cut his meeting short and headed to the great hall to finally eat a decent meal because he knew that was where she would be.

Dirty, smelly, and with a five days' growth of beard on his face, Bretton entered the great hall where the majority of his men were now supping. Everyone was exhausted from the battle, from the march, so there wasn't much excitement going on. Merely men stuffing their faces with bread, cheese, mutton in gravy, and great bowls of the bean and pork stew Allaston had made. In fact, the entire hall smelled delicious and Bretton sat at the end of the feasting table, being served his meal from an old man with stringy gray hair. Before the servant could leave, he spoke to the man.

"Where is Lady Allaston?" he asked.

The servant was another nervous mess. His lips trembled as he spoke. "In the kitchen, my lord," he said. "Shall I send for her?"

Bretton nodded as he tore apart a hot loaf of bread with garlic and peppercorns. "Send her to me."

The old servant dashed away as Bretton began to stuff his mouth with the bread, which was delicious. The mutton was delectable, surprising for mutton, as was the bean and pork stew. It was all flavored beautifully with onions and garlic and plenty of salt. He loved it. As he was slurping up the last of the mutton from his trencher, he caught movement from the corner of his eye. Turning his head, he saw Allaston standing by his left arm. When their eyes met, he actually smiled.

"This meal is the best I have ever had," he told her with complete honesty. "The nuns at Alberbury taught you this?"

Allaston nodded, her cheeks flushed from the warmth of the kitchen and perhaps even from his compliment. "Aye, my lord," she replied. "I told you that I had been assigned kitchen tasks and the nuns taught me what they knew."

He continued to stare at her. She was still nervous and he didn't like it, not in the least. He rather preferred the woman who was intent on defying him to this cowering female. There was such strength in Allaston, strength that had garnered his respect. This woman standing before him was not showing strength. Wiping his mouth with the back of his hand, he stood up and grasped her by the arm.

"Come with me," he said softly.

Allaston had no choice. Her arm in his grip, she trailed after him as he pulled her out of the hall and across the bailey. Dust kicked up as his big boots met with the dry soil and rocks, and Allaston was on the verge of panic. Why was he taking her away like this? Had she done something wrong? Sweet Jesus, she'd worked so hard to do everything *right*.

As he pulled her up the stairs, Allaston tripped out of sheer anxiety, and he carefully helped her back to her feet again. There was an odd gentleness in his touch, something quite unexpected. Well, was he angry with her or wasn't he? By the time he pulled her into the open room on the entry level, the room he used for his meetings, she was nearly in tears.

Once inside the room, Bretton let go of Allaston's arms and faced her. He crossed his arms, his head cocked pensively, as he looked into her eyes.

"What has happened since I last saw you that you would cower in my presence?" he asked quietly. "The woman I left a few short weeks ago did not behave as if she was afraid of me. But the woman I see before me behaves fearfully. Look at you. You are almost in tears. Why do you behave this way?"

Allaston didn't want to tell him but she had little choice. He was asking a civil question and expecting the truth. Were she to lie to him, she suspected his questions would no longer be civil. But, God help her, she didn't want to tell him. Yet, she had to. She backed away from him, rubbing her arm where he had gripped her.

"You wanted obedience, did you not?" she asked, having difficulty looking him in the eye. "I am simply being obedient."

He grunted. "There is a difference between obedience and abject fear," he said. "You are displaying the latter and I want to know why."

She looked at him, then. "You told me when you left those weeks ago that I was to stay to the keep and to the hall, that I was to be obedient," she said. "I have done that. I have done everything you told me to do. So now I have done something wrong because I am doing what you told me to do? I do not understand."

He saw a flash of the old Allaston, the fiery one, and it pleased him. So she was still in there, somewhere. He wanted to bring her out. It was that Allaston he liked.

"You behave as if I have a knife to your throat," he said. "I have never done anything like that to you, even when I took you from Alberbury. I have never held a weapon to you in any way. Why do you fear me so now?"

Allaston met his examining glare, seeing something so brilliant and beautiful in his face. Aye, it was true. She could see brilliance and beauty. She simply couldn't imagine he was behind the horror outside the walls, the horror of killing the Mother Prioress right before her eyes, but the truth was that the man was a killer. He had made it clear that he was capable of atrocities beyond her comprehension. It was this killer who was using her to lure her father to his doom. So how on earth could she think he was brilliant and beautiful? The dam she had held so tightly was beginning to burst and there was no stopping it. She was so confused, so fearful, that she could hardly control herself.

"As you seek answers to your questions, I also seek answers to questions of my own," she said quietly. "May I ask my questions first?"

He shrugged. "You may."

"Will you be completely truthful?"

"I always am."

Allaston considered that response before continuing. She was careful in the way she phrased her questions, not wanting to sound accusing or irrational. At least, not yet.

"When you were gone these past weeks, where did you go?" she asked.

Bretton met her gaze unwaveringly. "That is my business, lady."

"It was to conquer another castle. I heard you and your men speaking."

"Then if you already knew, why did you ask?"

Allaston's scrutiny was intense. "Was there a lord and lady at that castle, too?" she asked, her voice trembling. "Did you bash their children's brains out and put the parents on spikes like you did the lord and lady of Cloryn?"

All of the pleasant or warm reflections in Bretton's expression had vanished. Now, he was looking at her with the eyes of a man who had no regrets in life, no matter what he'd done. He regarded her coolly.

"Where did you hear such things?" he asked evenly.

Allaston shook her head, firmly and with resolve. "It does not matter," she said. "What matters is if those rumors are true."

He didn't hesitate. "They are."

She swallowed hard, staggering back a bit as if he had struck her. Even though she'd known the truth, it was still a blow to have him confirm it so callously. Tears began to pool in her eyes but before she could respond, he was moving towards her, stalking her, as if he was the hunter and she was the prey. His enormous body moved with grace and stealth.

"And before you think to denounce me for such things, remember this," he hissed. "Your father did such things along this border twenty-five years ago, such horrors as you cannot comprehend. Whatever I am doing, he did first, so before you tell me what a horrible murderer I am, you had better rethink your accusations. Your father was a brutal murderer who ran a spike through my father's anus, up into his guts and through his chest so that the end of it came out of his shoulder. Then he put one end of the pole into the ground and left my father, a truly good and decent man, to die an agonizing death, so every man I put to a stake, every woman I disembowel, and every child whose brains are splashed out over the walls has your father to thank for it. It is all de Velt's fault!"

He was in her face by the time he finished, leaning over her as she recoiled from him. Allaston couldn't tear her gaze away from his angry blue eyes. He was enraged, that was true, but oddly enough, she wasn't afraid of him. That pity she had felt for him before began to fill her veins yet again because she understood why he was doing it. She'd understood it back when he'd first told her but now, it was more evident than ever.

"I know what my father did to your father, for you have already told me," she said, her tone a breathy whisper. "Now you are doing what my father did, but for what? To somehow punish my father? Do you really believe this will hurt him somehow by emulating his reign of terror? Nay, that is not why you do this. Deep down, you are still that hurt, shattered five year old boy and you are taking your anger out on the world. The only person you are hurting is yourself."

Bretton was so close to Allaston's face that his breath was lifting tendrils of her hair. Her words sank in and his eyes narrowed, briefly, as a flash of anger rolled through him. As fast as lightning, he reached out and grabbed her, pulling her hard against his broad chest. His fingers bit into her tender flesh and she gasped, startled by his reaction. She could see something dark and painful brewing in his eyes.

"You know nothing," he snarled. "What do you know of that five year old boy who watched his entire world go up in flames? What do you know of that child who saw his mother kill his sister and then herself because she knew what her fate would be at the hands of de Velt? I watched as my mother stabbed my sister in the chest and then slit her own throat, but I was too young and too powerless to stop her. I was too young and too powerless to stop de Velt from impaling my father and destroying my castle. I escaped with some of the servants, a lonely bundle of humanity, who then kept me for a while, tending me, until I became too much of a burden and they sold me into slavery. I was too young and too powerless to stop the man who bought me from raping me from the time he purchased me until I grew old enough to fight him off. I killed him when I was ten years of age to finally free myself of the abuse. So do not judge me, Lady Allaston, by the way I treat the world. The world has never been kind to me. Therefore, I am not kind to the world."

Allaston stared at him, deeply surprised and deeply horrified by his admission. Her heart was aching for the man. Now, so much of what he did and who he was made sense. It was much more than Jax de Velt destroying his castle and killing his father. It was everything that came after that. He blamed Jax for destroying his life, as he'd once said. It would seem there was some truth to that.

"What you have had to endure is barbaric and terrible, and I cannot imagine the pain you must have felt," she admitted. "I would apologize for the sins committed against you but I do not believe that would make a difference. If… if my father apologized to you, would it help to ease this anger you carry?"

Bretton still wasn't over the fact that he had just told her his darkest secret. Gazing into those bright green eyes and beautiful face, it was as if he'd had no control. It all just came spilling out. He was both embarrassed and strangely relieved, as if a burden had been lifted from him, a burden he had carried most of his life. Now Jax de Velt's daughter shared that burden, too. Perhaps it was right that she did, considering her father had laid this heavy burden across his shoulders. Perhaps it was right that a de Velt helped him bear the unbearable.

"Do you truly believe it that simple?" he asked after a moment, the grip on her arms loosening. "The destruction of a man's life cannot be erased by condolences."

"Mayhap not," she said softly, "but mayhap it will ease you some-what. You have a terrible burden to bear. If I could make it easier for you, I would."

She had meant it innocently, in the course of attempting to be un-derstanding about his situation, but Bretton didn't take it that way. All he could think about was physical comfort, sexual comfort, as sexual contact with a woman he was attracted to was something of a rarity. In fact, he couldn't even remember bedding a woman he felt something for. Those kinds of relationships didn't exist in his world. Aye, she could make it easier for him. She could give him comfort where none existed.

His mouth descended on hers, abruptly, tasting a woman who was sweeter and softer than anything he had ever experienced. Allaston shrieked, into his mouth, but Bretton didn't release her. In fact, he pulled her tighter, kissing her so forcefully that she was nearly bent over backwards. As she squirmed and gasped, he forced his tongue into her mouth, tasting her, suckling her tongue as she continued to resist him. But the more she struggled, the more excited he became. It wasn't so much her resistance as it was her taste. She tasted delightful and he could feel himself growing hard. There was only one way to ease his desire.

Grabbing hold of the front of her surcoat, he gave one powerful yank and ripped it down to her navel. Allaston screamed as his big, warm, and dirty hand snaked between the torn pieces of fabric, grasping a warm and soft breast, fondling her. He pinched her nipple as she struggled to get away from him, and he ended up picking her up and plopping her down on the tabletop. As Allaston beat at him and fought to get away, he easily caught both of her flailing arms and pinned them over her head.

She bucked and wept as his hot mouth came down on a distended nipple, suckling furiously. As she struggled, he climbed upon the table and got on top of her, wedging himself between her kicking legs. With both arms pinned by his iron grip, he was free to do as he wished as he began to toss up her skirts.

"Nay," Allaston wept. "Please do not do this. Please! This is not the way for a man to behave, do you hear me? You must not do this!"

He heard her. However, he was so overwhelmed with his lust and want for her at the moment that it was clouding his common sense. All he could think of was satisfying his desire, of feeling his body in hers, of tasting her tender flesh. There was nothing else in his world. This is how the act of sex had always been done, ever since the merchant who owned him had tied him down and raped him. He'd been screaming and crying, subjected to unbelievable pain, but the old man had penetrated him anyway. He hadn't listened to the young boy's cries. Therefore, Allaston's struggle was nothing out of the ordinary. When his fingers began to probe the soft curls between her legs, she let out a scream of utter terror.

"Stop!" she howled. "Would you truly do this to me? I am meant for the cloister and if you do this, I will be stained forever! You have told me how terrible it was for someone to do this to you, yet you are doing it to me! I beg you, please stop! I swear upon all that is holy that I will hate you forever if you take what does not belong to you! *I will hate you!*"

He inserted a finger into her, listening to her scream with pain and terror. She was very tight around his finger and he could feel the proof of her virginity opposing him. He could only imagine how his manhood would feel inside of her, enveloped by the warmth and moisture of her body. He could imagine no greater pleasure. But her words began to sink in and he paused, his mouth on her breast and his finger in her body. He'd often wondered what it would be like to bed a woman whom he hadn't paid, or who wasn't screaming in terror.

To have a woman respond to him, to want him to touch her… it was a foreign concept, but one he'd always wondered about. Perhaps it was something to consider because he didn't want Allaston hating him. If he raped her, she would. Nay, he didn't want her hatred at all. Deep down, that part of him that understood decency was struggling to come forth. He'd known decency, once, as a child. He well remembered his kind mother and father, and how good they had been. If he could recollect the concept of decency, then perhaps it wasn't dead in him after all.

So he stopped suckling her breast and removed his finger. Pushing himself off the table, he watched Allaston leap off the other side, pulling the ends of her tattered surcoat together as she bolted from the room. He could hear her running up the stairs to the second floor and he heard the door to her chamber slam. He was sure she bolted it, too, but he hadn't heard that part. As he stood there, feeling guilty and confused, Dallan entered the keep. He could see the man approaching from the entry.

"Bretton," he said, extending what looked to be a rolled bit of parchment in his hand. "A missive has arrived for you."

Bretton forced himself away from thoughts of Allaston to focus on the message Dallan was bearing.

"A missive?" he repeated, confused. "For me?"

Dallan nodded. "A rider dropped it at the gatehouse and fled," he said. "It seems the army of the dead outside the walls frightened him sufficiently, but when the sentries collected the missive, it was addressed to Bretton de Llion."

Bretton eyed the man with both curiosity and suspicion as he took the parchment. He inspected it with great interest, turning it over in his hands so the seal was exposed. He squinted as he studied the red seal, attempting to discern the details of the seal. After a moment, shock registered across his bearded face.

It was the seal of the House of de Llion.

CHAPTER TEN

I T WAS DARK on the entry level of the keep now that the sun had gone down. Bretton sat alone at the scrubbed table with the open missive in front of him, listening to his men out in the bailey as night descended. Laughter and shouts wafted in through the three long lancet windows on the north side of the room, windows that faced the kitchen yard but the hall was near the kitchen and he could hear the sounds coming forth. Men were enjoying themselves now after a victorious campaign at Rhayder. It was the sound of mercenaries enjoying their latest bloody victory.

But Bretton wasn't interested in celebrating. In fact, he wasn't interested in much at the moment. He kept the missive at his hand, every so often glancing down at it, but the room had grown so dark that he couldn't see the carefully scribed letters anymore. But he really didn't have to, he knew what it said. He had been reading it all afternoon.

In the keep, there had been some movement during the time he'd sat and read the missive. Allaston had eventually come down from her bower, but he was sitting out of her line of sight as she descended the stairs and quit the keep, he assumed, to oversee the evening meal. In truth, he hadn't thought about her much since he'd received the missive. All of his energy had been directed at the contents of the parchment that contained the seal of de Llion. He'd smelled the aromas of cooking meat, of freshly baked bread as Allaston and the kitchen servants cooked for several hundred men, but he wasn't particularly hungry. In fact, he wasn't sure what he was.

In an emotionless limbo, he continued to sit as the evening deepened and the room around him grew dark and very cold. He sat and fingered the missive, pondering the contents, for minute upon minute, turning into hour upon hour. He had no real concept of time passing, lost in a world he didn't much like to reflect on. The world of his past. At some point during the passing of the hours, he heard the keep entry open and footfalls approach. Light was approaching, too. He glanced up, slowly, to see Allaston as she entered the chamber with an oil lamp in her hand. Two servants trailed behind her, one with a bucket of something and one with a tray of food. Allaston pointed to the dark hearth.

"Blandings, please light a fire," she said, and as the old man with the bucket moved for the black hearth, she directed the fat servant with the tray towards the table where Bretton sat. "Robert, please take the food to the lord."

Bretton sat there, not saying a word, as a tray of food was placed before him. Allaston moved around the table to a bank of tallow candles, impaled on an iron floor sconce, and lit them with the flame from the oil lamp. Soon, a warm glow filled the room as the candles gave off their significant light. She was business-like and polite as she set the oil lamp down on the table so he could see the food laid out before him. Taking the wooden pitcher off the tray, she poured a measure of dark red wine into the earthenware cup.

"Blandings, please make sure to bring in more fuel for the fire before you leave," she called over to the man who was stoking the hearth. "And bring more peat, it lasts longer."

The man responded in the affirmative as Allaston proceeded to take the trencher and other items off the tray, setting them in front of Bretton. Smells of garlic and meat and onions filled his nostrils and he realized that he was the slightest bit hungry. Allaston was pulling bread and butter off the tray, setting it within his arm's reach, working around the parchment without moving it aside. When she was finished with her task, she took the tray off the table and headed for the door but Bretton stopped her.

"Lady," he said, his raspy voice soft. "Hold, please."

Allaston came to a halt by the door, pausing to look at him. It was the first time she had looked him in the face since entering the hall. But Bretton didn't say any more, at least not until Blandings finished stirring up the flames in the hearth and left the room in search of more fuel for the fire. Only when he heard the keep entry shut did Bretton continue.

"Will you please join me?" he asked softly.

Allaston was clearly hesitant. She moved to the table, slowly, and took a seat that was well out of arm's length. It was obvious she was fearful of being grabbed again and Bretton was rather sorry. He knew his actions had terrified her. She said she would hate him forever if he completed his dastardly deed, and even though he hadn't completed it, it was quite possible she hated him simply for attempting it. Nay, he didn't want her hate. Oddly enough, he found he wanted her comfort. He'd never depended on anyone in his life but, at the moment, he wanted to depend on her. She was the only person in his entire life that had ever shown him the slighted amount of compassion and under-standing. That fleeting taste had given him a glimpse of what he had been missing.

"For my earlier actions…," he began, "I am a man not given to regrets but I fear that my actions… I cannot explain what it is I felt or why I did what I did. I did not mean to injure you."

Allaston's countenance was guarded. It wasn't exactly an apology but he was trying. Still, she wasn't ready to forgive him yet. If she did, it might show the man that he could get away with things like that and that certainly wasn't the case. He had crossed the line of propriety with her and she was unwilling to forgive and forget at the moment. He had hurt her feelings, scared her, and embarrassed her, and she wasn't ready to release those emotions against him.

"You did not injure me," she said after a moment. "Why have you asked me to join you? Is there something more you require for your meal or comfort?"

He shook his head, slowly, his eyes on the parchment that was lying on the tabletop a few feet away. He reached around the oil lamp to retrieve it, holding it up in front of him as he read the words again. His normally impassive expression was in danger of becoming something emotional.

"I received a missive earlier today," he finally said. "It is from a cousin I have not seen since before de Velt destroyed Four Crosses. This cousin is three or four years younger than I am, so in truth, I do not know the man. I only know *of* him. But he speaks of my grandfather, who is also his grandfather. I have only vague memories of the man."

In spite of her anger towards him, she was inevitably interested in what he was saying. She was also surprised by the news. "That seems strange," she said. "How would these relatives know where to find you?"

He frowned and tossed the parchment aside. "That is the question I have been asking myself," he said. "How did they find me? When I escaped Four Crosses, they certainly made no attempt to locate me, so how were they able to locate me now?"

Allaston could hear bitterness in his words. She was coming to think there was some resentment there. "Where does this cousin live?"

Bretton glanced at the parchment in spite of the fact he had tossed it away. "Bronllys Castle," he said. "It is well south of here. My grandfather is the garrison commander for the Earl of Hereford, or at least that is what my cousin says. I do not remember any of those particulars, but I do remember that my grandfather was stationed at Bronllys."

Allaston asked the obvious question. "If you have family there, why have you not contacted them before now?" she asked. "Surely they would like to know you are alive and that you did not perish with your family."

Bretton looked at her and she could see the turmoil in the bright blue eyes. "They would not care," he said flatly. "If they loved me so much, why did they not try to find me after Four Crosses was destroyed? They could have searched for me but they did not. In fact, I prayed nightly for such things, praying for my grandfather to come and save me. Instead, he left me to the mercy of others. Nay, my relatives do not care for me. This missive simply asks if I am the Bretton de Llion whose father, Morgan, commanded Four Crosses. They do not even know for sure if it is me. If they truly cared, they would have come personally and not have sent a cold and impersonal missive."

Allaston's eyebrows lifted. The man, in her opinion, couldn't have been more wrong. "How were they supposed to find you?" she asked. "Your entire family was killed at Four Crosses and they naturally assumed you were killed as well. There was no way for them to know otherwise. But now, somehow or someway, they have heard that you are here at Cloryn so they are reaching out to you."

He snorted rudely. "By sending a missive?"

"Do you think, given your reputation, that it would have been safe for one of them to have come personally?" she countered. "What if you are not the cousin they seek? It could have been a very hazardous situation in that case."

Once again, she spoke the truth. Bretton considered her a moment, pondering her words, before looking back to the parchment. He leaned forward, his elbows resting on the table, looking at the contents of the missive once again without touching the parchment. It was quite clear that he was torn, not knowing how to react to it.

"That is a logical conclusion," he said. "My cousin asks me to meet him at The Falcon and Flower Inn in Newtown. It is about twenty miles from here, to the south. He has asked me to meet him there on the first day of the new month, which is two days away. I have not yet decided if I will do this."

Allaston was curious. "Why not?"

He shrugged. "Because I am not entirely sure there is a need," he said. "What could my cousin possibly say to me? We do not know each other. We are simply related by blood and, I am sure, worlds apart in philosophies."

Allaston thought on that. "Mayhap you could discover how he knew where to find you," she said. "If it were me, I would be most curious to know."

He cocked his head in agreement. "I will admit that I would like to know."

"Then mayhap you should meet with him," she said, her eyes glimmering in the weak firelight. "I would also think… well, at least by my reckoning… that I would want to find out why they did not try to find me after Four Crosses burned. They could have a sound reason for it, you know."

He looked at her, studying her lovely face across the flicker of the oil lamp. "Why would you encourage me to seek people who abandoned me?"

"That is my point. You do not know if they did for certain."

"Aye, I do. No one ever came for me."

"Mayhap because they did not know where to look," she stressed. "You said yourself that you escaped with a few servants and that they took you away. If anyone is to blame, it is the servants. They should have contacted your grandfather but they did not. It's not for me to say, of course, but they could have even ransomed you to your grandfather. It seems to me that they thought there was more money to be had in selling you."

She always seemed to make sense. Bretton was coming to admire that quality about her. His men would essentially tell him what he wanted to hear, dependent upon him as they were for riches, but Allaston wasn't dependent upon him at all, at least not like that. She had the luxury of speaking without prejudice. Maybe that was why he had asked her to stay and listen to his tale of the mysterious missive. He knew she would have an opinion on it. He was glad she did.

"You have an excellent point," he said. "To be truthful, I never thought on it that way."

"Then mayhap you should meet your cousin and see what he has to say."

Bretton mulled her words over, thinking that perhaps her advice was sound. Truth be told, he did want to see Rod. He wanted to know why no one had ever looked for him and he thought Rod might have the answers to questions that had pestered him for years. It was a sorrow he buried deep, but something that had fed his anger against de Velt. Were he to admit it, there was a lot of anger against his family, too. He had felt abandoned.

As he sat there and deliberated what to do, Allaston rose from her seat. "If that is all you needed, then I have duties to attend to," she said, making her way to him at the head of the table and picking up the pitcher to see if it was empty. "Would you like something more to eat? There is plenty of stew left."

He shook his head, sitting forward with his elbows on the table as she moved around him. He watched her as she poured the last of the wine into his cup and collected the pitcher. But before she could move away from him, he reached out and grasped her left hand. Allaston stiffened, preparing to fight him off, when he brought her hand to his lips for a kiss. It was soft, gentle, and warm. Just as quickly, he released her.

"Thank you," he murmured.

Allaston could hardly breathe for the shock of that kiss had bolted through her. But it wasn't a frightening shock in the least. It was a thrilling one. After what had happened earlier in the day, she was torn and confused with her reaction. It didn't make any sense but, then again, nothing revolving around Bretton de Llion made much sense to her. She was attracted to a man who wanted to kill her father, a man who was reasonable and moderate one moment yet vile and terrible the next. He was a paradox. Without another word, she grabbed the empty wine pitcher and fled the room.

Bretton sat there, reflecting on the misty memories of his grandfather and family, for the rest of the night.

Cg

THE NEXT MORNING dawned clear and mild, a weather pattern that seemed to be holding. Allaston rose before dawn and stoked the fire in her chamber, heating some water over the flickering flame for her morning ritual. The day she had learned about the fate of the lady of Cloryn, she had gone to the room where the family's things were haphazardly stored and she had neatly bundled everything, a show of respect for the family that had so terribly lost their lives. She even returned the majority of the garments Grayton had brought her, and the combs she had borrowed, until she realized she had absolutely nothing of her own to use or wear.

It seemed sacrilegious to use Lady Miette's personal items and she was quite torn in her thinking that the lady no longer had a need for them. After saying a few prayers over the family's possessions, she thought perhaps that Lady Miette would not have minded if she continued to use a few things. At least, she hoped not. Therefore, she took back the garments she had borrowed, and the combs, and she also found a small phial of rose-scented oil, which she reluctantly took as well. Her skin was very dry to the point of cracking and she knew the oil would help. She silently said a little prayer of thanks to Miette for her generosity and tried not to feel guilty for taking it.

It was this rose-scented oil that ended up in her morning water, and she used a rag to wash her body down with the warmed water. With the weather warm, she tended to sweat, and she hated the smell of her body, so the water washed away whatever she considered an offensive odor. She couldn't help but notice the oil was getting very low and soon she would have none, which would present something of a problem. Even the nuns at Alberbury would let her use grease or oil on her cracked hands. She realized she would soon have to do the same thing here and end up smelling like a side of pork from the grease smeared on her skin.

The yellow surcoat from yesterday that Bretton had torn down the front was in a pile on the chair by the fireplace, waiting to see if it could be acceptably mended, so Allaston dressed in a linen shift and then a heavier linen surcoat the color of eggshell because it wasn't as heavy as some of the woolen dresses. It was a simple garment with a square neckline, long sleeves, and two strips of cloth fastened to the waist that were meant to tie in the back, pulling the bodice snug. She put it on, braided her hair, slipped on her worn leather slippers, and headed out for her morning tasks.

Coming down the steps to the entry level, she couldn't help but peer into the open room where she had last seen Bretton. She had left the man there after his meal and he was still there when she had gone to bed. He had been sitting with that open missive, undoubtedly pondering the many things the parchment represented. He was clearly still upset by it. She didn't disturb him as she went up to bed and half expected to see him still sitting in the same spot this morning. But he was gone and the room was cold and dark. The parchment on the table was gone, too. Opening up the keep entry, Allaston headed out into the mild gray dawn.

She came to a halt at the top of the steps, looking with surprise at the collection of armed and mounted soldiers gathering in the bailey. Grayton was also there, wandering among the soldiers, and another knight with long auburn curls. She kept her eyes on the group as she descended the steps, wondering why they had gathered, when her attention was pulled away by the sound of Bretton's voice.

He was emerging from the stable area leading a big, silver horse that was wearing expensive and heavy tack, including chain mail across the front of its chest. Bretton was in full armor, speaking to a big bald knight who was also in full armor. As she came to the bottom of the stairs, Bretton caught sight of her and he interrupted his conversation with the knight to lift a hand and flick a wrist, summoning her. Obediently, Allaston headed in his direction.

As she came close, the knight he had been speaking with quietly excused himself but Bretton stopped the man from going any further.

"Lady Allaston," he said. "This is Dallan de Birmingham. I do not believe you two have formally been introduced, so let me do the introductions now. Dallan will be in command of Cloryn while I am away. You will obey him as you obey me."

Allaston nodded nervously at Dallan. He had a very grim look about him that she didn't like. He acknowledged her politely but ran off before any words could be exchanged. Allaston watched him go before turning her attention to Bretton.

"Where are you going?" she asked. "You said nothing of leaving yesterday when we spoke."

Bretton's gaze glimmered at her in the early morning light. "I am taking your advice," he said. "I am going to Newtown to meet with my cousin."

She was pleased to hear that. She was also rather touched that he took her advice on the matter. She honestly didn't think he would.

"Then I will pray that the meeting goes well," she said. "I pray that you find the answers you seek."

He nodded, pulling tight his gloves. "We shall see," he said ambivalently, as if he held little hope for the truth. "Meanwhile, you will stay to the keep and to the kitchens. The majority of my army is in residence and I do not want men unnecessarily tempted by the sight of a woman."

Allaston's expression tightened with fear. "What do you mean?" she asked. "Will they harm me? They've not tried to harm me yet and I have been around them a good deal in the great hall."

He shrugged, his eyes moving out over the compound. "These are mercenaries," he said. "They do not conform to the rules of propriety. If they see something they want, they take it. With me gone, they may be bolder than usual."

Allaston didn't like that thought in the least. "Then I will go to my chamber and lock it until you return," she said. "I do not want to give anyone the opportunity to do me harm."

He looked at her, then. "That may be wise," he said. "I should only be a few days at the most. You can keep yourself occupied until then."

She nodded firmly, eyeing the soldiers on the walls with great suspicion. "There is much I can do," she said. "I have a good deal of sewing to be done. By the way, it would seem that I am almost out of thread and I do not have the means here to make any. If Newtown is big enough, there should be a merchant who carries all manner of sewing goods. Can you please purchase some thread?"

He looked at her as if she had gone mad. "Purchase *thread*?" he repeated, insulted. "Surely you jest. I will do no such thing."

"Then I will not be able to mend the things you have given me."

He scowled at her. "You can make your own thread."

She met his scowl. "Gladly," she said. "If I had a spinning wheel and raw wool, I could easily do it, but I do not have any of those things. Therefore, you will have to buy the thread."

He eyed her, unhappy. "I will not," he said. "*You* can buy it."

"How can I buy it? I have no money and no opportunity."

He shook his head as if he thought the entire situation ridiculous. "You will indeed have the opportunity because you are coming with me," he said, turning away. Then, he began muttering. "Thread buying. What a preposterous suggestion."

She heard him muttering and fought off a grin. She was coming to suspect he didn't think it ridiculous so much as it was an affront to his masculinity. It was rather humorous to watch him mutter to himself.

"You can always steal it," she suggested exaggeratedly. "Just knock his walls down and take as much thread as you can grab in one handful. It should not be hard for a man with your talents."

He looked at her as if she had grievously insulted him. The look on his face alone made Allaston break down into laughter. She couldn't help it.

"Do you think to taunt me?" he demanded without force.

She shrugged. "Mayhap, just a bit."

He was still frowning at her greatly, but it was all for show. He was in danger of breaking a smile. Allaston could see it. He finally wiped a hand over his mouth and scratched his face to mask it.

"Go inside and collect a cloak and anything else you might need for the journey," he said, trying to be gruff but it wasn't coming out very convincingly. "Do not delay. I do not have time to waste waiting for you."

Allaston grinned at him, gathered her skirt, and scurried back into the keep. Bretton watched her, and only her, until she disappeared. Even after she was gone he found he could think of little else but he did manage to send a soldier to the stables to saddle a horse for her. As she packed and the horse was being saddled, he made his way over to the cluster of soldiers waiting for him. Dallan, Teague, and Grayton were among the group and he sought them out.

"It would seem that Lady Allaston will be accompanying me to Newtown," he told his commanders. "It makes more sense this way, Dallan. You will not have to worry over her and I can keep her in my protection. Cloryn will be female-free."

Dallan nodded but didn't say what he was thinking. In fact, they were all thinking the same thing and had been for a while. It seemed to them that Lady Allaston had been on Bretton's mind more than she should have been, and not in a way that made them comfortable. It wasn't so much in his words but in how he behaved towards her. She was becoming less and less a prisoner and more and more an object that evidently had much free reign. Somehow, she had bewitched the man. As Dallan simply nodded, Grayton was braver and spoke up.

"She does not need to go with you," he said. "I can return her to the vault. She's a prisoner, after all. She should not be running about here freely as it is."

Bretton took the comment as a direct challenge to his authority right away. With this nasty band of cutthroats and murders, he had learned to be on his guard, always, even with his commanders. He looked at Grayton, the bright blue eyes poised for a fight.

"*You* were the one that told me to treat her with more courtesy," he said, hardness in his tone. "*You* took her out of the vault when I had her there for three long weeks, and now you tell me she belongs there?"

Grayton could see that the man's entire posture changed with that suggestion. If he'd had any doubt before that Bretton had feelings for de Velt's daughter, those doubts were now dashed. He could see in an instant that Bretton had interest in the woman simply by the way he was acting. The Bretton he knew would have dismissed him quickly rather than confront him. He was defensive, a tale-tell sign. The situation went from one of polite conversation to one of hazardous intent fairly quickly.

"I was wrong," Grayton said steadily, holding his ground. "She tried to kill you, Bretton. She has the same killer instincts that her father does. It is not safe for any of us to have her roaming the grounds freely. What if she poisons our food next? Have you thought of that?"

Bretton was surprised at just how furious he was that Grayton should verbally attack Allaston.

"Foolishness," he hissed. "If she wanted to kill me, she could have easily done so when she knocked me unconscious with the fire poker, but she did not. I told you why she did it. She was attempting to escape."

Grayton shook his head in a flustered gesture. "She is a prisoner," he stressed. "She belongs in a locked chamber at the very least."

"She stays to the keep and to the kitchen," Bretton countered through clenched teeth. "That is what I told her to do and she has obeyed. Until she destroys that trust, I see no reason to lock her up."

Grayton wasn't satisfied with the answer. He knew there was more to it than Bretton was telling them. A preoccupied liege meant an uncertain situation. He didn't want a change of plans, nobody did. Bretton had promised them wealth and power, and that was exactly what they wanted, woman or no.

"What happened to the man who killed a mother prioress to get to his victim?" he wanted to know. "You stopped at nothing to gain the daughter of your enemy and once she was in your grasp, you threw her in the vault and kept her there."

"She would probably still be there if you didn't demand I release her!"

"I was wrong! She belongs in that hole like the vermin that she is!"

Bretton balled a fist and hit Grayton squarely in the face, sending the man flying backwards. Teague and Dallan stood back, holding back the collection of astonished soldiers, as Bretton loomed over Grayton as the man struggled on the ground. When Grayton tried to sit up, Bretton hit him again, on the forehead, and the man went down for good. Bretton postured angrily over him.

"Right now, that woman serves a purpose," he snarled. "Much like you, or any of my men, she now serves a purpose. She serves *me*. If you have issue with this, then keep it to yourself for I do not want to hear it. You will not question my decision again, is that clear?"

Grayton was half-unconscious but nodded. He also wisely remained on his back, looking up at Bretton with unfocused eyes.

"Aye," he grunted.

Bretton wasn't finished with him yet. "She is a valuable prisoner, as you once stated," he growled. "If anyone moves against her, I will kill him. And I do mean anyone. Make sure that is well understood within the ranks."

"Aye, Bretton," Grayton replied.

Bretton loomed over the man angrily for a moment longer before standing up, coming into eye contact with both Teague and Dallan as he stood back from Grayton. He lifted his eyebrows at them.

"Do either of you have something to say about this?" he demanded.

The two warriors shook their heads, knowing now was not the time to express any concerns over the prisoner. But they, too, realized that their liege had some kind of feelings, or some sense of protectiveness, for de Velt's daughter. It was a sensitive subject that bore watching.

"Nay," Teague finally said. "But she should be much more careful about moving in the great hall. I have seen more than one soldier eye her rather hungrily. It would probably be best if she kept to the kitchen and the keep, for her own safety."

Bretton was still furious about his confrontation with Grayton and struggled to calm the rage. Taking a deep breath, he nodded as he turned away from his men.

"I would agree," he said, his tone considerably less hostile. "I will make sure she knows."

They let the subject die as he went back over to his charger, pretending to check the connections and straps, when what he was really doing was evaluating his reaction against Grayton. The man was his closest friend, someone he trusted implicitly. Was it possible that he was correct and that de Velt's daughter was truly a danger to them all? He couldn't honestly believe it but, then again, he had been having some very odd feelings where she was concerned. He wondered if his men were seeing something he wasn't, blinded by her beauty and kindness as he was.

The wait for Allaston wasn't long. Within ten minutes of Bretton's punch to Grayton, she came scurrying out of the keep with a small satchel in her hand. She also had a cloak on, the same one she had been wearing since Grayton had given her all of those garments. Brown, lined with rabbit fur, Allaston took great care of Lady Miette's cloak. As she approached Bretton, he pointed at the bag.

"Where did you get that?" he asked.

Allaston looked at the satchel in her hand, made from brocaded wool. It was quite nice. "I found it in the chamber above mine where I also found a comb for my hair and these clothes," she said, wondering how much she should say about whom, in fact, it had belonged to. "I am just borrowing it because I have nothing else to carry my possessions in."

He eyed the bag. "You may have any of those possessions that catch your eye," he told her. "They belong to me now."

Allaston looked at him as he spoke rather emotionlessly. *They belong to me now.* They belonged to him because the real owners were dead, killed by de Llion's war machine. She wondered how he could be so callous about such things. It was confusing, really. Last night, he had kissed her hand with tenderness only angels possessed, yet he spoke of a dead family's possessions as if they were nothing at all. It was difficult not to tell him what she thought of his attitude towards the bundle of lonely items that were the sole reminder of a family who had met a terrible end.

So she said nothing, following him as he took her elbow and pulled her over to a horse that was standing rather docile and half-asleep a few feet away from his charger. He took her bag from her, handing it over to the nearest soldier with the instructions to secure it to her saddle before taking her by the waist and lifting her up onto the horse. The saddle wasn't made for a woman, but rather for a man to ride astride, so she shifted a bit, trying to get comfortable, as he handed her the reins.

Bretton mounted his silver charger, snapping orders to the two commanders who were accompanying them, and the commanders began to form the men in loose columns. Someone shouted to the gatehouse and the gate, a big oak and iron monstrosity that was newly rebuilt in many sections, began to lurch open. The wider the gate yawned, the more the breeze from outside the walls began to infiltrate the bailey, bringing with it the horrible stench of death.

Allaston caught whiff, a horrible sweet and greasy stench, and she immediately sucked in her breath and pinched her nose shut. She glanced sidelong at Bretton and at the two other commanders, one of them being Grayton who was sporting a swollen nose, and she couldn't help but notice they weren't reacting to the smell. They were paying more attention to the party that was riding forth and when Bretton finally motioned her forward, she reluctantly kicked the horse in his flank and the animal began to move. The closer she drew to the open gate, the more apprehensive she became. Knowing what was outside those gates made her stomach lurch. And then, she saw them.

Dozens upon dozens of bodies, mounted on poles, exposed to the air like a ghastly army of scarecrows, only the crows weren't scared. There were flocks of them feeding on the flesh of the corpses. It was a grisly sight. Horrified, sickened, Allaston realized that the great army of impaled men stretched out for at least a quarter of a mile, flanking the road leading in to Cloryn. There were men on poles almost as far as she could see.

The scope was beyond comprehension. All of these men who had once fought for Cloryn were now dead within sight of it. As she absorbed the hideous sight, the full atrocities of de Llion's campaign of terror were becoming real. The stench, coupled by the vision before her, brought tears to Allaston's eyes and she hung her head, unwilling to look at the macabre scenery any longer. They were surrounded by it. As the horse plodded from the gate, she happened to catch a glimpse of something billowing in the breeze off to her left and she glanced over, a reflexive action, to see the most horrific sight she had ever seen, a horror of horrors that made everything else seem tame by comparison.

Lady Miette's dress was waving in the morning breeze, a dark blue garment of fine fabric that had been terribly weathered these months that it had been exposed to the elements. The woman herself was impaled on a pole that went in between her legs and exited her sternum, coming to rest just below her chin. Her head hung forward with copious amounts of dark hair blowing over her face. It was difficult to see her decayed features but her hands, small and boney, were clasped near her waist as if in prayer. Allaston could only imagine that the woman, as she was dying, set about to pray for her passing by folding her hands in prayer. It was a sad, horribly poignant sight.

Next to her were the remains of a man in pieces of armor and chain mail. He was impaled like the woman, without his helm, and the wind blew his dark blond hair gently as it framed his sunken features. Against his legs, a body of a small boy was trussed up with rope and secured to him. The child's face was buried between the man's legs so she couldn't see it, and his little body was all wrapped up in the rope. In death, the child was tied to his father. It was both horribly saddening and horribly touching.

Every terrible story Allaston had been told about the family and about the horrors de Llion's army cast against them came crashing down on her and, with a sob escaping her lips, she pulled her horse to a stop and dismounted, making her way through the ghoulish forest of bodies until she came to Lady Miette and her husband. She fell to her knees in front of Lady Miette.

"*Ave María, grátia plena, Dóminus tecum*," she prayed, tears streaming down her face as she crossed herself. "*Benedícta tu in muliéribus, et benedíctus fructus ventris tui, Iesus.*"

Her actions didn't go unnoticed by Bretton, or any of the others. Bretton was behind her as they'd exited the gates, too far away to prevent her from dismounting her horse. Quickly, he spurred his horse forward and dismounted, moving through the army of the dead until he came to Allaston as she prayed and wept over the family. He didn't even look at the bodies, for he had seen them before. But he knew she hadn't. He couldn't quite grasp why it upset her so, other than there was a child visible. He knew she was sensitive, he'd seen it. But the emotion she was displaying was foreign to him.

"My lady," he said quietly. "We must be...."

She cut him off, hissing. "How could you do this?" she demanded. "How could you kill this woman and her children? I do not understand what kind of monster would do this heinous thing."

He stiffened. "You are not to judge my methods, bearing de Velt blood as you do," he said, trying to keep the emotion out of his voice, which he wasn't very good at in any case when it pertained to her. "Your father did this to my family. This should not upset you so."

Her head snapped up to him, the pale green eyes blazing. "I am *not* my father," she snarled, tears and mucus raining down her face. "Whatever my father did was well before my time, and you and I have traversed this subject before. Whatever he did, it is in the past. I do not hold the same views as he once did. When I see things such as this, all I can think of is the pain and terror this woman must have suffered. And the child... Sweet Jesus, he was just a little boy. Why did you have to kill him?"

She was weeping loudly and Bretton knew everyone could hear her. Reaching out, he grabbed her so hard by the arm that he nearly snapped her neck. Pulling her up against him brutally, when he spoke, it was through clenched teeth.

"I told you to be careful how you spoke to me," he growled. "This will be your final warning."

Allaston wasn't intimidated. She was too emotional to care. "Or what?" she countered as if daring him to make good on his threat. "What will you do? Will you put me on a post as you did this woman? Then I say do it, do it now. You want to hurt my father, don't you? You want to draw him to Cloryn? Imagine how hurt and shattered he will be to see me on a pole by the gates. You will put me there, of course, won't you? In a place of honor to be seen by all?"

She was out of control and he shook her again. "Stop it," he hissed. "Keep your mouth shut and get on your horse."

Allaston shook her head, struggling to pull away from him. "I will *not*," she said. "I am not going anywhere with you. Lock me in the vault or put me on a pole as you did the rest of these poor people. I am not afraid of you, de Llion. You are a weak, pathetic man to do this to people who were only defending what belonged to them. You are a *monster!*"

Bretton almost struck her in that instance but something prevented it. He wasn't sure what because his emotions were running wild, but something stopped him from taking his hand to her. Somehow, he just couldn't do it. Still, she had embarrassed him, humiliated him, and there was only one way to deal with insubordination. If he didn't, he would lose the respect of his men and he knew it.

Men were watching him, men who would see any sign of weakness from him and exploit it. He had no choice. Everything was building up inside him, thoughts and emotions that were threatening to explode in every direction. *Damn her!* Pushing Allaston to the ground so that she fell squarely on her bum, he turned and marched for Lady Miette.

Bretton was a man of incredible strength. It took him little time to push the pole down so that Miette was lying in the dirt. Frustrated, infuriated, Bretton put a foot on the woman and held her firm as he yanked the pole out of her body, which wasn't a great feat considering she was mostly a dried cluster of skin and bones at this point. There was no blood, no innards. With the pole in his hands, he turned to Allaston, who was still sitting on the ground, watching him with a hysterical expression. His features darkened as he marched over to her.

"Get onto your hands and knees," he rumbled.

She looked up at him as if she didn't understand the question. "I…?"

"I said roll over onto your hands and knees!"

He shouted it so loudly that it reverberated off the walls. Startled, and realizing what he was about to do, Allaston showed surprising control. Hysterical one moment to calm the next, she gazed at him steadily.

God's Beard, had her mouth finally gotten her into trouble? Had she finally signed her death warrant with her uncontrollable tongue? Allaston could hardly believe it, but the proof was in front of her. Bretton was poised and ready to move. He was ready to ram the pole into her body, in one end until it came out of the other. She knew it was going to hurt. She understood the concept. She just hoped she could bear the pain without pleading forgiveness from the man. She'd rather die than ask for his forgiveness for what she said because she wasn't sorry in the least. He *was* a monster. Perhaps all of those silly notions about him having kindness and understanding beneath all of that warfare were just foolish dreams. Perhaps all of those feelings she thought she might have for him were simply bouts of madness.

"So you are going to kill me," she said. It was a statement, not a question. "I am not surprised. My death should not matter in the least to you considering how many people you have killed. When my father comes, you make sure to tell him that I met my death bravely. I am not afraid. At this moment, I have more courage than you do."

Bretton was so angry that he was grinding his teeth. "We shall see," he said. "Get on your hands and knees."

She simply stared back at him, mulling over the command. After a moment, she shook her head. "Nay," she said. "I will not make this easy for you."

Her attitude was only serving to infuriate him more. "I will have my men hold you if that is your wish."

She gaped at him, knowing he would probably do just that. Her fight was with him, not with the men who would try to hold her down. She didn't want to lose control of the situation, not now. She was coming to think that perhaps he wouldn't impale her after all. There was something in his eyes, some flicker deep in the brilliant blue depths that told her he had no intention of doing to her what he'd done to countless others. The man had confided in her, protected her, and laughed with her for these past few weeks. An odd relationship between a captor and captive. Something told her he wasn't going to kill her. It was a hunch she had. She decided to play it.

Slowly, she rolled over onto her belly, propping herself up on her hands and knees with her buttocks facing him. If he was truly going to impale her, that would be the point of entry. Presenting her arse to him, she lowered her head and waited.

His response wasn't long in coming.

CHAPTER ELEVEN

Lioncross Abbey Castle

"CHRIS!" EDWARD DE Wolfe stuck his head into de Lohr's solar where the man had been working over some documents. "Come quickly!"

Startled up from his desk, Christopher made haste from the solar, following Edward who was showing distinct signs of excitement, into the great hall of Lioncross. The big room was part of the keep and it was scented with fresh rushes that had been replaced that morning, giving off a strong greenery smell. There weren't any dogs in the hall because Lady de Lohr didn't like the smell of dogs, and Christopher entered the fragrant room on Edward's heels only to find one of his soldiers standing near the hearth, slurping up a cup of wine that a servant had brought to him. When the man saw de Lohr, he quickly put aside the cup.

"My lord," the soldier, bearing the blue and yellow de Lohr tunic, greeted his liege. "I have just come from the northern borders of your lands. I was on patrol with four other men and we saw it on the horizon, north of Pearl Lake."

Christopher was listening intently. Edward leaned over into his ear. "North of the River Arrow," he told the man helpfully. Christopher waved him off.

"I have no idea what the man is talking about yet," he said, focusing on the soldier. "What did you see?"

The soldier took a deep breath, his gaze moving between his liege and Edward. He was an older man who had been at Lioncross for many years. In fact, he had grown up on the Marches. He didn't like what he was about to say, as it dredged up old fears from days long past, days he hoped were gone forever.

"At least one thousand men," he said. "A very big army is heading in our direction."

Christopher's first reaction was that it was somehow the mercenary they'd heard tale of and his sense of concern grew. Perhaps the man, having grown weary of smaller targets along the Marches, was now moving to bigger game.

"Did you see any colors?" he asked. "Surely they were flying standards."

The soldier sighed heavily. "Aye, they were," he said. Then, he shook his head. "My lord, I grew up in these parts. I know the stories and I know the history. The last time I saw standards of black and red with a boar's head in the center, Jax de Velt was sweeping through the Marches."

Christopher stared at the man, trying not to show his astonishment. "De *Velt?*" he repeated. "That is impossible. Jax de Velt's reign of terror ended twenty-five years ago."

The soldier nodded firmly. "I know it, my lord," he said. "But unless someone else is flying the red and black boar's head, Jax de Velt has returned to the Marches and he is coming our way."

Christopher could hardly believe what he was hearing, but in the same breath, he remembered the conversation with Rod about the newest threat on the Marches and how the man had burned Alberbury Priory to get to de Velt's daughter. Christopher was terrified that his prophecy was about to come true; *and Hell followed with him.* Was it possible that de Velt was returning to the Marches to seek vengeance for his daughter's abduction? Christopher could only guess. But one thing was for certain. He had to be prepared for whatever was coming.

There was no time to waste. After a few moments of deliberation, he turned to Edward.

"You know what to do," he said calmly. "Get the men moving, Edward. We will prepare for de Velt as if the man intends to attack us. Warn the village and take all who will come inside to the safety of the castle. Time is critical, so move quickly."

With that, he turned away from the soldier and headed out of the hall with Edward beside him. Their manner was business-like and calm for the most part even though they were both rattled at de Velt's appearance. It was exactly what they hadn't wanted. Running a thoughtful hand through his thick blond hair, Christopher continued to focus on what needed to be done in order to secure Lioncross. He was certain he could hold de Velt off in any case, but he had to make sure they were fully prepared. He couldn't take any chances.

"Gather the officers in the bailey so we can tell them what has happened," he told Edward. "And find Max and Jeffrey. They must be given instructions. I need my knights, Edward."

Edward nodded grimly. "I wish we had Gart and Rhys and Lawrence with us," he muttered. "I would feel better about this whole thing."

Christopher grunted agreement as they reached the keep entry. Beyond, he could see the massive bailey of Lioncross, busy with commerce and activity. Men were going about their business and the gates were open because it was the time in the morning when the kitchens dealt with local farmers. It tore at him to think all of it would soon be under siege. His peaceful, lovely world would soon be under threat.

"I wish that as well, but we do not," he said quietly. "Gart is in France for my brother. As for Lawrence and Rhys… well, God rest their souls, they are no longer with us. And I sincerely wish my brother was here but he had to marry a woman who lives in Kent, so it would take him weeks to reach us. That being said, we must think of other options for assistance. De Boulers, mayhap?"

Edward nodded. "Unless de Velt has already torn him to pieces," he said. "The scout said that the army was approaching from the north, which meant they had to pass through Shropshire lands. But I will send a messenger to Shropshire."

Christopher agreed quickly. "Do it immediately," he said. "But provided Shropshire is compromised, we will send a request to assistance to someone else."

"Who?" Edward wanted to know. "Anyone else on the Marches is days away. Chepstow, mayhap? Or Gloucester?"

Christopher already had an idea of who to summon. "Nay, not them," he said. "There are English outposts in Wales that are closer to us, Keller de Poyer, in fact. We have sent men back and forth to each other since he has been in Wales, nearly eight years now. He is two days away on a swift horse. He carries almost a thousand men."

It was an excellent idea and Edward was already moving, preparing to send off messengers. Christopher caught sight of Max Cornwallis, one of his other knights, and summoned the man with a flick of the hand. From across the dusty bailey, Max came on the run and, soon, he too was off with orders from de Lohr. Much needed to be done in a short amount of time because from where the soldier said de Velt's army was camping, they could be upon them in mere hours. Time was of the essence.

Time moved swiftly, indeed. The messengers were sent off in short order to Shropshire and de Poyer as Christopher had a conversation with his wife instructing her and their children to remain in the keep. The Lady Dustin de Lohr, a spitfire of a beauty, was fearful but resolved to her husband's instructions to barricade the keep, and Christopher was better able to focus knowing his young family was safe.

And it was a very good thing that he was clear-headed with determination. A little more than a half-hour since Christopher had been told of de Velt's presence, he heard the sentries on the wall take up a cry. A rider had been sighted, heading towards Lioncross on the main road leading in from the north. Christopher raced up to the walls to catch a glimpse of what had the sentries so excited and ended up standing in a group with Edward, Max, and Jeffrey, watching the incoming rider. As the man drew close, Jeffrey, an older Germanic knight who had spent many years on the Marches, hissed under his breath.

"De Velt," he muttered in his thick accent. "He wears the red and black."

They could all see that, adding to their unease. The rider drew close to the castle as the men glared down from the walls, scrutinizing him, and the rider wisely came to a halt well before he reached the walls. It was clear that Lioncross had been warned because peasants were streaming in from the village and the gates were open. Christopher, seeing the man come to a halt, made his way down from the walls and to the open gates of his fortress.

Since Lioncross had been many things before it became a castle, it was not moated, nor did it have a motte or a keep in the general sense. Lioncross depended upon her massive walls for protection, walls that were twenty-five feet high in places, with extended fighting platforms and murder holes from which to destroy the enemy. At the moment, however, the gates were open to allow the villagers easy entry, and one lone rider was clearly no threat against the hundreds of soldiers at Lioncross.

With that in mind, Christopher made his presence known at the front gates, flanked by Edward and Max while Jeffrey remained upon the walls to keep watch on the horizon. Dust was being kicked up in their faces by the villagers scurrying in through the open gates of the fortress as the three knights eyed the rider in the distance.

"Max," Christopher said, his eyes still lingering on de Velt's messenger. "Go out and tell him to drop his weapons. Strip him."

Max, a massive knight with long, dark hair, made his way out to the distant rider. Christopher and Edward watched as Max explained the way of things to the rider, who dismounted his horse without a word of protest and began dropping his weapons to the ground. The sword and scabbard went down into the grass and so did a small array of daggers.

Max gestured to the man again, obviously giving him more instructions, and the rider peeled off his tunic and hauberk, followed by his mail coat and finally his boots. Nearly everything came off the man as Max had him strip down to his tunic and breeches. Even then, he patted the man down to make sure he wasn't carrying a concealed weapon. Only when he was convinced the man was weaponless did he gesture to Christopher and Edward, who came forward through the crowd of villagers trying to enter the fortress. When they came to within about ten feet of the messenger, Christopher came to a halt.

It was an odd standoff, three big and fully armed knights against a man in his dirty tunic and breeches with no shoes. Christopher studied the man a moment before speaking.

"State your business," he said evenly.

The soldier looked between the three men. "I come bearing a message for the Earl of Hereford."

"That would be me," Christopher replied. "State your business and be quick about it."

The messenger focused on Christopher. "My lord," he said politely. "Sir Ajax de Velt has asked me to extend his greetings. He is in need of your counsel and seeks audience. He comes in peace and asks if you will kindly see him."

That wasn't the message Christopher had expected. He could feel Edward's gaze upon him, curious and confused, but he didn't look at the man. He didn't want to give the messenger, who would undoubtedly return to de Velt and report his observations, any hint of his bewilderment or doubt. De Lohr was a master at keeping his emotions in check.

"If he comes in peace, then why did I receive a report that one thousand men bearing de Velt banners were camping on my lands?" he wanted to know. "Why does he field a massive army if he does not intend to use it?"

The messenger shook his head. "His quarrel is not with you, my lord," he said. "He is eager to seek your counsel on a terrible matter and seeks an audience. He has brought the army for another matter entirely but he wishes to speak with you first. Will you please see him?"

Christopher looked at Edward, then. They were both thinking the same thing. *He must be here about de Llion.* Knowing what they did about the events on the Marches involving de Velt's holdings and Alberbury, it was the obvious and logical conclusion. But they were still genuinely shocked that he had come to Lioncross. *My lord requires your counsel.* Evidently, the man wished to speak with him about de Llion. Or, that was what Christopher assumed. There was only one way to find out.

"What did he have in mind?" he asked.

The messenger had obviously been well-schooled by de Velt on the answers he should supply to the earl. "If you would be more comfortable, he will come to you, unarmed and alone," he replied. "If that is not acceptable, then he asks that you name your terms and he will obey."

Christopher was growing more bewildered by the moment. Scratching his cheek thoughtfully, he turned his back on the messenger and motioned Edward close. De Wolfe complied.

"What is your take on all of this?" Christopher whispered to the man. "Is this an honest request or is it a ruse?"

Edward eyed the messenger before replying. "I do not sense a ruse," he admitted. "De Velt's history suggests he does not operate that way. Moreover, if what Shropshire told us was true about the mercenary abducting de Velt's daughter, then this makes perfect sense. Mayhap de Velt is here to ask for your help?"

Christopher lifted his eyebrows. "Christ," he muttered. "I never thought I'd live to see the day that would happen."

Edward was forced to agree. "I have spent all of my time being terrified of de Velt," he said. "To consider that the man is requesting a peaceful conference... I do not know what to think."

Christopher pondered that a moment. "I am more afraid to think of what will happen if I deny him an audience," he said. "I suppose having him come to Lioncross, unarmed and alone, is harmless enough."

"I suppose so," he agreed. "But it is Jax de Velt we are speaking of. Even if he is unarmed by our standards, he may not be unarmed by his. The man is likely to draw a dagger out of his arse and kill you with it."

Christopher struggled not to grin. "Let us hope not," he said. "Mayhap I should do the man a courtesy and listen to what he has to say."

"As you said, to deny him might anger him, and that is something we don't want."

"I don't want him to take a dagger out of his arse and kill me with it, either."

"Then you have a difficult choice to make."

With a heavy sigh, Christopher turned to face the messenger. "Tell your lord he is welcome to come to Lioncross, alone and unarmed," he said. "I will meet him at the gatehouse. Tell him to come this day."

The messenger nodded. "May I dress, my lord?"

Christopher motioned Max away from the messenger. "Be quick about it," he said. "I will wait for de Velt's arrival."

The messenger began to dress swiftly as Christopher, Edward, and Max headed back to the open front gates. The trickle of peasants had lessened and the guards at the gate were preparing to lower the portcullis. Christopher made it inside the gatehouse, remaining with his men as the portcullis began to lower. Peasants made a run for it, some making it under the fanged grate just in time while still others hadn't been fast enough. The guards at the gate instructed those who didn't make it to return to the village but remain in their homes, so there was a wild scattering as people rushed back for the village. It was a mad dash for safety in uncertain times.

Inside the gatehouse, Christopher stood near the lowered portcullis with his knights, waiting for the moment Jax de Velt would show himself. He'd never met the man but he'd heard he looked like a wild beast with crazed eyes. He'd been lucky in his life not to have had any contact with him, or any conflicts, but all of that was about to change. He hoped that all de Velt wanted to do was talk because the alternative had him edgy. He wished his brother was here, a knight among knights. He wished he had more knights on hand. In fact, he wished every fighting man in England was here at the moment, at his disposal.

If de Velt became angry, it might take every soldier in the country to fend him off.

… and Hell followed with him.

CB

JAX HADN'T BEEN on a military campaign in two decades. True, he had traveled during that time, significantly, but this was different. He felt as if he was on a battle march, which was essentially the truth. Moreover, this march was different. He was heading into the realm of Christopher de Lohr who, in his opinion, was the most powerful man in England. The man had allies all over the place and he existed in a world that was somewhat foreign to Jax. If de Lohr needed assistance, all he need do was summon one of a dozen nearby allies. If Jax needed assistance, he had no one to really call upon, but that was his own damn fault. Even when he'd stopped his campaign of conquest, he'd never really made a huge effort to repair any of the damages he'd done.

His properties in Wales were a prime example. Twenty-five years ago, he'd plowed through a portion of the Marches with a ferocity that no one had ever seen before. He'd taken castles, killed people, burned villages, and generally destroyed everything he touched. He'd established his own commanders at the castles to oversee them and the wealth he received from those properties, to this very day, was significant. But when he'd stopped his conquest, mostly because his wife did not agree with what he did, he'd just left things as they were. He'd returned a couple of English castles to Yves de Vesci, his liege, but he'd kept the rest and never said another word about it. He never tried to mend any relationships or make any allies, as he'd told his wife. His properties were his own and he'd never cared much for alliances. Until now.

As he traveled towards Lioncross Abbey, de Lohr's seat, he was fairly certain that de Lohr was alerted to his approach. Any man worth his weight in steel and sweat would have patrols across his lands, searching for threats, and he was positive de Lohr was no exception.

Therefore, he didn't expect a particularly warm welcome, especially when de Lohr found Jax de Velt and an army of one thousand men at his doorstep. He would be lucky if de Lohr didn't lash out first and ask questions later. Given that possibility, when he was about an hour away from Lioncross, he sent forth a messenger to de Lohr to let the man know his intentions were peaceful and requesting an audience. He didn't think de Lohr would believe him, or even agree to see him, but he had to try. As Jax remained lost to his thoughts, a knight astride an excited destrier pulled up alongside him.

"My scouts tell me that Lioncross is over this next rise," the young knight said, flipping up his visor. "The messenger has yet to return, however."

Jax cocked an eyebrow at his second son, a young man who resembled him to a fault including the dual-colored eyes. Sir Julian de Velt possessed the brown eyes with a big splash of pale green in the right eye, just as his father did, only Julian's condition was a little less pronounced than his father's was. Still, the resemblance was eerie.

"I would not be surprised to find our messenger locked up and de Lohr preparing to unleash archers on us the moment we come in range," Jax told his son. "Therefore, the army will stay well back while you and I approach. Where is Cole?"

He was asking about his eldest son, a very powerful knight in his own right who possessed his mother's fair looks. Sir Coleby de Velt actually served the Earl of Northumberland, Yves de Vesci, but Jax had called the man home for this particular venture. Julian looked around, searching out his brother from among hundreds of men. He finally saw him.

"He is over to the east," he said, pointing. "He is riding along the edge of the column. I wonder what he is doing?"

Jax looked over his shoulder, seeing his eldest son in the distance.

"What we should all be doing," he growled as he faced forward. "Watching to see if de Lohr is launching an offensive our way. Ride point, Julian. Be well on guard. Stop the column when we come to within a half-mile of Lioncross and tell them to hold station."

Julian nodded, eyeing his father a moment. There was something warm glittering in the two-toned eyes.

"If I have not told you before, Father, allow me to tell you now," he said. "I am proud to be riding with you. I have never ridden to battle with you, you know. This is a momentous occasion."

Jax glanced at his enthusiastic son. At twenty years and two, he was still very young mentally, much younger than Jax had been at that age, but he was exceptionally skilled and intelligent. Still, he had a lot of growing up to do, something only time and experience would take care of. He gave the boy a half-grin.

"You have gone to battle with me before," he said. "When you were younger, we had to fight off the Scots a couple of times."

Julian shook his head. "I was only a child then," he said as if those skirmishes had been nothing of consequence. "I had not even gone to foster yet."

"You still rode with my men to defend White Crag against raiders."

Julian made a face. "That was nothing," he said. "This is *real* battle."

Jax didn't have the romanticized view of this campaign that Julian did. He shook his head faintly. "I hope not," he said quietly. "We are riding to retrieve your sister. I hope it does not go badly for us or for her."

Julian sobered as he was reminded of the reason for their campaign. "As do I," he said, thinking of his sister who was only two and a half years younger than he was. "I hope Allie is... you do not think they have harmed her, do you? I mean, she is probably locked away in the vault but they would not actually hurt her, would they?"

Jax couldn't even think on the possibilities. He didn't want to visit that horror unless he had to. "She is more valuable to them alive than dead," he said steadily. "One does not usually harm an asset, not when it can get you what you want in the end."

Julian eyed his father. "What they want is you."

"And I am coming to them," he said, looking at his son. "I am coming with one thousand men and two big knights to secure my daughter. They shall not get the better of me, lad, have no doubt."

Julian seemed comforted by that, as Jax had intended. Whether or not he believed his own propaganda was another matter altogether. Not wanting to discuss the situation further, he snapped his gloved fingers at Julian to prompt the young knight to head to the point of the column, as he had been ordered. Julian spurred his big bay Belgian rouncey forward, parting the soldiers along the way as he went. Jax watched the young man go, wondering if, indeed, they would see action before this campaign was through. Clearly, he knew one thing for certain – if Allaston was harmed in any way, there would be blood. The Dark Lord would see to it.

Another half-hour saw Lioncross Abbey Castle come into view towards the south, a massive bastion that sat atop a small rise like a great sentinel protecting the countryside. The walls were the color of sand, a beige-grayish stone that was local to the area. Jax focused on the legendary castle as they approached, relieved that there was no army waiting for him, or worse, riding out to fend him off. For once in his life, he wasn't looking for a fight. He was looking for help. As the army drew within the half-mile perimeter that Jax had discussed with Julian, Cole came riding up beside his father.

"The messenger is returning, Father" he said. "I can see him coming up the road."

Jax took a deep breath. He realized that he was actually nervous. Would de Lohr agree to see him? Or would he tell him to go away? "Very well," he said. "Let us hope that de Lohr is in an agreeable mood today, for I would very much like to speak with him."

"Will you ask for reinforcements from him?" Cole wanted to know.

Jax shrugged faintly. "I am sure it will be too much to ask," he said. "Who in their right mind would ally themselves with Ajax de Velt?

Certainly not a man with a reputation like de Lohr's."

"Then why did we come?"

"Because one can hold out hope that I am wrong and de Lohr will indeed join ranks with the likes of me."

Cole's lips twitched with a smile. "You are not so bad."

"You were not around twenty-five years ago."

Cole snorted softly. He knew what his father had done twenty-five years ago, more in-depth than anyone else did because Jax himself had told him. Since marrying Cole's mother, however, his life had changed drastically. He no longer surrounded himself with killers and mercenaries. All the men that served him now did so out of fealty, not rewards. Those generals who had been so instrumental in his conquest those years ago had moved on to other things. Unless it was in direct relation to a property he owned, Jax had little or no contact with those men from the past. It was true that men could be reformed and Ajax de Velt was a living example of that. But his reputation, the one of fear and death, still lived on. It was something he would never be rid of.

"Not to worry, Father," Cole said. "Someday, all will be forgiven or, at the very least, overlooked. In any case, I…."

A shout cut him off and both Jax and Cole looked to see a lone rider barreling up the dusty road that skirted the big village, heading in their direction. In the morning sun, light glinted off of the rider's metal protection and created a flashing effect. Jax emitted a piercing whistle from between his teeth, signaling to Julian, who called a halt to the column. Men began to shout, making sure everyone had heard the command, as the army of a thousand men and six wagons began to grind to a stop.

So they waited, watching, as the rider drew close. Jax moved forward to intercept the messenger as the man pulled his frothing steed to a halt, kicking up dirt and rocks from the road.

"Well?" Jax demanded. "Did you speak with de Lohr?"

The messenger nodded. "I did, my lord," he replied, struggling to calm his excited horse. "He says he will see you, alone and unarmed, at the gatehouse of Lioncross. He says that you must come now."

It wasn't the answer Jax had expected. He had fully expected denial and disappointment. His surprised showed.

"Truly?" he asked, incredulous. "He said he would grant me audience?"

Again, the messenger nodded. "Indeed, my lord."

"What did he say, exactly?"

The messenger didn't hesitate. "He asked me to state my business and I did," he replied. "He wanted to know why you had brought so many men if you did not mean to engage him and I assured him that your intentions were peaceful."

"Did he seem reluctant?"

"He did, my lord."

"But even so, he agreed to see me?"

"He did, my lord."

Jax turned to look at his sons, astonishment evident on his face. He had frankly been prepared to spend a few days at Lioncross at the very least, begging de Lohr to give him a few moments of his time, so this immediate agreement was something of a shock. He was so used to being alienated that a concurrence like this had him stumped, but not stumped enough so that he lost his ability to think. He could think very well and, after a moment's pause, he dismounted his horse. As his sons watched, the armor started coming off, per de Lohr's instructions.

"Father, should we accompany you?" Julian asked, concerned. "May we at least escort you closer to the castle?"

Jax shook his head as he pulled off his tunic. The mail coat was next and he bent over, deftly pulling it over his big body. His hair, which had always been shoulder-length, was gathered at the nape of his neck by a strip of leather and he smoothed the loose pieces of hair back and tightened up the leather tie.

"Nay," he said flatly. "De Lohr said that he wants to see me alone and unarmed, and that is exactly what he is going to get. If he sees you escorting me, he might think I am disobeying his terms and refuse to see me. And I very much want to see the man."

Cole and Julian eyed each other with concern but didn't reply. Their father was determined to do as the Earl of Hereford instructed because he didn't want to appear threatening or disobedient in any way. In fact, as Jax removed his mail and weapons, there was an excitement to his manner that neither man had ever seen. It was very clear how serious he was taking all of this. *De Lohr was willing to see him!* When the last piece of chain mail was handed over to the soldiers who were collecting the man's armor, he began stripping the armor off of his horse.

Pieces of armor came off the warhorse, including the chain mail near the chest and on the flanks, and the heavily armored saddle eventually came off, too, leaving the horse in his bridle only. Jax didn't care. Every piece of armor was removed from both him and his horse, and he vaulted onto the beast's back, gathering the reins.

"I will proceed alone," he instructed the men around him, including his sons. "You will remain here. I do not know how long this will take, so it is my suggestion that you make camp here. Do not wander into the town and do not go about stealing anything. Everyone will remain within the perimeter of the camp and behave properly. You will wait patiently for my return."

Cole's brow furrowed. "But what if you do not return, Father?" he wanted to know. "What will you have us do?"

Jax's looked over his right shoulder towards the bastion in the distance. "Give me at least two days," he said. "If you do not see me returned in two days, then send a messenger to inquire on my status. If you receive no answer or are not given a satisfactory reply, then we will assume that something has happened to me and you, Cole, will demand to speak to de Lohr personally. If he denies you audience or tells you something you do not wish to hear, then you have my permission to lay siege to Lioncross and destroy her. All of her. However, the Earl of Hereford has a reputation for fairness and honestly, so I do not think the man will move against me. I have faith that I will return to you. But if I do not, then you have your orders."

Cole was satisfied with the directive. Reining his horse over to where his father was, he extended a mailed hand to the man. Jax took it and held it tightly.

"Godspeed, Father," he said. "We will be waiting for word."

Jax squeezed the man's hand and let it go, reining his charger in the direction of Lioncross. As the beast picked up into a thundering canter, de Velt's army watched the man ride away, each soldier with thoughts on de Lohr, victory, Wales, and the future. No one had certainty of any of those choices.

The next move was de Lohr's.

CHAPTER TWELVE

T HE INHABITANTS OF Lioncross waited in tense silence mostly, watching the horizon, knowing de Velt's army was lingering in the distance, watching and waiting. The massive, oddly-shaped bailey was full of peasants as the soldiers tried to organize the refugees from the village, trying to put them into areas that were least likely to receive bombardment or projectiles should de Velt's army advance. The air was filled with uncertainty even though de Lohr seemed particularly calm. He stood with his knights in the gatehouse against the portcullis, watching the road and waiting.

And waiting.

But the wait wasn't a long one in the grand scheme of things. Less than a half-hour after the messenger returned to de Velt, the sentries on the walls of Lioncross began to take up the cry. A rider had been sighted in the distance. When the cry went up, Christopher turned to look at his knights, who peered back at him in various stages of apprehension. Soon, they would see what no man had ever seen and lived to tell the tale – Jax de Velt in the flesh. The Dark Lord himself would soon be on their doorstep and they were understandably apprehensive. Old fears died hard.

"I will wager that he is a tiny old man," Max finally said, his attention on the road beyond the portcullis. "All of these years we have feared a monster and, more than likely, rumors have been exaggerated.

He is probably a tiny old man with no teeth."

Edward, standing beside him, snorted. "Better still, what if he is really a woman?" he said. "Wouldn't that be a tale to tell? The great Ajax de Velt is female!"

Max grinned and opened his mouth to reply but de Lohr shushed his knights. "He is not a woman and he is not a tiny old man," he said, his sky-blue eyes fixed on the road. "He is as big as a mountain and as dark as the Devil, see for yourself."

Edward and Max rushed to the portcullis, pressing their faces against the heavy iron to see what de Lohr was seeing. The road stretched out before them, fairly flat, before curving to the right to circumvent the perimeter of the village. There was also a descent in elevation from the castle so that the fortress had an expanded view over the top of the village and to the countryside beyond to the north. As they watched, a figure could be seen galloping in from the north, following the curve of the road as he moved around the berg, and then heading towards them up the incline leading to the castle.

All eyes were fixed on the figure who was riding a very large war horse bareback. The man astride the horse was big, bigger still as he approached, with tendrils of his long hair blowing in the wind as the moved along at a clipped pace. The sun was up now, shining brightly as it headed towards its zenith, so it was easy to see the details of the rider as he approached. The closer he came, the more they realized that he was indeed an enormous man. Enormous and larger than life, as Ajax de Velt should be.

Christopher was well aware of the man's size and of the fact that he was beholding Ajax de Velt. He examined the man as he drew closer still before calling to one of the sentries at the gate.

"Open the portcullis!" he boomed.

Edward and Max looked at him as if he had lost his mind. "What are you doing?" Edward asked, clearly apprehensive.

Christopher cast his men a long look. "Stop acting like a bunch of frightened women," he scolded. "I am going out to meet the man and you will remain here. Whatever he has to say is between him and me, and I do not need a bunch of nervous women cowering behind me. He is a lone man on a lone horse with no weaponry. There is nothing he can do against me."

Edward didn't take kindly to be called a nervous woman, truthful though it might be. "Remember that dagger he has up his arse," he muttered. "If he cuts your throat with it, don't say that I did not warn you."

The portcullis was nearly a third of the way up and Christopher called a halt, moving to duck underneath it. But before he did, he looked at Edward. "If he pulls a dagger out of his arse, then tell the archers to aim for his heart," he said. "If the man makes any aggressive move towards me, tell them to shoot him down. Is that clear?"

Edward liked that command a great deal. It brought him comfort. "Aye, my lord."

Christopher ducked underneath the portcullis and ordered it lowered as he took a few steps forward, away from the portcullis as de Velt came near. Before the man could come too close, however, Christopher held up his hands to stop him. The rider obeyed, coming to an unsteady halt several feet away. Now, the moment of truth was upon them and it was a great and terrible silence that followed. The Dark Lord had arrived.

Christopher eyed the man atop the big bay stallion. He was utterly enormous, with long dark hair tied behind his head, enormous hands, and a muscular body. He was older now, with streaks of gray in his dark hair, and he was perhaps ten or twelve years older than Christopher. He was rather handsome and well formed, and he certainly didn't look like the monster de Velt had been accused of being, but as Christopher took another step or two in the man's direction, he could see that the man had two distinctly colored eyes. Christopher had seen horses with eyes like that but never a man. De Velt's left eye was brown and his right eye was a bright green. Now, some of the fear and lore of Ajax de Velt was starting to take on a bit of credibility. He did indeed look terrifying.

"Are you Ajax de Velt?" Christopher asked steadily.

Jax nodded his head. "I am," he said. "Are you de Lohr?"

Christopher nodded. "I am Christopher de Lohr," he said. "Your messenger said that you wished to speak with me. I am granting you that privilege but you will do it from a distance. Dismount your horse and remain beside it."

Jax didn't hesitate. He threw his leg over the horse and hit the ground. Then he just stood there as Christopher studied him, perhaps satisfying a deep curiosity, perhaps simply wondering what the man wanted. It was a natural inclination since Jax de Velt, when he hadn't been tearing up the land, kept to himself. He'd been quiet for many years. After a moment of scrutiny, Christopher spoke.

"Now," he said, putting his hands on his hips. "What did you wish to speak with me about?"

He wasn't being overly friendly but he wasn't being rude, either. It was better than Jax had hoped for.

"First, I would like to thank you for being gracious enough to see me," he said. "I did not think you would."

Christopher cocked an eyebrow. "I was afraid of what you would do if I did not," he said truthfully. "History tells us that it is not prudent to anger Jax de Velt."

Jax gave him a half-smile, ironic. "I suppose we should speak on the days of the past and get them out of the way before we continue with pleasantries," he said. "I have not engaged in conquest of any kind in twenty-five years, not since I met my wife. We have six children and I live a very quiet life in Northumberland as the vassal of the Earl of Northumberland. My life since those days of long ago has been peaceful. It is in peace that I come to Lioncross to seek your counsel."

Christopher listened to the man's word with interest. He certainly sounded sincere. In fact, he seemed rather docile, calm, and reasonable, not at all like the Jax de Velt of legend. It was rather perplexing and he struggled not to let that confusion show but he simply couldn't help himself.

"I *am* speaking with the Ajax de Velt that tore through the Marches twenty-five years ago and confiscated six castles, am I not?" he asked. He felt as if he had to. "You are the one who killed men, women, and children by impaling them on poles and then posting the bodies for all to see, are you not? It *is* The Dark Lord I am speaking to?"

Jax nodded patiently. "It is I," he said. "I am sorry to disappoint you. Mayhap you were expecting lightning bolts to shoot out of my eyes and fire to belch forth out of my mouth?"

Christopher nodded honestly. "I was expecting to see horns and cloven feet at the very least."

"I have yet to remove my boots so you may yet be satisfied."

It was spoken with humor, an unexpected element added to the conversation. Christopher's lips twitched with a smile.

"Don't do that," he said. "Leave some air of mystery about you. I have never met a legend before."

"Nor have I until now."

It was a compliment. Christopher had to admit that he was feeling more at ease with de Velt, a man who seemed to understand the terror he caused and was not beyond accepting it and even making fun of it, as dark as that period in time was. But there was still an air of uncertainty to the conversation and Christopher addressed it.

"You are not here to burn my town and lay siege to my castle, are you?" he asked. "This counsel request is not a ruse, is it?"

Jax shook his head firmly. "I swear that it is not," he said. "I come with entirely peaceful intentions, contrary to what you would believe of me. I have come to you because... because I need help."

Christopher's eyebrows rose. "The great Ajax de Velt needs help?" he repeated. "I am astonished. Since when do you need help from anyone?"

Jax nodded as if accepting what Christopher was saying. "It is a rare occasion but in this case, it is true," he said. His eyes took on a grim glimmer. "There is a mercenary along the Marches who has abducted my daughter. He has asked me to come to him if I wish to keep her in good health. I have come to see if you have heard anything about this mercenary and, if so, find out what you have heard. I know nothing about the man other than he has my child. I want her back."

So it was as Christopher had suspected. The man was here as a result of de Llion's rampage. But, truly, this wasn't a path he had ever considered, de Velt coming to him to discuss the situation. They had all believed Jax would go straight after the mercenary. But in reflection, it made sense because Christopher was one of the most powerful marcher lords and would inevitably know what happened along that stretch of border. The Jax de Velt he'd heard tale of was an inhuman beast bent on destruction. The man before him did not fit that mold.

Christopher's eyes studied Jax as he took a few steps closer, to within a few feet of him. Standing before him was the most feared warlord England had ever seen. De Velt's brutalities were legendary. But all Christopher could see at the moment was a father who wanted to save his daughter. Perhaps it was foolish of him to see that and only that, but having two young daughters of his own, Christopher could understand a father's anguish, even a father as fearsome as Ajax de Velt.

"We heard about Alberbury," he finally said, his voice quiet. "We heard that a mercenary took your daughter."

Jax's features filled with hope. "Then you know about this?" he asked. "Will you please tell me what you know?"

Christopher nodded. "I will," he said. "Inside, over a pitcher of wine and some food. I am famished."

He motioned to de Velt to follow, who hesitantly complied. Christopher called to the sentries to lift the portcullis and slowly, the big iron fangs began to lift. Like the great parting of the Red Sea, Christopher moved through the gatehouse with Jax next to him, and men fell away as if they'd been pushed. No one had been this close to de Velt and had lived to tell about it. Men backed off as if Lucifer himself had made an appearance.

The two men made it to the steps leading into the keep as most of the population of Lioncross looked on. It was the great benevolent earl who had guided the course of a kingdom and the warlord who had struck more fear into the hearts of men than anyone had ever done. It was a historic moment, not lost on those who witnessed it.

When they finally disappeared into the dark recesses of the keep, there were those who still couldn't believe what they had witnessed. It was a moment in time that would live in their minds forever.

☙

JAX WASN'T SURPRISED that de Lohr's men were staring at him with a mixture of apprehension and hostility. It was odd, truly, for a man who never really traveled much out of his home or comfort zone to be in a strange castle and surrounded by strange men. Jax didn't often get a chance to talk to men he didn't know and he was mildly nervous because of it. More than that, he was completely without his weapons and vulnerable. That, more than anything, made him nervous. It was a situation he had never found himself in. He was completely at de Lohr's mercy.

But de Lohr had been a gracious host so far. He had taken de Velt into his home, into his keep, and made him comfortable in the great hall. It was a long room with a minstrel gallery above and living quarters on the second and third floors. There was a massive fireplace and fresh rushes strewn about, but no dogs which Jax found strange. He sat at the long, scrubbed feasting table that filled up the center of Lioncross' great hall, his back to the hearth because it made him doubly nervous to have his back against anything else. He figured it would be more difficult for a man to sneak up behind him if he saw the shadows thrown from the firelight behind. Therefore, he sat tensely as de Lohr and a few of his men settled in across from him.

A handsome knight with ruddy skin and golden eyes gazed at him steadily from his position at de Lohr's right hand, while on the other side of de Lohr sat a knight who could have very well been Jax's brother with shoulder-length dark curls and brown eyes. He had the look of a barbarian about him. There were a few soldiers in the hall but they lingered near the entry. Jax made sure to keep track of everyone in the room, and everyone coming and going from the room including the servants. The longer he sat there, the more uncomfortable he grew.

De Lohr must have sensed that. He had servants bring in wine, bread, cheese, and fruit, and all of it was placed on the table between them. He indicated for de Velt to serve himself first, but Jax only took a small measure of wine. He wasn't hungry. He wanted to know what de Lohr knew about Allaston and was becoming increasingly impatient with the delay.

"So," Christopher began as he poured himself some wine. "Allow me to introduce to you two of my close friends and knights. This is Edward de Wolfe to my right and Max Cornwallis to my left. They have served me for many years, including in The Levant. You did not go to The Levant, did you?"

Jax shook his head. "Nay," he replied. "My fealty at the time did not include the King of England."

Christopher had an amused twinkle in his eye. "And now?"

"It does," he said, the paused before continuing. "But I do not much like him."

"Neither do I."

Jax cracked a faint smile. "As I recall, you were Richard's champion at one time," he said. "Since John hated his brother, how does the king treat you?"

Christopher grinned, scratching casually at his head. "Very carefully," he said. "Much as I do not wish to anger you, he does not wish to anger me. We have history, John and I. He tries to stay clear of me as much as he can."

Jax took a drink of his wine, a fine red varietal. He smacked his lips. "He has asked de Vesci to maintain the borders against Scotland that parallel Northumberland," he said. "My only brush with combat in recent years is where it pertains to the Scots borders."

"And how are the Scots these days?"

"Quiet," Jax replied. "William has some internal struggles, but he still holds his kingdom. Any action we see from the Scots are raids, not organized onslaughts."

That was interesting news for Christopher, sitting along the Welsh Marches as he did. Often, Scotland seemed like a world away. Besides, he had his own troubles in Wales, and ones that de Velt was interested in. He set his cup down.

"That is good to know," he said. "Trouble along one border is quite enough. That being said, let us address the reason for your visit. I will tell you what I know – we received word from Robert de Boulers, Earl of Shropshire, that there was a mighty army sweeping through his lands, conquering or destroying everything in their path. They laid siege to Clun Castle and Knighton, badly damaging the castles and stripping them of nearly everything of value before moving to the Marches and taking Cloryn Castle. Then, they moved north where they raided Dolforwyn Castle, moved north into Shropshire, and burned Alberbury Priory to the ground. That is where your daughter was, am I correct?"

Jax was listening intently. "Aye," he nodded, sounding disheartened. "Allaston wanted to join the cloister at a young age. She was always a very pious girl but she had an unfortunate stubborn and brash streak in her. Her mother and I told her that the nuns would not accept such behavior, but she insisted that she wanted to serve God, so when she turned nineteen years of age, we permitted her to commit herself to Alberbury. I am a patron, you see. I donate three hundred crowns a year to Alberbury, which is her dowry, so they were more than willing to take her."

Christopher understood something about stubborn women, considering he had married one. "How did you find out about the abduction?" he asked. "We were told the mercenary left one solitary nun alive to deliver the message to you."

Jax shook his head. "I know nothing about an old nun," he said. "I received a missive declaring terms from who, I assume, is the mercenary himself. A mass of my daughter's hair was enclosed with it. A week prior to that, however, I received a severed head that I determined to belong to my garrison commander at Ithon Castle. Although there was no written message, it was my first hint that something was amiss at my properties."

Christopher pondered that bit of information. "I see," he muttered. "Then Ithon is compromised also?"

"I would assume so."

Christopher fell silent for a moment, deliberating the conquest of Ithon. He hadn't heard that. But soon his attention moved from Ithon's conquest to the part about the hair. As a father himself, he could only imagine how de Velt felt receiving his daughter's hair along with the threatening note.

"De Boulers found out about the mercenary's activities because of the old nun," he said. "Somehow, someway, the commander of this mercenary army discovered your daughter was at Alberbury. The man bloody well destroyed the place to get to her."

Jax was trying not to appear sickened by the thought. "He wanted her very badly," he muttered. "He is using her to get to me. He knows I will not stay away if she is in danger and that is evidently what he wants – a confrontation with me."

Christopher glanced at Edward to see if he could read the man's expression. Edward seemed very intent on studying de Velt, analyzing the man. Edward was very good at that sort of thing. When he noticed that Christopher was looking at him, he cleared his throat softly and spoke.

"We were told that the mercenary army is from Ireland," he said. "They are not Welsh, and they are certainly not English, but whatever they are doing emulates the pattern you set twenty-five years ago when you moved over the Marches. Do you see the pattern with this, my lord?"

Jax looked at the older knight. "I do," he said. "If what you have said is accurate, everything on that list was a location I engaged except for Alberbury."

"Which means he will more than likely move on your other holdings very soon," Christopher said. "I was not here those years ago when you claimed those castles. Is he moving in the order you moved in?"

Jax nodded. "Indeed he is," he said. "If his pattern holds true, he will move on Comen next."

"Do your men still man those castles?"

"They do."

"Then mayhap you should tell them to vacate," Christopher said. "They may come here if they wish. I will shelter them until you can figure out what you need to do."

Jax looked at him with a good deal of astonishment. "You would *do* this?" he asked, trying to keep the incredulity out of his tone. Then, he shook his head as if he could not believe what he was hearing. "*Why* would you do this?"

Christopher kept an even expression. "You came to me for help," he said. "I am offering it. Your men are in the path of destruction. Will you leave them to die or will you move them out?"

Jax just stared at him. It was clear that he was having difficulty accepting that de Lohr was being so generous with him. After a moment, he began to shake his head in disbelief. "You know who I am," he said, showing more force in his personality than he had since his arrival. "You know very well what my name means. You know what I did along the Marches those years ago. If I wanted your castle, de Lohr, it would not have mattered who you were or how well respected you were. I would have taken it and I would have put you on a stake, you above all else because of your title and name, and I would have planted that stake right outside of the walls of this castle for all to see. I would have done it and I would not have cared about anything other than my victory. You understand that, do you not?"

Christopher could see a hint of the killer in the man as he spoke, but he responded calmly. "I understand," he said. "But I also understand that you haven't done that kind of thing in over twenty years. You said you stopped when you met your wife. I, too, was something of a focused man before I met my wife. I earned a reputation no one has surpassed and that was all I cared about. The men I killed were on the sands of The Levant, Muslims fighting for the land they were born in, but I didn't care. I cut their heads off and mounted them on spikes. I wasn't fighting for England at that point. I was fighting for me because I wanted the glory and I got it. But the man that I was long ago no longer exists, just as I believe the man you were long ago no longer exists. Am I wrong in this assumption?"

Jax shook his head slowly, his gaze riveted to Christopher's. "Nay," he said. "When I met my wife, all things changed."

"What a coincidence. The same thing happened to me."

The statement had a humorous ring to it and Jax fought off a smile. "The woman I married is stronger than I am," he said. "I suspect the same thing can be said for your wife."

Christopher nodded. "She is strong beyond comprehension," he replied. "But that brings me to the point – you are no longer the killer you used to be. I understand that. But I also understand that this mercenary has challenged the man who once existed. If you confront him now, as you are, then you will be confronting him as an emotional father and that will be your downfall. Do you want my advice in this matter? I hope you do because I am going to tell you whether or not you want to hear it. This mercenary is as you were twenty-five years ago, a soulless beast. When you confront him, you are going to have to draw on that monster that has long been dormant inside of you. He is still there. I caught a glimpse of him only a moment ago. You will have to become the monster again if you want to save your daughter. The mercenary commander is calling forth Lucifer and Lucifer must appear."

Jax listened to him seriously. Everything he said made perfect sense. He paused, sighed heavily and moved to pour himself more wine. He was coming to need it.

"May I tell you the truth?" he asked softly.

Christopher nodded. "Please."

Jax eyed him as he set the pitcher down. "My wife sent me here to see you," he said. "She is afraid that if I confront this mercenary, that it will only agitate him. She knows the man is out for my blood and she is terrified that she will lose both her husband and her daughter in this crisis. You are a man with a great reputation for wisdom and fairness. She wants me to ask you if you will be an intermediary between me and the mercenary. She hopes that by dealing with you, the man who holds my daughter will be less confrontational. He may even be willing to negotiate. I realize I do not know you, de Lohr. We are not friends or allies, and what I ask of you is terribly bold. But I ask on behalf of my wife who is terrified for my life and for the life of our daughter. I do not wish to pull you into a blood feud, but I pray that you will consider it. *That* is the help I was coming to ask from you. I swear to you that if you assist me with this, I shall ever be in your debt. All you need do is call and I will ride for you. My sword will be yours. Mayhap it is not much, but it is all I have to offer – myself."

Christopher didn't say anything for a moment. He just sat and looked at him and it was clear that there were many thoughts running through his head. Many, indeed. After a few moments of deliberation, he turned to Edward.

"Send Dustin to me," he said softly.

Eyeing de Velt, Edward stood up from the table and left the hall, taking the stairs just inside the entry to the living quarters above. Jax watched the man go and when he disappeared from view, he couldn't help but look to Christopher curiously. Christopher smiled weakly and picked up the pitcher of wine.

"A moment, please," he said, pouring more into Jax's cup as he shifted the subject. "I purchased this wine in London last fall. It comes from a region in France where the monks tend these tiny dark grapes. My wife is quite fond of it but I warn you, it will get you drunk quite fast if you do not pace yourself. That has happened to me a few times."

Jax took his cup and drank deeply. "It is very good," he said. "Sweet. My wife would like it as well, as she tends to like sweet wines. Anything else puts her to sleep."

Christopher set the pitcher down and collected his own cup. "Tell me of your wife," he said. "What is her name?"

"Kellington," Jax replied. "Lady Kellington Coleby de Velt."

"And how did your marriage come about? Were your families allies?"

Jax tried not to look too embarrassed. "Nay," he grunted, appearing somewhat uncomfortable. "One of those castles I confiscated… she was a captive."

Christopher was amused. "I suppose that is one way to meet women," he said. "Did you force her to marry you?"

Jax struggled not to grin. "We fell in love," he said. "After I had killed all of her friends, of course. It would be fair to say that our beginnings were quite rough, but in spite of everything, we managed to become fond of each other. I have loved the woman madly for twenty-five years."

Christopher grinned. "You sincerely do not appear to me like the killer of legend," he said. "You seem quite normal, in fact, because only a man with feeling and conscience would admit to loving a woman. I still can hardly believe you are Ajax de Velt, the Beast Who Destroyed the Marches."

Jax let his smile break free, grinning at Christopher over the top of his wine cup. "I will tell you a secret."

"What?"

"I really would not have gone after Lioncross Abbey those years ago. There are some men I will attack and some I will not. I am not entirely sure I would be victorious over you, so it is better not to try."

Christopher started to laugh. "I was not at Lioncross twenty-five years ago," he said. "My wife's father was the lord at that time and, I hate to say, you probably could have bested him. But I am glad you did not."

Jax's eyebrows lifted. "Do you mean to tell me that I missed a grand opportunity?"

They were snorting when Edward appeared in the hall again, followed by a woman clad in a fine linen surcoat. Jax turned to look at her. She was petite, with a glorious curvy figure and a mass of blond hair that trailed all the way to her knees. As she drew closer, Jax could see that she was truly an exquisite woman, exceptionally beautiful. The woman approached the table, looking at Jax rather curiously. Christopher held out a hand to her.

"My lady, thank you for coming," he said, kissing her hand before turning to Jax. "My lord, this is my wife, the Lady Dustin Barringdon de Lohr. Dustin, this is Sir Ajax de Velt. He is our guest."

Dustin's curious expression faded somewhat. Like everyone else on the Marches, or in England for that matter, she recognized the name. She didn't quite remember what she knew of him, but she had definitely heard the name. Something told her there wasn't a good association with it, but those years back when Jax had been tearing up the Marches, she had been far too young to remember.

"Welcome to Lioncross, my lord," she said. Then, she turned to her husband. "Did you need to speak with me?"

Christopher continued to hold her hand, not putting it against his cheek. "Indeed," he said, eyeing Jax. "It would seem that de Velt has a problem. A terrible man has abducted his daughter and he has asked me to mediate. What do you think of that?"

Dustin was immediately swamped with sympathy and outrage. It was written all over her face. She looked at Jax.

"I am so terribly sorry to hear that," she said sincerely. "How old is your daughter?"

Something about the woman reminded him of Kellington, although he couldn't put his finger on it. There was something in her eyes, a flame of strength that burned within the depths. Allaston had that flame, too.

"She has seen nineteen years, my lady," he replied. "She was a novice nun at Alberbury Priory."

Distress creased Dustin's features. "She is so young," she said sadly.

"Who is this man who has abducted her?"

"A mercenary," Christopher answered softly. "He is using the girl to lure Jax to him. He has a vendetta against the man, so de Velt has asked me to intervene. He wants his daughter back and wishes to keep his life in the process."

"Of course he does," Dustin said vehemently. "What does he want you to do?"

"Talk to the mercenary, I believe," he said, looking at Jax. "Is that what you meant?"

Jax nodded. "I was hoping you would."

"Of course he will," Dustin said before Christopher could reply. "If he will not, I will go in his stead. We have two young daughters, my lord. I can only imagine my agony if one of my daughters was in danger. Turn me loose on the man and I guarantee you shall have your daughter back."

There was such fire in the woman. Jax was rather taken aback at her passion, looking to de Lohr to see if the woman was serious. From the look on de Lohr's face, it was evident that she was. Christopher kissed his wife's hand again before gently pushing her back in the direction of the stairs that led to the living rooms above.

"Thank you, sweetheart," he said with mock patience because he was trying to get rid of her. "Before I answered de Velt, I wanted to see what you thought of it. Thank you for your input."

Dustin wouldn't leave so readily. She was still looking at de Velt. "My husband will make sure he pays for the crime of abducting your daughter," she said. "Have no fear that he will do what he can."

"Thank you, my lady," Christopher said, more loudly so she would get the hint and leave the room. He turned to smile at her to make sure she left before he continued the conversation. "Your advice is priceless. We thank you very much."

Dustin was still fired up over the abduction of the young girl, muttering threats to the abductor as she left the hall. Both Christopher and Jax listened to her as she quit the room and headed up the steps to the upper floors. When she was out of earshot, Christopher turned to Jax.

"She tends to get excited over things," he said, "but I must have her approval before I do anything and I had to make it seem as if it were her decision. Otherwise, she would give me extreme grief for involving myself in someone else's battle."

Jax laughed softly. He couldn't help it. "Your wife and my wife are cut out of the same cloth," he said. "I understand completely."

Christopher grinned but soon sobered as he thought on the task that lay before him. After a moment, he spoke.

"There is something more you should know about this mercenary," he said. "I assume he gave you a name when he sent his missive to you about your daughter?"

Jax nodded. "Bretton de Llion."

Christopher drew in a long, thoughtful breath. "I heard that name also," he said, "and it was familiar to me, so I contacted a vassal whom I believed to be related to the name. It turns out that the name Bretton de Llion was the name of my vassal's cousin, a cousin who lived at Four Crosses Castle when you attacked it. De Llion was the name of the garrison commander and Bretton was his son. We thought that somehow the boy survived the siege, which makes sense if this mercenary who calls himself Bretton de Llion is out for revenge against you. It would make him the son of a man you killed."

Jax appeared rather surprised by the revelation. He thought back to those dark and bloody days, thinking of Four Crosses Castle, which was the last castle he confiscated along the Marches. He had put one of his best generals in charge of it, Apollo l'Ancresse. The man still lived there with his wife and children and grandchildren. Unlike his other general, Orion, who no longer lived at Cloryn, Apollo still inhabited the castle he was assigned after the conquest. But along with that information, Jax also remembered something else.

"Four Crosses," he muttered. "I recall the place very well. A big castle with no moat and a big gatehouse. You say that this mercenary is a survivor of that siege?"

Christopher nodded. "That is the suspicion."

Jax thought hard on that possibility. "Four Crosses was different from the other castles I confiscated," he said. "It was the last one so mayhap I was feeling a bit more lenient because we did not kill everyone. We took some men and forced them into servitude."

Christopher listened with interest. "Do you have any of these men left in your service?"

Jax shook his head. "Nay," he said. "Those men have either died or have moved on. One man, a knight from Four Crosses, actually serves de Vesci. He is an older man and somewhat diminished mentally from a blow he received to the head during the siege of Four Crosses, but he is as strong as an ox. In fact, de Vesci keeps him as a bodyguard of sorts. The man can barely speak a full sentence but he can still kill."

"What is the knight's name?"

"John Morgan."

Christopher stared at him a moment. Then, his eyebrows lifted. "Morgan de Llion was the name of the commander at Four Crosses," he said, rather shocked at the potential implications. "Is it possible that de Llion's father lived?"

Jax was rather surprised at the implications, too. "I suppose it is," he said. "When we found the knight, he was incoherent. He gave his name as Morgan and we thought it was his surname."

"Is it possible it was his first name?"

Jax shrugged. "It is possible, but you know as well as I do that Morgan is a very common surname in Wales."

Christopher was thinking many different things at that moment, not the least of which was utter neutralization of the mercenary and the return of Jax's daughter. He was a man who thought quickly on his feet because his life often depended on it. The more he pondered the thought, the more enthusiastic about it he became.

"Agreed," he said. "But on the possibility that this could be de Llion's father, mayhap you should summon him from Northumberland. When I go to mediate with the mercenary, I will bring this knight with me. Even if it is not the man's long-lost father, mayhap he will recognize him and it will unbalance him enough for me to gain the upper hand. I am not beyond playing dirty tricks when the life of a young girl is at stake."

Jax whole-heartedly agreed. "I will send word to Northumberland today," he said. "But it will take time for Morgan to arrive. I am not sure I want to wait that long to begin negotiations for my child."

Christopher shook his head. "You will not have to," he said. "I have the luxury of thinking more clearly about the situation right now than you do, and I believe that we should send this mercenary a missive telling him that you have asked me to assist with the negotiations and we want to know what his terms are in exchange for your daughter. I might even tell him that we have an old knight from Four Crosses who survived the siege but nothing more than that. Let his imagination run wild. That should garner an immediate and, I would think, eager response."

Jax felt much better with Christopher taking the lead on the negotiations. It was what he had hoped for. This man was much better at communicating than he was and he could see why – he was gracious, well-spoken, strong, and highly intelligent. Aye, there was much to respect there. Finally, he felt as if he were one step closer to getting Allaston back and he was deeply grateful.

"Then I shall trust your judgment," he said. "And… thank you. I am not accustomed to showing gratitude to anyone, but please know that you have my most heartfelt thanks."

Christopher poured them both more wine, the last of the pitcher, and held up his cup. "I was content with having you swear your sword to me," he said. "Imagine how feared I will be when all know I have The Dark Lord in my arsenal."

Jax grinned, holding up his cup to the man. "Beware," he said. "It may bring you less awe than you think. There are those who still hate me a great deal."

Christopher shrugged, sipping at his wine. The sweet, potent alcohol had already gone to his head a little. "What do we care?" he said. "I will simply have you go out and kill them. Then no one will hate you because they will all be dead."

Jax laughed softly. "The last man I killed was fifteen years ago during a border raid against the Scots," he said. "I fear that I may be out of practice."

Christopher looked at him, suddenly appearing very sober. "If negotiations with this mercenary fail, then we will have no alternative but to take the field," he said grimly. "We will need your sword, out of practice or not."

Jax's gaze held the man steady. "Then you intend to go into battle with me?"

"You have not formally asked me to."

"I would not dare to hope. But I would be deeply honored if you would."

Christopher smiled. "Then that makes us allies, you and me."

Jax shook his head with awe. "I never thought I would see the day when Christopher de Lohr, the most respected knight in England, would ally himself with me."

Christopher's grin broadened as he brought his cup up again and tipped it against Jax's in a show of solidarity, of unity, and of a new alliance.

"It is better to be the right hand of Lucifer," he said softly, "than in his path."

Jax lifted an eyebrow. "So you have agreed to help me simply so I will not be insulted and turn against you?"

Christopher was ambivalent. "Think what you will."

Jax had to laugh at him. After that, the conversation moved on to other subjects and more food was brought out. Jax actually shared a conversation with Edward, who was able to overcome his fear of the man and behave intelligently. Lady de Lohr even returned with her children in tow, four of them, two young girls who were around five and six years of age, and two toddler boys. The younger girl, Brielle, had absolutely no fear of Jax and even came to sit next to him, very curious about the strange man in her father's hall. Jax lost himself in conversation with a five year old who reminded him very much of Allaston at that age. It made him miss her all the more.

Chatting with de Lohr and his family and his knights, Jax felt more at home and more comfortable with these strangers than he had with almost anyone, ever. He had never understood alliances or relationships outside of his own family, but at the moment, he was coming to. He understood that these people had overlooked his reputation, the darkness he perpetuated, and were willing to see the man beneath. They were willing to help the fearful father. Eventually, Jax sent word to his army that all was well, and Cole and Julian came forward to join their father in Lioncross' massive hall.

Before the day was finished, Christopher set out a missive to Cloryn Castle, the rumored seat of the mercenary. It contained all of the terms he had discussed with Jax earlier in the day with instructions to the messenger to leave it at Cloryn's gate and ride like hell home. They didn't want the mercenary getting his hands on one of Christopher's men.

All that was left now to do was to wait.

CHAPTER THIRTEEN

Cloryn Castle

ALLASTON WAS ON her hands and knees in front of Bretton, her buttocks in the air. It was such a perfect target and he knew it, but at this moment, he was so furious at her for pushing him in front of his men that he could hardly see straight.

He was a killer, and he was her captor, and he was more than capable of taking her life in a most heinous manner. Everyone looking at him was expecting him to do it, waiting for the moment when he would ram the sharp end of the pole into her intestines, punishing her for her insolence and disobedience once and for all. Aye, he knew what his men were expecting and had anyone else been the target, he would have complied without hesitation. But it wasn't just anyone else. It was Allaston.

He was angry with her. Positively furious. So much so that when she turned her round little buttocks into the air, he came up behind her with the pole and, just to scare her, rammed it underneath her so that it slid up between her knees and hands, underneath her body. Startled, she barely had time to shriek before he was grabbing her around the waist and spanking her within an inch of her life.

At least five good whacks, right on the backside, and Allaston howled in pain. Then, Bretton grabbed her by the long, dark braid of hair and pulled her through the forest of bodies until they reached his horse. She was weeping and gasping with pain, and fright, as he picked her up and tossed her, belly down, across his saddle. Mounting up behind her, he spurred his charger towards the group that was preparing to accompany him to Newtown. He positively bellowed at them.

"Return to Cloryn," he yelled. "I am going to teach this wench a lesson once and for all. Go back and wait for me!"

He was so mad that Grayton and Teague didn't question him in the least. They immediately directed the escort party back to the great gates of Cloryn while Bretton thundered off down the road with Allaston slung across his saddle. As the escort party moved back into the bailey, the two commanders lingered at the gatehouse, watching Bretton race down the road with the prisoner, suspecting he was going to do to the woman what he should have done at the beginning. He was either going to murder her and bury the body, or he was going to make her wish she was dead. Either thought pleased them greatly.

But Bretton wasn't going to kill her. He had to publicly beat her so he wouldn't lose the respect of his men, and even then, he was sure they were suspicious of his intentions towards her. He knew that Grayton's argument about the fact that she was Jax de Velt's daughter, their greatest asset and a prisoner to boot, would have some effect on his men. Grayton was very loyal to him but he also had strong opinions. Bretton was fairly certain Grayton wouldn't turn his men against him, but he would certainly turn them against Allaston.

So he had to remove her, to get her away from the situation, and as he pounded down the road from Cloryn, he came to a crossroads within a quarter of a mile and began to head south. Then, and only then, did he slow the animal's pace because he was certain the rough ride was not at all comfortable on Allaston as she lay on her belly in front of him. To her credit, however, she hadn't muttered a sound.

The horse slowed to a walk. Bretton shifted his reins to the other hand and promptly smacked her on the butt again, hard enough so that she grunted. He eyed her dark head.

"Are you conscious?" he asked.

Allaston nodded her head. "Aye."

She sounded ill. Grasping the back of her surcoat, he slid her off of the horse and onto the ground. Allaston hit feet first but she lost her balance and fell back onto her sore bottom, wincing as she did so. Bretton pulled the horse to a stop and looked down at her.

"Well?" he said, sounding displeased. "What do you have to say for your behavior back there?"

Allaston was slowly getting up, brushing off her bottom as she moved rather unsteadily. "What would you have me say?" she asked, refusing to look at him. "You killed that woman and her family. It was…."

He cut her off. "Allow me to clarify the situation," he said. "I did not kill her and her husband. My men did. As for the boy, I am not sure who did that, but everything that was done was completed at my direction."

She looked at him, then. "But why?" she wanted to know, pain in her voice. "Why would you do such a thing? You allowed that lady to be… abused horrifically and then killed. She committed no crime against you!"

Bretton would not be reprimanded and he struggled to hold his temper in check. "Such is the nature of conquest, lady," he told her. "Your father did the same thing. He killed everything that moved because anything left alive, no matter how seemingly innocuous at the time, can at some day or some time be a threat. I am a perfect example of that. I escaped to live as Jax de Velt destroyed my home. Now, I have come back to kill him. And I shall."

Allaston wasn't going to be sucked into another argument against kill her father. They'd had that conversation too many times. "You had the chance to hurt him very badly back there," she said. "You should have put me on a pole."

"And, yet, I did not," he said. "You are more valuable to me alive than dead at the moment, but that may change."

"So you have said."

"You do not believe me?"

Allaston wasn't in any mood to be toyed with. "I believe you like to play games with me," she said bitterly. "You have moments when you are quite rational and quite human, and I feel comfort with you, and then you have times like this when you are mad with vengeance and all you do is threaten. Do you know what I think? I do not think even you know what it is you want out of life. You want to kill my father, that is true, but I do not think you know what you want to do after that is accomplished or even what you want to do with me. Sometimes you treat me like a prisoner, other times like a companion. You are a man in great turmoil, de Llion, and you have sucked me into the turmoil with you."

As always, she was quite astute. His first reaction was to rage at her but he found that he couldn't because she was right. Everything she said was correct. Puzzled, and feeling reprimanded, he did what he often did when faced with such things – he withdrew. He didn't want to talk about it anymore because he didn't want her to get the better of him. This novice nun, this prisoner, and this beautiful woman he couldn't seem to get out of his mind, had increasing control over him.

When Bretton fell silent and turned away from her, Allaston studied the man closely. He tended to brood when he didn't have an answer to what she was saying. She'd seen it before. *Be kind to him.* She'd tried that before but it hadn't worked. She's tried to fight him, too, and that hadn't worked, either. However, now they knew each other better and she was coming to understand him a bit more. Deep down, his vengeance was a result of a horrible sadness, something inadvertently perpetrated against him by Jax de Velt.

Just like everyone, Bretton wanted to be satisfied in life. He was not satisfied now and he believed that killing Jax would lead him to gratification. Allaston thought a moment on how she could help him find contentment and perhaps save her father at the same time. After the man had refused to put her on a pole, even after she'd provoked him, she had a feeling he might be more apt to listen to her persuasion.

"De Llion," she said softly, moving in his direction. "*Bretton.* May I call you Bretton?"

He looked at her, seeing that she was coming towards him. "You will whether or not I want you to," he said, rolling his eyes with exasperation. "You never do anything I want you to do."

She smiled agreeably. "Bretton," she began quietly. "When my father set out to conquer Four Crosses those years ago, it was not with the express intent to hurt you or ruin your life. You were simply collateral damage. Surely you understand that."

"I do."

She thought carefully on what she would say next. "I do not believe that we are all born predisposed to what we will become," she said. "In other words, you were not born to be a killer. I am sure you were born a very sweet little boy who loved his parents very much. You probably had pets and toys like all children do. What you have become since that time… you chose to become a killer and to seek vengeance against my father, who inadvertently ruined your life. Killing him will not bring your parents back and it will not suddenly make you a happy and content man. On the contrary, I believe it will leave you more empty and angry than before. You will not find the true happiness you seek in another man's murder. Therefore, I want to make you a proposal."

He was trying not to look interested. In fact, he waved her off. "There is nothing that you can propose to me that will satisfy me."

"Will you at least hear me?"

He rolled his eyes again. "I am sure I have little choice but I will tell you again that it will do no good."

Allaston was going to give it her best try. She had always been persuasive. She hoped her luck would continue to hold.

"I decided when I was twelve years old that I wanted to become a nun," she said. "I have always wanted to serve Our Holy Father as a Bride of Christ, but I am not sure anymore if that is something that will make me happy. Let me explain… my happiness lies within my family.

It took me a long time to realize that and even as I served at Alberbury, it was not happy. I missed my family, my parents and siblings, because I believe the love of a family is something God has given to us to enjoy and to appreciate. Even before you came and abducted me, I was coming to think that I had been misplaced at Alberbury. I was not particularly happy for the reasons I just outlined. I wanted to go home and spend time with my family, and mayhap someday have a family of my own and a home of my own. Isn't that something you would like to have as well? A wife who is loyal and children who love you?"

Bretton was looking at her again, the bright blue eyes guarded. "I would like heirs but only to carry on my name," he said. "A wife and children will simply be something else that belongs to me – possessions."

It was a cold way to view it and she wasn't entirely sure she believed him. There was something about the man that suggested he wasn't completely emotionless as he wanted others to believe. He was simply afraid of being hurt again, of losing someone he loved. In many ways, Bretton was still that little boy who had been so devastated by the loss of his parents and sister. She went forward with her proposal.

"I do not want to see my father killed, especially when it will not bring you the relief or happiness you seek," she said. "I understand the love of a family, Bretton. I understand how it can fill you like nothing else and my father, after those years of warfare, understands it, too. The love of my mother was strong enough to make him stop his dreams of conquest. Love is the greatest thing of all. Therefore, because I love my father, I am willing to make this sacrifice – I know I told you that I would kill myself I you ever touched me, and I swore I would not agree to marry you, but the situation has changed. I will offer myself to you as your bride if you will cease your vengeance against my father. When you marry me, I come with a dowry – my father has several castles and since I am his eldest daughter, I have been given Belford Castle on the Scots border. My dowry was promised to Alberbury when I took my final vows, but since I have not taken them, the property still belongs to me. I have an annual income of three hundred gold crowns a year as well. All of this will be yours if you marry me and cease your vengeance against my father. Will you at least consider it?"

Bretton gazed steadily at her. He couldn't quite bring himself to deny her but he didn't understand why. Perhaps there was a part of him that wanted to have her by his side, as his wife, because clearly, she had grown on him since the day he had abducted her. In fact, he couldn't imagine not having her around. But he wasn't yet ready to give up on his vengeance against de Velt, not when it had been part of him for so long. Torn, he averted his eyes, sighing heavily as he did so. Allaston, not receiving any manner of answer, moved towards him so that she was standing by his left leg. She looked up at him earnestly.

"Remember when you were a child and your father meant so much to you?" she asked, trying to tear down his walls of resistance. "Think of the family we might have – a son or two, or even three. Mayhap even a few daughters. Think of what they would mean to you and how you, as their father, would be proud of them. That kind of pride is so much better than the empty victory my father's death will bring you. Can you understand that?"

He looked at her, sharply. "I understand a boy's adoration of his father," he said. "Your father deprived me of that."

"But you can find it again with your own son," she insisted, daring to put a hand on his leg. "Will you at least consider it?"

He could feel her hand on his leg, searing him through the leather of his boot. He was so bloody confused and conflicted that he could hardly see straight. He simply couldn't give her the answer she wanted and it tore at him because so much of what she said made sense. So much of what she said was attractive to him. But he couldn't tell her what she wanted to hear. Reaching down, he took a firm grip on her wrist and pulled her up, onto the saddle behind him.

"Now, sit still and be quiet," he told her as she seated herself comfortably behind him. "I do not want to hear another word from you."

Allaston complied, mostly because she didn't want another spanking should she disobey. Her bum was already quite sore. But she had planted the seed within him and she hoped it would take root. She hoped that her offer was something he would consider for it was all she had to give. Her life, her servitude, in exchange for her father's life. She'd tried before, begging the man not to kill her father, but this was different. She was offering him the rest of her life. But she kept quiet as he directed the horse back down the road, south, on a direct course for Newtown twenty miles away.

There would be time enough to discuss such things later.

⚃

THE FALCON AND Flower Inn was an older establishment in Newtown, having been only The Falcon Inn about a hundred years ago, adding the "Flower" by the current owner's wife. Eleven years ago when she had married her husband, she had set about making the place a little more "lady friendly". She cleaned up the rooms, kept whores away from the place, and she even had a small room where one could take a bath and freshen up. The inn was more expensive than most, but it catered to a finer clientele.

Rod sat at a table in the inn's main room. He'd arrived yesterday and slept on a mattress that had been stuffed with feathers, dried lavender, and dried rose petals, and he'd never slept so well in his life. He'd even taken a bath in the inn's special bath tub, a large copper trough that was about the size of a coffin. A big male servant had helped him bathe and had even shaved him, so he was clean and shaved and prepared to meet whatever came. And something was indeed coming. He could feel it.

The missive Rod had sent to Bretton de Llion had asked the man to meet him on the first day of the new month, which was tomorrow. Rod had come alone, that was true, but he was meeting the man in a public place so he doubted there would be any trouble. There were too many witnesses. He had also told him that he would be wearing a tunic bearing the de Llion colors of yellow and black, which he was, so he could be easily identified.

So here he sat, cleaned and shaved and bearing colors, waiting for a killer to enter the room. He was fairly certain that de Llion was coming, whether or not he was truly his cousin. If it was indeed his cousin, then perhaps he would come, eager to be reunited with his kin. Or if he wasn't his cousin but simply a man using the de Llion name, then… perhaps Rod would discover why. Either way, he was fairly certain the man was coming.

The morning came and went, as did the nooning hour. The inn-keeper's wife brought him a delicious meal of a thick chicken stew with big dumplings in it, stewed plums with cinnamon, a big loaf of hot cream-colored bread, and plenty of tart red wine. Rod stuffed himself silly because they didn't eat this well at Bronllys. His grandfather only liked lamb and beef, and too much bread gave him gas, so he was enjoying the change in diet and ate to his heart's content.

But mealtime soon passed and the afternoon set in. Rod continued to sit at the table he had been sitting at since early that morning, his back to the wall, watching as people came and went from the inn. There were some interesting characters, too. A very old man and a very young girl who was his daughter, at least, that's what he'd told the innkeeper's wife. But Rod doubted it from the look of fear on the girl's face. There had also been a pair of swarthy men with strange accents, a very wealthy older woman and her two homely daughters, and finally three knights bearing the colors of Lancaster. The knights had fortunately ignored him, eaten their meal, and then left.

At some point he could hear thunder and the rain began to fall, gently at first but then with increasing power. Soon, there was a full-blown storm overhead that was lashing the walls of the tavern. More people were streaming in to get out the rain and as the sun began to set, the innkeeper's wife stoked the hearth into a roaring blaze to dry off those who had been caught in the rain. People began to crowd around the spitting hearth, drying wet heads and hands, as Rod sat back and sipped at his watered wine.

Time passed and he found himself watching a man who had come in off the street with his young son. He wasn't sure if the man was a merchant, or a lord, just passing through town, but he was rather well dressed and the boy was, too. They were both soaked through and the man was undressing the lad in front of the fire so the child would warm up. As Rod watched, it made him think of his own father, Renard.

Crusty, sometimes tactless, but an excellent knight and a man of honor, Renard de Titouan was a wonderful father. He was thankfully still alive, living at Whitebrook, the family home in the Wye Valley, along with the rest of Rod's family – his mother, Orlaith, his mother's older brother, Rhett, who had also once been a fine knight but had suffered a painful affliction of the joints that left him no longer able to bear a sword, Rod's younger brother Dylan, and finally his nephew, Maddoc, son of his eldest brother, Rhys. Aye, Rod knew he was very lucky to still have both parents alive and a big family to love. It was something he cherished. He wondered if he was about to meet yet another member of his family to add to the happy group.

As he sat and watched the man deal with his young son, the front door to the tavern opened and two people blew in with the wind and the rain. It was fairly dark over by the entry but Rod happened to glance over to see a very large man in armor and a small woman in a wet cloak. The moment the man looked around the room in search of someone in charge, Rod's breath caught in his throat. The man had black hair, a growth of beard on his square-jawed face, and brilliant blue eyes that were the same color as Rod's. In fact, the entire de Llion family had them – him, his mother, Uncle Rhett, his brother Rhys, Rhys' son Maddoc, and even Berwyn. It was a family trait. Rod stood up from the table, his eyes riveted to the man who was now dragging his companion away from the door and towards the fire. He'd know that de Llion face anywhere.

"Bretton?" he asked, rather loudly.

Bretton came to a halt, his hand still clutching Allaston's arm, as he came face to face with a man that looked very familiar to him. He noted the yellow and black tunic and knew instantly who it was. Rather than be standoffish or guarded, as he had planned, all he felt was relief. And perhaps some shock.

"Rod?" he responded quietly. "Is it you?"

Rod nodded, staring at him, before reaching out to grab him. Before he could stop himself, he was throwing his arms around Bretton and squeezing him within an inch of his life. There were tears in his eyes, too, as he pulled away to look at the astonished man.

"Sweet Jesus," he breathed. "It *is* you. I can hardly believe my eyes. *It is you!*"

Bretton wasn't quite sure how to react. His cousin was hugging him and kissing his cheeks, so very excited to see him. He was also tearing up, wiping at his eyes because he was so emotional. Before Bretton could say a word, Rod was dragging him over to his table.

"Please, sit," he insisted. "And your lady? Greetings, Lady de Llion. I cannot tell you how thrilled I am to see you and my cousin. This is like... like a dream. Never did I imagine I would ever see my cousin again. I cannot adequately express my joy."

Allaston looked at the big knight as he gushed out his happiness. He did indeed look a good deal like Bretton, although he was a bit taller and not quite as bulky. Still, the family resemblance was uncanny. She let the knight remove her cloak and put it on a peg next to the hearth so that it would dry out.

"Sit, please," Rod said, practically shoving her into a chair. He pulled up another for Bretton, hugging the man again before he pushed the chair at him. "Bretton, you have no idea how happy this makes me. After losing Rhys last year, I feel as if... as if God has given me back another brother."

Bretton was still rather stumped by Rod's enthusiasm but he managed to take the chair. He also managed to understand something about his cousin, Rhys, passing.

"Rhys is dead?" he asked. "I barely remember the man but I remember he was sort of a big, quiet lad. What happened?"

Rod's jaw ticked. "The king," he said quietly, perpetuating the fabrication that everyone knew about Rhys. "John executed him."

Bretton wasn't upset by it. He didn't even really know his cousin. But it was clear that Rod was upset. Still, this entire meeting had his head spinning and he struggled to gain control of his thoughts and emotions. Rod was bowling him over with his enthusiasm and Bretton wasn't sure he wanted such eagerness. He wasn't sure he wanted anything at all, except perhaps a few questions answered.

"Then I am sorry for you," he said evenly.

Rod nodded, his gaze riveted to his cousin. He simply couldn't look at anything else. "It really *is* you," he exclaimed again. "I still cannot believe it. I do not even know where to start except at the beginning. How is it that you escaped de Velt? We thought you were dead!"

Rod had taken the conversation right to the core of the situation and it was difficult for Bretton to collect his thoughts. The entire situation was overwhelming him and he struggled to gain his bearings. It was difficult for him not to lash out right away, too, and he labored with his self-control.

"I was not dead," he said steadily. "I escaped with a few servants and we ran for freedom."

Rod listened with great interest. "And you are just now returning to Wales?" he asked. "But why have you not contacted us before now? I do not understand. And what is all this about you leading a mercenary army?"

Bretton could see that Rod was genuinely puzzled and evidently had no idea of the truth behind his questions. That ignorance made him furious and the control he was struggling with shattered.

"You have the boldness to ask such foolish questions?" he hissed. "Let me ask *you* a question. Why did no one ever come looking for me? Do you have any idea what happened to me after I escaped Four Crosses? I was kept as a slave and abused in ways I cannot speak of before I escaped and began to learn the life of a mercenary. I had no other choice, Rod, because my loving family, who is evidently so glad to see me now, never made the effort to locate me back then. Stop acting as if you care about me because your actions over the past twenty-five years tell me otherwise. I am here today for one reason and one reason only, and that is to discover why my family left me to the mercy of others. Well? Why did no one ever come looking for me?"

Rod was taken aback by the passion coming forth from Bretton and he was frankly astonished by the questions. He sat back in his chair, bewildered, as Bretton's venom poured forth.

"Because we thought you were dead," he said simply. "Four Crosses was taken over by de Velt and he killed the occupants. We naturally assumed you were one of the dead."

"But you never made the effort to find out for certain?" Bretton said angrily. "How could you do that? How could you just assume I was dead and not find out for certain?"

Rod could see that the man was more hurt than angry. Given the circumstances as he saw them at this moment, he didn't blame him.

"Bretton, please," he said softly, trying to calm the man down. "I do not know the exact circumstances because I was a child myself, so I suppose this is a question you must ask our grandfather. I know he mourned your family deeply. He still does."

Grandfather. The mention of the man took Bretton down a peg or two. His anger cooled a bit, thinking on the man he had loved so very much as a child. But his hurt, that deep despondency of abandonment from long ago, was overtaking him.

"Grandfather is still alive?" he asked quietly.

Rod nodded. "He is," he said. "When I told him you might be alive after all, he went rather mad. He has been in a depression ever since because he does not believe it to be true. He thinks you are still dead."

"Is that why he did not come?"

Rod shook his head. "He did not come because I did not tell him where I was going," he said. "I wanted to see for myself if it was true first. I did not think the man could take a disappointment like that if the man calling himself Bretton de Llion was, in fact, not his lost grandson."

Bretton eyed him. "Will you tell him it is me?"

"Of course I will."

Bretton thought on that a moment. For the first time, he glanced over at Allaston, who was sitting quiet and still, watching the exchange. He couldn't help but think that this was the same thing she had told him. *They assumed you were dead. How were they to know where to look?* In hindsight, he supposed she was right, but he still couldn't get over that little boy who had prayed nightly for his grandfather to come and get him.

"I am sure he will not care," Bretton said. Now, he was starting to feel sorry for himself. He reached out and poured himself a measure of Rod's wine. "Now, I would ask you something, cousin. How is it you knew where to find me? And how did you know it was me?"

Rod watched Bretton take a long, deep drink of wine. "When you burned Alberbury, you gave a message to an old nun to deliver," he said quietly. "The nun delivered it to some of Shropshire's men, who in turn delivered it to my liege, Christopher de Lohr. De Lohr, knowing that I was related to the de Llions, summoned me to ask me if I had ever heard the name Bretton de Llion. You told the nun that you were at Cloryn Castle, so that is where I delivered the missive."

It made sense. Bretton poured himself another cup of wine. "Did the nun do as she was told and deliver my message to de Velt?"

Rod shrugged. "I can only assume that de Boulers did," he said. "Since the missive involved the capture of de Velt's daughter, I am sure de Boulers did out of courtesy."

Rod's attention immediately moved to Allaston, sitting next to Bretton, and he was coming to think that she wasn't so much Lady de Llion as she was his cousin's prisoner. The knight in him, the protector of all that was good and pure, began to take over.

"And you, my lady," he said quietly. "I assumed you were Lady de Llion but I am guessing that was an incorrect assumption. Am I wrong?"

Allaston, now at the forefront of the conversation, met Rod's gaze steadily. She didn't dare look at Bretton because she didn't want to see his expression. It could have been one of intimidation or one of resignation. Either one was prone to upset her so she answered Rod of her own accord.

"Nay," she replied. "I am Lady Allaston de Velt. Jax de Velt is my father."

"Then you are his prisoner."

"Aye."

Rod nodded understandingly, drawing in a long, steadying breath. After a moment, he stood up, kicked the chair back, and withdrew his broadsword.

"My lady, please back away," he said evenly. "My horse is around back, a black steed with four white feet. You can make it to my horse as I hold off my cousin. Ride hard south to Bronllys Castle and tell my grandfather who you are. He will help you."

Allaston's eyes widened with shock, looking at Bretton, who remained calmly in his seat. But his eyes were fixed on Rod.

"Is this truly what you wish to do, Rod?" Bretton asked. "I will not let her go, so you are in for a fight. If you think you can best me, I invite you to try."

"Wait!" Allaston stood up, putting her hands out, eventually rounding the table and putting herself between Rod and Bretton. "I am not leaving, Sir Rod, although I appreciate your chivalry. I must remain with Bretton."

Rod's brow furrowed as he looked at her. "Why would you do that?" he asked. "He has abducted you. He burned an entire priory and killed dozens of nuns for the privilege. And you say that you must stay with him? I do not understand."

Allaston faced off against Rod, a big man with a big sword. "Because he wants to kill my father," she said, wondering if he would understand her logic. "As long as I remain with him, mayhap I can convince him otherwise. If I flee now, he will continue with his vengeance against my father and I do not wish to see my father killed."

Rod did indeed understand her reasoning. He didn't like it, but he understood. "So you are voluntarily remaining with him?"

Allaston nodded firmly. "I am," she said. Then, her eyes glimmered with pain. "I must."

Rod sighed heavily and, giving the woman a somewhat sorrowful expression, sheathed his broadsword. As if he hadn't just drawn his sword against his cousin, he collected his seat, took the cup away from Bretton, and drained the contents. He found that he needed it.

"This is all so damn confusing," he said, pouring more wine. "Since when do prisoners want to remain with their captors? I was prepared to go head to head against my own flesh and blood for you, my lady."

Allaston was still standing up, now closer to Rod than she was to Bretton. "And I appreciate your chivalry, as I said," she replied. "But I will not leave Sir Bretton. I choose to remain."

"I am not 'Sir' Bretton," Bretton muttered. "I am simply Bretton. Slaves and mercenaries are not usually knighted, as it is a noble profession. My profession is not noble and I was never knighted."

Both Rod and Allaston looked at him with some surprise. "All de Llion men are knighted," Rod said frankly. "We have never had a man in our family who has not been knighted. I can knight you right now, as I was knighted personally by King Richard. So was my brother, Rhys. I will knight you, Bretton."

Bretton's first reaction was one of surprise and gratitude. Of course he had always wanted to be a knight. It had been a dream of his since he had been very young. He was certainly skilled enough, but there was more to it than that, enough so that he knew he would never make a true knight. He had committed too much wrongdoing against the church, against mankind in general, for him to be an honor to the knighthood. It was something that was not possible in his world.

"Nay," he said, shaking his head. "Knights are sworn to uphold the chivalric code and that is something I cannot and will not do. I respect the knighthood enough not to want to sully it."

Rod was perplexed. The man before him was not what he had expected, although he wasn't sure what, exactly, he had hoped for. It was clear that Bretton de Llion was a complex man, one that Rod didn't entirely relate to or understand. His hopes for forging a relationship with the man were slowly being dashed because it was clear that Bretton wanted no such thing. After a moment's pause, he shook his head.

"There are strange forces at work around you, Bretton," he said. "Although I am still very glad to find you alive, I am not sure what goes on with you. You are not the cousin I expected."

Bretton looked at the man. "What *did* you expect?" he asked, a tinge of anger in his tone. "My family was killed when I was five years old and I escaped with a few servants although sometimes I wonder if it would have been better had I died. The servants sold me into slavery to a man who raped me repeatedly, and when I was old enough to escape him, I squired for an Irish mercenary who would get drunk and beat me to a pulp until I was old enough to best him in a fight. Unlike you and your posh life where you were loved and taken care of, I have had to fight for every breath I've ever taken. I've had to fight for everything I have. Vengeance against Jax de Velt has been the only thing keeping me alive and I swear to God that I will finish what I started. So do not judge me, cousin. You have no right. No right at all."

With that, he stood up and grabbed Allaston by the arm, pulling her up with him. But Rod stood up, reaching out to grasp Bretton before he could get away.

"I am sorry, Bretton, truly," he said. "Do not leave. I did not mean to offend you. I understand that it has not been easy for you and, believe me, I am not judging you. No matter who you are or what you've done to get there, you are still my cousin and I am very glad to know you have returned. As for the rest... well, I would never judge you in any case whether or not I agree with your methods."

Bretton eyed his cousin, somewhat soothed by the man's words. Slowly, he regained his seat, as did Allaston.

"I do not even know why I came here today," Bretton muttered after he'd sat back down. "Wild curiosity, I suppose. I wanted to know how you found me. I wanted to know why no one ever came looking for me. Now, I know everything. You have heard about me and I have heard about you. I am not entirely sure if there is much more to say between us."

Rod was still holding on to Bretton's arm as if fearful the man was going to run off. "Mayhap there is not," he said softly. "But we are family. I would like to come to know you better, Bretton."

"Why?" Bretton wanted to know. "It is not as if we shall be allies or friends. I am your cousin and nothing more. We share blood and that is all."

Rod could sense the wall of resistance up around Bretton. He'd sensed it from the beginning. "Will you at least come and see Grandfather?" he asked softly.

Bretton shook his head firmly. "Nay," he said. "The man remembers an eager five year old lad. Let that be all he remembers about me, not the man I am today. I am not entirely sure he would be proud of what I have become."

Rod felt a distinct sense of sorrow on his grandfather's behalf. "Then you do not want me to tell him I have found you?"

"Nay."

Rod nodded. "If that is your wish."

"It is."

Rod's gaze moved between Bretton and Allaston. He was so very disappointed with the way things turned out. Somehow, he'd held out hope that Bretton would want to come with him to be reunited with the family again, but Bretton wanted nothing to do with them. He was his own man, with his own world, and his long-lost family didn't fit into that world. He was a mercenary, the very worst kind, and he had a mission of destruction. Rod couldn't help him with it and he couldn't turn him away from it. There was nothing left for him to do or say. After several moments, he squeezed Bretton's arm and let him go, taking a last drink of wine before rising from his chair.

"You are my cousin, Bretton, and I will always love you as such," he said, but there were tears in his eyes. "I will not tell grandfather about you. I wish you the very best in life and I truly hope that someday, you will find what you are looking for. I hope you find something that makes you happy. But know you can always call upon me, no matter what. I will be there for you. My lady, I wish you the best of luck, too."

With that, he left the table and headed out into the rainy night beyond. Bretton and Allaston watched him go, each lost to their own sense of sadness. Bretton most of all. He wished he could be more like Rod. He wished he could have accepted the man and they could have been family and allies once again, but it was not to be, mostly for Rod's protection. Rod had no idea how turbulent Bretton's world was or how terrible. It was best just to leave everything between them on this somber note.

When Rod was gone, Allaston turned to Bretton, who was staring off into space as if reflecting on times gone by, times when he and Rod were young and carefree. Reflecting on the times that children share. She wasn't quite sure what to say.

"He seems very nice," she said hesitantly. "He seems genuinely concerned about you."

Bretton was still staring off. "Aye," he said. "He does. But it is best that he stay far, far away from me."

Allaston nodded. "He knows that," she said sadly. "I could see it in his face."

Bretton sighed heavily. "I always wanted...," he began, then stopped and collected himself. "It is best for him to remain away from me, but I will admit that I miss him already. I never had a brother. I suppose this moment that we spent here with Rod is the closest I will ever come."

Before Allaston could reply, Bretton was on his feet, looking for the innkeeper so he could secure two rooms for the night. Allaston got the distinct impression that he wanted to forget about Rod and their conversation. Perhaps it was too painful for him to reflect upon. In any case, Bretton was moving on, pushing Rod and the de Llions out of his mind. Now that Bretton knew the truth of why no one ever searched for him, it was time to leave the abandoned little boy in the past.

CHAPTER FOURTEEN

A LLASTON HAD NEVER seen an actual bathroom before. As nice as her home of Pelinom Castle was, there were no rooms dedicated purely to bathing. Therefore, when the innkeeper's wife showed her into the small, windowless room that was lit with several candles, all Allaston could do was look around in wonder.

After Rod had left, Bretton had arranged for a room and a bath for Allaston, of which she was extremely grateful. The bathing room had a big oiled cloth spread over the floor and atop the oiled cloth was a mat of woven grasses so that the water would drain through the mat to the oiled cloth below and keep the bather's feet dry. There was a very large bathtub, half-full of warm water, a stool in the corner, and a table upon which sat precious glass phials that were filled with some kind of liquid. There was also a painted wooden box on the table and a bowl that contained flower petals, some of them dried and some of them fresh. The innkeeper's wife pulled out the big screen that was over in one corner, positioning it near the bathtub to protect the bather from the open door.

"Now," the woman said. "I will bring ye a robe so that ye may wear it whilst I clean up yer clothing. Is that all ye have with ye?"

Allaston nodded, looking down at the dark blue dress she was wearing, made from heavy wool for traveling. "Aye," she said. "I have nothing else."

"Not even a shift to sleep in?"

Allaston shook her head. "Nothing but what I am wearing."

The innkeeper's wife eyed her. "Ye look about my daughter's size," she said. "I will bring ye something to sleep in. Can I help ye undress, my lady?"

Allaston shook her head. "I will do it," she said, casting the woman a long glance. "I will also bathe alone. I do not need help."

The woman nodded, not at all offended by the statement. She went to the small table and pulled forth a phial, pulling out the stopper. She sniffed deeply before pouring a measure of the clear liquid into the bath.

"Lemon rind and rosemary oil," she said. Then, she pulled the top off of the painted box to reveal three lumpy bars of soap. "Ye can use these if ye wish, one is rose, one is lavender, and the other is Castile soap. Ye may use any of these."

Allaston nodded, waiting until the woman left before going and smelling all three of the soaps. It was something of a novelty. At the priory, they bathed with a soft soap made from lye and animal fat. The Mother Prioress didn't believe in anything sweet-smelling, thinking that it only fed the vanity, so the soaps often smelled terrible. Therefore, to smell these deliciously-scented soaps was a very special treat. Allaston took her time in selecting her soap, choosing the lavender, and in little time she had all of her clothing off and climbed into the tub.

It was warm and wonderful, and she quickly submerged her entire body, including her head, luxuriating in the lemon-rosemary water. It had been a while since she'd last had a bath. The last time she could remember was when she had been released from the vault those weeks ago. Therefore, she was enjoying this one.

Her hair, long and dark, was washed with the lavender soap and she wrung it out, braiding it tightly and winding up around her head as she scrubbed every inch of skin. All the while, her mind kept going back to the meeting with Rod and the things that had been said. It had been a depressing conversation, in her opinion, because loving her family as she did, it was hard for her to understand Bretton's resistance to becoming close a cousin who very badly wanted to know him. If she thought hard about it, she felt badly for Bretton in general. The man was terrified of letting anyone get close to him.

It wasn't as if he was a truly heartless man. Allaston had been around him long enough to know that was far from the case. She'd seen him around his men and he came across as very ungiving and demanding, but when he was with her, there was humanity and warmth to him. Those days when she was in the vault and he was her cold captor were long gone. The Bretton she had come to know was a man, she believed, who was indeed capable of feeling. He simply had to warm up and overcome his fear of attachment. He had to overcome his fear that the person he cared for was going to be ripped away from him.

She was jolted from her thoughts when the door to the room suddenly opened and then promptly closed. Assuming it was the innkeeper's wife, she turned casually to look at the woman and was completely startled to see Bretton standing there.

"Oh!" she shrieked, rolling up into a ball in the tub, hugging her knees. "Why are you here?"

Bretton stood there with a lazy half-grin on his face. "I have come to help my wife bathe," he said.

Allaston frowned deeply. "*Wife?*" she repeated, outraged. "What madness is this?"

He shrugged and planted himself on the stool, his eyes glimmering with mirth at Allaston as she tried to maintain her modesty.

"It seems that there is only one room left," he said. "The inn is full because of the nasty weather so I took what they had, and the only way the old woman would rent the room to me is if we were married, so… you are my wife."

Allaston scowled. "I'll not sleep in the same bed with you if that is what you are hoping for."

"Then sleep on the floor. I will be most comfortable on the bed."

She made a face at him. "Will you *please* get out?"

He cocked his head. "Why?" he asked. "I have seen a naked woman before."

Allaston was furious. "You have not seen *me*...," she stopped herself, thinking of that frightening and embarrassing moment when Bretton had nearly taken advantage of her, and re-thought her statement. "Let me rephrase that... you have not seen me naked when I was a willing participant!"

He grinned. "Your modesty is admirable but unnecessary," he said. "I am staying in here because the innkeeper's wife suggested I wash up as well since my wife was. She thought mayhap that two clean bodies in the same bed would be more pleasant."

Allaston groaned and rolled her eyes. "This has all played into your master scheme, hasn't it?" she asked somewhat sarcastically. "You had this planned all along."

Bretton was enjoying her embarrassment. "For once, I had no plan," he said, watching her frown. "I am not entirely sure why you are upset about this. Did you not offer yourself to me in marriage earlier today?"

She looked at him, eyes narrowed. "You may *not* try the merchandise before we wed," she said firmly. "There are no samples to be given or a foretaste of what is to come."

"Who says I need your permission?"

He was serious. Or, at least, he was pretending to be. She couldn't really tell. Allaston glared at him, emphasizing she would not be a willing party to whatever he was planning. Still hunched into a ball, still trying to cover herself up, she awkwardly stuck out her right foot and scrubbed at her toes.

"My marriage proposal came with certain conditions," she said. "If I marry you, then it would be to shift your focus to me and our family. You must forget about your vengeance against my father."

His good humor faded. "You seem to think that you can dictate my life to me, lady," he said reproachfully. "I will never forget my vengeance against your father."

In a split second, the mood between them had gone from one with some levity to one of grim reality. The atmosphere no longer saw them jesting but once again reminded them both of the seriousness of the situation. Allaston was still looking at her toes, scrubbing the dirt from them, feeling her disappointment and frustration rise. She also felt tears, close to the surface.

"I am willing to give you everything I have, including myself, but that is not good enough for you," she complained. "I have tried to reason with you, to argue with you, and everything else in between, but still, you will not be deterred. Do you not understand? I do not want you to kill my father. I love him, as you loved your father. I know you can understand the love from a child to a parent because you had it once. Because of what my father did, that love turned to hate, and that hatred is eating your soul away like a tumor. If you will not accept my marriage proposal, then hear me now – if you kill my father, I will hate you for the rest of my life just as you hate the very name de Velt. The hatred you have towards my father will be nothing compared to the hatred I will have for you. I know you do not care if I love you or hate you, so I am sure this conversation is pointless. But I speak it just the same so you understand how things will be should you follow through with your threat."

Bretton understood hatred very well. He knew how much he hated de Velt for what he had done, so he understood clearly what Allaston was saying. He didn't want her hatred and the very thought made him feel both very sad and very angry. *Why did the woman have to be so bloody difficult?*

"By what right do you believe you can dictate what I feel or how I live my life?" he wanted to know. "You presume too much, lady."

She looked at him, then. "This is a conversation we have over and over," she said. "I grow weary of discussing the same subject, your hatred of my father and me trying to talk you out of such a thing. You have my offer. It is your choice to take it or not."

He thought on that. "I have decided to take it," he said. "I will take you and your castle and your dowry. But my vengeance against your father is my own."

She returned her attention to her toes. "Then you will have a wife who hates you," she said simply. "I hope you can live with that."

Bretton could see that she meant every word. That was not what he wanted. He wanted a wife who was pleasant to talk to, someone to keep his house, bear his children, and someone he could even grow fond of. He realized, as he looked at her, that he was already fond of her. God help him, he was. The feeling both frightened and uplifted him. But to know that she would hate him if he carried out his revenge against her father… he wasn't sure he wanted to live with that. He was fairly certain he couldn't. He cleared his throat softly.

"When I came to Alberbury to find you, it was with one goal in mind," he said gently. "I wanted to capture the daughter of my mortal enemy and use her as bait to lure her father to me. I kept her in the vault for the first three weeks of our association before a comrade pointed out that a living prisoner was of more use to me than a dead one. That is the only reason I permitted you to be released from the vault, you know. Had you remained there, you were going to die."

Allaston kept fussing with her toes and Bretton, not receiving a reaction, continued. "I tried to stay away from you in the beginning because the very name of de Velt was like acid upon my tongue," he said. "Every time I looked at you, I saw your father. But I eventually realized that you were *not* your father. You have traits I have not seen in a very long time. You have compassion and understanding, and the comprehension of those traits are buried deep in my memory. My mother and father had them, but thinking of them brings me back to that five year old boy who had his parents brutally torn away from him. Seeing you, coming to understand you as I have, takes me back to the time in my life when I was the happiest. I am not sure I want to go back there, knowing how badly it can end."

Allaston was looking at him by the time he was finished, surprised by his admission. She thought seriously on her reply because she didn't want him to think she was mocking him, or worse, taunting his show of emotion.

"What you say is very deep and thoughtful," she said, eyeing him a moment before grunting with both confusion and hesitation, as if she were at her wit's end. "You have moments, like now, where I can see a man of feeling, but then you have moments when I truly believe you are a barbaric beast. You are a paradox, de Llion. I do not believe you are this ruthless mercenary because you want to be. I think you became him because you have had no choice. That soft, tender boy is still in there, somewhere, and he wants to become a man who shares in the same happiness as the boy did. You must not be afraid to love or feel emotion. You had it once and you can have it again."

He shook his head, hanging it. "I do not know how," he said quietly. "I am not sure I can let go of what I have become."

"I will help you if you will let me."

He looked up at her, feeling an ache in his heart that he couldn't begin to describe as his eyes locked with hers. The ache spread out from his chest, into his limbs. He very much wanted her to help him but he truly didn't know where to begin. The only love or affection he had ever received had been long ago, or post-de Velt, if he had paid for it. Was it really possible that affection, even love, would cost him nothing if it was with the right woman?

"Do you...," he began, swallowed, then started again. "Do you think... that is, as my wife, that you could feel something for me? Mayhap even become fond of me?"

Allaston had the same aching feeling he did, something that made her limbs tingle and her heart flutter. The way he was looking at her made her feel so warm and liquid inside. She'd never known such feeling until she had met him and now, as she came to know him better, the feelings only grew strong. Strange, wonderful, alien feelings. But she was deeply torn.

"You are a killer," she said softly. "You have killed so many. You want to kill my father. But I think you are correct when you said you had no choice in what you have become. You had to become this killer, this mercenary, in order to survive. I could not have feelings for the killer. But I could have feelings for the man beneath. I think I already do. And I want to help him."

Her unexpected response hit him like a hammer, so much so that he actually emitted what sounded like a strangled gasp. He could hardly believe what he was hearing but, in the same breath, it was empowering. All of his thoughts and feelings started to come out whether or not he wanted them to.

"Already, I know I cannot be without you," he said. "You have grown on me but I cannot describe what I feel more than that. All I know is that I want you with me, for always, and if you were to hate me, I could not abide it. But my hatred against your father... it has made me what I am."

"It also brought me to you," Allaston reminded him quietly. "How can you hate my father when he has given you someone you have feelings for?"

Bretton shook his head, baffled and bewildered. Then, he came off the stool, slowly, crawling the few feet to the tub and sitting next to it. Allaston unwound herself from her protective ball and leaned against the side of the tub, next to him, her head very close to his. He was looking at his lap and she was looking at him.

"I do not know," he whispered. "I find myself in a great quandary. I have plans and aspirations, plans that have been set for twenty-five years. Now, suddenly, I find myself uncertain about those plans. I do not want you to hate me, but I swore vengeance against Jax de Velt and I must see that through."

The mercenary, the killer, the warlord was fighting against something stronger than all of the armies and all of the hatred in the world. He was fighting against love, something that was creeping into his heart. He was so very afraid of it and so very confused. Allaston could see that confusion in everything about him. Sympathetically, she impulsively leaned over and kissed him gently on the cheek.

"Mayhap that vengeance could take the form of something else," she whispered. "You do not have to kill a man in order to seek vengeance."

He felt the kiss lingering on his cheek as if she was still touching him. It was warm and wonderful. He looked up at her. "How could I possibly accomplish that?"

Allaston's green eyes twinkled. "By marrying his daughter who was meant for the cloister."

He looked at her a moment before breaking down in a weak grin. "I am already going to do that," he said. "That will not be any of measure of vengeance against him."

"Untrue. He will consider it a great insult against him."

Bretton chuckled again and shook his head. "Mayhap, but not enough of an insult."

She looked stricken. "It is not enough to marry me?"

He lifted his eyes, looking at her. "It will be everything, I think," he said, resignation in his tone. "But my vengeance against your father...."

Allaston could see that he was weakening his stance slightly and she leapt on the opportunity to expand the gap. "Mayhap if he gives you more properties, that will help ease your sense of conquest and vengeance against him," she suggested helpfully. "And... and if he were to apologize, Bretton... would you accept? I told you that the man he is now is much different from the man he was those years ago. The man he is now, the man I know, would feel badly for depriving a young boy of his parents. I am sure he would feel badly to know how you have suffered since then. Won't you at least consider these things as an alternative to such vengeance?"

He was looking at her seriously. "You truly believe that an apology will right all wrongs?" he asked. "I will not consider it. I cannot."

"Then what will right the wrongs?"

"His death."

"Then what happens after you kill him?" she asked. "We have had this conversation before, too. Will it instantly make you a happy man?

Will it cause your father to rise from the dead? It will do neither of those things. But something will result from it, I assure you – my hatred of you. If you are willing to risk that, then there is nothing more I can say."

He just sat there, looking at her. He was torn and indecisive. *Damn her!* She had made him that way. She was tearing away at his resolve. For lack of a response that she hadn't heard before, because he too was growing weary of their circular conversations, he reached over to the table against the wall and grasped a folded linen rag that was on top of it. Dipping it in the warm, scented water, he wiped it over his face. Perhaps cleaning up would make him think more clearly as his clear-cut vengeance against Jax de Velt was growing less clear-cut by the minute and it was all Allaston's fault. She made him think about something other than revenge. She made him think about her.

Allaston sensed his conflict and she was glad, glad that she was causing him to reconsider killing her father. She could only pray that she could sway him enough. Too many times had they argued about this, fought even, but this was the first time she started seeing any progress. He was weakening. As she watched him wash his face, lost in thought, she patted him on the shoulder to gain his attention.

"Will you please hand me that drying linen over on the table?" she asked, pointing to it as he turned around to see what she meant. "I would be grateful."

Silently, his mind wracked with confusion from their conversation, Bretton reached over to grab the linen, but the moment he did so, the door to the room opened and the innkeeper's wife entered, shutting the door swiftly behind her. She nearly tripped over Bretton, sitting on the floor.

"God's Bones!" she cried, catching herself from falling. "Forgive me, my lord. I didn't see ye!"

Bretton waved the woman off as he rose to his feet. He noticed she had something in her hands. "What is that?"

The old woman held up some kind of garment made from unbleached linen. "A robe for my lady," she said, pointing to Allaston, still in the bath. "I will take her clothes with me and clean them. I will leave them outside yer door so she will have something clean to wear come morning."

Bretton took the robe from the woman, handing her Allaston's dark blue dress and shift in exchange. "Make sure her clothes are ready before dawn," he told the woman. "We are leaving before sunrise."

The old woman took the garments. "Will ye be wanting a meal?"

Bretton nodded. "We will eat it on the road."

The old woman departed, shutting the door behind her. When she was gone, Bretton held up the robe to Allaston, but she shook her head at him.

"The drying linen first," she said. "I will put the robe on after I dry my skin."

He silently set the robe down and picked up the drying linen, handing it to her. Allaston reached out to snatch it from her position sitting inside the tub.

"Turn around," she said. "I will not dry myself with an audience."

He just shook his head at her as if baffled by her stance. "Must we go through this again?" he said. "I have seen many naked women in my time. Unless you have a third teat or something out of place on your body, nothing you can show me is any different from what I have seen before."

Allaston tried not to laugh at him because he sounded genuinely perplexed. "Turn around."

He sighed with exasperation. "Why?" he demanded. "I will marry you soon. Let me see what I will be getting."

She scowled. "You cheeky devil," she said. "Turn *around*."

Fighting off a grin, he did. He pretended to be quite put out by it because that was the tone of the conversation. They were actually laughing at one another, a rare and unexpected occurrence. He could hear the water sloshing behind him as she got out of the tub. The linen was still in his hand and she grabbed for it, but he held it fast.

"God's Blood," he hissed. "Is there something you do not want me to see?"

Wet and naked behind him, Allaston tugged on the linen. "Give it to *me*."

He wouldn't let go, his back to her. It was rather fun taunting her and he had so little opportunity to taunt anyone. It was rare, rarer still with genuine humor involved. He was actually enjoying himself.

"You are hiding something, aren't you?" he asked, suspicious. "What is it? Do you really have a third teat? Or mayhap a fourth? Do you really look like a nursing dog, with rows of breasts down your torso, and you just do not want to show me?"

Allaston started giggling as she yanked at the linen, finally getting it away from him. Snatching the robe, she scurried behind the screen that had been partially blocking the tub. Once behind it, she began to quickly dry herself.

"You should know what I look like because you stole a glimpse of it," she said, reminding him of two days ago when he had tried to take advantage of her. "You do not need to see it again until it rightfully belongs to you."

He bit his lip to keep from smiling, crossing his big arms across his chest. "You clearly do not understand the concept of being a prisoner," he snorted. "You are one of two things to me – either my captive or my wife. In either case, you belong to me and I can look at you any time I please."

Allaston tossed the robe on and tied the fastens at the side. It was a rather luxurious piece of goods for belonging to the daughter of an innkeeper because it was lined with something very soft, lamb's wool, she thought. In any case, it was clean, warm, and wonderful. She ran her hands over the sleeves as Bretton spoke, not particularly concerned with his view of their relationship.

"Mayhap that is true but you shall not be doing any looking to-night," she told him as she stepped out from behind the screen. "I am hungry and I am weary, so if you will kindly direct me to my room, I would be grateful."

He eyed her as she came out from behind the screen. In the pale robe, with her hair wound up around her head, she looked like an angel. He just stood there a moment, gazing at her, thinking she was the most beautiful woman he had ever seen.

Seeing the odd expression on his face, Allaston cocked her head at him. "Why do you look at me so?" she asked.

He simply shook his head. "I have not had much experience telling a woman of my thoughts," he said. "At least, I've not had much experience telling a *lady* what I am thinking. I've not been around many of them and when I have, the situation has not been particularly calm."

Allaston tightened up the tie on the robe as she approached him. "You mean the women you have killed when you have laid siege to their homes?" she asked softly.

He nodded slowly. "Mayhap."

Allaston couldn't help her thoughts from turning to Lady Miette. She sighed sadly. "It could have so easily been me," she said quietly. "You could have very easily attacked my home and you would have killed me without care. I simply do not understand how you can do those things to people who could not possibly harm you."

She wasn't being combative but he didn't like it when she brought up his methods. It made him feel so very guilty and that, in turn, frustrated him.

"You could very well ask your father the same thing with all of the carnage he created twenty-five years ago," he said. "Whatever you ask me, and whatever you disapprove of, know that I am simply emulating what your father did those years ago. My methods are nothing new."

She thought on that. The entire thing left a bad taste in her mouth. "May I ask you something?"

He lifted his eyebrows at her. "You are going to whether or not I give you permission."

That was true and she pursed her lips wryly before continuing.

"Lady Miette," she ventured. "You... you did not personally kill her or defile her, did you?"

His gaze was steady. "Would it make any difference to you whether I did or not?"

She had asked the question. Perhaps she wasn't brave enough to hear the answer. But she answered with her usual honesty.

"Aye," she said softly, "it would."

"It would make you look at me differently?"

"Aye."

He realized he wasn't prepared to risk it. They'd spent the past several minutes with a warm mood between them, something extremely rare in his world. It had lifted his heart and spirit in ways he couldn't describe. Still, he was truthful with her. He could be nothing else, for he was not ashamed of his life or what he had done. The sooner Allaston accepted it, the better it would be for them both.

"Then in answer to your question, I am the commander and commanders to not usually follow through with tasks better left to the subordinates," he said. "I simply give the commands, lady. I do not partake in the actions, but I do ensure that my orders have been followed. I look for the end result."

Allaston digested the information. Her expression was guarded, sad. "Did you give your men orders to rape that poor woman?"

He shook his head. "It is considered spoils of war," he said emotionlessly. "If they consider it a reward, then I will not stop them. These men fight for me not because they love me but because I provide them with reward. The lady of Cloryn, as well as the lady of Rhayder, was a part of the spoils."

Allaston winced and lowered her gaze. "The lady of Rhayder, too?" she asked, feeling sickened. "Bretton, if you could do one thing for me, I would beg you to please call your men off from defiling any more women. Please leave them some dignity since you are taking away their very lives. Had you not been seeking me as part of your plan to lure my father, then it could just as easily have been me that your men defiled and murdered. How would that make you feel, knowing me as you do now? Would you like for your men to abuse me to the point of death, touching me in a way that only... only my husband should touch me?"

That hard, guarded expression came over his features again, but Allaston wasn't sure if it was because he was growing angry with her or because he was thinking on nameless, faceless soldiers violating her body in all possible ways. She reached out to touch his arm, feeling the hard sinew and muscle beneath her fingers.

"I am not trying to upset you, truly," she said. "But it is so barbaric and terrible to do this to women whose only crime is to be lady of the castle. I am only asking you to consider showing a measure of mercy to them, Bretton. It would mean a great deal to me."

His expression was still hard. "Why?"

She grew serious. "Because I do not believe that you are all monster," she said. "I believe there is some good left in you. You would have killed me long ago, as Jax de Velt's daughter, if there was not some measure of decency left in you. I would like to hope the man I marry allows for that decency to show."

He very much wanted to disregard her but there was a large part of him that wanted to listen to her. It gave him hope. She wanted to respect him, which was an utterly foreign concept in his world. There was no respect in the dominion of Bretton de Llion, only fear. But he couldn't give her an answer. Would that long-buried decency she spoke of surface for her because she wished it and asked for it? Only time would tell.

"I cannot know for certain what will happen in the future," he said. "As for showing mercy, some would perceive that as weakness and I will not show weakness to my men. Remaining as I am, with ruthlessness, is the only way to maintain control for my purposes."

Allaston knew that would be his answer but she was not discouraged. "Then mayhap you will at least think on what I have said when the time comes," she said quietly. "Mayhap you will think of mercy the next time you are faced with a frightened woman whose only crime was living in a castle you want as your own. Throw her in the vault, or do whatever you have to do in order to keep her from your men, but I would pray that whatever comes, you consider showing mercy in all things. I... I want to be very fond of you, Bretton. Mayhap even love you. Please give me a reason to."

Bretton refused to look at her, as he was in the process of removing his mail and tunic, thinking to use some of that sweet-scented water on his dirty, weary body. More than that, he thought that he needed some time to think on all of this. There had been a great many things said over the past several minutes. He needed time to digest it all. He was, at the moment, overwhelmed by everything. He wasn't accustomed to such personal conversations. *Give me a reason to love you.* He just couldn't bring himself to speak on it. The mere thought made him feel wildly uncomfortable and wildly joyful. Since he couldn't adequately respond, it was best not to until he could.

"The room I rented is directly across the corridor," he told her, ignoring her last statement altogether. "You may go to bed. I will be there shortly. If you run into any hazardous situations in the three steps it takes to cross the corridor, then scream. I will come."

Allaston watched him as he peeled off his tunic, revealing a magnificently scarred and sculpted chest. She was beginning to feel disappointment that he hadn't responded to her statement regarding mercy and love, but seeing his bare flesh quickly diverted her attention. Having never really seen a naked man under such intimate circumstances, her cheeks immediately flushed red and she averted her gaze. But she wasn't embarrassed enough that she didn't sneak a couple of glances before quitting the bathing room. He was rather delicious to look at and the sight set her heart to racing. It didn't take much imagination to think of his flesh against hers, something completely foreign to her but utterly titillating. She was so caught up in stealing glances of his naked skin that she smacked into the door as she went to open it. Startled, she grasped the latch and threw open the door.

"I will bid you a good sleep, then," she said, trying to cover up her embarrassment.

Bretton was running a rag along the back of his neck. "Why?" he asked. "I will be with you in a moment."

Allaston didn't reply. She was too busy trying to get away from the sight of all that naked flesh. Once inside the small but comfortable chamber across the hall, she noticed that someone had put food on the small table near the very warm hearth, and she delved into the bread and cheese hungrily. She even took a piece of cheese to bed with her, eating it lying in bed as she thought of her conversation with de Llion.

There wasn't much to think about, really. The conversation had been circular, as she had mentioned, rolling over the same subjects again and again, only now there was the added element of a marriage between them. She could only pray that she could eventually break de Llion down of his hatred against her father. Perhaps if she could make him happy, if she could fill those big holes inside of him that drove the man to do what he did, then maybe he would be willing to forget about de Velt. Perhaps she could fill his mind, and his heart, with something better. It was all she could truly hope for.

I am not sure I can let go of what I have become.

His words kept rolling over in her mind but she pushed them aside. She wouldn't dwell on them, not tonight. Finishing her cheese, she said her prayers and rolled over, falling asleep almost immediately. Exhaustion and a full belly saw to it. She was sleeping so soundly that she didn't hear Bretton enter the room a short time later.

Noticing Allaston was asleep, he wasn't really surprised. He was almost relieved. He just didn't have the energy to continue their conversation. Therefore, he finished the food that was left on the table and lay down on the floor next to the tiny bed. It wasn't where he wanted to be but he suspected she would not take his presence on the mattress next to her very well, undoubtedly leading into more of an exhausting conversation and a restless night. And he very much wanted to rest and to think about what had been said.

For him, there was so much more at stake, things she would never understand. It was much more than showing mercy. It was trying to change the unchangeable. Did he want to do as she asked? He did. Whether or not he could was another matter altogether. Her hand was hanging over the side of the bed, right over his head. Reaching up, he stole a secret touch of her soft flesh, as light as butterfly wings, as he thought on the things she had said to him. *Give me a reason to love you.* He wanted to. With God as his witness he did. But he wasn't sure he could.

The entire ride back to Cloryn the next day was completed in brooding silence.

CHAPTER FIFTEEN

*D*E LOHR MUST *know.*

Rod's first impulse upon leaving The Falcon and Flower Inn in Newtown was to go to Lioncross Abbey and tell de Lohr of his meeting with his cousin. The man would want to know, so in a blinding rainstorm, Rod set out for the southern Marches and de Lohr's fortress. It was a fair distance away, at least a day's long ride, so he set off at a steady pace, but it soon became clear that traveling in a rainstorm in the dead of night was unsafe at best. His horse had tripped twice and the second time, he had nearly pitched off the animal.

Therefore, he had been forced to stop at a farmer's hovel along the way. The old farmer provided him with his stable to sleep in, and it was dry and fairly warm so it wasn't entirely miserable. The rain let up before dawn and Rod was back on the road again, heading for Lioncross Abbey.

The rain the night before had created divots on some of the roads where the mud had washed away and holes remained, which slowed his pace somewhat. As the sun came out and began to dry up the water, the fields were alive with foraging creatures, and he passed more than one farmer on his trip south. He even passed a man who had an entire cart full of small green apples, he told Rod, from a tree that he had pruned in the wintertime and was now producing fruit. He gave Rod a few to take with him. They were extremely sour but, hungry, Rod managed to choke them down. It was better than nothing. He gave his horse the apple cores and let the beast graze for a few minutes, watching it chomp down the fat, wet grass along the road.

But he didn't take too long for eating. He had someplace to be, so he continued along the road that was growing increasingly better to travel on as the rain dried up. With his steady pace and the better road conditions, he was able to make it to Lioncross well under what he had estimated. As he reached a crest in the road overlooking de Lohr's great fortress in the distance, he could immediately see a rather large encampment about a half mile to the north.

It took him a moment to realize it was an army. He could see standards flying. Startled, he watched and waited to see what the army was doing. It seemed to be sitting there, camping, minding its own business, and Lioncross seemed unruffled. He could see men in the distance as they moved freely on the road in and around the castle, so clearly, the castle wasn't under siege. Curious, he spurred his charger onward.

True to form, Lioncross' main gate was open, the portcullis up, as people moved about without a care in the world. It was sunset and Rod knew the great portcullis would soon be closing, sealing in the castle for the night. As he thundered beneath the gatehouse and entered the bailey, his gaze fell upon Max Cornwallis standing near the smithy shack. Max spied him, waving a big hand in his direction, as he made his way towards him.

Wearily, Rod dismounted his charger and asked a soldier to take the beast over to the stable. Just as the soldier walked away with the exhausted horse, Max and Rod met up.

"Back, I see?" Max asked. "I thought you were staying at Bronllys."

Rod lifted his eyebrows, an exhausted gesture as well as a knowing one. "I was," he said. "I had to go on an errand. Where is de Lohr?"

Max gestured to the keep. "Inside," he said. "But before you go into the keep, you should know that we have a visitor."

Rod nodded. "I know," he said. "I saw an army camped about a half mile to the north but I couldn't make out the standards. Who is it?"

Max recited the name deliberately for maximum impact. "Jax de Velt."

Rod's eyes widened. He had never been any good at hiding his feelings, so his measure of surprise was more dramatic than most.

"Ajax *de Velt*?" he repeated, astonished. "What is he doing here? And why isn't he burning down the fortress and sticking us all up on poles?"

Max snorted. "Because he has come on a peaceful mission," he said, sobering. "He received a missive that his daughter has been abducted. He came to see Chris because, being a major marcher lord, he thought de Lohr would know something more about it."

Rod scowled. "He is here *peacefully*?"

"He is indeed."

"Is that even possible?"

Max nodded. "It is," he said, turning Rod in the direction of the keep entry. "Go inside and see him."

Rod was afraid to. He was torn between curiosity and terror. In fact, he started backing away, his gaze moving nervously over the keep. "We discussed the scenario should de Velt come to the Marches, bent on blood," he said. "You were there, Max. You heard what was said, what we feared."

Max nodded patiently. "I know what we feared," he said. "But trust me when I tell you that de Velt is here to seek help in saving his daughter and nothing more. Chris has offered to help him."

Rod still wasn't sure about the entire situation but at least he'd stopped backing up. His dubious gaze was on Max. "How long has he been here?"

"Two days."

"No executions? No men on poles?"

Max laughed softly. "None of those things," he said, pointing to the keep again. "Go inside. The man will not tear the hide from you. He's actually not so bad once you come to know him. Suffice it to say that time has matured and changed him, I think. He is as normal as you and

I are."

Rod's eyebrows flew up. "Normal? De Velt?" he shook his head, now moving towards the keep. His curiosity had the better of him. "This is something I must see for myself."

Leaving Max grinning in the bailey, Rod took the steps up to the keep and entered the cool, dark foyer. Directly in front of him was the great hall of Lioncross and he could hear soft voices deep inside the room.

As he approached the hall entry in the shape of the classic Norman arch, he saw a few servants moving around inside the room and there were four soldiers, de Lohr soldiers, near the door. Rod entered the hall to see Christopher and Edward with their backs to him, and a very large man with his long hair tied back at the nape of his neck all sitting at the feasting table. There was also another unfamiliar knight at the table and as Rod approached, the unfamiliar knight stood up, glaring at him with hostility. Rod glared back, insulted by the expression, as Christopher turned around to face him.

"Rod," he said with surprise, rising to his feet. "I was not expecting you. What brings you back to Lioncross?"

Rod showed due respect to Christopher but the truth was that he couldn't keep his focus off the big man and the unfamiliar knight at the table. The man had oddly colored eyes and was rather intimidating. At least, Rod thought so. Something about those eyes unnerved him.

"My lord," he greeted Christopher. "I have come with more news about the mercenary. I hope my appearance is not inopportune."

Christopher waved him off. "Of course not," he said. "In fact, it is most welcome. Allow me to introduce you to Sir Ajax de Velt and his son, Sir Coleby de Velt. They, too, have come to Lioncross because of the mercenary. My lords, this is one of my finest vassals, Sir Rod de Titouan."

It was a polite mutual introduction and Rod nodded respectfully to Jax, less respectfully to his arrogant son. Coleby seemed to have an arrogant attitude and Rod had visions of punching the young knight in the face should he continue his mental chest-beating. But his focus soon returned to Christopher.

"I have much to tell, my lord," he said. "Things that will, coincidentally, interest Lord de Velt. May I sit? It has been a long ride."

Christopher indicated for him to sit on his left hand, pouring the weary knight a measure of wine as Rod sat heavily. As Rod downed the entire cup of wine, Christopher eyed him with growing concern. He appeared exhausted, that was true, but there was something more, something he didn't like.

"Tell us, Rod," he quietly encouraged the man. "What more do you know?"

As Rod gazed at the two great knights, he almost didn't know where to start. In truth, he was still a bit rattled to be sitting across the table from the infamous Jax de Velt, so he struggled to overcome that issue. So much had happened in his conversation with Bretton and, worse yet, with a captive who seemed less like a captive and more like a companion, a woman who also happened to be de Velt's daughter. As Rod had told Bretton, strange forces were at work around the man. Pouring himself another cup of wine, Rod sighed heavily.

"I suppose it is best to start from the beginning," he said, looking at Christopher. "Did you tell Lord de Velt about the de Llion connection?"

Christopher nodded his head. "I did," he said quietly. "He knows that you are connected to the de Llion name but he also knows we do not have confirmation that the mercenary is, in fact, your cousin."

Rod wriggled his eyebrows ironically as he took a long swallow of wine. "We have confirmation now," he said, looking between Christopher and Jax. He finally settled on Jax. "My lord, the name the mercenary commander gave was Bretton de Llion. Lord de Lohr came into this information and knew that my family has connections with the de Llion family. In fact, my grandfather, whom I serve at Bronllys Castle, is a de Llion. When you conquered Four Crosses Castle twenty-five years ago, my grandfather's son, my mother's brother, was the garrison commander. He was killed in the siege along with his wife and two children, or so we thought. But then this mercenary commander surfaced, emulating your exact path of destruction along the Marches, and gave his name as Bretton de Llion. Bretton de Llion was the son of the garrison commander, whom we believed to be dead. He is my cousin."

Jax bobbed his head in understanding. "De Lohr told me all of this," he said. "You say you have confirmation that it is, in fact, your cousin?"

Rod nodded, facing the two lords. "After Lord de Lohr told me of the alleged identity of the mercenary commander, I returned to Bronllys to tell my grandfather of our conversation," he said. Then, he shook his head sadly. "My grandfather refused to accept that Bretton had somehow survived Lord de Velt's siege and would not speak of the possibility, but for my part, my curiosity grew. I was determined to know if Bretton, in fact, was alive and tearing up the Marches, so I sent a missive to Cloryn Castle and asked Bretton to meet me in Newtown if he was, indeed, Bretton de Llion, son of Morgan. I wanted to know if my cousin was still alive. I can confirm that he is."

Christopher's eyebrows lifted. "Then it *is* your cousin?" he said, somewhat stunned. "And you met with him?"

Rod nodded and drained the rest of his wine. "I met with him," he confirmed. "There is no mistaking he is a de Llion. He looks just like the rest of the family. But it is much worse than we could have ever expected, for the man is nothing as I had hoped. He was not glad to see me. He is very bitter towards my grandfather for not trying to find him after Four Crosses was taken. But that bitterness aside, he holds a massive sense of vengeance against Lord de Velt and blames the man for ruining his life, so much so that the burned Alberbury Priory to abducted Lady Allaston de Velt. He plans to use her to lure Lord de Velt to his death, but you already know that. Here is where it becomes complicated – Lady Allaston de Velt was with him when he came to Newtown. I gave her the opportunity to escape and she would not take it. She says that she cannot leave Bretton because if she does, he will stop at nothing to kill her father, and she is quite convinced she can talk him out of it if she stays by his side. Lord de Velt, she stays with him willingly to protect you."

Jax just stared at him, those dual-colored eyes wracked with emotion. After an eternal moment of staring at Rod, digesting what he had been told, Jax let out a hissing sigh and rolled his head back. He ended up staring at the ceiling with the expression of a man who could hardly believe what he'd just been told.

"Allie," he whispered. "God's Bones, is it true? Is she really doing such a thing?"

Rod cast a long glance at Christopher, who seemed equally concerned. As Jax reflected on the state of his foolish, brave daughter, Christopher addressed Rod.

"Did she seem in good health?" he asked. "Good spirits?"

Rod nodded. "She was healthy and whole," he said. "But when I challenged Bretton to a fight to allow her to escape, she refused to flee."

Jax was still staring up at the ceiling, now shaking his head in disbelief. "She was always a head-strong, foolish girl," he muttered, eventually looking at Christopher and Rod. "But she is much like her mother in that she is extraordinarily brave and stubborn. If she thinks she can talk de Llion out of his vengeance, then she will not give up. She will be like a dog with a bone in her persistence."

Christopher understood a woman like that, as did Jax. The older knights could comprehend the strength of women but Rod was still puzzled by it. With no wife, and no lady love, he wasn't seasoned in the ways of woman like Christopher and Jax were. In fact, Rod came across as being rather insulted that the lady didn't take him up on his offer to release her.

"I tried to help her escape," he said, "but she flatly refused. But rest assured that she seemed quite healthy and sound."

Jax did take comfort in that. "Then my mind is eased as far as her health is concerned," he said, disgruntled. "But the fact remains that she has been abducted by a man who shows no fear as he murders and burns. She is at the mercy of a madman."

Christopher couldn't disagree. He looked at Rod. "Did de Llion seem unstable to you?" he asked. "How was the man's demeanor?"

Rod shrugged. "As I said, he is very bitter against my grandfather and full of hatred against de Velt," he replied. "He did not seem unstable, only resentful and determined."

"How did he behave towards Lady Allaston?"

Rod thought back to his meeting with Bretton and the lady. "He was not unkind to her," he said. "He was not cruel to her and, frankly, did not treat her like a prisoner. When I first came into contact with them, I thought she was his wife."

Jax's brow furrowed. "Wife?" he repeated, terrified and disgusted. "*Wife?* Was he... God's Blood, he wasn't affectionate towards her, was he?"

Rod shook his head. "Nay," he assured him. "I mean that they coexisted relatively peacefully. She was not resisting him and he was not being dominant over her."

Jax fell silent, contemplating that scenario. Although he was vastly uncomfortable with it, it was better than the alternative – acting brutally towards her. As he contemplated the relationship between his daughter and her captor, Christopher spoke.

"Is there anything the man said that would be helpful to us in re-gaining Lady Allaston?" he asked. "Did he discuss any plans with you? Anything of value?"

Rod shook his head. "He did not speak of anything I would consid-er valuable to use against him," he said. "Are you planning on launching an offensive any time soon?"

Christopher glanced at Jax before speaking. "Not immediately, at any rate," he said. "Two days ago, I sent a missive to Cloryn Castle acting as a mediator on Lord de Velt's behalf. Since I am not directly involved in the situation, Lord de Velt came to me to ask for assistance. He thought using me as a mediator might ease some of de Llion's volatility. I will act like a buffer, as it were. But the same day I sent a missive to Cloryn, I also sent a missive to Keller de Poyer at Nether

Castle asking for reinforcements. I do not want to ask for reinforcements from any marcher lords because it would deplete their force should de Llion decide to move against them, so de Poyer is the logical choice. He is buried deep in Wales and not in the direct line of sight of de Llion's activities."

Rod nodded in understanding. "I know Keller," he said. "He and my brother were good friends. Rhys spoke very well of the man."

Christopher moved to pour himself another cup of wine as he spoke. "It is my hope that he sends me what I requested in order to reinforce my ranks," he said. "In any case, I believe it prudent to wait and see what kind of response I receive from de Llion. If he is as determined as you say he is, he may look at my attempt at mediation as interference. It might earn me his wrath, so I am taking a serious chance doing this."

"And I appreciate it," Jax said, making sure Christopher understood just how pleased he was to have the man's help. "But something is concerning me now that we have heard from de Titouan. If what he says is true and Allaston is remaining with de Llion willingly, and is in good health, I am hesitant to move on the man. I know my daughter. If she is working on a plan, we must give her time to complete it. If she thinks she can single-handedly bring de Llion to his knees without violence or blood, then I am wondering if we should not give her that opportunity."

Christopher looked at him. "Do you believe she is truly capable of negotiating with a mercenary who is out for your blood?"

"You've not met my daughter."

That was true. Christopher had never met her so he didn't know how persuasive she could be. Still, he didn't like, not in the least.

"What would your wife say to you right now if she heard that?" he asked. "She is the girl's mother, after all. Would she agree with you?"

Jax cracked a grin. "She would demand I go and get her."

Christopher's lips twitched with a smile. "Then I will suggest this," he said. "Let us wait a nominal amount of time for three important reasons – the first being that we should give de Llion time to respond to my missive and the second being that we should wait to see if de Poyer can spare reinforcements from Nether. And the third... oh, Christ, I did not even think of this. Rod, do you remember what your Uncle Morgan looked like?"

Rod's brow furrowed at what he thought was an odd question out of the blue. "I was a very small boy when I last saw him," he said. "I remember images of the man and not much more. He was very big and he had big, booming laughter. He was also missing most of the little finger on his right hand. I remember being fascinated with that as a child. My grandfather said he lost it when horse bit it off. That made me frightened of horses for a very long time. Why do you ask?"

Christopher looked at Jax. "Did you hear that?" he asked. "The man was missing his little finger on his right hand. Did you notice this on your John Morgan?"

Jax's dual-colored eyes were glittering with the possibilities as he looked at Christopher. "I do not know," he said truthfully. "I cannot recall. We sent a missive to Northumberland to send his bodyguard to the Marches the same day we sent off the missives to de Llion and de Poyer, so I suppose now all we can do is wait and see."

Rod was confused, looking between Christopher and Jax. "You sent a missive to Northumberland, too?" he asked. "I do not understand what is being said. Why did you do this?"

Christopher turned to him. "Brace yourself, lad," he said. "There is much more to this situation from de Velt's perspective. There is a chance your uncle is alive and living in Northumberland at Alnwick Castle. Several men were taken after the fall of Four Crosses and not killed outright because their labor was needed, and it is possible that your uncle was one of them. The man in question is now serving the Earl of Northumberland as his body guard. We have sent word to Yves de Vesci to send that man, called John Morgan, to the Marches. If he is Bretton's father, then we intend to present him to de Llion in exchange for Allaston, and you just gave us a very definitive clue to identifying the man – the missing finger."

Rod's jaw popped open in sheer astonishment. "God's Blood," he hissed. "I can hardly believe it. Could it be true?"

Christopher nodded. "It is possible," he said. "Was his body ever positively identified at Cloryn? Did your grandfather ever dare to seek the truth?"

Rod was ashen with shock. "I… I do not know," he said. "I know that he was told of Cloryn's siege and how everyone was killed, including the garrison commander."

"*Who* told him?"

Rod shook his head. "I do not know," he said. "Rumors, fleeing villagers… who is to say?"

Christopher cleared his throat softly, eyeing Jax as he did so. "Rod," he said casually. "I realize this was an extremely difficult thing for your grandfather to go through, but mayhap it would be wise to bring him to Lioncross. If Northumberland's bodyguard arrives and it is indeed your uncle, mayhap your grandfather would like to be here when he comes."

Rod was growing overwhelmed and saddened by the entire circumstance. "And what if it is not?" he said. "It would hurt him more to get his hopes up after all of these years."

"Then do not tell him the truth behind my summons," Christopher said. "Ride to Bronllys and tell your grandfather I wish to see him. I will then keep him on hand until Northumberland's man arrives. If it is your uncle, then your grandfather will know it right away. If it is not, then no harm done and I will make up an excuse as to why I summoned him in the first place. You haven't told him about the confirmation of Bretton's identity, have you?"

Rod shook his head. "Nay," he replied. "I came here first. I am not sure what I am going to tell my grandfather. Bretton did not want me to tell him at all."

Christopher agreed. "For now, I concur with that," he said. "Let your grandfather live in ignorance for a while, at least until Northumberland's man comes. Then, we will determine how to proceed in any case."

It was sage advice and Rod simply nodded wearily. In fact, he was quite exhausted and wanted to have some time to rest and reflect on the most recent information. He was still quite stunned. Finishing up what was left in his cup, he wiped his mouth with the back of his hand and stood up.

"Agreed, my lord," he said. "But there is one more thing. Since Lord de Velt destroyed Four Crosses Castle and my uncle along with it, my grandfather bears a great deal of hatred towards him. When he comes to Lioncross, inevitably, he will come into contact with Lord de Velt at some point. That will upset him as much as anything else will."

Christopher scratched his head. "I will explain to Berwyn the way of things with de Velt now," he said. "He will understand that now is not the time for old grudges to play out. We have other things to focus on, to be aware of, and your grandfather will simply have to accept the way of things. If he cannot, then I will lock him in the vault until such time as I feel it is safe to let him out. Although I understand his grief at losing a son to de Velt, I cannot have Berwyn running amuck, Rod. Surely you know that."

Rod nodded sadly. "I do," he said. Then, he scratched his head and sighed heavily, the sign of a man with a great deal on his mind. "For now, I would like the opportunity to wash and rest, if I may. I find that my exhaustion has the better of me and I want to be fresh in the morning for my ride back to Bronllys."

"Bring your grandfather back as quickly as you can, Rod," Christopher said. "I believe time is of the essence considering what you have told us."

Rod nodded wearily. "I will return in three days with my grandfather," he said. "A day to reach Bronllys, a day for my grandfather to prepare before he leaves, and then a day to return to Lioncross."

It was a sound schedule. Christopher gave the man his leave, watching Rod wander wearily from the hall. When the young knight was gone, he returned his attention to Jax.

"It would seem that you and I have some waiting to do," he said. "I was never much good at that."

Jax snorted. "Nor me," he said. "What can we do to fill the time?"

"We could suit up the men and have sword practice or battle drills," he suggested. "Pit my men against yours?"

Jax had an annoyed expression on his face. "Never mind that," he said. "Let us discuss games of the mind. At my age, those are more appealing to me."

"Like what?"

"Chess? Fox and Geese? Nine Men's Morris?"

"I should warn you that I am the reigning game champion at Lion-cross."

Jax let out a burst of laughter, a rude sound. "That is because you are the lord and everyone is afraid of what will happen to them should you not be permitted to win," he said. "I am not afraid of you, so be prepared to defend your honor."

Christopher had a massive grin on his face as he went to hunt down his Nine Men's Morris board.

CHAPTER SIXTEEN

Cloryn Castle

I T WAS ODD, really, since their return from Newtown. Odd because Bretton seemed… different somehow. As Allaston shelled a basket of peas from the garden in the sunny kitchen yard, her thoughts revolved around Bretton, who was in the great hall with his men. Even in the kitchen, she could hear voices being raised in the hall. Whatever was being said was clearly a contentious subject.

The day after their return from Newtown, things at Cloryn seemed rather strained. None of Bretton's commanders – Grayton, Teague, or Dallan – would talk to her or so much as look at her. They kept to themselves, moving away quickly when she came around. She knew they didn't approve of her being out of the vault and she knew that Grayton in particular seemed averse to her. She suspected that it was because he felt betrayed. He let her out of the vault only to have her turn around and clobber Bretton over the head with a poker. She wasn't about to apologize for her actions so she, too, stayed clear of the commanders. There was no real cause for them to interact.

So she stayed to the kitchens with Blandings and Uldward, shelling peas and helping bake bread. Even now, nearing noon, the smell of baking bread was heavy in the air of the kitchen yard, wafting over the bailey to entice those who smelled it. It was almost stronger than the stench of the dead army outside the walls, but not quite, making for a rather disgusting smell once the winds changed.

I am not sure I can let go of what I have become.

Those words kept rolling over and over in Allaston's head. She wanted to make the man forget about his vengeance against her father by marrying him, and by being his wife and providing him with heirs, but since the time they'd spent in Newtown and the serious conversations they'd had, she was coming to think that she most definitely felt something for the man. He was such a lost soul and she wanted to help him find his way. He was very funny at times, awkward at others, and frightening at still others. But she could see the man beneath the façade and it was that man she felt something for. It was that man who needed her.

So she continued to shell peas, thinking of Bretton, when she began to hear a good deal of activity coming from the bailey. From her position in the kitchen yard, she couldn't see what the fuss was about but dared to walk to the edge of the kitchen yard, bowl of peas in her hands, to see what was happening. Whatever it was revolved around the gatehouse and she could see men swarming around the portcullis, which was slowly lifting. Curious, and perhaps a bit apprehensive, she wondered what all of the fuss was about. She doubted they were under attack but, still, the uproar was perplexing.

Curious, she stood there and watched, still shelling peas, as men began to emerge from the great hall directly in front of her. She could see Bretton and his commanders make their way towards the gatehouse while the sentries at the portcullis shouted excitedly. She lost sight of Bretton as he disappeared into the crowd of armed men, all of them milling around the gatehouse.

Whatever was happening seemed to be confined to the castle entry so after a few minutes of watching the activity, Allaston grew bored and went back to her stool next to the kitchen door and finished shelling her peas. There was another big basket that was full of unshelled peas so she began shelling those as well. She was halfway through the basket when she caught sight of someone entering the kitchen yard. When she saw who it was her entire manner changed dramatically. She softened and there was a smile already on her lips to greet him.

Bretton came through the gate, his eyes immediately finding Allaston near the kitchen door. She was smiling at him, dressed in the yellow surcoat he had torn down the middle, now mended and with an apron covering the repair. Her long hair was braided, draped over one shoulder, and a kerchief was tied around her head, keeping the dust off her hair and her hair out of her face. She looked, as always, like an angel. That was the only way he could describe her because he'd seen so much hell in his life that he was positive she was his first, and only, glimpse of heaven.

The sight of her did things to him that he'd never experienced before. It was as if his heart was lighter and his mood was better instantly. Something had changed for him since Newtown – if the woman had been on his mind before, now he could think of nothing else. She was never far from his thoughts no matter where he was and, as such, he found himself becoming fiercely protective of her. Just now, in the great hall when Grayton had brought up the fact that she had gotten away with her terrible behavior on the morning they'd left for Newtown, Bretton had reacted just as he'd reacted before – he punched Grayton in the face and sent the man onto the floor.

No one brought up Allaston after that and Bretton knew it was because his men sensed there was much more than a captor/prisoner relationship between them. Even if it was the case, Bretton wouldn't elaborate on it and he wouldn't explain it away. It wasn't any of their affair, anyway. But he knew the uncertainty was making his men edgy and that edginess was beginning to create a divide. He'd been feeling that divide since before Newtown, but now in the aftermath, it had gotten worse.

It was tension between him and his commanders that was interrupted by the commotion at the gatehouse. It had been enough to divert the attention away from his relationship with Allaston. A messenger had evidently ridden to within a few dozen feet of the gatehouse, dropped an envelope that contained a missive, and had just as swiftly left. The army of the dead did its job to frighten away those who would approach Cloryn. Bretton's men ran out to grab the envelope and a couple even gave chase to the messenger, but he was astride a very swift horse and able to lose those who were trailing him. Meanwhile, the envelope was delivered to Bretton.

The first thing he saw on the leather envelope was the seal of Hereford and Worcester burned into the animal hide. *De Lohr*, he thought. Curious, he had gone into the keep with Grayton, Teague, and Dallan trailing after him, opening the envelope by the time he entered the keep. By the time he entered the small, open room, he had broken the seal on the parchment and carefully unrolled it. There was a good deal of writing on it and the first thing he looked at was the signature on the bottom. He could make out de Lohr's signature.

His curiosity grew. He had no idea what message de Lohr would have for him but he soon found out and as he read down the parchment, the veins on his temple began to throb. He was absolutely enraged by what de Lohr had to say, not at all the reaction the earl was going for but one that he had feared. Bretton read the missive four times before turning it over to Grayton, who read it once in its entirety before reading it aloud to Teague and Dallan. As the three commanders discussed the possibilities of de Lohr's missive, Bretton left the room. He had to, or he was sure to get in another confrontation with his commanders. They were amenable to de Lohr's suggestions, he was not. He knew the only reason the commanders were agreeable was because the missive involved removing Allaston from Cloryn, which was something he suspected they were increasingly inclined towards. They wanted her out.

So Bretton found himself in the kitchen yard staring at Allaston as she sat and shelled peas. The mere sight of her gave him pause to breathe, to collect himself. He could feel himself calming. As she smiled at him, he returned the gesture and made his way over to her.

"More peas?" he asked. "I swear I have never eaten so many peas in my entire life until I came here. Is that all that grows in the garden?"

Allaston giggled. "Practically," she said. "Peas, carrots, and a few cabbages. But the peas are my favorite. I like to eat them when they are young and green. They are soft and delicious."

He nodded, grinning because she was. When she coyly lowered her eyes and turned back to her peas, Bretton's attention stayed on her a moment longer before he turned away, leaning against the support beam for the kitchen's roof overhang as he studied the immediate area. He found that he really didn't have to say anything. Their silences had become comfortable ones, as if they were content simply to be next to one another. All the while, however, his mind was reflecting upon de Lohr's missive. He was trying to determine just how much to tell her. Normally, he wouldn't have involved her in his business but because she was mentioned by name in de Lohr's message, he felt she had a right to know something about it.

"I saw some commotion near the gatehouse earlier," Allaston said, breaking into his thoughts. "What was happening?"

Bretton, leaning against the support post, folded his enormous arms against his chest. "We had a messenger," he said casually.

Her head came up and she looked at him curiously. "A messenger?" she asked. "Another message from your cousin?"

Bretton shook his head. "Nay," he replied. After a brief hesitation, he decided to tell her all of it. He couldn't come up with a good reason not to. "It was a message from Christopher de Lohr. It would seem that the Earl of Hereford and Worcester has offered to mediate my dispute with your father. He wants to know my terms to return you to your family."

Allaston set aside the basket of half-shelled peas and stood up. "What are you going to tell him?" she asked. "I do not want to go back, not now."

Bretton glanced at her. "Why not?" he asked. "You had a mind to escape me once."

She calmed down a bit, her expression uncertain. "I know," she said. "But the situation has changed. It is as I told your cousin. If I can deter you from killing my father, then I am more than willing to stay."

Bretton turned to her, looking at her full-on. "Is that the only reason you stay?" he asked softly. "I told you that my vengeance against your father is my own. You shan't change my mind."

Allaston gazed at him, steadily, thinking many things at that moment. He was asking for truth. Perhaps he was even asking her how she felt, as if there was more in her heart than the mere desire to save her father's life. Their conversation in Newtown had been very deep and very revealing. Perhaps he was asking for more than what she was willing to tell him. Allaston has the distinct feeling that he was demanding to know what was in her heart. Simply by the way he was looking at her, she could tell. She began to feel warm and quivery all over.

"What do you want me to say?" she asked quietly. "Do you want me to tell you that somehow, someway, you have grown on me, too? I will tell you that if that is what you wish to hear."

His expression was surprisingly soft. "I only wish to hear it if it is the truth," he said. "Is that why you wish to stay? Because I have grown on you?"

Allaston wasn't comfortable speaking on her feelings when it came to a man. As a woman committed to the cloister from a young age, it was something she had never had to face. She felt a bit embarrassed, that was true, but not so embarrassed that she did not want to answer his question. After a moment, she simply shook her head.

"There is more to it," she said, gazing into his bright blue eyes. "I cannot tell you what more, or how much more, but there is more to it. I want to stay because… because I think you need me somehow. I told you in Newtown that I want to be fond of you but I think I already am."

His eyes roved her lovely face, devouring her as he had never devoured a woman in his life. All things fine and soft and beautiful were standing before him, things he never knew to exist. He never knew feelings like this to exist, something that took his breath away yet made him strong all in the same moment. It was astonishing.

"You told me that you wanted me to give you a reason to love me," he murmured. "How can I do that? What can I possibly do to earn that love?"

Allaston was growing giddy with the conversation, feeling an odd liquid warmth spreading between the two of them, enveloping them both. She's never known anything like it and it was enough to make her feel light-headed. But she didn't mind in the least.

"I... I am not sure," she said. She couldn't help notice that he was moving closer to her. "A man of goodness and mercy would surely earn it. I have asked that you show mercy in your dealings, Bretton, that you spare women and children in your quest to conquer their homes."

He reached out, timidly, and grasped her by the upper arms. His grip was warm, strong, and reassuring. "I told you that I would try," he said. "But even if I do, you will not be there to witness such things. How can I do something that you will witness, something that will please you?"

She peered up at him, his touch causing her heart to race. "Does it mean so much to you to earn my love, then?"

"I would not ask if it did not."

It was a beautiful answer. Allaston gazed up at him, feeling his heat and power enveloping her, thinking it was about the most wonderful thing in the world. The man was a killer, that was true, and by all rights she should not love the man. But she was a woman of religion, and religion taught her to forgive and not to judge. Even though he had done some terrible things, it was truly not her place to judge him. She needed to show him mercy and compassion, too, in the hopes it would bring forth that man, that good man, she knew to be buried deep within him. She opened her mouth to reply but the wind shifted and she caught a whiff of the rotting dead outside the walls. In that stench, she had her answer.

"Bury the dead of Cloryn," she said softly. "It would be a great act of mercy and compassion, Bretton, something I could see. Something I could be proud of. Would you do this for me?"

Bretton didn't outright deny her but she could tell that he was unhappy with her request. The hands on her arms began to caress her, ever so slightly.

"Why would this mean so much to you?" he asked. "You do not know these people. They mean nothing to you."

She fell silent a moment, contemplating her answer. She had to make him understand. "Nay, I do not know them," she said. "But someone did. Someone mayhap even loved them. Think on it this way. If it was your father out there, wouldn't you hope that someone would have the decency to bury the man and put him to rest?"

He let go of her arms, his bright eyes studying her, deliberating on her reply. With her calm questions, she was making him face the most horrific thing in his life rationally, without anger or fear. It was not a pleasing or simple answer that he gave her.

"As far as I know, no one did," he said quietly. "My father was left on a pole for all to see and I do not know how long he remained there. Everyone knows that de Velt left his victims impaled for at least six months. But what he did with them after that, no one seems to know. More than likely, he threw the bones into a mass grave or into a river."

Allaston sighed heavily. "But why do you leave them up?" she asked the same question she had asked before. "You are not hurting my father by doing this. You are not even sending him a message because he truthfully doesn't care. I told you that the only way to truly hurt him would be to put me on a pole so he can see me when he comes to Cloryn, but you would not do it. I even gave you the opportunity."

His expression was one of displeasure. "You were counting on the fact that I would not do it," he said. "You knew I would not. You did it to bait me and to humiliate me in front of my men."

Allaston shook her head. "I did not mean to humiliate you," she said truthfully. "At the time, I truly meant what I said."

"That may be, but you caused me some dishonor with your behavior. Surely you realize that."

"Then tell me how I can prove my remorse?"

His attention focused on her, thinking of all the ways she could make good on her apology, but they were ways she would more than likely not agree to. In fact, she was quite likely to fight him on it because his ideas involved naked bodies. He had to think of something she would be agreeable to, something they would both find satisfaction from. He was on such unsteady ground with her, not knowing what to say, unfamiliar with the art of gentle conversation. He wanted to be polite and courteous, but it was utterly foreign to him. He simply wasn't an eloquent man so he said the first thing that came to mind.

"No more peas," he said, pointing to the basket she had set down. "I will eat carrots, but no more peas."

Allaston grinned, turning to look at the basket he was pointing to. "I must prepare those or they will rot," he said. "You will not have to eat whatever I make. Is that truly all you can think of to make amends? No more peas?"

He shrugged his big shoulders, eyeing her after a moment. There was a hint of mischief in his expression. "I might forgive you for a kiss."

The statement has been spoken almost fearfully, as if he knew she was going to deny him even before he asked. It was an utterly innocent statement, too, coming from a man who had no more innocence. It had been taken from him long ago. But not everything in him was ruined. Allaston could see it in his expression. There was still something good and fair underneath. But he was also being a bit impish about it and she played along.

"Cheek or hand?" she asked.

He cocked is head. "What do you mean?"

She signed with mock impatience, as though he was an ignorant fool. "The kiss," she said. "Where do you want it? Cheek or hand?"

He could see she was jesting with him. "You can plant it on my arse."

Allaston shrieked in disgust, trying not to giggle as she did so. "I am *not* kissing your arse," she said. "It is the cheek or the hand."

Bretton was fighting off a grin. "Those are my only choices?"

Allaston nodded firmly. "Your only choices," she confirmed. "In fact, if you…."

She was cut off when he suddenly grabbed her, slanting his warm mouth over hers. Allaston was startled, initially a little scared, but she quickly succumbed to his hot, seeking lips. He suckled her lower lip gently, running a tongue over it, and Allaston shuddered. Fueled by her response, Bretton's onslaught grew more intense and his arms tightened around her.

Although the initial grab had been rough and tactless, the kiss was searing, speaking of untapped desire. Bretton had never kissed a woman in a manner that wasn't pure lust or physical need, so this was something quite different to him. He was kissing her because he wanted to, because it seemed like the right thing to do, and because doing so somehow satisfied something deep inside him. She was warm and luscious, and so very soft, her body against his. He was losing himself in the kiss, letting himself go, when Uldward the cook suddenly came through the doorway. The next thing Bretton realized, he was standing about five feet away from Allaston with his heart pounding in his ears.

Allaston looked a bit startled as well. She gazed at Bretton, wiping at the moisture on her swollen lips. As Uldward bustled around in the kitchen yard on a hunt for something he evidently needed, she eyed the man, knowing he had seen them in a passionate embrace. Her cheeks began to flame as she struggled to pretend that Uldward hadn't seen any of it.

"What do you intend to do about de Lohr's missive?" she asked, simply to move onto another subject far away from the heated kiss. "Will you respond to him?"

Bretton had the back of his hand to his mouth. He could still taste her on his flesh and he wanted to keep that taste as long as possible. He could smell her, too. She smelled like flowers.

"It is none of his business," he said. "De Lohr has no cause to interfere in something that does not concern him."

Allaston's head was still swimming from his kiss so she wandered back over to her stool, next to the pea basket, and sat heavily.

"I find it quite surprising that my father asked him to broker my release," she said. "As I said, my father has no allies. He keeps to himself."

There was something in that statement that caught Bretton's attention. "Then the question is *why* he would involve de Lohr," he said thoughtfully. "Why ask someone you do not know to mediate a conflict? There must be a reason."

Allaston began shelling the remainder of the peas. "Maybe he did not want come himself," she said. "Mayhap he was fearful of what would happen if he did. I'm sure he fears that you will harm me. Mayhap he believed that de Lohr can better negotiate my release given the fact that you are not angry with de Lohr."

Bretton looked at her with a cocked eyebrow. "I wasn't angry with him until he sent his missive," he said. "No man will stand between me and Jax de Velt, and especially not Christopher de Lohr. De Lohr had better be careful that I do not kill him in order to get to de Velt."

Allaston said nothing. Her focus was on her peas. She wasn't going to argue with him about his vengeance towards her father any more. He knew how she felt about it but he was determined to go through with it anyway. At least, he said so. She could not give up hope that she could change his mind. She could only hope that God would work a miracle in her favor.

"When you reply to his missive, will you tell him that I wish to remain here?" she asked. "I am sure he will not believe you, but you will make sure to tell him, won't you?"

Bretton's gaze lingered on her. "It is your father I want," he said. "I will make sure de Lohr understands that. Your purpose in this situation has been pre-determined from the beginning. You are to draw your father to me."

She looked up. "Is that what you will tell him?"

Bretton drew in a long, pensive breath. "I will tell him that if he wants to negotiate, then he must see me face to face. That is the only way I will conduct business with your father or with de Lohr."

Allaston looked down to her peas. She didn't have much more to say to that so she let the subject die. Bretton seemed preoccupied, anyway, now thinking of de Lohr's missive and not of the heated kiss they had shared. As she sat there and harvested tiny green peas, Bretton walked over to her, gathered her dirty right hand to kiss it gently, and then promptly turned and headed out of the kitchen yard. Before he could get away completely, Allaston called after him.

"Bretton?"

He paused, turning to look at her. "Aye?"

Allaston looked up from her peas, her green-eyed gaze swallowing him whole. "Please consider burying the dead of Cloryn," she said. "If it was your father up there, you would want someone to bury him. That man of mercy... let me catch a glimpse of him today. It would mean a great deal to me."

Without another word, Bretton left the yard. Allaston wasn't sure her request had much impact with him simply from the stubborn expression on his face so she went back to her peas, hoping that someday he might have more respect for her requests.

Within the hour, the army of the dead outside of the walls started to come down.

⚃

BY THE EVENING meal, the smell of burning bodies filled the air, mingling with the smell of roasting meat. The pig that had been butchered a few days prior was now being roasted over an open flame, creating a stench with the burning dead that truly had to be experienced to be believed.

Although Allaston has asked him to bury the bodies, Bretton had decided to burn them and bury the ashes because there was very little left of the bodies as it was. It was easier to burn and bury the ashes. As Allaston stayed to the kitchen to make sure the food was amply, and properly, prepared, Bretton was in the keep in the entry-level room that he had claimed for his own.

Sitting at the head of the long, scrubbed table, he had a quill in his left hand as ink and sand sat off to his left within easy reach. A piece of vellum was spread out before him, a section he had torn off from another missive he found at Cloryn addressed to the former commander. He was scribing a missive to de Lohr, basically telling the man to stop protecting de Velt and send the man to him. He proceeded to tell de Lohr, under no uncertain terms, that Allaston's life would be in danger until de Velt presented himself. He was just finishing up the missive when he heard boots approaching, glancing up to see Grayton, Teague, and Dallan approach from the keep entry.

He put his head back down, finishing his message, as his commanders entered the room. The strain between him and his commanders had been great ever since he had returned from Newtown and he wasn't particularly in the mood to speak with them. He'd done enough of that earlier in the day when they'd had a fine yelling match in the great hall. As he continued to write, the three commanders sat down at the table, remaining silent as Bretton finished scribing. When he paused enough to make them think he was finished, Grayton spoke.

"Is that the response to de Lohr?" he asked.

Bretton nodded, his eyes on the parchment before him. "It is," he said, unfriendly. "I have told de Lohr not to interfere in what does not concern him and to produce Jax de Velt on my doorstep or Lady Allaston will suffer. Grayton, prepare a messenger to send this immediately."

Grayton's eyes assessed Bretton. "I will," he said, "but we must speak with you first."

Bretton grunted sharply. "If you are going to fight with me about placing Lady Allaston in the vault again, then my answer is still no," he said, finally looking up at them. "What else could you three possibly have to say to me beyond that?"

Teague, who was the most level-headed of the group, spoke. "The men are concerned, Bretton," he said honestly. "Before the yelling started in the great hall, we were going to relay those concerns, so I will relay them now. Our next target is Comen Castle and we were supposed to be there now, as per your word. But it seems that you have grown complacent and Lady Allaston seems to be at the center of it. You must understand that perception is everything, Bretton, and she is perceived as having bewitched you with her wiles. The men grow increasingly suspicious and if you allow her to roam the castle freely, it is quite possible that her life will seriously be in danger purely because they believe her to be a threat to the dreams of wealth you promised them."

So it was out. Now Bretton heard the real reason behind his commanders' aversion to Allaston because earlier in the hall, they hadn't been truthful about it. They had made it seem as if they, personally, wanted her imprisoned. The problem was that Bretton could see the logic and he believed every word Teague said. He knew how mercenaries thought. If they perceived something as a threat, they would stop at nothing to eliminate it. That being the case, it was time for total truth between Bretton and his men. Perhaps if he could make them understand his mindset, he could sway them to his side. Right now, they sided with the men. He could see that plainly. Rather than fight with them about it any longer, he decided to try reason.

"Their dreams of wealth have not been quashed, no matter what they think," he said. "I am planning on moving on to Comen the day after tomorrow, which should give us enough time to prepare the army. As for Lady Allaston… I must be completely honest with you for I fear I have not been. I have treated her like a personal possession, a personal whipping post, and I have not let any of you get close to her. She represents all I hate and every reason behind our conquest of de Velt's properties."

Teague leaned forward on the table, his serious focus on Bretton. "There is more to it than that," he said quietly. "We can all see it. When you tell us to take down the bodies posted outside of the walls, bodies you were determined to keep out there for six months, then we can only assume the lady has had some hand in this decision."

Bretton's expression was guarded. "Why would you assume that?"

Teague lifted his dark eyebrows. "Because we all saw her weep at the feet of the former lord and lady of Cloryn," he said. "She was very upset about it. Must I really explain this, Bretton? It is apparent that you are doing it to appease her."

Bretton shrugged. "Does it matter why I have ordered the bodies cut down?" he wanted to know. "I seem to remember a battle commander telling me that the smell was unappetizing. God's Blood, I cannot seem to please any of you these days – if I cut the bodies down, I am appeasing Lady Allaston, and if I do not throw her back in the vault, then Grayton is furious with me. When did every command I make fall under such scrutiny? I grow weary of having to justify myself constantly."

Teague nodded, glancing at Grayton. He had been at the head of the anti-Allaston campaign and had been speaking out the most against her. Teague also knew why and it was time to settle the matter once and for all because the conflict between them and their liege was growing unhealthy. It was time to air their grievances and hopefully solve them.

"You cannot blame Grayton for his concern over the lady," Teague said. "The woman tried to kill you once. She could very well be luring you into a false sense of security with her feminine charms so you will trust her. She only needs to get a poker in her hand again, or worse, to do some real damage."

Bretton shook his head as if the entire suggestion was ridiculous. "She will not kill me."

Grayton couldn't remain silent any longer. "She has tried once and she will try it again, but you do not want to listen to me."

It was a struggle for Bretton not to become angry with him. "I will not repeat the shouting match we had in the hall earlier," he told the man. "I appreciate the fact that you are concerned for my health, Grayton, but I will not put the woman in the vault so you may as well stop bringing the subject up. Besides, I do not believe that is the truth behind your grudge against her. I believe it is because you let her out of the vault and then she betrayed your kindness by assaulting me with the poker. If that is the case, then you need to move beyond that humiliation, which was no humiliation at all. I am not upset about it and you should not be, either."

Grayton simply shook his head and looked away. Bretton watched the man, feeling remorseful with the situation between them because before Allaston had come into their lives, he and Grayton had been good friends. He trusted the man. Now, there was tension, and he was sorry. But he wouldn't dwell on it. Still, there was more he had to say.

"I will, however, calmly address the subject of Lady Allaston," he said. "Mayhap you feel as if I have left you out of my decision making process when it comes to her, and you could be correct. As I said before, she is my captive and she is my property, and I have considered the woman a great deal and how best to use her against her father. I believe I have a solution."

Teague was the only one who didn't seem guarded in his reaction. Grayton was still sitting there, his eyes averted, and Dallan was much more a follower than a leader. He was simply listening to what had been said. Therefore, Teague headed the conversation.

"Proceed, Bretton," he said. "We are listening."

So he had their attention. Bretton didn't even know where to start. He didn't want to come across as weak or indecisive or, worse, foolish. He decided to simply come out with it all but convince his men that there was less of his emotion involved in the situation than there was. It would be a struggle not to come across as emotionally invested in her because he was. He wanted his men to believe that she was a tool to gain his ends and nothing more.

"I have decided to hit de Velt where it will hurt him the most," he said. "Holding Lady Allaston captive will not suffice. Killing her will bring me nothing but a dead captive. I must strike and strike hard at the man. I have therefore decided to marry Lady Allaston, impregnate her, and breed an army of de Llion sons who will be brought up to hate de Velt as much as I do. An enemy will be bred from the very blood that flows through de Velt's veins. According to Lady Allaston, de Velt is quite the family man these days. I intend to infiltrate that family."

It was a brilliant, unemotional summation and Bretton was rather proud of himself for it. By the time he was finished with his speech, Grayton was looking at him, too, and he could see a semblance of approval in their expressions. It was Dallan who finally spoke.

"Humiliation," he confirmed. "You will humiliate de Velt through his daughter."

Bretton nodded. "Exactly," he said. "Do you understand that logic?"

Teague and Dallan nodded but Grayton wasn't so sure. "You would marry the daughter of your enemy?" he asked. "She will only hate you more and possibly deny you sons."

Bretton groaned inwardly. "Then tell me what *you* would do with her, Grayton?" he asked, with some irritation. "You once told me I had a valuable bargaining tool in her, but all that seems to have changed. When I had her in the vault, you wanted to release her, so I permitted it. Now, you do not trust her and you want to put her back into the vault again. The messages you are sending me are both confusing and infuriating. Tell me what you would do with her and tell me now. I grow weary of your constant contradictions."

Grayton, with all eyes on him, was defensive and uncertain. After a moment, he finally shook his head, exasperated that Bretton, who so often took his advice, had been choosing to ignore his suggestions when it came to Allaston. He was coming to feel left out of Bretton's decisions, which was perhaps the root of his problem.

"I have already told you what I think you should do with her but you do not want to listen," he said. "Marry the woman and fill her full of your sons, but do not be surprised if those sons turn against their father. You are playing a dangerous game by allowing the enemy so close to you."

Bretton watched the man as he fidgeted angrily. "I am doing what battle commanders have been doing for centuries," he said. "I am marrying the enemy to achieve my ends."

Grayton knew his argument against the lady was at an end. He could see it in Bretton's features. "Your ends are to capture de Velt's castles," he reminded him, embittered. "You promised us the wealth from these raids and unless you want a rebellion on your hands, I would suggest we continue our conquest before you marry the woman and live your life with her. *We* are your priority, Bretton, and not de Velt's daughter. As you said, she is a possession like a castle or a horse – she is merely a tool. If you delay too long with your focus on the lady, then you risk your men growing restless and either turning against you or deserting you."

Bretton's eyes darkened. "Are you threatening me?"

Grayton shook his head as Teague stood up, placing himself between Bretton and Grayton. He'd seen that look on Bretton before, always before he lashed out. Teague didn't want any bloodshed between them because it would end up destroying everything they'd worked for.

"He is not," Teague assured him. "He merely speaks the truth. The men are already growing restless, waiting to march on the next castle. You said you were planning on heading to Comen in two days. Let us focus on that. We will have the men prepared to leave at dawn the day after tomorrow. How far is Comen Castle from here?"

Teague knew the answer but he was trying to distract Bretton from his deadly glare against Grayton. As he hoped, Bretton's focus shifted.

"It will take us a day at most," he said, tearing his gaze away from Grayton and returning his attention to the message on the table before him. "Comen will be under siege by the next morning."

"Excellent," Teague said, motioning to Dallan to remove Grayton from the room. "We will spread the word. The men will be happy to hear it."

Bretton had returned to his missive but he called out before the commanders left the room. "Grayton," he said, and all three paused in the doorway. "Do not forget to send me a messenger. I must deliver this missive to de Lohr today."

Grayton, upset and disillusioned, simply nodded. "Aye, my lord."

"And, Grayton?"

"Aye?"

Bretton's head came up, the bright blue eyes narrowed. "Make sure the men understand that if Lady Allaston is harmed or molested in any way, in any fashion, my wrath shall be deadly. I will strike first and ask questions later. Is that clear?"

"It is, my lord."

"Then go."

Grayton left the room, followed by the other two. When Bretton heard the entry to the keep open and then softly close again, he tossed down his quill and ran his hand through his hair in a pensive gesture. He wasn't sure if his commanders were supportive of his marriage to Allaston and that concerned him. Without their support, he would have a difficult time maintaining the fealty of the army.

But without Allaston, he would be nothing at all. Difficult choices were coming in his future. He could sense it.

CHAPTER SEVENTEEN

Comen Castle

O UT OF ALL the castles so far on Bretton's list of conquest, Comen seemed to have fallen the fastest. A rather large, spread-out castle with inadequate walls and a very vulnerable postern gate near the kitchens, Comen fell in only two days. On the evening of the second day, the hall and stables were in flames and Bretton's men were mounting the walls, killing everything that moved. At sunset, when the sky was turning shades of orange and yellow, the blood and destruction of Comen was something unparalleled in recent times. It was as if the very gates of Hell had opened up, revealing the horror of Satan's realm inside. In truth, Comen, that night, became Hell personified. The Devil had expanded his dominion and no one was safe because of it.

The soldiers defending Comen had suffered the worst. Bretton's men had rounded up the ones who were able-bodied and those wounded but still strong enough to stand, and crowded them all into one corner of the bailey while gangs of Bretton's men had cut down trees in the nearby forest, making posts to impale the submissive army on. The impalings began just after dark and the agony of those who were put to the stakes filled the smoky, cold air.

The keep of Comen had held for another couple of hours after sunset, finally being breached when Bretton's men had managed to reach the entry door by way of ladders, as the retractable staircase had been burned away. Unfortunately, the door was solid oak and after a half-hour of chipping away at it to make the wood raw enough to flame, they ignited the door and it burned steadily for an hour, finally falling away to ash sometime before midnight. Teague and several de Llion mercenaries were the first ones into the keep, rounding up the lady of Comen and her three frightened daughters.

Bretton was with Grayton and a few soldiers, coming in after the damage had been done to take stock of what was left. The hall was almost in total ruin, as were the stables, but several fine horses had been saved that Bretton immediately laid claim to. The rest of the bailey seemed relatively intact and that included a very nice armory. Bretton was inspecting the kitchen yards, noting that the cooks, or someone, had destroyed most of the supplies once the castle began to fall, when Dallan appeared.

"My lord," he addressed Bretton formally. "We have the commander of Comen. Would you like to interrogate him before we put him to the stake?"

Bretton's gaze was lingering on the castle garden where there seemed to be an abundance of peas before, shuddering in disgust at the peas, turning to Dallan. He noted that Dallan seemed particularly weary, covered in soot and sweat.

"I will see him," he said. "Where is he?"

Dallan pointed to a group near the smoldering ruins of the hall. "Over there," he said as he and Bretton headed in that direction. "It seems his father is with him, too, a man who was one of de Velt's original commanders."

Bretton looked at him with interest. "Indeed?" he said. "What is his name?"

"Sir Ares de Gault," he replied. "His son, the garrison commander, is Sir Augustus de Gault. It is Augustus' family that we took from the keep, his wife and three daughters."

Bretton could spy the two beaten knights ahead, surrounded by his soldiers. Being in possession of one of de Velt's original knights was quite an unexpected event and he wasn't quite sure how he felt about it.

"Where are the women?" he asked.

"I think the men have them."

A note of warning sounded in Bretton's head. "Are they having their fill of the women?"

"I believe so."

Bretton suddenly came to a halt. "Go stop them," he said, giving Dallan a shove. "Tell them not to touch the women until I give permission. Hurry and do this now. Then, I want you to take the women to the kitchen and keep them there until I arrive."

Dallan nodded and ran off to find where the soldiers had taken the women. He didn't give a second thought about Bretton's command, mostly because he assumed Bretton wanted to see the women before anything was done. Perhaps he wanted to interrogate them or perhaps he even wanted them for himself, but that would have been unusual. Bretton had never taken a woman by force in all the time Dallan had known him. But he didn't give the command much thought beyond that. He simply moved to carry it out.

Bretton watched Dallan head off, wondering if he was too late to prevent his men from defiling the women. He kept thinking about what Allaston had said about showing mercy. The concept was foreign to him but he sought to try. So many things Allaston had spoken of were alien in his world, compassion and mercy being the two largest issues, but he understood that those two attributes meant a good deal to her. Her words, spoken in Newtown, were haunting him:

Mayhap you will think of mercy the next time you are faced with a frightened woman whose only crime was living in a castle you want as your own. Throw her in the vault, or do whatever you have to do in order to keep her from your men, but I would pray that whatever comes, you consider showing mercy in all things. He seriously wondered if he could.

But he pushed those thoughts aside as he came upon the commander of Comen and his aged father, an original de Velt knight. A man who had helped de Velt conquer the Marches and perhaps even a knight who'd had a hand in killing his father. His initial reaction to an original de Velt knight had been curious but ambivalent, but now he was starting to feel some anger. Pure, unbridled anger that fed off his sense of vengeance. Ignoring the son altogether, he walked straight to the old knight to get a very close look at him. He wanted to see the face of those who had killed his father.

As Bretton scrutinized the old man, he was met with a fearless expression. The old knight was big, perhaps a bit round, but he had been very muscular in his youth. He was still handsome as far as old men went, with very big hands. Bretton looked into the old knight's eyes and saw nothing but courage and resignation. He wasn't sure if it impressed or infuriated him. Here was a man who had seen all of de Velt's dealings, who had experienced everything that had ruined Bretton's life. The man before him, essentially, had made Bretton what he was. A killer.

"You are Sir Ares de Gault?" Bretton finally asked.

The old man with a full head of salt-and-pepper hair nodded. "I am."

"I am told you are one of de Velt's original knights."

De Gault merely nodded, the gesture of a man who saw no need to announce his accomplishments in life. It was an understated gesture, but Bretton merely cocked an eyebrow.

"This is a rather momentous moment for me," he said. "I never thought to meet one of de Velt's original knights."

The old knight regarded him carefully. "And so you have," he said. "Now that you have me where you want me, what are your intentions?"

He spoke with strength, which fueled Bretton's respect for him. But it also fueled that five year old boy in side of him, the one who had lost his father at the hands of men such as de Gault. The questions that came next were natural.

"Were you part of de Velt's siege at Four Crosses Castle?" he asked.

De Gault nodded. "I was part of every siege de Velt planned," he said. "Why do you ask?"

Bretton could see hardness in his eyes, the ruthless stare of a man who had killed and killed again. No remorse to his answer, but no pride, either. It was simply a statement of fact, and Bretton's rage began to build. He didn't answer the man's question, not yet. But he would in time. He wanted this man, this knight of de Velt's, to know why he was here. He wanted to see his expression when he saw that retribution for all of his past sins had come.

"Did you notice what we are doing to your army?" he asked, pointing off to the destroyed gatehouse. "I am employing the same tactics that you and de Velt used in your conquest."

The old knight's gaze moved across the bailey, to the gatehouse, where men were being led to slaughter. He could hear the screams and groans of men as they were impaled.

"I see," he said after a moment. "I assume you are going to do the same thing to me."

Bretton's expression remained impassive. "It would be justice for all of those people you put to the pole back in your day," he said, "my father included."

That brought a flicker of a reaction to the old knight. A flash of understanding, of realization, and nothing more. Now, the old knight knew why the enemy had come and things were starting to make some sense.

"Who was your father?" he asked calmly.

Bretton shook his head, feeling increasingly angry and embittered by the conversation. "Just a knight who was protecting his home," he said. "You killed my father and, as a result, my mother killed herself and my sister. I was the only one who survived but because there was no one to take care of me, as a child, I was sold into a life of unimaginable horror. The only thing that kept me alive was knowing that, someday, I would be able to exact my revenge against de Velt. And here I am, preparing to exact my revenge against you and your family. How does it feel knowing that you will watch as I put your son and his family on poles? I will make you watch them as they squirm and bleed and die.

How does it feel, de Gault?"

The old knight's jaw was ticking slightly, the only indication of his emotion. He knew better than to beg. "I am an old man," he said. "I have done things I am not proud of and if it is vengeance you seek, then I ask you to punish me. It is I who deserve it. Spare my family, for they have done nothing wrong."

"My father did nothing wrong, either, but you killed him anyway!" Bretton exploded, yelling so loudly that it ruffled the front of de Gault's hair. "My father was defending what belonged to him but you and de Velt took it anyway and you killed him for doing his duty. To Hell with you, de Gault. To Hell with you and the others who committed such atrocities against my family because now you are going to know what I suffered. You are going to feel that anguish, too."

De Gault was a steely old man. He met Bretton's gaze without emotion, at least outwardly, but the dark eyes were flickering with horror.

"I am sorry for what we did to your father," he said evenly. "I am sorry for your pain, but it was a byproduct of conquest. If I could take it back, I would, but I beg you to spare my family. Please do not make them pay for my sins."

Bretton was close to throttling the old man. He really was. How dare he beg for the life of his family when he, in his prime, would hear the pleadings of others to spare their loved ones but would pay no mind to them! Yet, somewhere in that swirling mist of turmoil that was in Bretton's mind, a ray of light shone forth. *I believe there is some good still left in you.* Allaston's word echoed in his head. Was it true? Or was he truly all monster, all Devil?

It seemed, to him, as if this was a pivotal moment. When he told Allaston of events at Comen Castle, he wanted to be truthful about it. He didn't want to lie. Therefore, he needed to show mercy when he truly didn't want to. But perhaps that was the true sign of a decent man – showing compassion when one was reluctant to. Pondering that very question, he turned to the nearest soldier.

"Keep these two here until I decide what's to be done with them," he told the man. "Under no circumstances will you listen to anyone else's orders on their fate but mine. Is that understood?"

The soldier nodded. "Aye, my lord."

Bretton had meant Grayton or Dallan, the two commanders who were very eager about putting men on spikes. Bretton didn't want anything done with those knights, especially de Velt's original knight, until he'd had a chance to decide their fates personally. Meanwhile, he headed to the kitchen to see to the lady of Comen and her daughters.

As he passed through the kitchen yard, which was twice the size of Cloryn's kitchen yard and included a big chicken coop that his soldiers were raiding, he headed into the kitchen structure itself. Oddly, the box-shaped kitchen was built from a mixture of rock and wood, with a thatched roof that could easily catch fire. Poking his head inside, he could see a big bread oven and a butcher's block. But there were no women waiting for him and he was coming to think that he'd been too late in sending Dallan to stave off his men's lust.

Just as he was emerging from the kitchen, he heard a commotion off to his right and saw Dallan rounding the keep with a woman and thee girls in tow. The girls were weeping hysterically as the mother tried to comfort them, especially the oldest girl, who looked to be around six years of age. The mother was practically carrying her as the girl wept. As they drew closer, Bretton could see that the girl's gown was badly torn.

Bretton stood there impassively, arms folded across his broad chest as they approached. Silently, he indicated for Dallan to take the women into the kitchen structure. Once the women were inside, Bretton had Dallan and the soldiers vacate the kitchen and take station outside in the kitchen yard until they were needed further. Then, Bretton went into the kitchen were the four women were trying to comfort one another.

It was a distressing scene to watch. The mother was being mostly stoic about the entire thing but it was clear she was quite terrified. Bretton had never given any thought to that kind of fear before but, because of Allaston, he was noticing now. The younger girls were perhaps five and four years of age, respectively, and they were clinging to each other in terror. After several moments of watching the group, Bretton cleared his throat softly.

"You, lady," he said quietly. "What happened to your daughter?"

He pointed to the eldest girl with the torn dress. The mother, quivering, responded.

"The enemy soldiers did this," she said. She wasn't accusing, simply stating a fact. "They took her to sport."

Bretton eyed the pale young girl with a big bruise on her left cheek. "Did they accomplish their task?" he asked. "Or did they simply beat her?"

The lady sighed heavily. "One of them mostly accomplished the task," she said, trying not to cry. "But the others were prevented from following suit. It could have been much worse."

She was trying very hard to be brave, which strangely impressed him. He saw something of Allaston there.

"What of the other two?" he asked. "Are they intact?"

The lady nodded. "They are," she replied, now getting a better look at him. "Whom may I have the honor of addressing, please?"

Bretton shook his head. "My name is not important," he replied. "Suffice it to say that I am the new Lord of Comen and you and your daughters are my prisoners. Do you comprehend, madam?"

The woman nodded respectfully. "Indeed I do, my lord," she replied. "We are your humble servants. May… may I ask a question?"

For a woman whose home had just been overrun and her daughter raped, she was exceptionally brave and level-headed. A measure of respect sprouted for the woman.

"Not until I have finished with my questions," he said. "You will tell me your name and the names of your children."

The lady nodded. "I am Lady Amalia de Gault," she said, then indicated her daughters in order from the eldest to the youngest. "These are my daughters Lucy, Isla, and Aurora."

Bretton eyed the girls, who were still quite shaken. "No sons?"

Lady Amalia shook her head. "None living, my lord," she replied. "There was one, but he died in infancy last year."

Bretton absorbed the information. Strange that he was starting to see these women as living, thinking creatures and not objects. Usually, those he conquered were simply items, possessions to be had. With this foursome, he had names and he had a tragic event in their past. He was feeling emotion whether or not he wanted to.

Please show mercy....

"You had a question to ask me, madam," he said. "What is it?"

Lady Amalia maintained her composure as she spoke. "I would simply like to inquire as to the condition of my husband," she asked. "We saw the men taken away and saw... saw what was done to them. I would like to know if my husband was..."

She trailed off, trying to find the right words, and Bretton interrupted her. "Impaled?" he supplied.

The woman was incredibly brave, nodding stoically. "Aye, my lord."

Bretton shook his head. "Nay, he is not among them," he replied. "I have your husband and his father held in another location. I have not yet decided their fate."

For the first time, Lady Amalia showed some emotion. "My lord," she said. "I understand that we are your prisoners and you may do with us as you will, but I was wondering... I was hoping... might I see my husband one last time? I would consider it a great show of mercy and would be forever grateful, no matter what comes."

A great show of mercy.

There was that word again. He looked at the family of girls. There was no point in killing them or letting his men have them. He remembered something Allaston had said to him once, that it could have quite easily been her castle he had conquered and then she would have been fodder for his men. Looking at these girls, he could see Allaston among them, terrified and cowering, and he didn't like that thought one bit.

God's Bones, what is happening to me? Am I becoming weak in my old age? Is that what emotion does to a man, weaken him? Or does it create bonds so strong that a wife would risk my wrath by asking to see her husband one last time? He wondered.

"Remain here and do not move," he told them. "If you do, I will kill you. Is that clear?"

Lady Amalia nodded and Bretton left the structure, ducking underneath the low doorway and emerging into the kitchen yard where Dallan and several soldiers were waiting. He went to Dallan.

"Bring the two knights to me," he told the man. "Make sure they are both stripped of all weaponry and armaments."

Dallan nodded, heading off to complete his orders. Meanwhile, Bretton sent the soldiers gathered in the kitchen yard back out to the bailey where all the action was happening. The men left without question, happy to get back to the process of securing the castle and destroying their enemy. When they were gone, Bretton stood in the kitchen yard, alone for several minutes, until Dallan returned with the prisoners.

The old knight's expression never changed but the younger knight, who wasn't so much young as he was an adult male who had seen at least twenty-five years, appeared rather anxious. Bretton knew why – if Bretton had a wife and three daughters held captive, he would have been anxious, too. Crooking his finger at the men, he indicated for them to follow him to the kitchen structure. When the three of them reached the doorway leading into the warm, cluttered kitchen, Bretton stood back and indicated for the two knights to enter first. They did, and Bretton could hear the squeals of delight and relief as he entered behind them.

Bretton stood just inside the doorway, watching Lady Amalia hug her husband tightly. The woman's stoic demeanor had broken down and she was weeping softly, kissing his cheeks, her hands on his face, studying him closely in an expression that was nothing short of adoring.

As Bretton watched, he realized that he wanted to see that in Allaston's expression when she looked at him, too. He wanted that great, all-encompassing adoration that came with true love, something he'd always believed to be a fool's dream until now. Watching Lady Amalia and her husband, he wanted what they had. He wanted that fool's dream, too.

In fact, the entire family was hugging and weeping, and Bretton's heart began to break, just a little. He remembered having that kind of love with his mother and father, too, a love that kept them safe and comforted no matter what happened in life. Even if Bretton was to kill the two men, or the entire family for that matter, they still would have shared something he himself had only had a fleeting taste of – true and pure love. All men searched for it but only the good, the true and spirited man, ever found it.

But he was not a true and spirited man. He was a man who had let vengeance and hatred eat him from the inside out. He was damaged and broken in many ways, whilst Allaston, who had lived a life of such love as he was seeing before him, was true and pure in many ways. She was, in fact, too good for him and it was only just occurring to him now that he did not deserve a woman such as her. She deserved better than what he was. She deserved that love that all women would be grateful for. At that moment, his heart, which was a closely guarded and fragile thing, shattered into a million pieces because he knew he didn't deserve what he so badly wanted.

Allaston.

As the family before him hugged and wept softly, Bretton knew what he had to do. He couldn't bring himself to destroy such purity, such unbridled emotion. It was so very rare and he hadn't the right to destroy it no matter how envious he was of it. No matter if that old knight, one of de Velt's original knights, had taken it from him. Allaston had been right in so many ways. Killing her father, or any of her father's original knights, wouldn't bring his family back again. It wouldn't even make him happy again. It would just be more deaths in a long line of many, deaths that would never bring fulfillment to anyone. With that stark realization, as the pieces of his heart scattered to the wind, never to be reclaimed, he cleared his throat softly.

"You will all listen to me and listen well," he said. "You will remain in this kitchen. If I see one of you outside of it, even in the kitchen yard, I will kill the lot of you. Is that clear?"

The younger knight, the father, still clutching his wife, nodded. "It is, my lord," he said in a beautiful, deep voice.

Bretton eyed the man. He felt such envy for what he had. Something Bretton now realized he would never have.

"Stay hidden and stay low," he said. "I will close the door to the kitchen but there may be soldiers who enter, looking for valuables. That being the case, you must stay hidden. When night comes, I will come for you, but until then, remain out of sight. If you do not, your lives will be at risk. Do you understand what I have told you?"

The younger knight nodded again. "Aye, my lord," he said. "We will hide ourselves."

Bretton nodded shortly but he didn't say another word. He couldn't. He was all broken up inside. Leaving the kitchen structure, he returned to the bailey where his men were impaling what was left of de Gault's army. An army of the dead and dying once again rose outside the walls of Comen Castle as it did twenty-five years ago when de Velt had done the same thing. When Bretton was finished supervising that madness, he had his men settle down in the bailey into individual groups with a cooking fire between them, cooking their booty of stolen chickens and other ill-gotten food stuffs. It was Bretton's way of avoiding anyone using the kitchen where the old knight and his family were hiding out.

His men drank and ate into the night while Comen's army, on spikes outside of the walls, groaned and gasped into the darkness, men dying out like lights being snuffed, lives dimming one by one. Bretton remained with his commanders around a fire of their own, eating and drinking as if all was well between them again, with no mention of

Allaston or the troubles they had experienced because of her. Talk was on their next target, Erwood Castle, and Bretton assured them that they would march on Erwood once Comen was secured.

Bretton decided that Grayton should remain at Comen to oversee the rebuild, and Grayton was more than happy to comply because Comen was a truly big and rich castle. With Grayton appeased, Bretton could think a bit more clearly. His thoughts were on the family in the kitchens, hiding out, waiting for his return, until Grayton brought up the subject of the fate of the commander of Comen and his family.

Bretton looked at Grayton, realizing he was going to have to lie to the man. In order to show mercy, he was going to have to be under-handed about it unless he wanted real trouble on his hands. It seemed rather ironic that in order to do something good, he had to do something bad.

"I am sure you all saw the older knight that we captured," he said, looking at all three commanders as he spoke. "He was, in fact, an original knight of Jax de Velt and he was present when Four Crosses Castle was sieged. He more than likely had a hand in killing my father, so I consider his capture a stunning stroke of luck. Therefore, I am keeping the family alive until I decide what to do with them. My first thought is to kill the family and leave the old knight alive to watch, but I am mulling over other opportunities as well."

"Such as?" Grayton wanted to know.

Bretton looked at the man, seeing suspicion in his eyes. It infuriated him and he struggled not to show it. It also disappointed him because he had always considered Grayton his closest friend and colleague. It was evident that things had changed with the introduction of Allaston. Bretton wondered if things would ever been the same again.

"Very well, Grayton," he said snappishly. "Let me ask you what *you* would do to them? Keep in mind that the older knight had a hand in killing my father. What would you do to the lot of them to exact your revenge?"

With the focus turn on Grayton, the drunk knight tried to think clearly. "I suppose I would make the old man watch as we kill his family," he said. "Make him feel what he made you feel, Bretton. Make the man watch while you put his family on spikes."

Bretton eyed Grayton steadily. "I have thought of that," he replied. "But I have thought of something else, too – putting all of them to death together. Having the old knight's last memories be those of sorrow and grief, knowing he could not save his family because he, too, was dying. I have them in the kitchen right now, in fact. I am thinking of simply burning it over their heads and letting that be the end of it."

Grayton liked that idea, as did Dallan. Teague didn't give an indication either way. "Why would you not want the old knight to feel the pain your father felt?" Teague asked. "Put the man on a spike and let him rot there. Let him feel what your father felt in his last moments."

Bretton turned his gaze to the fire, snapping softly in front of him. "Because there is not enough pain in that death," he said quietly. "Burning of the flesh… there is extreme pain in that, mayhap even enough pain to ease some of my vengeance. I would want the man to suffer more than my father did, whatever death I choose for him."

It made sense to the commanders and they were very pleased to see that Bretton's sense of vengeance was still intact. They had feared, over the weeks, that Lady Allaston had somehow taken the edge off of it with her pleading. They were comforted to see that it was very much alive, that hatred that fed every move Bretton made.

It was mostly small talk after that, speaking on Erwood Castle and, the ultimate prize, Four Crosses Castle. Bretton sat with his men well into the night, telling stories and drinking, until Grayton and Teague finally fell asleep and he was only left with Dallan. The big Irish knight wandered over to the destroyed gatehouse, drunk, and Bretton didn't see him after that.

So he left the fire, wandering among several other fires where his men were either still drinking or had fallen asleep after a most strenuous day. He made his way around Comen's big keep to the kitchen yard in the back, near the stables, and he noticed as he moved into the yard that there were six soldiers stationed at the destroyed postern gate. That awareness made him shift course and he headed to the postern gate instead.

He sent all six soldiers away from the gate under orders to search the keep and see if they could find any bedding that the men in the bailey could use. He also told them they could keep anything of value they came across since the keep hadn't been fully looted yet, which thrilled the guards and they readily did his bidding. They were also under instructions to return to him once they'd raided the keep, which they agreed to. When the six disappeared into the keep, Bretton made a break for the kitchen structure.

He found the old knight, the father, and the mother awake, each one of them holding a sleeping child. Indicating for them to remain silent, Bretton freed them from the kitchen and led them out into the dark night and to the postern gate, where he told them to flee and never return. He also told them that if they informed anyone of Bretton's merciful gesture, that he would hunt them down and kill them, so it was best for them to keep their mouths shut on how they truly escaped Comen.

The mother and father were the first ones through the postern gate, down the narrow path that led to a wooded area below, but the old knight, holding his youngest granddaughter, was the last to go. He held Bretton's gaze a moment, wondering why this conqueror, this killer, had spared his life, especially given that the old man had been with Jax de Velt during his campaign of terror. Old Ares was going to ask for the reasons behind the show of mercy but decided better of it. He simply thanked Bretton and fled after his son and daughter-in-law, down the shadowed path and into the darkness that signaled freedom. They didn't have any weapons, money, food, or clothing, but they were alive and free, and that was all that mattered. Bretton stood there and watched them go, wondering if he had done the right thing. There was an odd lightness in his heart that told him he had.

I would ask you to show mercy. In his own way, he had.

An hour later, when the six soldiers returned from raiding the keep, Bretton ordered them all into the kitchen structure, which he then closed and locked from the outside with an iron fire prong wedged against the door latch, preventing it from being opened. He then proceeded to burn the kitchen down with the six inside so that, in the morning, well after the hot cinders had reduced bone and flesh to mostly ash, all anyone was able to find of those who had been in the kitchen were small pieces of bone and teeth, and portions of six charred skulls.

It was enough to convince the commanders, and anyone else, that Bretton had burned the commander of Comen alive along with his aged father, one of de Velt's original knights, the commander's wife, and their three daughters. No one was the wiser to the truth, and no one would ever know the mercy Bretton showed that night.

Except for Allaston. Bretton meant that she should know.

C3

IT WAS EARLY morning at Comen Castle and the stench of smoke and burning bodies hung heavy in the moist morning air. It was just before sunrise when the sky was turning shades of dark blue and pink, and Bretton's men were up and moving, preparing to return to Cloryn. Bretton himself hadn't slept all night and was back in the kitchen yard, watching the kitchen smolder in ruins, leaving his commanders in the bailey to organize the men. Word had gotten around that he had burned one of de Velt's knights in the kitchen blaze, so everyone assumed he was reconciling the death against his sense of vengeance. He was rightly lingering over a personal victory.

Grayton had already agreed to remain behind at Comen to oversee the rebuild, leaving Teague and Dallan to return with Bretton back to Cloryn. The four commanders would then be down to two, and those two would be taking charge of future castles on Bretton's list of conquest. Still, all three had suffered through the strained relationship with Bretton as of late and Olivier, having been at Rhayder Castle since it had been taken over by Bretton, had not been aware of the fact that there was increasing distance between Bretton and his commanders. Therefore, the two that were remaining were the ones to deal with Bretton's distraction with Lady Allaston.

She was the reason for the separation, the reason why the men weren't entirely close with Bretton any longer. They had tried to reason with him about her, but it was clear the man was obsessed. Whether it was because she was de Velt's daughter, or because he was simply infatuated with her, no one seemed to know. All they knew was that she seemed to have more power over him than they did, and no one liked that. Least of all Grayton.

As Bretton pondered over the smoldering kitchen, Grayton gathered Teague and Dallan. It was time for the three of them to discuss the future as they saw it, the future that Bretton had promised them. Even though they had conquered Comen Castle, as Bretton had promised, the future was uncertain. Mostly, to Grayton, it was not as he had envisioned.

In the burnt hall of Comen, the three commanders gathered. Amid the smoldering ruins and rubble, they remained out of sight as the men outside prepared to depart. Grayton backed Teague and Dallan into a corner, away from prying eyes and ears.

"You two are heading back to Cloryn Castle today," Grayton said, his voice low. "I must remain here to see to the rebuild, which means I will not be able to keep an eye on Bretton. That is something you both must do. I fear… I fear that Bretton has lost his direction in all of this. I fear that we are on the verge of a change that none of us will appreciate."

Dallan's brow furrowed. "What do you mean?" he wanted to know. "Bretton has not lost his focus. He has done everything he said he would and we have the riches to prove it. You have been sour since the day de Velt's daughter smacked Bretton over the skull, Grayton. Now you are being a doomsayer to things that do not exist."

Grayton's lips tightened into a flat, angry line. "I am closer to Bretton than anyone and I am telling you that the man is verging on a change," he insisted. "I can see it in his manner, especially when he gets around that de Velt woman. She changes him. We have all seen it. She even convinced him to take down the impaled bodies at Cloryn and burn them. He told us that he intended to leave those bodies up for six months, yet she asked him to take them down and he did!"

That was an undeniable fact that had the commanders perplexed since it had happened, but Dallan eventually shook his head.

"It means nothing," he insisted. "The stench was so bad that it was affecting everyone's appetite. He took them down for that reason."

"He took them down because she begged him to!" Grayton fired back. "But it will not end there, nay. I fear that she will convince him to go back on everything he has promised us. Do you not understand? That woman has bewitched him!"

Dallan sighed heavily, looking at Teague, who was the most level-headed out of the three. Teague didn't cushion his opinion.

"You speak treason," he said to Grayson. "I think Bretton is obsessed with the woman for the sheer fact that she is de Velt's daughter. You seem to think she has hypnotized him so that he will only do her bidding. I do not see that happening."

Grayson was flustered that the commanders were not on his side, not seeing what he was seeing. He jabbed a finger at them.

"Mark my words," he said. "He will not kill de Velt because she will beg him not to. If that happens, I can guarantee that everything we have been promised will be for naught. He will go back on his word to us because of her."

Teague shrugged his big shoulders. "If it comes to that, then we will deal with the situation accordingly," he said. "I, for one, do not intend to allow de Llion to break his promise to me. I am well on my way to being a very rich man and I plan to be richer before this campaign is through. If Bretton does not provide me what he promised, then I will act accordingly, but not until, or if, that moment comes."

Dallan was already heading out of the hall, moving for the door.

When Grayton called to him, he waved the man off irritably. He didn't want to hear his nonsense. As Teague turned to leave, Grayton grasped him by the arm.

"Listen to me, Teague," he said. "I have seen what a woman can do to a man. A woman's will can topple the mightiest of men, Bretton included. Watch and be wary… if she convinces him not to kill de Velt, the only thing that has kept him driven and has kept us rich, then everything shall crumble. Remember that."

Teague just looked at him, eyeing the fingers on his arm until Grayton reluctantly removed them. Even as he left the ruins of the hall, Grayton's words echoed in his mind as much as he didn't want them to.

Watch to see if she convinces him not to kill de Velt….

Try as he might, Teague couldn't seem to shake Grayton's sense of foreboding.

CHAPTER EIGHTEEN

Lioncross Abbey Castle
Nine days later, mid-August

"COMEN HAS FALLEN," Edward was standing in the doorway of Christopher's solar. "There are some refugees streaming into the village, people who used to live at the base of Comen Castle. They said a massive army moved in almost six days ago, laid siege, and infiltrated Comen in two days. They further say that the conquering army has posted all of Comen's inhabitants on poles, impaling them, leaving them exposed for all to see."

Christopher had been sitting at his desk, as was usual with him these days, working on some documentation that would see him purchase a great deal of land in Devon, but with Edward's news, he set the quill down and stared at the man with some shock.

"De Llion," he muttered.

Edward nodded grimly. "It certainly sounds like him."

Christopher sighed weakly, pondering the news. "Does de Velt know?"

Edward shook his head. "I do not believe so," he said. "The man is back at his encampment. I will send someone to retrieve him."

Christopher nodded. "Go yourself," he said. "Bring him back here. We must discuss this."

Edward nodded and was gone, rushing out to the bailey of Lioncross in order to collect his horse and ride for Jax's encampment. As Edward went along his way, Christopher pondered the event of Comen's siege. He'd sent the missive to Cloryn regarding terms for Lady Allaston de Velt's release but the missive he'd received in response had been terse and to the point – produce Jax de Velt or his daughter would suffer.

That had been over a week ago and he'd sent another missive back to Cloryn, telling de Llion that he wanted to see if there was anything else to be done before they went to all-out war. Surely there was a way that would satisfy them all. Christopher had made it plain that he would provide support to de Velt in a military conflict, hoping that would give the mercenary cause to reflect on his demands, but so far, he'd received no reply and now he knew why. The mercenary had been laying Comen Castle to waste. The man was making a statement to de Lohr and to anyone else who would think to oppose him.

The lack of written response to de Lohr's second missive was making Jax very nervous, too. Christopher had come to know the man a bit over the past few weeks. He was rather quiet, stoic, but brilliantly sharp and very humorous at times. Christopher and Jax had spent one night sitting before the fire, trying to out tell each other's battle stories. Christopher's knights, as well as Jax's sons, had sat in on the fun and it had turned into an eye-opening experience for both sides. Christopher came to understand why Jax had done what he had done twenty-five years ago, how his father had set a grim example of greed and conquest, why he had set out to conquer a section of England and the Welsh Marches for himself, and why he had subsequently given it all up. He had given it up for love.

Edward, aware of the historical significance of such a conversation, had even written most of it down. When Christopher asked him why, Edward said that someday, someone would find it important. Christopher wasn't entirely sure who, in the future, would care about battle stories, but Edward seemed to think it might mean something to someone, someday.

But the conversation with de Velt that night had indeed been enlightening for all concerned. Christopher also came to understand just how frantic de Velt was about regaining his daughter, which was why today's news about Comen's fall was not welcome news in the least. He knew it wouldn't sit well with de Velt and it was very possible they were going to have to mount up and march into Wales to meet the mercenary head-on. In the end, it was very possible that de Velt was going to go to the mercenary, as de Llion had wanted. Perhaps favor was going to lean in the mercenary's direction, after all.

Christopher was lost in thought as he approached the steps of the keep, only to glance up and see Rod and Berwyn standing there. The pair had arrived from Bronllys four days before and Christopher had done his best to avoid the old man, who was seriously wondering why he had been summoned to Lioncross and away from Bronllys during this time. More than that, Comen Castle was very close to Bronllys, and that was likely to make Berwyn very edgy when he found out Comen had been taken. When Christopher saw the two men, he spoke first as to not give old Berwyn the chance to speak and demand to know why he had been summoned.

"Good knights," Christopher said as he approached them. "It seems we have some news. Let us go into the hall and speak of this over a pitcher of fine wine."

Rod knew that Christopher had been avoiding his grandfather for days, too. They were trying to keep the man in the dark until John Morgan from Northumberland arrived, but every day that passed saw Berwyn growing increasingly impatient. In private, Christopher and Rod had spoken of John Morgan's imminent arrival, which Christopher estimated would come at any day. At least, that was the hope.

It had been almost a month since he'd sent the missive to Northumberland, probably longer, so a man on a swift horse could make it from the Northumberland to the Marches in eleven or twelve days, depending on the road conditions. It was summer, and the summer had been relatively mild, so he was hoping good road conditions had provided for swift travel. Their entire plan was predicated on the arrival of John Morgan. It was an agonizing wait.

"I am eager for news, my lord," Berwyn said as Christopher clapped a big hand on the old man's shoulder, directing him into the keep. "I am eager to know why I have been summoned. I do not like to be gone from Bronllys overlong, you see. It is my home and I am an old man. I am most comfortable there."

Christopher feigned hurt feelings. "Do you mean to tell me that you do not like Lioncross?"

Berwyn grinned. "I did not mean that at all," he said. "Your wife is gracious and your children are well-behaved. Well, all except for your boys, but they are very young. They have not yet learned obedience."

Christopher gave him a wry expression. "If they take after my wife as I suspect they do, then they will never learn it," he said, watching the old man laugh. He eyed Rod over Berwyn's head. "Rod, take your grandfather inside. I will join you in a moment. I must find Max and speak with him."

Rod nodded and escorted his grandfather a few feet into the keep, but then he directed the old man to continue on into the hall as he ran back out to catch Christopher before the man could get away. He caught him at the bottom of the steps, just as the man was heading off into the dusty bailey.

"My lord," Rod called quietly.

Christopher came to a halt, turning as Rod caught up to him. "Where is Berwyn?" Christopher wanted to know.

Rod threw a thumb in the direction of the keep. "I told him to go inside," he said. "I wanted him out of earshot. What is this news you speak of? Is it something we need to be concerned with?"

Christopher's sky-blue eyes were grim. "Comen Castle has fallen to de Llion," he said quietly. "We have refugees flooding in from the countryside, telling tales of blood and terror."

Rod sighed heavily. "Christ," he muttered. "How many does that make now?"

Christopher lifted his eyebrows in thought. "Cloryn, Rhayder, and now Comen," he said. "We think he also has Ithon because de Velt was sent the head of Ithon's commander several weeks ago, prior to the abduction of his daughter. De Velt's two remaining properties on the Marches are Erwood and Four Crosses."

Rod winced. "Did de Velt tell you about the head?"

Christopher nodded. "He did," he said. "He fears that more heads might be sent to Pelinom that he doesn't know about. His commander at Pelinom has promised to send word if any arrived but, so far, we've received no confirmations."

Rod shook his head in disgust. "Praise God for that," he said. "Then I shall go into the keep and sit with my grandfather and await you. He will be very worried to hear of Comen Castle. It is only a day's ride from Bronllys."

Christopher knew that. "And it is less than a day's ride from Lioncross," he said quietly. "It is closer to me than it is to Bronllys and for that reason, I will have Max bring in de Velt's army so we can house them in the bailey and seal up the castle. I am uncomfortable leaving everything wide open with a madman close by."

Rod couldn't disagree. He went inside to sit with his grandfather as Christopher continued out into the bailey, locating Max near the stables, and instructing the man to make preparations for housing de Velt's army in Lioncross' massive bailey. There was plenty of room for them and it was imperative he bring the men into the protective embrace of the castle. With no reply from de Llion to Christopher's last missive, he couldn't be sure what the man was thinking and he didn't want to give him any opportunity to compromise Lioncross.

Orders given and men on the move, Christopher was heading back across the bailey towards the keep when he heard his sentries take up the call. He paused, cocking his head, listening to what was being said. Someone shouted down to him that an army was sighted to the northeast and, in a fit of great concern, Christopher mounted the battlements to where Jeffrey and several soldiers were watching the northeast horizon.

A black tide in the distance signifying men on the approach met with Christopher's apprehensive scrutiny. Given the uncertainty of the Marches at this point, he had to assume the worst was approaching.

"Seal up the castle," he told Jeffrey calmly. "Edward is to the north with de Velt and his army, but they are going to have to fend for themselves. I must make Lioncross secure."

Jeffrey nodded swiftly and was on the move, bellowing to the soldiers to begin sealing up the keep. The massive gates of Lioncross and the equally large portcullis began to shift, preparing to move, as men ran about with great intensity. The fear in the air was palpable, given what happened to Comen, and Jeffrey made it down to the gates, rushing in any peasants that were running to the castle for protection. On the walls overhead, Christopher had two men who sounded big bronze *lurs*, like trumpets, in times of trouble, and the peal of the lurs could be heard for miles.

As the haunting notes blasted overhead, Christopher and several sentries were still trying to figure out who the approaching army was. Christopher assumed it was de Llion but he hoped he was wrong. As the army drew closer, banners could be seen waving in the breeze, although no one could make out the colors quite yet. The men standing around Christopher were straining to see, straining to make out anything they could about the approaching army. Christopher's eyes weren't what they used to be so he let the younger men make the call. When someone spouted out that the banners were black and green, a bolt of realization shot through Christopher. Running to the parapet, he yelled to Jeffrey down below.

"Kessler!" he boomed. "Send out a rider to the approaching army! They are bearing the black and green banners of de Poyer!"

De Poyer! Word started to spread like wildfire as Jeffrey sent a young, skinny soldier out on a swift horse to make the confirmation. Christopher watched the soldier race off, thundering down the road that led off to the northwest to intercept the approaching army, and breathed a sigh of relief. He'd sent word to de Poyer what seemed like years ago but, in truth, it had only been weeks. Now, de Poyer had come and it looked as if he was bearing several hundred soldiers. His relief was palpable.

The halls of Lioncross would be filled with men of legend tonight.

℘

LIONCROSS HAD SEEN its share of important people within her walls, kings and great counselors included, but tonight was different. The men within the walls of Lioncross tonight were men of power, men who had shaped the course of a nation. They were soldiers at heart, born and bred for war.

Keller de Poyer was one of the premier knights of William Marshal, a man who could only be described as the consummate knight. He was a big, muscular man with massive hands, dark hair flecked with gray, and an awkward social manner when he wasn't with people he knew and respected. He was also one of the most highly intelligent men ever to walk the earth, a razor-sharp mind that the Marshal had greatly depended on. Eight years ago, Keller had been awarded Nether Castle in Powys, Wales, for his dedicated service to the crown. He had married the Nether heiress and, at last count, had five children. For Keller, life had been very good and Christopher was happy for his friend.

Since Keller had manned Pembroke Castle for years as the garrison commander before assuming his property at Nether, the man had a very good handle on the workings of Wales in general. It was this knowledge that he brought to the table, confident and unflappable as always, but even Keller raised an eyebrow when he was introduced to Jax de Velt.

Keller had been a young knight when Jax had ripped through the mid-Welsh Marches, so he was well aware of what the man was capable of. He was surprised to see that de Velt had come peacefully to Lioncross, but in reality, he wasn't particularly surprised to see him in general. He, too, had heard what was happening on the Marches again and he had even heard about Alberbury. But once he heard that de Velt's daughter had been abducted by the same mercenary who was claiming de Velt properties, one by one, he began to understand more of what was going on. Something sinister was afoot that could affect them all. If they didn't band together, there was no telling what would happen.

"We received word of the fall of Cloryn Castle and Ithon Castle," Keller was saying, "but we had not heard of Rhayder or Comen. I take it these are recent events?"

The men were sitting around Christopher's feasting table, a long, heavy thing that had seen much action over the years, both good and bad. In the great hall, the knights gathered, and their retainers stood behind them, on the outskirts of the conversation, and this included Keller's two knights, Sir William Wellesbourne and George Ashby-Kidd, as well as Jax's two sons, and Christopher's men. Rod and Berwyn were standing behind Christopher, listening to every word spoken.

Therefore, the hall was crowded with knights, all of them concerned with what was happening in Wales and along the Marches, so it was time to settle things and establish a plan. They had families and property to defend, and a young woman to save. What was happening along the Marches not only affected Jax, but all of them as well. There was much at stake.

As servants brought forth food and drink, putting it on the table within arm's reach, Christopher answered Keller's question.

"The fall of Comen and Rhayder was recent enough," he replied. "You say you heard of Ithon's fall?"

Keller nodded. "We received word about it."

Christopher glanced at Jax, who merely shook his head in disgust. Christopher returned his attention to Keller.

"De Velt received the severed head of Ithon's garrison commander several weeks back," he said. "He assumed Ithon had fallen but this is the first we've heard independent confirmation."

"A traveling merchant told me he had seen it with his own eyes,"

Keller said. The dark eyes narrowed curiously. "When I arrived, you briefly explained what was going on, Chris, but surely there is more to it."

Christopher nodded, with great reluctance. "Unfortunately, there is," he said. "The mercenary in question landed in Liverpool back in May, from Ireland we believe, and made his way down the Marches to the area that de Velt claimed twenty-five years ago. Everything this mercenary has done has mimicked de Velt's actions from twenty-five years ago with the exception of torching Alberbury Priory. That was accomplished to abduct de Velt's eldest daughter. De Velt came to me for assistance, believing a mediator might help his daughter's cause, so I sent the mercenary a missive at his seat of Cloryn Castle asking for terms of the daughter's release. What I received in reply was a demand for de Velt himself or his daughter would suffer. Therefore, I sent a second missive, but the answer to that missive seemed to come in the form of the conquest of Comen Castle. At the moment, the mercenary is charging through the mid-Marches unopposed. I fear the time has come for someone to stand in his way or we may risk greater chaos."

Keller was listening to Christopher with great interest, as were the rest of the knights. Jax, seated across from both Keller and Christopher, seemed to be the most pensive about the situation, and for good reason. In fact, the man struggled not to appear distraught. Keller glanced at the great Dark Lord of legend for a moment before replying.

"It is clear this mercenary is bent on destruction against de Velt," he said. "Do we even know who it is?"

Christopher turned to look directly at Rod, standing behind him. He nodded slightly to the man, encouraging him to come forth in spite of the fact that Berwyn was standing next to him. *Go ahead, lad. Tell them what you know.* In the interest of making sure everyone who would be going to battle against the mercenary knew exactly what they were getting in to, there was little choice. Rod cleared his throat softly.

"Back in May when the mercenary first began his raids, Lord de Lohr summoned me to Lioncross Abbey because of a missive had had received from the Earl of Shropshire, Robert de Boulers, detailing the activities of a mercenary creating chaos along the Marches," he said. "The reason I was summoned was simple – the mercenary gave a name as something Lord de Lohr believed I would recognize. The name was Bretton de Llion."

Berwyn, standing beside his grandson, grunted with disbelief and hung his head. Rod, hearing his grandfather groan and sigh, continued with more information that Berwyn was not aware of. He had no choice. A glance at Christopher saw the man nodding encouragingly, spurring him onward. The time had come for Berwyn to know the truth of the matter, whether or not he wanted to believe it.

"You must understand that Bretton de Llion is the name of my young cousin, a young man we believed killed when Jax de Velt conquered Four Crosses Castle where my uncle, Bretton's father, was garrison commander," Rod said. Then, he shook his head as if at a loss for words. "When I told my grandfather what name the mercenary had used, he refused to believe it. You see, as far as he knows, his son and grandson lost their lives twenty-five years ago at Four Crosses Castle. I, too, believed that until this mercenary appeared, following the path of destruction that de Velt had carved out those years ago. I was curious, nay, *more* than curious about the identity of this mercenary so, unbeknownst to my grandfather, I sent a missive to Cloryn Castle, the mercenary's seat, asking if Bretton de Llion, son of Morgan, would meet me in Newtown. I wanted to meet the man on neutral ground to see if it was, in fact, my cousin whom we believed to be dead. I am sorry to say that it was him. He has returned from the dead as a killer of men."

Behind Rod, Berwyn had been listening with growing horror, now completely overwhelmed to realize that the mercenary commander was indeed his long-lost grandson. He grabbed hold of Rod's arm in sheer astonishment but he wasn't able to speak. His knees gave way and Rod found himself catching his grandfather before the man collapsed completely. Edward, also standing behind Christopher, helped Rod guide his grandfather onto the bench. Gasping for air, his face a mask of disbelief, Berwyn clung to Rod.

"It is *not* true!" he breathed.

Rod held his grandfather tightly. "It is," he confirmed quietly. "I am sorry I did not tell you. I did not want to upset you. But it seems that you must know, for it is indeed Bretton tearing up the Marches. It seems that he escaped the carnage at Four Crosses and has spent all of this time gathering an army to return for revenge. He did not want me to tell you that he is alive, but I fear I must break my vow to him. He is alive and he is not a man you or I would hope to be associated with. He is death."

For the most part since Berwyn's arrival at Lioncross, Christopher had made sure to keep Berwyn and Jax apart for obvious reasons. The old man had been aware of Jax's presence, as told to him by Christopher, but it had been explained to him in no uncertain terms that Jax was at Lioncross peacefully and any past hatred or grudges would not be played out at this time.

It had taken Berwyn two days to come to terms with the fact that de Velt was at Lioncross but he still hadn't met the man face to face until today, at this moment, in this council. He'd remained remarkably silent about everything, as he had been instructed, but at this moment, all he could feel was utter hatred and agony. He looked over at de Velt, seated across the table from them, and his careful control shattered.

"*You*," he gasped. "You did this to my family. You destroyed Four Crosses Castle and my son and his family along with it. You put my son on a stake and let the birds pluck his eyes out, and you murdered his wife and my grandchildren. You did this, you bastard! You brought this all down on yourself, do you hear?"

Rod grabbed his grandfather, yanking him up from the bench and dragging the old man from the room.

"Quiet," Rod hissed at him. "Be quiet before you say something you will regret."

Berwyn struggled against his grandson. So much, in fact, that Edward came up behind them and helped Rod take his grandfather from the hall. But not before Berwyn fired off his last terrible curse.

"I hope your daughter dies the same way my son died!" he yelled, his voice muffled as Rod slapped a hand over his mouth. "I hope you feel my pain, do you hear? *I hope you feel it!*"

He was finally gone, carried away by Rod and Edward. Christopher sat still as stone, his eyes trained on de Velt, who was watching the old man as he was dragged from the room. When he was gone, Jax turned to look at Christopher. They simply looked at each other for a moment, both men unsure what to say. Finally, Jax looked around the table at the other men, at Keller and his knights, at Christopher's men standing behind him.

"Please," he said, lifting his hand in an ironic gesture. "If there is anyone else at this table I have wronged, please speak your peace. We have all done things in our lifetime that we are not proud of but I suppose I was the worst of it. I have no excuse except to say I was young and full of ambition, and saw what I did as a means to achieve an end. It was not until later in life that I realized the gravity of what I had done. Therefore, if anyone else has anything to say to me, I will accept it."

Next to Christopher, Keller spoke softly. "You killed a cousin of mine at Ithon Castle those years ago," he said. "He was a rotten excuse for a human being, lying to my mother, beating his own mother, and once he even stabbed his father in an argument over a horse. I have always wanted to thank you personally for doing away with him. You saved me the trouble."

Jax looked at Keller, surprised, until William Wellesbourne, standing behind Keller, broke out in soft laughter. The giggles were infectious because George Ashby-Kidd started giggling, followed by Max. Hearing Max and his high-pitched laugher set Christopher off and, soon, the entire table was roaring with laughter. It was a welcome bit of respite after Berwyn's outbreak, easing the tension. Keller, with little sense of humor, looked around at those laughing as if they had lost their minds.

"I am serious," he insisted. "My cousin was a boil on the buttocks of our family; sore, ugly, and difficult to pop. Had de Velt not done away with him, I would have had to. He saved me the trouble!"

Everyone screamed with laughter and even though Keller was serious, he, too, started to snort just because everyone else was. He supposed it was rather humorous, a light touch in the midst of such seriousness. Wellesbourne slapped him on the shoulder in his revelry, causing Keller to lose his humor immediately. But William didn't. He clapped him again.

"God help you, Keller," he said. "Sometimes, your honesty is the best part about you."

Keller wriggled his eyebrows. "I sincerely hope that is not what my wife thinks," he quipped, returning his attention to Christopher. "If everyone will stop laughing at me, I would like to return to business. It sounds as if we have a blood feud on our hands. De Llion is seeking vengeance for what de Velt did to his father. There is nothing worse than one relative seeking justice for another."

Christopher still had a smile on his face as he replied. "That is true," he agreed. "But my fear is that de Llion will not be content with capturing de Velt's holdings. He is painfully close to Lioncross right now with his latest conquest at Comen Castle. Who is to say he will not set his cap for my castle or Shropshire's castle? He may even move into Wales and move for Nether. Nay, we cannot know his mind and that is what concerns me. It is best to stop this mercenary before he does too much damage. I fear that if we wait, we will have a massive problem that will be difficult to control."

Keller wasn't hard pressed to agree. "Wales has been, as of late, relatively peaceful," he said. "This mercenary along the Marches is the first serious threat I have encountered in several months. In fact, knowing his scope in Powys, I took the long way around him from Nether Castle, mostly because I did not want to engage him. I know he is moving his army around in the mid-Marches and did not want to chance running into him, so we moved straight across Wales into

Shropshire and then down to Lioncross."

Christopher nodded. "I can understand your caution," he said. "I am inclined to move on Cloryn Castle, the mercenary's seat, before the week is out if we can agree on a strategy. But before we convene a war council, you should know something else. Now that Berwyn has left, I can speak freely about it. It may be a gift from heaven or it may be a great disappointment. In any case, in speaking with de Velt I learned that he did not kill everyone at Four Crosses. He retained some men for slave labor, including one knight with a serious head injury who calls himself John Morgan. You must understand that Bretton de Llion's father's name was Morgan, and it is quite possible that John Morgan is really Bretton's father. John Morgan current serves Yves de Vesci as his personal bodyguard and I have sent word to de Vesci asking him to send John Morgan to us so that we may see if he is, indeed, the mercenary's father. If he is, then it is quite possible the battle will be over before it begins. But if it is not his father, then we must be prepared to strike and strike hard."

Keller digested what he was told. After a moment, he shook his head with some amazement. "That is an incredible story," he said. "Let us hope the man is indeed de Llion's father."

"Agreed."

"How long ago did you send word to de Vesci?"

"About a month. I expect to see John Morgan any day now."

Keller reached for a wine cup in the middle of the table, pouring himself a measure of rich, red wine. "That is a reasonable time frame, even traveling from the north," he said. "And you say Berwyn does not know that his son may indeed be alive?"

Christopher shook his head. "Nay," he replied quietly. "You saw how he reacted to de Velt. One more shock and we may lose him altogether."

Keller took a long drink of wine. "But you are going to have to tell him, eventually."

Christopher glanced at Jax, who shrugged. "I thought it would better if we did not tell him anything," he said. "Let John Morgan show himself and then we shall see if Berwyn recognizes him. If he does, then it will be a wonderful reunion. If not, then we did not get an old man's hopes up."

Keller sat there, toying with his wine cup, thinking on Christopher's strategy. Although the story of John Morgan was an incredible one, something didn't make sense to him. After several pensive moments, he spoke softly.

"Do you not think that if John Morgan was really Bretton de Llion's father, he would have contacted Berwyn long ago?" he asked softly. "I would think that he would have contacted his own father simply to let him know that he was alive."

Jax interjected himself into the conversation. "John Morgan suffered a head injury during the siege of Four Crosses," he said. "He could only tell us his name was Morgan and not much more. It was my men who gave him the name John Morgan. He was as strong as a bull but his head injury was severe enough that he could not think well for himself. I gave him over to de Vesci as a personal guard because the man didn't have much of a mind of his own and de Vesci wanted someone close to him who could be easily ordered about. John Morgan fit that role well. I had no more use for the man so de Vesci took him."

Keller listened intently, reasoning through the situation. "If John Morgan really is Bretton de Llion's father," he said, "then will he even know it? What if he is the father and we present him to de Llion, but Morgan has no knowledge that the man is his son? Worse yet, what if he shuns him? That could go very badly in our favor, worse than if we hadn't presented the father at all."

Christopher could see his logic. "That is a good point, but I am willing to take the chance," he said. "In any case, we must unbalance de Llion and take advantage of that chaos. We must stop the man once and for all, and regain de Velt's daughter in the process."

Keller poured himself more wine. "Then what do you have in mind?"

Christopher, too, poured himself some wine from another pitcher. He found he needed it. "We have two options, in my opinion," he said. "We present John Morgan to de Llion and pray the man is his father. If he is, then we do an exchange – Morgan for Lady Allaston."

"But Berwyn will know his own son," Jax interjected. "If Morgan arrives at Lioncross first, and Berwyn is still here, then surely the father will recognize his own son, therefore, we will know *before* engaging de Llion if John Morgan is really his father. If he is not, then we must make a secondary plan."

Everyone fell silent for a moment, assessing the possibilities. Jax had made a very good point. Behind Keller, William Wellesbourne cleared his throat softly to gain their attention.

"If I may, my lords," he said, leaning forward on the table so he could better look those around it in the eye. "If John Morgan is not de Llion's father, we still have a man related to him within our grasp – his grandfather. Mayhap Berwyn would use himself in exchange for de Velt's daughter."

Christopher nodded. "It is as good a plan as any," he said. "I will approach Berwyn with it when the man has sufficiently calmed. Until then, let us enjoy this wine and this food and entertain further possibilities. I, for one, am more interested in learning about Keller's terrible cousin that he was going to have to kill. Keller, you have my interest. Who was this awful man? Did I know him?"

Keller didn't want to discuss his terrible cousin as wine was passed around and bread was distributed. The serious meeting had loosened up and soon they were speaking of things other than war and destruction. Christopher had just launched into a story that involved himself, his brother, a knight named Sir Kieran Hage, and an encounter with an angry potentate in The Levant when Edward suddenly entered the hall.

"Chris," he called gravely. "You had better come."

Christopher knew that tone and he didn't like it. He set his wine cup down and turned to Edward.

"What has happened?" he demanded. "Is Berwyn well?"

Edward was oddly pale, avoiding the question about Berwyn.

"We just received two riders," he said. "One rider is the messenger we sent to Northumberland those weeks ago, and the second rider is a man he brought with him from Northumberland by the name of John Morgan."

Everyone at the table stood up at that moment, including Christopher. The air was instantly full of anticipation, of foreboding, as the entire future hung in the balance with the course of the next few words. They all knew the stakes. They all knew what this moment would mean. Now that it was upon them, the air was fairly crackling with anxiety. Christopher could hardly spit the words out.

"Where is Berwyn?" he asked.

"He was in the bailey when the men rode in."

"Has he seen the man?"

"Aye."

Christopher was ready to explode. "And?" he demanded, charging away from the table as he headed for the keep entry that led out to the bailey beyond. "Damnation, what has happened? Is John Morgan missing a finger?"

Edward grabbed Christopher before the man could storm past him, an unusual gesture but one wrought with the emotion of the moment. All eyes were on Edward as the man, his hands on Christopher's big arms, looked him squarely in the eye. The next two words sealed the fate of the future.

"*He is.*"

CHAPTER NINETEEN

CHRISTOPHER'S FIRST GLIMPSE of what should have been a happy family reunion was, in fact, not happy at all. By the time Christopher and the other knights raced from the hall and reached the bailey, they saw Rod picking Berwyn up off the ground several feet away. Standing in front of Berwyn was a very big man with a bald-shaved, scarred head and brilliant blue eyes. Once Rod picked Berwyn up, the old man ran at the bald man again and, as it had happened before, the bald man shoved the old man away, causing him to fall to the ground. Berwyn lay there and wept.

Christopher ran up, putting himself between Berwyn and the big, bald warrior so that Berwyn wouldn't charge him again. Jax, who was right behind him, walked up to the bald man and caught his attention.

"John Morgan," he said. "I am de Velt. Do you remember me?"

The bald man's attention shifted from Berwyn as he studied Jax for several long seconds before nodding. "I do, my lord."

Jax glanced at Berwyn, who was now being held up by Rod. "Why did you push that man down?" he asked.

John Morgan looked at Berwyn as if confused by the question. "He attacked me, my lord."

Rod, holding on to his grandfather, grunted. "He did not attack him," he said quietly, with great remorse. "He ran to hug him."

Berwyn was weeping into his hands. "My son," he cried softly. "My

Morgan. He is alive!"

So it was true. John Morgan was, in reality, Sir Morgan de Llion, only he had no knowledge of it and no idea that Berwyn was, in reality, his father. There was no recognition there whatsoever. Looking at the scarred head of the man and listening to his slurred, simple speech, it became clear that John Morgan was a dense and damaged individual.

Christopher sighed heavily, thinking the circumstance to be tragic on so many levels. Now, he had his answer about John Morgan but it didn't turn out as he'd hoped. He faced the big, bald man with the brilliant blue eyes.

"I am Christopher de Lohr, Earl of Hereford and Worcester," he told the man. "It was I who summoned you from Alnwick. Do you understand what I have told you so far?"

Morgan nodded. "Aye, my lord."

Christopher eyed Jax, thinking how to simply phrase the situation, before continuing. "Do you remember how you came into the service of de Vesci?"

Morgan nodded. "I was gifted to him by Sir Jax, my lord."

"Do you remember how you came to be in Sir Jax's service?"

That question seemed to stump Morgan. He began to look around, confused, as if someone would clue him into the correct answer. Jax picked up where Christopher left off.

"You came into my service during the siege of Four Crosses Castle in Wales," he said. "Does that name sound familiar to you?"

Morgan still had that blank look about him. "Nay, my lord."

Jax sighed and looked to Christopher for help. It was clear that Morgan remembered nothing of his distant past, at least prior to the head injury during the battle at Four Crosses. Jax hadn't been around the man in years and truthfully didn't remember much about him except he had been found at Four Crosses crawling out of the moat with a terrible head injury, the scar of which could be seen across his forehead. It ran the length of his forehead and back onto the left side of his head. No one knew how he got it but it looked as if an axe blade had been leveled at him and, it was suspected, he had toppled off the walls and into the moat. It was a miracle the man survived at all but the damage to his mind, his memory, was evident. As Morgan's father wept a few feet away, it was obvious that Morgan didn't recognize him in the least.

Christopher, realizing the devastation of the scene, met Jax's gaze but he was at a loss as to what to do about it. With a faint shrug at Jax, he turned to Rod, standing behind him with Berwyn.

"Rod," he said quietly. "Take Berwyn into my solar. I will join you shortly."

Rod did as he was told but Berwyn did not want to go. He wanted to be with his son, even if the man had no memory of him. Edward had to step in again and help Rod remove Berwyn to the keep, and the weeping of the old man faded away. But that left Jax, Christopher, Keller, and several other knights standing around, wondering what to do. Christopher finally motioned Jax away from Morgan, pulling the man into a private huddle which Keller joined. The three of them had some hard decision to make.

"Now what?" Keller asked. "Do you mean to tell me that de Vesci's man is, in fact, the father of the mercenary? A man thought to have been killed twenty-five years ago?"

Jax and Christopher both nodded. "It has been confirmed," Jax said. "But it is apparent John Morgan has no memory of his life as Morgan de Llion."

"Then mayhap we should tell him," Christopher said, looking between Jax and Keller. "Mayhap he needs to have his memory rattled because, one way or the other, I intend to use him as a bargaining tool to regain de Velt's daughter. Do you not understand? This is better than we could have hoped for."

Jax sighed heavily. "I agree with you," he said, "but what if Morgan does not want to go? He remembers nothing. Being presented to his son will mean nothing to him. What if he refuses?"

Christopher looked pointedly at him. "He cannot refuse a direct order from you," he said flatly. "How badly do you want your daughter back, de Velt?"

Jax didn't have to answer that. He nodded his head to Christopher's statement, knowing they were going to force Morgan into a pivotal position in their negotiations against de Llion whether or not the man knew his true identity and regardless if he didn't want to be put in that position. He glanced over his shoulder at Morgan, still standing where he had left him.

"We have spoken of unsettling de Llion with the appearance of his father and creating a diversion while others seek out my daughter," he said. "It will not work, you know. We would have no idea where to look for her and running about an enemy castle will only see us come to ruin. It is not an efficient way to tackle this issue."

"Then speak," Keller said. "If you have an idea, I will listen."

Jax was plain. "It seems to me that if we simply present de Llion with Morgan, he will no longer have a need to seek vengeance against me," he said. "It is my suggestion that we simply ride to Cloryn Castle, present Morgan to de Llion, and tell him that we will exchange his father for my daughter. It is as simple as that."

Keller let out a hiss. "I approve of a plan of reason," he said. "Ultimately, I would think that de Llion will want his father returned to him. But, for some reason, if he is unable to let go of his vengeance and refuses to trade de Velt's daughter for his father? What then?"

Christopher's expression was grim. "Then we lay siege to Cloryn," he said. "We breach her walls and kill everything that moves in the hunt for de Velt's daughter. If she is a prisoner, then she will more than likely be in the vault or some other secure location. It should not be difficult to find her."

Jax shook his head. "I am reluctant to lay siege to the castle," he said, "for fear that de Llion might harm my daughter in retaliation. In the event that he refuses to trade her for his father, I will have no alternative but to trade my life for hers."

Christopher and Keller looked at him. Both men had children, and daughters, and well understood the lengths a man would go through to save his child. Neither one could argue with him. Christopher reached out and put his hand on de Velt's shoulder.

"Let us hope it does not come to that," he said. "But if it does, I will not let him kill you. I swear I will do what I can to save you and your daughter. We must make sure you live long enough to see her wed and give you grandchildren."

Jax looked at him, realizing he'd never had another man swear to defend him. Jax's entire life had been about him defending himself. He'd always been a loner. Now, he was starting to realize he was a loner no longer. It was a rather astonishing awareness.

"You would save The Dark Lord?" he asked, his eyes twinkling with the irony of the situation.

Christopher grinned. "I have come to discover you are not so bad," he said. "Over the past few weeks, I have come to know you and have found you to be intelligent, humorous, and respectable. Moreover, if I do not save you, who will play Nine Men's Morris with me?"

Jax shook his head, fighting off a smirk. "I have beaten you six games out of ten," he said. "If you save me, I will only beat you more."

Christopher laughed softly. "I am willing to take that risk."

Jax's smile faded as his dual-colored gaze fixed on Christopher, a man who he was coming to realize was actually his friend. Somehow, someway, over the past few weeks, a friendship had developed and he hadn't even been aware. He was both touched and grateful.

"Thank you for taking that risk," he whispered sincerely, then glanced at Keller. "And thank you for taking that risk, also. I realize you do not know me, but I am grateful nonetheless."

Keller, humorless at times and awkward socially, could nonetheless have moments of true warmth. He crossed his arms and shook his head.

"I am not so certain that at times like this there is room for old fears and doubts," he said. "Much like Chris, I cannot deny a father the chance to see his daughter grow up and marry. I, too, will make sure you live to see it. But you will do me a favor."

Jax nodded. "Anything you wish."

Keller scratched his head, eyeing the big man with the two-toned eyes. "Continue to beat de Lohr in Nine Men's Morris," he said. "He is too cocky as it is."

Jax laughed softly. "Agreed," he said, sobering. "Now, we must make plans to march on Cloryn. There is a man holding my daughter hostage and I want her back. She has been his prisoner long enough. Let us meet after the evening meal to lay out our plans of victory."

The tone was set. What lay ahead of them now was a battle march to regain Lady Allaston, and the three of them broke from their huddle, each man moving off to make preparations for the war council that would take place later that evening. But as Jax and Keller went about their business, Christopher went over to John Morgan, still standing where they had left him, and motioned the man with him. Obediently, John Morgan followed.

"My lord?" he asked Christopher, curious as to where they were going.

De Lohr didn't say anything for a moment. He kept walking and Morgan kept following, heading towards a section of Lioncross Abbey that they called The Cells because it was part of the original Roman structure. There were cubicles where the Roman soldiers had slept, later converted to cells for the monks who followed when the structure was converted into a Benedictine abbey.

It was quiet and private, and Christopher wanted to speak with Morgan to explain why he had been beckoned. He thought it only fair. As they neared the narrow stairs that would lead down into the cold, dark realm of The Cells, Christopher looked over his shoulder to the big, bald man following him.

"I would like to tell you why you have been summoned," he told him. "And I would like to tell you what I know about you."

Morgan was confused. "Know about *me*?" he repeated.

Christopher nodded and led the man down into one of the cells where they proceeded to have an hour-long conversation. Morgan heard about his life before his service to de Vesci, something that both puzzled and frightened him. Christopher also told him about Berwyn and how the man had not been attacking him, but merely glad to see him. He was, in fact, Morgan's father.

The last part of the conversation dealt with Bretton and what was happening on the Marches. Christopher told the man as much as he dared, fearful that too much information would scare him off. The man had a very simple understanding of even the most basic things due to his head injury and Christopher took that into account, and by the end of the conversation he ended up sending the man off with Max, instructing Max to not let the man out of his sight. It would not do them any good to locate Morgan de Llion only to have him run off because he was confused or scared about his true identity. So much hinged on a man who could hardly comprehend what he had been told.

With John Morgan being monitored, Christopher headed into the keep to see Berwyn and Rod. When Christopher explained to Berwyn that John Morgan had now become their primary bargaining chip with Bretton, Christopher had never seen such sorrow in a man. To have found his son only to risk losing him again was something the old knight was having trouble reconciling. In fact, he was having difficulty with the entire experience, very badly wanting to speak with John Morgan but Christopher wouldn't let him. John Morgan had his own issues to deal with at the moment. It was better if both men calmed down before addressing each other.

Therefore, Christopher had Rod take Berwyn to the chamber they had been sharing and put the old man to bed. What his old bones needed most, at the moment, was rest.

The worst was yet to come. By sunrise, they were on the march to Cloryn Castle.

CHAPTER TWENTY

Cloryn Castle

A LLASTON HAD WATCHED the army returning from Comen Castle from her chamber high in the keep. They had been gone almost nine days, a much shorter time than when they had gone off to Rhayder, and she was curious to know why they had returned so soon. She certainly hadn't expected it, but rather than race down to see the returning army for herself, she remained in the bower, waiting, watching for her first sighting of Bretton.

He wasn't difficult to spot. Astride his charcoal charger, he entered the gates of Cloryn when about half of his army was already into the bailey. In the colors of sunset, the hues of orange and yellow flashed off the armor, creating bolts of lightning in the growing darkness. Allaston stood at the window, watching, until the rest of the army came through and the provisions wagons brought up the rear. When one wagon lost a wheel right at the gatehouse and got stuck, she decided to make her way down to the entry of the keep and watch from there. Somehow, she wanted to be closer to Bretton that way. She wanted him to know she was there.

Dressed in one of Lady Miette's surcoats, a brocaded blue silk that was extraordinarily fine, she smoothed at her hair, making sure it was properly braided and neat, before heading down the narrow inner stairs and ending up at the keep entry. As she opened the heavy oak and iron door, watching the commotion outside, Blandings mounted the steps and met her at the top.

"My lady," the old man greeted, eyeing the soldiers in the bailey. "What should we do for their supper? No one told us the army was returning until a half hour ago. Uldward has chicken carcasses stewing in a pot and he is baking bread, but it will not be ready right away."

Allaston looked at him. "We had a good deal of cooked mutton left," she said. "What about that?"

The old man shook his head. "It has gone sour," he replied. "We cannot serve it to the men."

Allaston sighed distantly. "Unfortunate," she said. "It was fine yesterday when I checked it. We were storing it in the coldest part of the vault."

"Would you like to check it for yourself, my lady?"

She shook her head. "Nay," she replied. "I trust you. If you say it has gone sour, then I believe you. But now we must figure out what to cook for the men on a large scale that does not take too much time."

Thoughts of greeting Bretton pushed aside for the moment, Allaston headed down the steps with Blandings in tow, both of them heading around the keep towards the kitchens to the rear. Once inside the kitchen yard, she met up with Uldward and had a discussion about the stewed chickens and how they could possible stretch it to feed hundreds. Allaston eventually came up with an idea that they had used at the priory to feed great groups of people. Dividing the stewing chickens into three large pots, she added more water and a mixture of rye and wheat flour and butter, which thickened up the liquid in the stew and made it richer and more filling. Then, she had Uldward pour precious white wheat flour into a bowl and she added water and salt to it, making it into a massive pile of dough.

Uldward carried the heavy dough out to the pots, simmering away with their stew, and Allaston began to break off little pieces of the dough, roll them into balls, and toss them into the simmering pots to make dumplings. She also tossed in chopped onions, carrots, peppercorns, and lots of salt into the stew to flavor it. Soon, both Uldward and Blandings were making little dough balls and putting them into the stew to cook.

As Allaston stood over one of the pots, checking the consistency of the dumplings, she heard movement behind her and glanced up from the pot, startled to see Bretton standing there.

"Oh!" she gasped, accidentally dropping her spoon into the simmering cauldron. "I did not know... what I mean to say is welcome home, my lord."

It was rare when she used "my lord" to address him and Bretton grinned. He couldn't help it. Moreover, the sight of her was something he had missed terribly. He had seen her briefly at the keep entry when he had entered the bailey but she had soon disappeared, so he had hurried through his duties so he could once again locate her. Now, all he seemed capable of doing for the moment was staring at her, drinking in his fill, and feeling his heart lighten. Something about the woman made him feel giddy and carefree, as if nothing else in the world mattered.

"My lady," he greeted, noting the bubbling pots. "I see you have a fine feast prepared for our return."

Allaston's gaze was still riveted to his weary but handsome face but she managed to nod in answer to his statement. "It should be ready soon," she said. "We have bread and stew."

"No peas?"

She grinned at his expression of disgust when he asked the question. "No peas, I swear it."

He laughed softly. "Then I am content."

Her eyes twinkled at him. "I did put carrots into the stew, however," she said. "Do they disgust you as well?"

He shook his head. "They do not," he replied, his levity fading as he looked at her. He couldn't seem to do anything other than stare at her. "Has the situation at Cloryn been quiet while we have been away?"

Allaston's smile faded as well. "It has," she replied. "You... what I mean is that you seem to have returned fairly soon. Did everything go as planned?"

As the lightheartedness faded from the conversation, the reality of the situation took hold. As Bretton gazed at her, all he could think of was the conclusion he had reached at Comen, how he simply wasn't good enough for the woman. She deserved a fine man and an acceptable marriage, certainly not a marriage with a mercenary who could not give her the respectability that she deserved.

Allaston was a good woman with a good heart, and he had realized sometime between last night and today that he loved her deeply. He had been fighting his emotions where they pertained to her, thinking himself merely fond of her, but he knew that was a lie. He loved her, with everything that he was, he loved her. But she was better off without him. Moreover, he had to kill her father and he could not bear looking into her eyes and seeing the pain he would cause as a result. He couldn't bear to see the hatred. He swallowed hard before replying.

"It did," he said. "I was hoping I might tell you about it."

Allaston was both surprised and curious at the statement. "Of course," she said. "I am happy to listen."

He reached out and took her, gently, by the arm. "Come inside," he said. "I will tell you... everything."

Allaston willingly went along with him, feeling his big hand on her elbow, so very thankful he had returned whole and sound. It was true that she knew why he had gone; to conquer another castle. He had gone to kill men and steal from them. But that didn't mean she wanted to see him cut down in the process. She still believed there was good in the man and, with time, she hoped she could turn him away from this terrible life. After all, her mother had done it with her father. She hoped she could do the same. Since he had left for Comen Castle, she had thought of little else.

The keep was cool and dark, smelling of fresh hay on the floor that Allaston would sprinkle about to catch scraps and waste, only to be shoveled or swept out at a later time. Instead of taking her into the open room on the entry level that he used as his private solar, Bretton took Allaston up to her chamber on the second floor, a comfortable room that was warm and nicely furnished. It was also more private. As they entered the room, Allaston turned to Bretton just as he closed the door behind them.

"Before you begin, I should like to say something," she said, gazing up into his weary, handsome face. "With all of the preparation prior to your departing to Comen Castle, I did not have the chance to thank you for burying the dead of Cloryn. What you did, Bretton… it meant a great deal to me. Thank you for showing such mercy to those who had perished."

Bretton's gaze was steady upon her. "Did it give you a reason?"

"A reason for what?"

"To love me?"

Allaston smiled knowingly, hearing her words echoed in his voice. "That is possible," she whispered coyly. "I missed you while you were away. I am happy to see you have returned whole and healthy."

God's Blood, how he wanted to give over to the feelings he was experiencing. Feelings of joy and contentment that he never knew existed. Feelings that all men dream about but seldom experience. Aye, he wanted to experience all of it but he knew he couldn't. He couldn't do that to her. He had to make her understand that they were not meant to be, in any aspect.

With a dreadful sigh, he moved towards the bed, sitting heavily, feeling it sink beneath his weight. His gaze was on Allaston as she moved towards him, her expression still alive with warmth. Already, what he must say to her, what he must do, was killing him.

"Comen Castle was not difficult to breach," he told her. "The walls were surprisingly inadequate. It took us two days to gain control. When we rounded up the commanding officer and his family, I was faced with the surprising fact that the commander's father was one of de Velt's original knights."

The warmth, the smile, disappeared from Allaston's face. In fact, she looked a bit bewildered as she sank down into a chair near the hearth.

"I see," she murmured, eyeing Bretton uncomfortably. "May I ask who it was?"

"Ares de Gault."

Allaston looked sick and tears immediately popped to her eyes. "He is my father's cousin," she said tightly, fighting the tears. "We used to visit with him quite frequently. He brought his wife and sons to Pelinom a few times, usually around Christmas, and we would celebrate the season with them. His wife, Lady Destanne, used to take all of the children out to the bailey and teach us how to shoot a bow and arrow. She was very good at it. And they had three sons, Augustus, Asher, and Harrison, and we would all play together. They were very nice boys. They were...."

She suddenly came to a halt and hung her head, unable to continue, knowing what he had done to the family, or at least thinking she knew. Bretton watched her as she struggled not to weep.

"I only met Ares and his son, Augustus, and Augustus' wife and their three daughters," he said. "I did not meet Ares' wife or the other sons."

Allaston simply nodded her head. She didn't ask any further questions, knowing she would hate the answers. Bretton stood up from the bed, exhausted, and made his way over to the chair next to hers. He sat down, watching her lowered head.

"They are alive," he admitted. "I let them go."

Allaston's head shot up, her eyes wide with shock. She could hardly believe her ears and it took several seconds for the news to sink in. Then, she threw her arms around his neck and began to weep pitifully, out of relief and joy, hugging him tightly. Bretton knew he shouldn't put his arms around her. God, he knew he shouldn't. He didn't want to torment himself with something he could never have, but he ended up holding her anyway. He simply couldn't stop himself.

"Thank you," Allaston sobbed. "Thank you so much for showing mercy, Bretton. I knew you could. I am so thankful that you did."

He hugged her, feeling her body against his, or at least as much as the awkwardness of the chairs and his chain mail would allow. It was a stolen moment, something to tuck back in his mind and revisit during the times he was particularly lonely. He patted her on the back gently.

"Aye, I did," he said quietly. "I did as you asked. I showed mercy. Stop crying, now. There is no need."

Allaston nodded quickly, releasing him as she wiped at her face. But she couldn't help kissing his cheek.

"Thank you," she whispered, patting the cheek she had just kissed. "Thank you for letting that good man come forth. I knew he was in there. I have always known."

She latched on to Bretton's hands, squeezing, and he was increasingly distraught with what he must do. It would be so easy to ignore it, to pretend he would make her a fine husband, but he knew it would not be possible. He stared at her hands, holding his, until the angst exploded in him and he pulled his hands away, standing up and moving away from her, wandering in the direction of the lancet window that overlooked the bailey. He found he couldn't look at her, terrified he would weaken.

"Mayhap there is a good man inside me, but not good enough," he said, gazing out into the wide evening sky beyond the window. "I told you once that I am not sure I can let go of what I have become. During this entire campaign to Comen Castle, it was all I thought of. *You* were all I thought of. The truth of the matter is that I am your captor and you are my prisoner. If I wanted to marry you today, I could. I could also impregnate you and fill you full of those sons I once spoke of, sons that would be conditioned to hate their grandfather. I could relegate you to nothing more than a broodmare. If I wanted to do all of these things, I could. But the reality is that I do not want to do this to you. I cannot. Allaston, I love you with all my heart and soul and then some, but this love I feel for you is not enough to overcome the need for vengeance against your father. It would always come between us and I could not do that to you. You must have a man who will love you wholly and give you the respect and station that you deserve. I cannot do that. I cannot give you what you deserve."

Allaston rose from her chair, her expression full of sorrow and foreboding. "What do you mean?" she asked, fear in her tone. "What do you mean to do with me?"

Bretton could feel her question like a dagger to the heart. He knew what he had to do and he turned around, looking at her with an expression of utter grief.

"I am going to send you home."

Allaston exploded. "Nay!" she hissed. "I am *not* going home. You asked for my hand in marriage and I agreed. I am staying here with you! You cannot send me home!"

She was furious. He was cowering. Bretton tried to reason with her. "Allaston, listen to me," he said. "You deserve an excellent match, something I cannot provide you. You deserve to have a husband who is good and pure, and who does not have a driven hatred against your father. Don't you see? No matter how much I love you, my sense of revenge against your father is what will drive us apart. I must kill him and I cannot stomach the grief and hatred in your eyes when I do. It will destroy me."

Allaston was beginning to weep, stricken with anguish. "You do not have to kill him," she sobbed. "I have begged you not to, I have pleaded with you, and I have even offered myself in marriage to you if you will only forget your vengeance. Whatever you have inside of you, this hatred you hold, is killing you. It will destroy you. You must under-stand that I would not have made the offer of marriage to you unless I loved you, too. I did not want to tell you for fear it would make no difference to you whether I did or not, but I will tell you now that I love you, Bretton de Llion. I love you and I will be your wife, and you will *not* send me home!"

She was sobbing loudly by the time she was finished. Bretton stood there, watching her, his heart breaking. He found that there was a lump in his throat, something very unfamiliar to him. The last time he had felt such a thing had been a long time ago. As he watched Allaston weep, all of his defenses crumbled. Everything he held strong and fast was laid to waste, dissolved by her tears.

"I am a broken man," he replied tightly, trying to make her understand. "I was five years old when I was sold to a merchant who raped me repeatedly. He tore me up inside, not only of the body, but of the mind. Things still… still do not work right at times. When I left him, I served an Irish mercenary for a time who not only taught me his craft, but beat me bloody in the meanwhile. When I was old enough, I left him, too, to seek my fortune, but I discovered that one needed money in order to build a fortune or pursue one's dreams. I therefore prostituted myself as a young man until I had saved enough money to buy weaponry and a horse, and then I hired myself out as a soldier of fortune. It took me years to amass the army you see now, years to find myself in the place I am this night, and all of it was possibly only because of the hatred I had for your father. It drove me, it molded me, and it has made me what I am. I cannot let go of it, Allaston, and I cannot let you marry a man who is purely filth and rancor. It would pull you into my world and I cannot let you live there."

Allaston was still weeping even though the hysterical sobbing had faded somewhat. She was listening to his horrible story, one that had seen the man survive some of the most terrible times imaginable. She felt such pity for him, such incredible pity. She wiped her face as she made her way over to him, sinking to her knees before him. When he tried to turn away, she threw her arms around his legs and refused to let him go.

"I understand your world is a terrible one," she cried, relishing the feel of his warmth in her arms. "I know you have had unspeakable things happen to you, but instead of seeing filth and rancor before me, I see a survivor. I see a man who was so strong that nothing could stop him. I see a man who had a goal, even if was a brutal goal, and he fought to achieve it. He did everything he could to fund that dream and here you are, the head of your own mighty army."

Her body against his legs was causing him physical pain. Bretton put his hands down, trying to pry her away from him, but she held fast. Tears popped to his eyes because he couldn't stand the contact between them. It was sweet beyond words, horrible beyond imagining. The tears in his eyes began to run down his face.

"Let me go," he commanded hoarsely. "Allaston, release me."

Allaston only held on tighter. "I will not," she whispered. "Not until you hear me out. You are a survivor, Bretton, a brilliant man of great determination. You have lived in a world that has been trying to kill you since you were five years old and when you came to Alberbury, it was because God, who knew he had ignored you for your entire life, directed you to come to me. He directed me to go to you. Don't you see, Bretton? God has given me to you as a reward for your terrible life. With me, you will find peace and love and happiness. I am your reward for a life gone wrong."

It made utter and complete sense to Bretton, but he refused to believe it. He couldn't. "God has never done anything for me," he muttered, wiping at the tears on his face. "I find it hard to believe he has taken an interest in me now."

"He has," Allaston assured him. Her cheek was against his armored thighs and she turned her head, kissing his legs tenderly. "You must also understand something. I will never have the opportunity for a respectable marriage given the fact that my father is Ajax de Velt. What family in their right mind would marry their son to a daughter of The Dark Lord? So your assertion that I should find a good and true man to marry is invalid. I cannot. Furthermore, the moment you abducted me, you announced to the world that I was your property. No one will want me after I have been in your custody. Therefore, if you do not want me, then I will have no choice but to return to the cloister. I am meant for you and no other, Bretton."

She was absolutely right on both accounts and it fueled his confusion even more. He tried to move away from her but she wouldn't let him go, and he ended up dragging her across the floor.

"Let me go," he told her again. "Allaston, release me. I demand it."

Allaston shook her head, holding his right leg tighter than she ever had. "I will not," she declared. "Please, Bretton, do not tell me you love me and then abandon me. I cannot stomach living my life without you."

He ended up stumbling, falling against the wall and sinking to the floor as Allaston maintained her grip on him. As he fell, she released his leg and pounced on him, her arms around his neck. Bretton, slumped against the wall, sat on his hands to keep from holding her. He knew if he did, all would be lost.

"Listen to me," he hissed. "Allaston, listen. It is true that I love you and, God knows how honored and touched I am that you would love me as well. Hearing those words from you has somehow made my life worthwhile. I have lived my whole life to hear it. But it does not change what I must do... it does not change the fact that my vengeance against your father must be exercised. It does not change that I must kill him."

Allaston didn't say anything for a moment. After a lengthy, brittle pause, she released her grip around Bretton's neck and sat back, pulling away from him. He watched her, distraught, as she sat back on her heels, eyeing him, seemingly confused or lost in thought. In either case, it was evident that there was a good deal on her mind. She was at the end of her wits and pure instinct took over. She appeared pale and disoriented as she stumbled over to the chair she had once sat in, near the hearth, and plopped down on it. As Bretton began to push himself up from the floor, Allaston spoke.

"I understand that my love cannot stop your revenge against my father," she said, her voice dull and hollow. "But hear me now. The day you kill him is the day I take my own life. I cannot live knowing the man I love would choose vengeance over my love. Life would not be worth living. There would be nothing left for me."

Bretton felt as if he'd been hit in the gut. He rose to his feet, slowly, and went to stand before her. His expression, as he looked down on her, was a mixture of horror and sorrow.

"Nay, Allaston," he beseeched. "You must not say that. You must not…."

"Why not?" she looked up at him, cutting him off. "If my father's life is not of value, then surely mine is not of value. I am a de Velt, after all. What difference does it make if one or more of us dies?"

His jaw ticked. "It matters to me," he said, his voice hoarse. "It makes all the difference in the world to me because I love you."

"You do not love me more than you love your vengeance against my father."

He growled, frustrated and grief-stricken. "Can you not understand that this is something I must do?" he begged. "It is a part of me, it is who I have become. Why must you threaten to kill yourself unless I give up this one thing that has kept me alive all these years?"

Allaston was shattered, cold, alone, and empty. She looked away from Bretton, devastated that her love was not enough to deter him from his revenge. She was not enough. Therefore, it didn't matter what became of her. At the moment, she didn't care one way or the other.

"Go away, Bretton," she told him, a lone tear trickling down her cheek. "I do not wish to speak with you any longer. Go and do what you must do. I will do the same."

He felt as if he couldn't breathe. "Please do not do this, Allaston," he begged softly. "Do not leave me with this horror."

She wouldn't answer him and Bretton had never felt so broken or hollow. Allaston's head was turned away from him and it took all of his strength not to reach out and stroke that dark, lovely head. He couldn't stand it and his control broke. A big hand extended, the dirty fingers barely touching the dark strands, like the brush of butterfly wings. Allaston felt the touch, gentle and faint, and she broke down into gut-busting sobs. She wanted to grab his hand, to kiss it and touch it, but she couldn't bring herself to do it. The hands meant to touch his ended up covering her face.

Bretton fled the room before he started weeping, too.

IT WAS DAWN.

Allaston hadn't slept the entire night. She'd been up thinking about Bretton, about their life that was never to be. It was odd, truly. Thinking back to the moment she met him as Alberbury burned around them, she would have never imagined falling for a killer. Aye, he was a killer. She had always acknowledged that. But Bretton de Llion was a complex creature. He was intelligent and skilled, driven by something that happened to him in childhood, something that had both fed and destroyed his soul.

She wondered what he would have been like had Jax de Velt never killed his father. He would have probably grown up with love, fostering in the best homes, and emerging a stellar knight with a bright future. Instead, Bretton had been forced to scratch and claw and fight for everything he had. It was all he knew. And now, she was asking him to change that way of thinking. Perhaps she had been wrong all along. Perhaps it was unfair of her to ask him to become something he wasn't. That very question had been tearing at her all night.

Shades of sunrise were beginning to color the eastern horizon. Allaston could see it clearly as she sat in the oriel window that faced over the eastern portion of the castle and a section of the bailey. She could see men moving around down below, going about their tasks, and she could smell the scent of baking bread. It would grow strong when the winds changed after sunrise.

Thinking that perhaps she should go down to the kitchen and help Uldward, she slid off the bench seat of the window and headed over to the wardrobe against the northern wall, the one that held the clothing she had borrowed from Lady Miette, garments Grayton had brought her so long ago. She hadn't seen Grayton for quite some time and was told he had remained at Comen Castle. Not that she cared. The man had been against her ever since the day she hit Bretton with the poker. In fact, she sensed that all of Bretton's men were against her to varying degrees. But none of that mattered now.

Bretton. She hadn't seen him since he fled her chamber the night before, and it was probably best that she hadn't. They were both too emotional about the situation and needed time to gather their wits. As Allaston changed into the yellow garment that Bretton had torn down the front during his fit of passion, the mending of which was now covered up with the bib of a white apron she had stitched on, Allaston knew without a doubt that she would never leave the man. He could try to send her back to her parents but she wouldn't go. She was determined to remain with him, to convince him that they belonged together, because she knew once she left him that her life would be a lonely and desolate thing. She didn't want to leave the only man she had ever loved.

So she cinched up the surcoat, tightening it over the linen shift, and pulled on her boots, boots she had borrowed from Lady Miette. She combed her hair thoroughly and braided it, pulling a kerchief around her head to keep loose strands out of her face and out of any food she would work with. On the table was a small polished mirror she had found in Lady Miette's possessions and she held it up, inspecting her face, seeing a woman of determination gazing back at her.

She seemed to have aged over the past several weeks. When Bretton had first abducted her, she had been a somewhat naïve girl. Now, she felt as if she had done enough growing to spread over a lifetime. She had seen much, and experienced much, and the love she felt for Bretton was engrained in her very fabric. Nay, she would not leave him, not even if he tried to force her. The only thing that was going to separate them was death.

As she set the mirror down, she began to hear a commotion down in the bailey. She could hear men shouting and, curious, she went to the window to see what the fuss was about. Her gaze was naturally drawn to the men below, running around, and she could see a portion of the gatehouse but not beyond it. She could, however, see over the wall towards the east where there was a sharp slope and groves of trees, and then the rolling green hills of Wales beyond. As she looked off to the east, it began to occur to her that, upon the horizon, a black tide seemed to be moving.

There it was, spreading across the green fields, moving towards Cloryn in a long, dark line. She watched, curious, until she realized that she was looking at the approach of an army. She had no doubt who was at the head of the army. Her blood ran cold.

Allaston bolted from the chamber, racing down the dark, narrow stairs towards the keep entry. Bolting through the door, she took the steps far too quickly and almost stumbled at the bottom, but she caught herself and began to run towards the gatehouse. All she could think of was warning her father off, of telling him to go back and away from Bretton's wrath. She was halfway across the bailey when someone caught her around the waist.

Frightened, she looked up to see that it was Teague who had a hold of her. She had never had much interaction with the warrior but she knew, like the rest of Bretton's commanders, that he was not friendly towards her. Panicked, she began to fight him, kicking and hitting, until he was forced to loosen his grip. But he didn't release her entirely. He held on to her. A shout filled the air and they both stopped their wrestling.

Bretton was heading towards them from the direction of the gate-house. As he drew near, he brusquely waved Teague off, who obediently let the lady go and vacated. As the big knight with the piercing dark eyes headed off, Bretton moved closer to Allaston, his eyes riveted to her.

"Where were you going?" he asked softly. "I saw you running out of the keep."

Allaston looked at him, defiantly. "I saw the army to the east," she said. "You know it is my father. I was going to warn him off. I do not want him coming near this place for obvious reasons."

Bretton gazed steadily at her. He hadn't slept all night, either, trapped in a world that was tearing itself apart, an engrained hatred against a love that consumed him. He'd been fighting with himself every hour of the night, trying to determine if he was doing the right thing by maintaining the hatred that had kept him alive all these years. Would he be a traitor to himself if he gave in to Allaston's love? God only knew how happy he could be with her. But how happy could he be if her father was still alive, reminding him of his discarded vengeance at every turn? More than that, would he end up resenting Allaston because she had taken away that which had kept him alive? He could only wonder. Gazing into her lovely face now in the soft light of morning, he could feel himself starting to weaken.

"We are not certain it is him," he said quietly.

Allaston scowled. "Of course it is him," she said. "You sent him a missive telling him to come to Cloryn Castle and, more than that, you told de Lohr the same thing when the earl tried to intervene. Of course it is my father – who else could it be?"

She was correct and he knew it. Of course it was de Velt, and de Lohr was more than likely with him. Reaching out, Bretton tried to grasp her arm but she pulled away from him, unwilling to let him touch her. A look of genuine pain crossed his features.

"Please go back to your chamber," he said. "I am asking you politely to do this. If you refuse, I will put you in the vault until this is over. Is that clear?"

Allaston's first reaction was to run from him, but he would only catch her. She knew that. Her rebellion turned to sadness, and sadness to pain. She struggled against the tears that were already threatening.

"Will you please tell me what you are planning to do?" she asked. "Please, Bretton. This day will see me lose one man that I love dearly and I would like to know what you are planning, I beg you."

He was in no mood to argue with her but on the other hand, he couldn't quite seem to make her go.

"Much depends on your father," he said. "My actions will be dictated by his."

"He will want me returned," Allaston said. "Will you show him that I am in good health? Will you at least let me speak with him?"

Bretton didn't think that was a particularly good idea but he was curious about it. "What would you say to him?"

Allaston thought on that a moment. "More than likely the same thing I would say to you," she said quietly. "I would tell him that I love him and I am sorry it has come to this."

Somewhere overhead, the sentries sounded out a cry that the army was drawing closer and Bretton acknowledged it with the wave of a hand. But his attention was on Allaston. With a gentle sigh, he reached out, taking her hand. Feeling her soft, warm fingers in his grasp nearly undid him.

"I could not sleep last night for thoughts of you," he murmured. "No matter what this day brings, Allaston, please know that I love you deeply. I always will. I have never loved anything in my life as I have loved you."

She wanted so badly to believe him but she knew it wasn't true. She pulled her fingers away from him.

"You do not love me more than you love your sense of vengeance," she said. "I wish it was true that you loved me more than anything, but it is not."

"I am sorry you feel that way."

"So am I."

They simply stood there and stared at each other, thoughts and emotions as tangible as rain filling the air between them. It was a painful moment, one that perhaps made them realize that they were two individuals with two destinies rather than two individuals with one destiny, a destiny of marriage and love and a future. Allaston couldn't stand the tension or the agony and eventually lowered her gaze.

"Will you please let me speak to my father?" she asked. "If you are going to kill him, then at least let me say what I will to him. Do not deny me what my father denied you. Let me speak to my father one last time."

He couldn't refuse her. "Very well," he said, sounding dull and defeated. "When it is over, I would expect to turn you over to de Lohr.

He will ensure that you are returned to your mother."

Allaston was so full of anguish that it was difficult for her to think straight. To face losing her father, and losing Bretton, was more than she could appropriately deal with.

"If… if you kill my father, then I will be taking his body with me," she said, her throat tight with tears. "I will not return home without him."

"Agreed."

"But if you should die, Bretton," she turned to look at him, tears in her eyes, "I will not leave here without you, either. I will make sure you have a proper burial, someplace that I can visit, if only in my dreams. I will make sure that, at the end of your life, you are treated with the dignity and respect you were denied while you were living."

Her words stunned him, touched him, as he had never been touched before. He'd never heard anything more gracious. "Why would you do this?" he asked, perplexed. "I have killed people and left them to rot. I have not treated the dead with any dignity whatsoever. Why would you treat me with dignity after death when it is not deserved?"

Her tears spilled over. "Because I love you," she said. "That is reason enough."

Bretton didn't think it was possible for him to feel worse than he already did, but he was wrong. Peering into Allaston's beautiful eyes, he felt cruel and shallow, wicked and shattered… all of those things he had felt when he realized she deserved someone better than him, he was feeling them again, more strongly than before.

"This will more than likely be the last time you and I will have the opportunity to speak to one another, privately," he said softly. "I want you to know that… that the day I abducted you from Alberbury was the day my life changed forever, only I did not know it at the time. You have shown me life and love and beauty, Allaston, such things as I had forgotten to exist. I pray that, in the future, no matter how this day turns out, that when you think of me, there is a measure of kindness in your heart towards me. Forgive me for not being the strong, virtuous knight you deserve. If I could be that man for you, please know that I would be. But my path is set and my world is dark. As I told you before, I do not want to pull you into that world. I love you enough to know that I must set you free."

Allaston listened to him, tears trickling from the corners of her eyes. She flicked them away. "I have pain in my heart such as I cannot comprehend," she replied. "I fear that no matter what happens here today, I will love you until I die, regardless of the outcome."

Bretton was feeling the same pain in his heart that she was. "Do you still plan to kill yourself if I kill your father?" he asked.

"I do."

"I will do all in my power to prevent it, you know."

She shook her head. "You will not be fast enough."

He grunted. "I will lock you in the vault for your own safety, then."

"I can still kill myself in the vault," she whispered. "Do not think to presume you can stop me. If you kill my father... my life is over. I will have nothing left to live for because you will have proven to me that your love for vengeance is greater than your love for me."

He sighed sadly. "Please," he pleaded softly. "Please...do not do anything rash or foolish. Allaston, I beg you."

She wouldn't answer him. She simply hung her head and Bretton stood there, staring at her. He knew there was no way to prevent her from killing herself if she was truly serious. He could only pray she wasn't, that somehow, someway, some bit of reason in her mind would stop her from doing it. He wasn't a praying man but, at that moment, he found himself saying a prayer for divine intervention. If she, in fact, killed herself, then he would have nothing to live for, either. At the moment, he was coming to hate himself for his sense of duty, his sense of revenge. But he could not stop that which was already in motion.

With nothing more to say, he impulsively reached out, again taking her warm fingers in his, but this time she did not pull away. He lifted her hand to his lips, kissing the flesh softly and feeling her tremble at his touch. Her hand, at his lips, moved to his face and she wedged herself closer to him, both hands on his face as she hung her head. It was as if she couldn't bear to look at him but she had to touch him one last time. Bretton moved to put his arms around her but she pulled away, abruptly, and shook her head. However, she did grasp his fingers again, pulling him with her as she moved, unsteadily, towards the keep. Bretton followed blindly, even when she let go of his fingers and ran up the stairs as if the Devil himself was chasing her.

The Devil, in fact, was. Bretton raced up the stairs after her, sensing that she wanted him to follow her and being unable to resist. Once he entered the keep, he slammed the door only to find her standing in the shadows of the keep entry. Before he could speak, she ran at him, her mouth fusing to his and her arms around his neck. Bretton responded wildly and instantly, his arms around her, his lips on hers, kissing her so hard that she was gasping for air. Still, he kissed her harder. There was finality in his touch, knowing this would be the last time he ever tasted her. It would be the last, and only, time he would ever touch a woman he loved. Emotion fed his passion to a frenzied level.

Allaston was in his arms as he carried her into the open room and sat her on the scrubbed table, the one he had molested her on those weeks ago. This time, there was so much fever and fire to their touch that it was raging out of control. Allaston began to weep softly as he kissed her, his hands moving to her body, touching her through the dress he had ripped once, feeling her warm flesh beneath the fabric. When he brushed over her right breast, unwilling to spook her, she grabbed his hand and put it squarely over her breast.

"Touch me," she whispered against his mouth. "I beg of you, take me as your own, Bretton. We will never know this moment again and I want to remember you against me, within me, as the only man who was ever meant to be my husband. In my heart, you *are* my husband. Please do not deny me this memory of you. Let me feel your love as it was meant to be."

Bretton didn't need to be told twice. With a growl, he picked her up again and took her to the end of the room that was dark and shadowed.

There was more privacy there. He loosened the fastens on the surcoat this time rather than tearing it, easing the shift and dress off her shoulders, enough so that he could get to a warm and tender nipple. When he suckled her furiously, Allaston cried out softly, holding his head to her breast as if he were a starving child nursing against her. As she held him tightly, his hands snaked underneath her skirts, hiking them up, revealing her virgin core beneath.

Pushing her back on the table, Bretton nursed hungrily at her breasts as his hands, far more gently this time, caressed her buttocks and stroked her thighs. When he gently stroked the dark fluff of curls, she leapt with uncertainty but he stilled her with gentle words and soft caresses. Allaston wanted this, after all. She wanted to feel the man within her, just this once. It would be the one and only time she did.

Bretton slipped a finger into her tight, wet sheath, feeling her gasp at the new and strange sensation. She was very moist and he refused to wait. He had been anticipating this moment since nearly the day he met her and he refused to wait any longer. He unfastened his breeches and let them fall to his ankles and as he put the tip of his hard, throbbing phallus at her threshold, he lifted his head and looked her in the eye.

"I love you, Allaston de Velt," he murmured, gently kissing her chin, her mouth. "What I do now, I do for no other reason than that. You are my heart, my soul, my wife who will never be. I have never loved anyone as I love you and I have never taken a woman who meant something to me. You are the first, in many ways. You are with me forever."

With that, he thrust into her, listening to her gasp with pain as he breached her maidenhood. She cried out softly as he thrust again and again, seating himself to the hilt, feeling her tight wetness around him. It was beyond pleasure. It was passion and desire such as he had never known. Once fully seated, he held her buttocks against his pelvis and began to thrust into her.

Allaston clung to him, feeling the proof of his passion buried deep inside her, filling her as she could have never imagined. As he pounded into her, she ended up gripping the edge of the table so he wouldn't push her off of it with the force of his movements. With every thrust, he ground his pelvis against hers and she could feel sparks every time their bodies met. His lips were against her forehead, kissing her softly as he made love to her, and Allaston was overwhelmed with it.

"I want your son," she breathed, daring to reach down and touch herself where their bodies were joined. She could feel his smooth phallus as he entered her, again and again. "Give me your son, Bretton. Give me your seed so that I may bear your child. If I cannot have you, then at least I can have him. Please... give me your son."

Bretton gasped heavily as he heard her words, sending lust and desire through him that fed through his loins. It fed him for another reason as well. A woman who was planning on killing herself would not be thinking of bearing a child. Perhaps this was the divine intervention he had been hoping for. He found himself imagining that he would impregnate her, filling her with his son, a child that would bear his good looks and her intelligent mind. He'd barely thought of heirs until he met her and now he could think of nothing else. When her fingers brushed his phallus again, he couldn't hold back his climax and he released himself deep into her body, feeling her own release as she joined him.

Gasping, sweating, Bretton gathered her up into his arms, holding her tightly, still embedded in her as the last of his arousal died away. He was savoring the feel of her against him, tenderly kissing the side of her head, when the sounds from the bailey grew louder and he knew it was because his men were looking for him. He could hear someone calling for him. An army was approaching, coming closer, and Bretton knew the time had come to leave her. But he didn't want to let her go, knowing this would be the last time he ever held her in his arms.

"I must go," he conceded. "If I do not, they will come in here looking for me."

Allaston pulled her head from the crook of his neck, looking up at him. Her bright green eyes were full of emotion.

"I love you," she whispered.

"And I love you, forever and always."

There was nothing more to say. Allaston released him and Bretton stood back, pulling his breeches up and securing them. Allaston slipped off the table, noticing a small amount of blood and bodily fluid on her shift. But it didn't matter. She didn't regret anything. Without looking at him, she headed towards the chamber entry.

"If it is your wish that I remain in my chamber, I will do it," she said quietly. "But I would like to speak to my father before… well, before anything happens. I would consider it a great favor if you would allow it."

Bretton looked at her, anguish in his eyes. "I will send for you."

"Thank you."

She took a few steps but he called out to her. "Allaston?"

She paused to look at him. "Aye?"

Bretton's gaze never left her as he crossed the floor, taking her into his arms one last time and kissing her with all of the power and anguish he was feeling. Allaston felt it, too. When he let her go, she ran up the stairs. He could hear the chamber door slam on the second floor. He swore he heard her sobbing, too.

With a heavy heart, yet with great determination, he headed out to the bailey to greet the incoming army.

To greet de Velt.

CHAPTER TWENTY-ONE

J OHN MORGAN HAD spent the past two days trying to figure out why he was in Wales. He was surrounded with people he didn't know, men who had told him he was really somebody else. It was damn confusing and he didn't like being confused.

The trek into Wales had been steady and methodical, as de Lohr, de Poyer, and de Velt were moving a fairly large army and they had thirteen provision wagons between them. De Velt had brought almost a thousand men from Pelinom, de Poyer had brought eight hundred men with him from Nether, and de Lohr had eleven hundred, making for a massive movement of men and material. All of these soldiers and knights heading into Wales, preparing to take on a mercenary who held de Velt's daughter hostage with John Morgan right in the middle of it. According to de Lohr, he was a very important part of it.

Unhappy, John Morgan followed de Lohr and de Velt into Wales because he had been ordered to, but he kept to himself. Unfamiliar people always made him nervous. On the morning of the third day out from Lioncross Abbey and after a restless night on John's part, the army was in sight of a castle in the distance and word spread through the ranks that it was Cloryn Castle. The sunrise was behind them, as they were coming from the east, bathing the castle in a golden glow. It looked rather pretty, to be truthful, but being that it was their destination, something evil await them there. John Morgan didn't like the look of it.

As he pondered the castle in the distance, riding off to his left was a young knight and an old knight astride their big war horses, men that de Lohr had told him were relatives of his. The old man was even his father, although John Morgan hadn't recognized him. But that wasn't unusual. He was very bad with faces and names. In fact, he was pretty bad at most things. He wasn't a bright man.

"I have been noticing your horse," came a voice beside him. John Morgan looked over to see a handsome young knight smiling back at him, a young knight he was told was his nephew. The knight gestured to the big bay stallion John Morgan was riding. "He has the long-legged look of a Belgian charger. Is that where you got him?"

John Morgan wasn't comfortable in conversation with men he didn't know so it was an effort for him to answer. "Nay," he said. "He was given to me."

"How old is he?"

"I am not sure. I think he is ten years old."

Rod had wanted to engage his uncle in conversation for two days but de Lohr had told him to stay away. He was afraid of upsetting John Morgan and possibly upsetting the entire campaign if the man decided to run off. But Rod was very sociable and he was also very concerned. Berwyn had been a wreck since the day he met John Morgan and Rod very much wanted to ease the way for his grandfather to have a conversation with his son. It was a heartbreaking circumstance.

"Have you had him long?" Rod continued.

John Morgan shook his head. "Not too long."

Rod wouldn't let the conversation die. He forged onward. "It looks as if he has a smooth gait," he said. "I had a fine Belgian charger once that was as smooth as silk but he had a nasty habit of farting all the time. It made travel rather unpleasant. Do you travel much, then?"

John Morgan shook his head. "Not much."

Rod was coming to see that the man wasn't much of a conversationalist but it didn't deter him. "How was your trip down from

Northumberland?" he asked. "I've actually never been to Alnwick. I hear it is a big place."

John Morgan nodded. "Big enough," he said. "My trip was bearable."

Rod eyed the man, trying to think of something that would possibly engage him in more of a conversation. So far, he wasn't doing very well. "I am pleased to hear that," he said, eyeing the horse again. "Have you ever used that horse in a tournament? He has a big chest. I imagine he would have a lot of power in the joust."

John Morgan shook his head. "I do not joust."

"Have you ever?"

Again, John Morgan shook his head. "I have not."

Rod was struggling to keep the conversation going. "I notice you're missing a finger," he said. "How did it happen?"

John Morgan lifted his right hand, looking at his little finger, taken off to the second knuckle. He inspected it a moment. "A horse took it off."

Rod felt a jolt of hope roll through him. *It happened long before his head injury. How did he know that?* "A shame," he said, eyeing the man. "I had an uncle who lost the same finger to a horse. As a child, I was scared of horses because of it. I thought they ate fingers for the longest time."

John Morgan didn't say anything. He continued plodding along, occasionally looking at his missing finger. "You mean me," he finally said.

Rod nodded, his heart softening. He found himself praying that somehow, someway, the man would remember them. For Berwyn's sake, he prayed.

"Aye," he said softly. "I mean you. I loved you very much, Uncle Morgan. I still do. Although you do not remember me, or your family, you were very loved. We are very happy to know you did not die those years ago."

John Morgan sighed with confusion. He kept looking at his missing finger, struggling to recall those years that had vanished from his mind. He didn't seem as uncomfortable or stiff as he had earlier.

"That old man," he said after a moment. "That man who attacked me. He is my father?"

Rod nodded slowly. "He is," he said quietly. "He did not attack you. He was happy to see you and was trying to hug you. He did not know that you did not remember him."

John Morgan was still staring at his hand, evidently pondering the information. "I do not know him."

"His name is Berwyn."

John Morgan looked up from his hand, his brilliant blue-eyed gaze roaming the land. He seemed to grow thoughtful, as if his damaged mind was working on something. He scratched his chin, his lips moving as if to bring forth words he couldn't quite grasp. When he finally spoke, Rod barely heard him.

"Fair flower," he muttered.

Rod was stunned. "Fair flower," he repeated softly. "*Blodwyn.* That was your mother's name. Why did you say that, Uncle Morgan? Do you remember her?"

John Morgan shook his head unsteadily, still looking over the landscape. He pointed to a patch of yellow flowers by the road. "Fair flower," he said again.

Rod turned around and frantically motioned to Berwyn, who was riding several feet behind them. Berwyn looked as if he had aged fifty years in the past two days, distraught over a son returned from the dead who did not remember him. But he dutifully spurred his charger forward, looking at Rod with as much curiosity as he could muster. Rod whispered to his grandfather as the man grew near.

"He said *fair flower*," he muttered. "That was grandmother's name, Blodwyn."

Berwyn looked at his son, brow furrowed, but John Morgan was staring at the flowers at the side of the road, seemingly in a world of his own. When Berwyn saw what he was looking at, it sparked a memory in him from long ago, something that his beloved wife used to say to their children. A child's rhyme that he pulled from deep in his mind.

"Fair flower, fair flower, you greet me each day," he said, loud enough so that John Morgan could hear him. "Fair flower, fair flower, do not go away. Fair flower, fair flower, your beauty won't fade. The sun from above is your soft fairy maid."

Rod had heard that rhyme from his grandmother once, too, but he hadn't made the connection when John Morgan had mentioned fair flower. He had only thought of his grandmother's name and its meaning. But the moment Berwyn repeated the rhyme, John Morgan looked at Berwyn with the most curious of expressions. Berwyn gazed into his son's eyes, his heart breaking that the man didn't know him. But there was something in his face that suggested he was trying. Something was going on in that wounded brain, sparks of long-lost memories beginning to stir.

"Do you know that rhyme, John Morgan?" Berwyn asked calmly. "Have you heard it before?"

John Morgan stared at Berwyn a moment longer before nodding his head, briefly. Then, he faced forward again, all but ignoring Rod and Berwyn. It was evident that the conversation was over. Still, contact had been made. There was something there, something that suggested memories were buried deep. They simply needed to dig them out. When Rod finally turned to Berwyn to see how the man was reacting, he was surprised to see a smile on his lips.

He had hope.

The ride continued in comfortable silence from that point forward. Rod's attention turned from his uncle and grandfather to the head of the column where de Velt and de Lohr were beginning to signal to the men. Cloryn Castle was drawing close and a call went up in the column, and everyone ground to a halt.

De Poyer, covering the rear, barked orders and sent the provisions wagons away from the rest of the column, back into a line of trees that was off to the northeast. They would have protection there and tents would be pitched out of the range of archers from the castle. Word then spread back through the lines, calling Rod forward. De Lohr had need of him.

Rod charged forward, along the column, until he reached Christopher at the head. "Aye, my lord?" he responded as he brought his charger to a halt.

Christopher was in full battle armor, as was de Velt. It was an impressive but odd sight, seeing the two great commanders in full regalia as allies with a common cause. De Velt was as frightening as always in his red and black tunic with his battle-scarred older mail, something he hadn't worn in quite a long time, while Christopher's recognizable blue and yellow tunic covered expensive and well-maintained mail. When Rod approached, Christopher lifted his visor.

"We can see movements on the parapets, so they are alerted to our arrival and are undoubtedly preparing," he told Rod. "Since you have already made contact with your cousin, I am going to ask you to ride to the gate and summon him. Since he knows you, he is less likely to shoot you down."

Rod pursed his lips wryly. "I am *not* comforted by that, my lord," he said. "What would you have me stay to him?"

Christopher fought off a smile at Rod's humorless answer. "Announce our arrival," he said. "Tell de Llion that we have come to make an exchange for de Velt's daughter. Tell him that we wish to see her and make sure she is in good health before we proceed."

Rod nodded, affixing the strap on his helm that had loosened. "Am I alone to view the girl and determine her health, or do you want me to summon you when she is being brought forth?"

"I want to see her," Jax said before Christopher could reply.

Christopher shook his head. "If you go any closer, you will be within range of the archers and they can cut you down," he said, telling the man what he already knew. His attention returned to Rod. "You can determine if the woman is in good health."

Rod wriggled his dark eyebrows knowingly. "He is going to expect de Velt for the exchange," he said. "What should I tell him?"

Christopher glanced at Jax before replying. "Tell him we have no intention of attacking Cloryn and we will keep our army at bay providing he brings de Velt's daughter and meets us on neutral territory, away from the walls of Cloryn." He could see the castle in the distance, the road, and a wide field on the opposite side of the road, away from the castle. He pointed at it. "That field will do. We will be in full view of the castle at all times. In fact, Jax and I will bring John Morgan and go there to await the exchange. De Llion will be able to see us and, if nothing else, it will pique his curiosity."

Rod nodded in understanding. "And if the girl is not in good health?" he asked. "What do you want me to do?"

Christopher didn't look at Jax, afraid to see his expression. "If she is not, then you will return to us immediately and tell us what you have seen. We will determine how to proceed at that time."

He meant plans for a siege. Rod sighed heavily, with regret for what might come. "And do you want me to tell him who we have with us?" he asked. "Do I tell him about his father?"

Christopher shrugged. "I would prefer that you not, but if it is the only way he will meet us on neutral ground for the exchange, so be it."

Rod nodded and spurred his charger forward, across the dusty road that doubled back on itself as it rose up the incline to Cloryn Castle. Meanwhile, Christopher and Jax plowed back through the lines until they came to John Morgan, back at mid-pack with Berwyn several feet away. Christopher focused on John Morgan.

"We have arrived at the castle your son has confiscated from Lord de Velt," he said in simple terms. "Do you recall I told you of this back at Lioncross?"

John Morgan nodded. "Aye, my lord."

"I told you that your son, Bretton, has seized Lord de Velt's daughter and he is holding her hostage to seek vengeance for your death."

Again, John Morgan nodded. "Aye, my lord."

Christopher leaned forward on his saddle, fixed on John Morgan's bright blue eyes. "We are going to present you to your son in exchange for de Velt's daughter," he said. "I told you this before. It is very important that you accept that Bretton de Llion is your son. We will explain to him that you do not remember him and I am not entirely sure how he is going to accept that, but it is very important that you go with the man so we can secure de Velt's daughter. You are a soldier, Morgan. This is your duty to help save this young woman. Do what you can to keep your son calm, at least until we can spirit her away. Is this clear?"

"Aye, my lord."

Even though John Morgan acknowledged the order, it was anyone's guess as to how much he really understood. Christopher's gaze considered John Morgan before seeking out Berwyn.

The old man was several feet away, looking pale and worn. Of anyone, this entire venture seemed to be taking the greatest toll on Berwyn with his long-lost son and grandson involved. Christopher's heart hurt for the man but there wasn't time for that now. They had a job to do.

"You will come with us, Berwyn," he said. "Mayhap we can overwhelm de Llion with his father and grandfather, enough so that we can get Lady Allaston away without harm. I would much rather handle this peacefully if we can."

Berwyn nodded with resignation. "I will come, my lord."

As Jax took John Morgan with him and headed for the clearing in the distance, Christopher reined his charger next to Berwyn as the old man secured his helm atop his head. There was lethargy to his movements, something that was sad to watch from the usually spry old man.

"I am sorry things have turned out this way, Berwyn," Christopher said quietly. "Although I am glad for you that Morgan and Bretton have been discovered alive, the circumstances of their lives are less than desirable. Hopefully, with time, that will change."

Berwyn nodded stoically. "We shall see, my lord," he said. "But, at this moment... I wish they were still dead to me. My memories of them are fond ones, but this new reality... I am not so sure I like it. I do not want the new, sad memories to destroy the old."

Christopher reached out and patted the old man on the shoulder before they drove their chargers onward, across the road and into the field opposite Cloryn's front gates. As the day around them deepened, the bright blue sky above was cheery and clear, hardly indicative of the turmoil about to happen beneath it.

The turmoil of a dead father returned to a dead son.

⁂

As Rod approached Cloryn's gates, he noticed a small forest of poles stuck in the ground surrounding the road leading up to the gatehouse. It looked like a bunch of tree trunks, reduced to stumps, emerging from the soil. As he slowed his charger to a walk, it occurred to him that these were the remains of the poles upon which people had been impaled. It was no secret that Bretton had been emulating Jax de Velt's pattern of conquest and as Rod plodded up the road towards the gatehouse, he couldn't help but feel the terror and pain that must have gone on at this place. He could almost hear the screams of the men as poles were rammed up their anus. The mere thought made him shudder and he swallowed hard, trying to push aside the horrific mental images.

His gaze moved to the walls of Cloryn, tall barriers constructed from mottled gray stone. Evil and fear radiated from the very walls, and the phantoms of the dead swirled about him. God, there was so much wickedness here. Rod could see men at the top, looking down upon him, so he slowed his pace as he drew near the entry and lifted his visor. The two-storied gatehouse loomed before him, the drawbridge raised and the moat, soiled with mud and muck and unspeakable filth, filled the air with its stench. Wary, and cautious, Rod finally pulled his steed to a halt. The time was upon him to speak.

"My name is Sir Rod de Titouan," he bellowed. "I am a cousin to Bretton de Llion. I have come to speak with him!"

He could see men moving around on top of the parapets and he could hear voices. There was a good deal of scuffling going on but no one called back to him or acknowledged him. Rod waited a nominal amount of time, watching them move about, before shouting again.

"I would speak with Bretton de Llion," he yelled. "I have come with the armies of de Lohr and de Velt. Tell de Llion I am here!"

More shuffling and voices. As Rod waited with some impatience, a voice eventually called down to him from the junction where the wall met the gatehouse.

"Rod?" Bretton called down to him. "What are you doing here?"

Rod looked up, spying Bretton on the wall above. He could see his face but little more. He waved a hand at the man.

"Greetings, cousin," he said. "I suppose you did not think you would see me again so soon."

Bretton didn't say anything for a moment. "Why are *you* here?" he asked again. "I asked only for de Velt."

"And he is here," Rod said. "He received your demands and has come. But first, I have been instructed to see his daughter to ensure that she is in good health. Will you produce her for me, please?'"

"And if I do not?"

Rod cocked his head. "Do you really think that every demand you make will be met without question?" he asked. "There are times when you must give a little in order to receive. It is not an unusual or terrible request to want to see if your hostage is still in good health, is it? You should not be reluctant to show that she is."

Bretton was displeased by Rod's reply but he sent Teague, who was standing near him, to fetch Allaston. As the big knight headed off the wall, Bretton remained fixed on Rod down below.

"She is in very good health," he finally said. "You saw her when we met in Newtown."

Rod nodded, pulling off his helm and wiping at the copious amount of sweat on his forehead. "I did indeed," he replied. "But I want to make sure she is still healthy and whole before we move forward in this process."

"And what would moving forward entail?"

Rod put his helm back on, looking up at Bretton with a rather guarded expression. "I would like to relay terms but I will not shout them for all to hear," he said. "Will you come down off the wall and face me? Or do you prefer hiding away to meeting me face to face as you did in Newtown?"

It was a moderate insult, surprising from usually-congenial Rod. Bretton sighed heavily. Nay, he didn't particularly want his men hearing everything that was spoken, especially where it pertained to Allaston. He thought it best to keep control of the situation by not having communication between him and Rod so spread out. Meeting the man face to face was a better alternative.

"Remain where you are," he told Rod. "I will come to you."

With that, he climbed off the wall and made his way to the gate-house, instructing the sentries to lower the heavy drawbridge. As the ropes and chains holding the panel in place began to creak and groan as the bridge was lowered, Bretton stood in the entry, waiting for Allaston to be brought forth. The bridge was almost down entirely by the time Teague brought her out of the keep. Bretton could see them heading towards him and the sight of the woman, after what had happened between them earlier, had his heart racing. The emotions, the love he felt for her, were running wild and he was having difficulty keeping his head.

Allaston had changed from the yellow wool and back into the dark blue brocade that made her pale skin look smooth and milky. Teague had her by the arm as he brought her to Bretton, who waved his commander off as he took Allaston by the wrist. Their eyes met and the flood of emotions burst forth, each one feeling so much more than they ever dreamed possible. Making love that morning had been a glorious mistake. Now, things were even more entrenched between them. Bretton's heart ached simply to look at her.

"My cousin, Rod, has come as a messenger from your father's ar-my," he told her quietly. "He has been sent to ensure you are still in good health."

Allaston nodded reluctantly. "Is my father here?"

Bretton led her towards the portcullis, still lowered, as Rod remained on the road just beyond the drawbridge.

"He is," Bretton said. "I have not seen him yet. Rod has been sent as an advanced messenger to relay their terms."

Terms that would involve her. Allaston stood against the portcullis, peering at Rod on the other side. When Rod saw the lady looking at him, he waved at her.

"My lady," he said. "I have come to makes sure you are well."

Allaston's eyes met the well-armed knight. "I am," she replied. "Where is my father?"

Rod turned around, looking over his shoulder at the field behind him. He could see four riders there, in the distance, watching him from amongst the green grass and scattered trees. He returned his attention to Allaston.

"Out there," he said, pointing back to the field. "Bretton, may I come closer so I may speak privately to you?"

Bretton nodded. "Come forth."

Rod dismounted his charger and, leaving the animal to graze next to the road on fat green grass, he made his way across the drawbridge, his boots creating great clodding noises as he walked. When he came to within a few feet of the portcullis, he came to a halt. His bright blue eyes met with those of his cousin and he could feel himself becoming emotional about the situation. After a moment, he shook his head as if suffering a loss of words.

"So much of my family is involved with this," he finally muttered. "It is very hard not to feel badly for what is happening. I have been instructed to tell you that de Lohr has no intention of attacking Cloryn and will keep the army at bay providing you bring de Velt's daughter and meet him on neutral territory, away from the walls of the castle."

Bretton looked over Rod's shoulder, seeing the four horsemen in the distance. "Who has de Lohr brought with him?"

Rod was careful in how he answered. "De Velt is with him," he said, avoiding most of the question. "That is who you want to see, is it not?"

Bretton's gaze still focused on the men in the distance. "There are more than just two riders there," he said, looking at Rod. "Who else is with him?"

Rod met his gaze steadily. "No one who will hurt you or be a threat to you," he said quietly. "Bring Lady Allaston and whoever else you feel you want to accompany you and come with me."

That wasn't the answer Bretton was looking for. Now, he was becoming suspicious. "*Who* else is there, Rod?"

Rod could see that Bretton wasn't going anywhere unless he told him. He wanted to lie about it but he wasn't sure that was wise. In fact, it was probably better if he was truthful with him. There was so much at stake here, for all of them.

"Grandfather is there," he finally said, watching Bretton's expression flicker with surprise. "And... and someone else."

"*Who* else?"

Rod sighed heavily. "Do you fear the fourth rider so much that you would refuse to come unless I tell you?"

Bretton crossed his big arms. "Nay," he said. "I do not fear anyone. But now you have made me wildly curious and until you tell me who all four riders are, I will not come and neither will the lady."

Rod met his cousin's gaze with steely determination. "And if you do not come, then they will let loose almost three thousand men on Cloryn. This castle will not survive such a siege and you know it."

"Then why will you not tell me who the fourth rider is?"

"Because I am afraid you will not believe me."

"Would you lie to me, then?"

"Never."

"Then tell me and I will believe you."

Rod had no choice. He eyed the lady, still standing there, listening to everything that had been said, before refocusing on his cousin again.

"I would prefer to tell you in private," he said softly.

Bretton shook his head. "I have no secrets from Lady Allaston," he replied. "She is involved in this situation as much as I am. You may speak freely in front of her."

Rod wiped a weary hand over his face, turning to look at the four riders in the field, pondering their identities, before returning his focus to Bretton.

"Very well," he said reluctantly. "But in order to tell you who the fourth rider is, I must give you some background. When de Velt came to de Lohr those weeks ago and asked for his assistance in mediating Lady Allaston's release, it was inevitable that there were discussions of de Velt's past events. It was also inevitable that the siege of Four Crosses was discussed. In the course of discussing the dead of Four Crosses, your family included, we came to discover that de Velt had not killed a few of the men. He took some of them for forced labor. One man in particular was discussed during the course of the conversation. He had a terrible head injury that had prevented him from remember-ing anything other than his name. He was a big man, very strong, and after de Velt was finished with him, he went to Alnwick Castle and served as a bodyguard to the Earl of Northumberland. This man gave his name as Morgan, and over the years he became known as John Morgan. Bretton, I am here to tell you that I have met John Morgan. Your father did not perish during the fall of Four Crosses Castle. By some miracle he survived and has been living in Northumberland under the name of John Morgan. John Morgan is the fourth rider."

Allaston gasped at the news, but Bretton's expression held steady. His brow was furrowed, listening to every word his cousin spoke, and when Rod was finished, he continued to stand there with a furrowed brow, frozen, as if he had forgotten how to move. He simply stood there, looking at Rod, until very slowly, his eyes moved beyond Rod to the four horsemen in the distance. But he simply stood there, unmov-ing, and more than likely not breathing. Allaston finally put a timid hand on his arm.

"Bretton?" she asked hesitantly. "Did you hear him? Your father is here! He is not dead!"

Bretton blinked. Then, it was as if he had been hit in the gut, for he exhaled loudly and painfully, suddenly grasping the portcullis for support.

"It… it cannot be," he breathed.

Rod could see how stunned he was and he moved closer, putting his hand on his cousin's fingers as they gripped the old iron grate.

"It is true, I swear it," he said. "Come with me, Bretton. Come and see your father. He is waiting for you."

Bretton yanked his hands off the portcullis, away from his cousin's touch. "You are lying!" he roared.

Rod shook his head. "Bretton, I swear upon my oath as a knight that I am not," he said. "Grandfather is there, too. They are all there waiting for you. Won't you please come and see them?"

Bretton was in a world of denial. "It is a trick," he hissed. "Witch-craft! My father died twenty-five years ago!"

Rod shook his head firmly. "Your father was very badly injured twenty-five years ago," he said. "He survived but he had no recollection of who he was. He does not remember me or grandfather. Will you please come and see him? Mayhap he will remember you."

Bretton was seized with shock and disbelief. He stumbled back, slumped against the wall of the gatehouse. His hands were at his mouth as if to hold back his astonishment.

"Why did you bring him?" he demanded. "*Why*?"

Rod watched his cousin, the mighty mercenary who had so flaw-lessly planned the destruction of Jax de Velt's empire, crumble before him. The man was falling apart.

"Because we want to exchange Morgan de Llion for Lady Allaston," he said urgently. "Your father is not dead, Bretton. If he is not dead, then there is no cause for vengeance against de Velt. If you will not come and see your father, then we will take him away and you will never know the truth!"

It was a plot to force Bretton to come to de Velt and de Lohr, but it worked. Bretton bellowed to the sentries to raise the portcullis and they did, chains grinding as the iron grate slowly lifted. When it was about three feet off the ground, Bretton darted underneath it and started running, running for that field where the promise of seeing his father waited. He was blind to anything else.

So was Rod. He ran after his cousin, unaware that Allaston, as she tried to duck beneath the grate, was grabbed from behind by Teague. The man slapped a hand over her mouth and spirited her away from the portcullis, but neither Bretton nor Rod noticed.

As a life-changing event was about to take place in the field below Cloryn, a life-or-death struggle was about to take place inside the walls.

CHAPTER TWENTY-TWO

B RETTON HADN'T RUN in this manner since he had been a child. He was running wildly, swiftly, so fast that his chest hurt from the exertion. He was sailing across the road, down the slope, and into the field where the four horsemen await in the distance. As he ran, he began to hear the sounds of children's laughter deep in his mind, sounds of his sister, Ceri, as she would chase him about. That was what running reminded him of; his beloved sister. He'd not thought of her in twenty-five years. Odd how he could hear her laughter as he ran for his life beneath the bright blue sky.

The four horsemen were drawing closer, three of them dismounting while a fourth remained on his steed. As Bretton drew close, the first thing he saw was Berwyn as the man ripped off his helm and moved to intercept him. But Bretton came to a halt before Berwyn could grab him, and he stared at his grandfather, so much older than he had remembered him, as the man broke down into tears.

"Bretton," he breathed. "It *is* you. Somehow, I imagined that Rod was wrong. Not until this very minute did I truly believe him."

Breathing heavily, Bretton focused on his grandfather. "It is me," he said. "It has been a long time, Grandfather."

Berwyn simply nodded, smiling through his tears, but he didn't try to hug him as he'd tried to hug John Morgan. That had only ended in heartbreak. So he stood there, wringing his hands and drinking in the face of the grandson he thought he'd lost. Rod, who had been slower to run because of the heavy mail he was wearing, came running up behind Bretton, breathing so heavily that he nearly collapsed.

"I told him," Rod said, panting, to Christopher and Jax. "He wants to see John Morgan."

Before anyone could react, the fourth rider, still astride his steed, removed his helm. Bretton caught the movement and turned to look at the man, realizing the moment he removed his helm that Rod had not been lying. Morgan de Llion no longer had his head of dark, curly hair, and he was missing his beard, but the face was the same and the eyes were the same. They were Bretton's eyes.

The emotion in the field was palpable as Bretton faced down the man he thought he'd lost. There were no words to describe his joy, no song beautiful enough to describe the moment. It was something he'd never thought he'd see again and he was at a loss. He could only think of four simple words, the four greatest words he could have ever used to define the moment.

"Papa," Bretton breathed, tears coming to his eyes. "It *is* you."

John Morgan gazed down at the warrior impassively. Stiffly, because he knew it was expected of him, he climbed down off the horse and faced Bretton, a man who looked a good deal as he had in his youth. He had difficulty meeting his gaze at first, that open and emotional stare that made him uncomfortable, but after a few moments, he found that it was nearly hypnotic to look into those bright blue eyes. There was something in them, something deep inside the depths that made him unable to look away.

"I am told that I am your father," John Morgan said.

Bretton nodded, tears falling from eyes and onto his stubbled cheeks. "You are," he whispered. "I thought you were dead."

John Morgan eyed the man who was coming increasingly more interesting for him to look at. He wasn't sure why, but something made him study the man who was supposed to be his son. He was still uncertain, however, and nervous. He was surrounded by strangers and struggling not to back away as he normally did.

"I do not know you," he said. "But you will take me in exchange for de Velt's daughter. Where is the girl?"

Bretton wasn't finished looking at his father. All he could do was stare at the man. "Look at me," he begged softly. "You do not know me? You used to call me Fish Bait. Do you remember that, Papa? You would take me fishing with you and tell me that you would throw me in the water to attract fish, and that they would nibble my toes. Don't you recall?"

Bretton was moving closer to John Morgan and the man took a step back, uncomfortable with Bretton's close proximity. "I do not," he said. Then, he tore his eyes away, looking up to the imposing walls of Cloryn Castle. "But what have you done here? My son would not kill people and abduct women. I have heard that about you. Why did you do such a thing?"

A hint of guilt began to creep over Bretton, an odd sense of shame as his father's words registered. When he replied, the words that came forth were the truth. "To avenge you," he said. "I thought you were dead at the hands of de Velt. I am here to avenge you."

John Morgan frowned. "Did I teach you that?" he wanted to know. "Did I teach you that vengeance is the way to live? I would not teach my son that. Where is this woman? Her father wants her back and you will turn her over immediately."

Bretton's joy at his father's appearance was dashed as shards of disapproval poked holes in his happiness. In fact, he felt as if he'd been slapped in the face, shamed for all to see, scolded by a man he had held up as nothing short of saintly. As he stood there, realizing this joyful event was becoming not so joyful, Jax walked up behind him and put a blade to his throat.

"It was foolish of you to come out here without protection or weaponry," Jax growled in Bretton's ear as he grabbed the man from behind. "You will tell your men to bring my daughter forth or this will end very badly for you."

Christopher hadn't seen Jax's action coming and he stepped towards the pair, holding out a quelling hand. He didn't want to see Jax do anything rash, at least not until they had Lady Allaston in their possession.

"Jax," he said, calmly but firmly. "Let him go. He will bring Allaston forth of his own free will but if you harm him, I fear what his men will do to her."

Jax had Bretton by the hair, pulling his head back and exposing his throat. He heard Christopher but he ignored him. "You called forth The Dark Lord and now you have him," he snarled. "If my daughter is harmed in any way, I will make you pay the price with every bone in your body. What made you think you could challenge me and win, boy? I will filet you as I have fileted countless others, better men than you. I will make you feel pain as you have never experienced it in your life."

Bretton wasn't afraid. He was fairly certain de Velt wouldn't do anything to him with de Lohr so close but, then again, he was dealing with an enraged father so it was impossible to know just how serious the threat was. Still, he kept calm.

"Your daughter is in perfect health," he told him. "She is at the gatehouse."

Rod, concerned for his cousin's life against an angry Jax de Velt, turned to look for Allaston. He had last seen her standing at the portcullis.

"I do not see her," he said. "Where could she have gone?"

Bretton couldn't turn his head because Jax had him by the hair. "She was standing with me," he said. "She must still be there. She must...."

A distant scream filled the air, echoing against the castle walls. It was a woman's scream. There was no doubt about it. Another one came right after it, hysterical and piercing. Rod looked at Bretton, his eyes wide with shock, only to see Bretton as he struggled to get away from Jax.

"Allaston," Bretton breathed, throwing up an arm and catching Jax in the face. As de Velt fell back, struck in the nose, Bretton took off at a dead run towards the castle. "*Allaston!*" he yelled.

Christopher grabbed Jax and shoved him toward his charger. "Mount up!" he bellowed. "Follow him!"

Christopher vaulted onto his horse, taking off after Bretton, passing Rod as the man took off running, too. Jax, nursing a bleeding nose, leapt onto his horse, followed by Berwyn and John Morgan, all three of them thundering towards the castle and the source of the screams, but Jax held off Berwyn as the man raced beside him.

"Return to the army!" he yelled. "Send de Poyer and a contingent of infantry immediately. Then have Wellesbourne and de Wolfe bring up the rest of the troops and position them at the gatehouse. We may need them!"

Berwyn obediently broke off from the men racing for the gatehouse, heading back to the army camped about a half-mile away. Jax, however, continued on, passing Rod and Bretton, on foot, and making it to the gatehouse just behind Christopher.

As the big knights dismounted their chargers, someone inside the gatehouse began to lower the portcullis. Christopher rolled under it, followed by Jax, before Bretton or anyone else could get beneath it. Suddenly, it was just Christopher and Jax against several hundred mercenary troops. Christopher quickly realized they were in a very bad position and he unsheathed his broadsword, as did Jax. Eyes on the mercenaries who were staring them down, he spoke to de Velt.

"Go find your daughter," he told Jax. "I'll try to lift the portcullis."

Jax was deeply torn. "You cannot do it alone," he said. "You will need my help."

As they stood there, backs against the portcullis, Bretton reached through and grabbed Jax. "I have two armed commanders," he said, breathless and wild with worry. "It is possible… oh, God, anything is possible. But if you come across them, do not underestimate them."

Jax nodded as Bretton turned to the others. "There is a postern gate," he said. "It is possible we can breach it. We must try."

As Jax and Christopher faced off against the mercenary army, trapped like dogs by the lowered portcullis, Bretton, Rod, and John Morgan made haste for the postern gate near the kitchens. As Rod ran to collect his charger, still grazing by the side of the road, Bretton began to run but a hand in his face prevented his forward momentum. Startled, he looked up to see John Morgan extending a hand to him.

"Ride with me," John Morgan said. "We will move faster."

Bretton looked at the hand in his face. *His father's hand.* He had visions of being a young boy again as his father offered him a helping hand. The emotions were swirling again, now joined by emotions of fear for Allaston's safety. As he heard another scream from inside the castle, he grabbed John Morgan's hand and vaulted onto the back of the horse. Holding onto his father, touched deeply by the feel of his father's big, warm body for the first time in twenty-five years, he gripped him tightly as the man spurred his big Belgian charger along the massive curtain wall of Cloryn Castle in search of the postern gate.

In search of Allaston.

☓

TEAGUE HAD DRAGGED Allaston away from the gatehouse and across the bailey. He had her around the waist, hauled up against his body, as she struggled and fought. He was very strong, however, and managed to carry her up into the keep even as she tried to kick his knees out. It was a vicious battle.

Once inside the keep, Allaston managed to make contact with his tender inner thigh and he faltered, tripped, and ended up dropping her to the ground. Allaston hit heavily on her right hip but she scrambled up and away from the warrior before he could grab her again. She ran into the open room with the table where she and Bretton had made love, rushing to the other side of the table, as far away as she could get from Teague de Lara. He was a big, frightening man and she was understandably terrified.

Teague stumbled into the room behind her, seeing that she now had a big, heavy table between them. His handsome face was dark with anger.

"You thought you could make a difference," he said, breathing heavily from their struggles. "You thought you could stop that which was already in motion. You cannot stop us, do you hear?"

Allaston, panicked, shook her head at him. "I do not know what you are talking about," she said. "Why did you grab me like that?"

Teague began to move around the table, noting that with every step he took she took another step away from him. "Grayton was right," he said. "You are a danger. You have bewitched Bretton. He owes us a measure of glory and I will not let you stop it."

Allaston was edgy and frightened. Teague was trying to get close to her again and she would not permit it. "I have no idea what you could possibly mean," she said. "I have not bewitched Bretton."

Teague came to a halt, wondering how he could get across the table and grab her again. "Aye, you have," he said, "whether or not you realize it. He is obsessed with you and that means his focus on our campaign, our plans to confiscate your father's Welsh holdings, is in jeopardy."

Allaston noted he had stopped attempting to pursue her but she didn't trust him. She knew he was going to come at her again and was trying to anticipate his next move.

"I want to go home," she said, her lower lip trembling. "I want to leave Cloryn and never look back. My father is here. Let me go to him."

Teague studied her. "Bretton is with your father now," he said. "What do you think they are discussing? If I hold you, I can control them both. They will have to do what I say. You are my path to riches, lady, and I will use you to my advantage."

His declaration made her blood run cold. "What do you intend to do?"

Teague shrugged, trying to make it look casual. "Lock you up as you should be locked up," he said. "Or mayhap I will tie a rope around you and dangle you from the top of the keep. Your father would do anything to keep you safe. And so would Bretton, I suspect."

She frowned. "What good will that do?" she said. "It will not make Bretton fall under your command. He is *your* commander."

Teague shook his head. "Not after this day," he said. "Even if your father exchanged himself for you, having Jax de Velt as his prisoner would only cause Bretton to become complacent. He would have what he wanted – he would have your father. There would be no incentive to conquer the remaining two de Velt castles as we had planned. You see, I have no emotional investment in you or in Jax de Velt, but I do have an army under my command. And I intend to use it."

Allaston shook her head. "You are mad," she hissed. "Those mercenaries will not follow you. They follow Bretton."

"We shall see."

With that, he suddenly vaulted over the table and Allaston screamed in surprise, ducking under the table and scrambling to the other side. Once on her feet, she made a dash for the front door, screaming again when she realized Teague was right behind her. She flew down the stairs, realizing he was making a grab for her as she ran, and suddenly ducked to the side so he sailed right past her, falling down the last several stairs and landing in a heap. As Teague picked himself up, Allaston went on the run again, screaming once more when he made a swipe at her legs.

Running around the side of the keep and heading for the kitchens and, hopefully, the postern gate, she saw the other commander, Dallan, coming at her from the direction of the great hall. He didn't seem particularly concerned until he saw Teague staggering after her, and at that point, he headed in Allaston's direction.

Terrified to see the second commander coming after her, she screamed yet again as she darted off towards the kitchen yard, racing through the opening in the wall. Her goal was the postern gate but she could see that it was guarded by several men, so she changed direction and ran for the kitchen itself. There were several things there that she could use to protect herself with. There was no way to escape so she knew she would have to fight.

Now, it was coming down to defending her own life. Those weeks ago when she had been abducted from Alberbury, she had believed she was already dead. Those weeks in the vault, she had wished for death. But she realized she wasn't ready to die. If these bastards wanted her, then they were going to have to work for it. She was a de Velt, and a de Velt was a fighter.

Uldward was in the kitchen when she ran in. Dallan was right behind her and she tried to slam the door in his face, catching his hand in the doorjamb. As Dallan howled, Allaston ran through the kitchen, past a shocked Uldward, and launched herself from the small, square window that faced the keep. By that time, Dallan and Teague had shoved the door open again and were knocking things over in their haste to grab her legs before she could make it completely through the window. Seeing this, Uldward let the mass of hot coals that he had been stoking for the bread oven tumble onto Dallan's right leg, burning through his breeches in a second. It also ignited the tattered edges of his linen tunic.

Dallan howled as his tunic began to go up in flames, knocking back into Teague, who made a desperate swipe for Allaston's leg just as she fell from the window to the other side. There were many implements leaning against this side of the kitchen and she grabbed an iron spit, one used to roast carcasses over an open flame. It wasn't too heavy and it was sharp on both ends, but as she started to run away, she saw Teague emerge from the kitchen and head in her direction. Caught, she doubled back and ended up trapped between the keep and the kitchen, boxed in, as Teague was closing the gap.

"Stay away!" Allaston yelled, wielding the iron spit. "If you come any closer, I will be forced to defend myself!"

Teague came to a halt. "You are trapped, Lady Allaston," he said. "Put down the spit and I will not harm you. Use it against me and I will not be so kind to you when I capture you. And I will capture you, so consider your actions from this point on very carefully."

Allaston wouldn't back down. It wasn't in her nature. "Nay," she shook her head. "I will not surrender without a fight. I will not let you take me, do you hear? You shall not have me."

Dallan came out of the kitchen, beating down his burnt tunic, and he came up behind Teague, looking between the commander and the lady with a good deal of curiosity and irritation.

"What goes on here?" he demanded of Teague. "Why are you chasing her?"

Teague wouldn't take his eyes off Allaston. Like any good hunter, he kept his eye on the prize. "Because she will ensure that Bretton behaves and does what he is told," he said. "Help me capture her. She cannot fight off both of us."

Dallan shrugged, as he didn't really know what was going on and didn't particularly care, but he nonetheless did as Teague asked and moved wide, trying to distract the lady while Teague moved up on her from the other side. She was boxed in, with nowhere to go, but they wanted to capture her without anyone losing an eye. A frightened lady was a fearsome thing.

Their movements terrified Allaston. She knew it was only a matter of time before they captured her but she wasn't going to surrender easily. She began swinging the spit wildly, daring them to come close, hoping to clip someone very badly in the process.

"Stay away, I say!" she screamed at them. "I will not let you have me, do you hear? I will kill you if you try!"

"And I will help you."

The deep, booming voice came from the entry to the kitchen yard. Allaston looked up to see Jax coming through the gate his massive broadsword gleaming wickedly in the morning light. Fully armored and looking every inch the terrifying Dark Lord of legend, Jax approached with the stalking grace of a cat, scoping out his enemy as he moved. It was clear he was heading in for the kill.

All of the poets in the world collectively could not have described the joy and relief of that moment as Allaston's gaze beheld the father she hadn't seen in well over a year. Tears sprang to her eyes at the sight and it was an effort not to run to him.

"Papa!" she gasped.

Jax didn't look at his daughter as he moved. To do so would have been to take his eye off his enemy and that action could be deadly. So he didn't take the chance and continued to stalk, moving Teague and Dallan away from his daughter. It was a slow, tense dance they engaged in as Jax circled them, waiting for the moment to strike.

"Are you well, Allie?" Jax asked from behind his terrifying helm.

Allaston nodded. "I am fine," she said. "How did you find me?"

Jax swung the broadsword in a very controlled, very threatening maneuver that caused both Teague and Dallan to back up, moving away from Allaston. The man was death personified and even though they were experienced warriors, engaging Ajax de Velt was something neither one of them was prepared for. Dallan was armed with a broadsword but Teague wasn't. He was at a distinct disadvantage.

"De Velt!" Dallan hissed, his eyes wide. "Good Christ, as I live and breathe, 'tis The Dark Lord himself!"

Teague kept his eyes on Jax as he spoke to Dallan. "Hold him while I go get my weapon," he said. "I will meet him on equal ground."

Dallan's eyes widened. "Hold de Velt?" he said. "Are you mad? I will do no such thing! Let him take his daughter and leave. My life is not worth trying to keep de Velt from his daughter."

With a heavy sigh, Teague turned to Dallan, grabbed his broadsword, and gored him with it. Dallan grunted as the broadsword cut into his chest, carving through bone and vital organs. He was dead before he hit the ground and Teague removed the broadsword, facing off against Jax.

"Now I am properly armed," he said evenly. "This will be much more of a battle because if you want your daughter, you are going to have to fight for her."

Jax wasn't amused. "Then stop talking and get on with it. I grow weary of your stalling."

The sound of metal upon metal pierced the morning air like a thunderclap.

തു

BRETTON SAW THE moment when Teague killed Dallan, and he further watched as Teague went after de Velt with a vengeance. De Velt was powerful, more powerful than Teague, but he hadn't held a broadsword in hand to hand combat in many years. Unfortunately for Jax, it made the battle more an even playing field in Teague's favor.

"Damnation!" Bretton roared, standing at the postern gate where several of his soldiers were lingering, watching the fight between Jax and Teague. "Open this gate!"

The soldiers, having no idea why de Llion was outside of the walls, complied, and Bretton entered with Rod and John Morgan on his heels. All three men were armed and as Bretton charged Teague, he unsheathed his broadsword, preparing to gore the man any way he could, but unfortunately for him, Teague saw him approach. He caught movement out of the corner of his eye and, seeing Bretton on the offensive, lashed out a booted foot and caught Jax in the knee, causing the man to buckle. As Jax went down, Teague bolted in Allaston's direction.

Allaston, who had been watching the fight with horror, had lowered her spit and wasn't able to lift it fast enough as Teague came after her. He grabbed her by the neck and she dropped the spit, screaming because he had hurt her. When Bretton, Rod, and John Morgan saw that Teague had Allaston in his grasp, their onslaught came to an instant halt.

"Now," Teague said as Allaston squirmed in his grip. "It would seem I have the power. Bretton, unfortunately, that means your army is now mine. You are far too distracted with personal issues to be an effective commander and I want what you promised me, do you hear? That means that I will take the army, and Lady Allaston, with me first to Erwood Castle, and then on to Four Crosses Castle, insuring that you will behave yourself as long as I hold her hostage. In fact, Lord de Velt, since those castles belong to you, it would be wise of you to simply hand them over to me. If you do not, things could go very badly for your daughter."

As Jax struggled to his feet, Rod went to him and helped him up. "I will turn them over to you, but you must give me my daughter now," Jax said. "If you keep her, you get nothing."

"And if I get nothing, she will rot away in a vault somewhere and there is nothing you can do about it."

"Teague," Bretton stepped forward, putting himself between Teague and Jax because he wanted the man's attention. "Listen to me now so that we may come to an agreement. You do indeed hold the power with Lady Allaston. I do not dispute it. And you are correct. I am distracted with personal issues. I am distracted with Lady Allaston. She belongs to me, Teague. Return her to me and I will give you everything I have, all of the wealth I have accumulated over the years. Everything shall be yours if you will give her back to me."

Teague's grip on Allaston tightened and she gasped in pain. "That is a fair bargain," he agreed. "But until I have everything you own deposited before me, she will remain with me. Not to say I do not trust you, but this is business. You promised to make me a wealthy man and you will fulfill that vow."

Over Teague's left shoulder, where the kitchen structure was located, Bretton could see movement in the window that Allaston had escaped from. He didn't dare look for fear of tipping Teague off, but he swore he could see an arm extending from the window, and the hand at the end of the arm held something. He began to suspect that a distraction of some kind was coming so he braced himself, moving in a direction that would make Teague blind to what was going on behind him. He had no idea what anyone else was doing around him and he didn't care. All he cared about at the moment was keeping Teague's focus. He had to gain the upper hand.

"I have done everything I told you I would do," he said. "I have never gone back on my word with you and I certainly will not do it now. Give me Lady Allaston and I swear to you that you shall have all that I own."

Teague glanced at the woman writhing in his grip. "Why is she worth so much to you, Bretton?" he asked, genuinely curious. "She is your prisoner. You treated the woman worse than a dog when you first abducted her but now you consider her something of a treasure. I do not understand."

Bretton drew in a long, steadying breath. He couldn't stand to see Allaston in pain as Teague twisted her neck. If he squeezed any harder, he might possibly snap it. Bretton struggled not to feel a sense of panic.

"Have you ever been in love, Teague?" he asked. Then, he shook his head. "I have never been. My entire life has been full of horrors that I will not describe here, but suffice it to say that loving someone was the furthest thing from my mind. But that has changed. *I* have changed. I didn't want to admit it before now, but it is true. There is a man standing a few feet away from me whom I swore vengeance upon because he killed my father, but I've come to learn that he did not kill my father at all. My father is alive and well. Have you met my father, Teague? He is here, beside me as I have always wanted him to be."

He turned to John Morgan, who was standing a few feet away, a grim expression on his face and a broadsword in his hand. Bretton smiled at the man.

"He does not know me, but that does not matter," he continued. "The moment I saw him alive, it was as if all of the pain and hatred I'd ever held in my life was sucked right out of me. That vengeance that has driven me is diminished. I no longer need it, for my father is not dead. It is a truly odd sensation to realize I no longer need that hatred to keep me alive. But what I do need is Allaston."

Bretton returned his focus to Teague and Allaston, struggling with each other a few feet away. Teague gazed back at him, something hard and dark within his eyes.

"What are you telling me, Bretton?" he asked. "That you no longer hate? I can give you a reason to hate, my friend. If that is what it takes to drive you, to give me everything you promised me, then I can indeed give you a reason to hate."

Bretton shook his head, knowing what Teague was leading up to. "Do not do it," he said quietly. "I had my family taken away from me when I was very young and it took me twenty-five years to learn to love again. Allaston has shown me what it means to love and to be loved. If you take her away from me... I doubt I would feel hatred. I would feel hollowness and grief such as the world has never seen. I have promised you all that I have in exchange for her. I beg you to take it and give her back to me."

Teague opened his mouth to reply but was cut off when he was hit on the side of the head by a small iron pot that came flying out of the kitchen window. Uldward the cook had hurled it at him with great aim and Teague, without his helm, was struck square-on, enough so that he pitched forward, losing his grip on Allaston as he fell.

Everyone standing around the man swooped in. Bretton grabbed Allaston while Jax, Rod, and John Morgan jumped on Teague, stripping him of his arms and beating him within an inch of his life. Bretton swept Allaston into his arms, carrying her towards the gateway that led into the kitchen yard, noticing that, out in the bailey, there was a tide of de Lohr and de Velt soldiers pouring through the open portcullis.

Cloryn was breached but Bretton could not have cared less. He had Allaston and that was all that mattered. The world was crumbling around him but he was oblivious – he had his world in his arms.

"Are you well?" Bretton asked as he lowered her to the ground. His big palms cupped her face, studying her. "Did he hurt you?"

Allaston was gasping softly, with joy and relief. "He did not," she said, her hands moving to his lips, watching him kiss her flesh. "Are *you* well?"

He laughed softly, pulling her into a warm embrace. "I am very well."

Allaston collapsed against him, savoring the feel of his body against hers. As she held him, she began to weep.

"My father is here," she sobbed. "Bretton, please… I have begged you so many times not to kill him. What more can I say that will make a difference to you? I will never stop asking you. I cannot. I cannot watch the two men I love best fight each other until the death."

He shushed her softly. "Did you not hear what I told Teague?"

She sniffled and wept. "I… I am not sure," she said. "I suppose I really was not listening. I was too afraid he was going to break my neck."

Bretton squeezed her and released her, holding her back at arm's length so he could look her in the eye.

"My father is *alive*, Allaston," he said softly. "It is as I told Teague. The moment I saw him, alive and well, it was as if all of the pain and hatred I'd ever held in my life was sucked right out of me. I felt the vengeance that has driven me diminish because I no longer needed it, for my father is not dead. I no longer need that hatred to keep me alive. I cannot describe what I feel better than that. It is as if… as if I feel whole. That black hole inside of me, the one you once described, is gone."

Allaston's hysterics had faded as she gazed up at him, listening to his words. *Was it possible?* She could only shake her head, amazed at what she was hearing, amazed at the words that were coming forth. She could have never hoped for, or imagined, such a thing from Bretton.

"But… how is this possible?" she asked softly. "That hatred drove you. It made you who you are. You told me I could not take it away from you, no one could. You told me once that you were not sure if you could let go of what you have become."

Bretton sighed. "I know," he nodded. "I will never be perfect but all I can tell you is that, at this moment, I feel like the most fortunate man on the face of the earth. You told me once that God gave you to me for a life gone wrong. Look around you. My father is here and you are here… this is the most perfect life I can imagine. Nothing else matters, not vengeance or your father or the horrors of my past. Those things will always be a part of me, but they will not rule me as I have let them. I have you now and I've come to see that is the most important thing of all. You were right when you said I loved my vengeance more than you, but that is no longer the case. That vengeance has been swept away. I am not sure I can explain it better than that."

Gazing into his face, Allaston was coming to believe him. She didn't know why or how it was truly possible for the man to suddenly forget and forgive twenty-five years of hatred, but she wasn't going to argue with him. If he felt whole, and if he felt like the most fortunate man on the face of the earth, then that was all she could ask for. A smile spread across her lips, one of joy and hope, and Bretton smiled in return. It was time to believe in something other than vengeance. It was time to believe in each other. As Allaston threw her arms around his neck and hugged him tightly, she heard a familiar voice behind them.

"Allie," Jax was standing a few feet away, his visor lifted and his dual-eyed gaze moving between her and Bretton. "I cannot help but notice that this is not the behavior of a prisoner."

Allaston laughed softly, rushing to her father and giving the man the biggest hug she possible could. Jax squeezed his child, tears stinging his eyes with utter joy and relief. When she let him go, he grabbed her face with his two big hands and looked her right in the eye.

"Are *you* well, sweetheart?" he whispered hoarsely. "Your mother and I have been worried sick for you."

Allaston nodded, kissing her father on the cheek. "I have been fine, Papa, I swear it," she said, turning to look at Bretton, who was standing where she had left him. His expression was rather uncertain but Allaston smiled at him. "Bretton... well, he is much like you. I think you two have more in common than you can imagine."

Jax's gaze found Bretton and he groaned loudly. "You sent a missive to me to come to you at Cloryn," he said quietly. "Here I am. I am offering myself in exchange for my daughter."

Bretton held the man's gaze steadily. "There was a time when those words would have meant everything to me," he said. Then, he shook his head, reflecting on bitter memories of the past. This was a defining moment for Bretton, one that would see him move beyond the hatred and accept what life had dealt him, as a true man would. "I had a speech planned for you when we finally met, de Velt. I was going to tell you what you did to my life, how you took my family from me, how I had to fight to survive, and how I spent my life being fueled by thoughts of vengeance against you. I took your castles and I took your daughter and, when you came to me, I was going to take your life, too. You ruined my life and I was going to punish you for it. But... a very strange thing happened."

Jax stood there with his arm around Allaston's shoulders, listening to a man who had thoughts that were very much like his own had been many years ago. Anger, greed, vengeance... aye, he had experienced those things, too, so he understood them well.

"What happened?" he asked softly.

Bretton's gaze moved to Allaston. "A woman happened," he said quietly. "I abducted her but she turned the tables on me and captured everything about me; my heart, my soul, my mind. But that still wasn't enough to quench my vengeance against you. I was still going to go through with it which, I am coming to realize, would have cost me the most valuable thing I have ever had – Allaston's love. Yet, when you and de Lohr showed up with my father, it was as if everything suddenly started to make sense. I have based my entire life on a lie – the lie of my father's death. I believed you killed him and I hated you for it. I tried to hate your daughter, too, but I couldn't bring myself to do it. And with my father returned... my sense of vengeance is gone. It is true that you set about a chain of events that saw me lead a terrible life for quite some time, but in hindsight, mayhap it all happened for a reason. Ultimately, it brought me to your daughter."

Jax considered the man before looking to Allaston, who was gazing at Bretton with that same dreamy expression that Jax had seen on his wife, Kellington. It was the look of love, and Allaston had it. Jax lifted his eyebrows in resignation.

"I cannot condemn my daughter for falling in love with a mercenary because my wife did the same thing," he said with some irony. "I am living proof that the right woman can change a man for good. I cannot say that I am entirely in favor of this union, but I am the last person to condemn this relationship when my wife and I started out much the same way. Therefore, we will speak on it. I am willing to listen."

Bretton grinned at Allaston before looking over his shoulder at the state of Cloryn's bailey. De Lohr and de Velt's men had moved in and were corralling his soldiers. It was clear that Cloryn was returning to the custody of de Velt, but Bretton hardly cared. He had the greatest prize of all in Allaston.

"We do indeed have a great deal to discuss," he said. "I have a few properties of yours that I am sure you wish returned."

Jax lifted an eyebrow before kissing his daughter on the head and releasing her. "That is quite possibly true," he said. "For now, I am going to see what you have done to Cloryn. Mayhap I do not want it back. Mayhap I shall give it to you and Allaston as a wedding gift. I've not yet decided."

He moved past Bretton, heading out into the bailey to see what was happening with his men and with the situation in general. Moreover, he suspected his daughter and Bretton had a few things to say to each other. Well did he remember the newness of his relationship with Kellington and the moments, in the early days, that they had spent alone. Those were precious times. Besides… he had a feeling he would be seeing a good deal of Bretton in the future. There would be plenty of time to get to know the man with a mercenary heart to mirror his own. Aye, they would understand each other well.

As Jax headed out to the bailey, de Lohr brushed past him, heading towards the kitchens. As Bretton and Allaston watched, there was a brief conversation between Christopher and Jax, ending with Jax pointing towards the kitchen and mentioning something that set Christopher to grinning.

The great Christopher de Lohr, perhaps one of the greatest knights to have ever lived, looked off towards the kitchen, seeing a man who looked like Rod standing along with a woman who had her father's dark hair, and knew he was gazing upon Bretton and Allaston. No one had to be obvious and point it out, he just knew. And he also knew that all was well. Whatever the trouble, whatever had caused them to come to Cloryn, no longer existed. Jax de Velt said so.

Allaston and Bretton watched Christopher turn and walk away with Jax, two legends heading towards the bailey, two men who were now allies as well as friends. As they headed towards Keller de Poyer, who now had control of the gatehouse along with a few hundred of his men, Allaston turned to Bretton.

"Thank you," she murmured, "for giving me my father back."

Bretton smiled at her. "I got my father back, too," he said, stroking her dark head. "I cannot say what manner of relationship we will have, but I intend to try and forge one. He is my father, after all. I feel… I feel as if I have been given a second chance with him, even if he doesn't remember me. I am going to do my best to help him try."

Allaston agreed, noting that Rod and John Morgan were now leaving the kitchen yard, having tied Teague up to one of the supporting posts that held up the kitchen roof. The man was bound and gagged, ridiculously so, and Rod grinned brightly at Allaston as he walked past her.

"I kicked him a few times for you, my lady," he said, leaning his head in the direction of Teague. "I even pinched his neck for good measure."

Allaston giggled at him. "I think I am going to like you, cousin Rod."

Rod winked at her boldly, his gaze moving to his cousin. His expression softened as he beheld the man and, after a moment, he reached out to lay a hand on Bretton's broad shoulder.

"Welcome back from the dead, cousin," he exclaimed. "I am very glad to have you back."

Bretton softened toward his cousin, a man who had been so happy upon their first meeting to see him alive. Bretton hadn't been very nice about it. Now, he was feeling the same joy that Rod had felt. Before Rod could get away, he grasped him and pulled him into a tight embrace, reaffirming bonds that had been shattered those years ago. Now, the bonds were being re-forged, stronger than before.

"I am glad to be back," he said softly as he released the man.

Rod was grinning from ear to ear as he walked away, heading back to the bailey where the rest of the de Lohr and de Velt men were gathering. Behind him trailed John Morgan, a big man with a battered head, and Bretton watched the man as he walked away, feeling a mixture of joy and sorrow in his heart. His father didn't know him now, but soon he would. Bretton vowed this to be true. He was just about to turn to Allaston when John Morgan came to a sudden halt, paused, and retraced his steps to Bretton. He stood there a moment, looking at the man, as Bretton returned his stare curiously.

"Is something the matter, John Morgan?" he asked.

The man stood there a moment, seemingly confused. When he finally looked up and fixed Bretton in the eye, there was something there, something more than just cursory recognition.

"Bretton," he finally said in his raspy voice, one that sounded very much like his son's tone. "Your name is Bretton."

Bretton nodded encouragingly. "It is."

John Morgan's mouth worked as if he was trying very hard to say something, words that he couldn't quite bring forth. Finally, he spit them out.

"Bee," he muttered. "Your name… it used to be Bee."

Bretton's breath caught in his throat and tears came to his eyes as he gazed back at the man he loved with all his heart. Once, there had only been his father in his world, a man who was bigger to him than a mountain. His life that was and would be again. He swallowed the lump in his throat.

"Aye," Bretton breathed. "You used to call me Bee when I was small."

A twinkle came to John Morgan's brilliant blue eyes. "I… remember."

Bretton started laughing. They were the sweetest words he had ever heard.

EPILOGUE

Year of Our Lord 1206 A.D.
Month of May
Pelinom Castle, Northumberland

T HE WEDDING DRESS was pink and Kellington had been extravagant with it. The train was twelve feet long, embroidered by Kellington, Allaston, Effington, and Addington as sort of a group project of the mother and daughters. While Kellington had been very specific on the designs, which were to be hummingbirds, flowers, and angels, Effington, the best embroiderer out of the group, and also the jokester, had stitched two small cherubs with big buttocks that she had tinged red right at the tip of the train. Addington had been in on the joke but she had kept her mouth shut, and the sisters had embroidered beautiful vines and flowers all around, so much so that Kellington hadn't see the cheeky cherubs until the day of the wedding. Mother exploded, and Addie and Effie ran to their father for protection after that, which he struggled to give. There was no holding off an angry mother.

Allaston, however, had grinned at her sisters' naughtiness and she had calmed her mother down about it. It didn't really matter in the long run and the cherubs *were* beautifully done. Dressing in the pink silk gown with the rounded neckline, long belled sleeves, and snug bodice, Allaston had looked like a goddess in spite of the cherubs with the red buttocks lining her train. When Jax came to get her in her bower to take her to the carriage, the one that would take her into town to St. Peter's Church where her wedding to Bretton would take place promptly at Vespers, he had to fight off the tears. His first born daughter was all grown up.

Addington and Effington were dressed in blue silk to complement their sister, with a band of small white roses around their heads, in contrast to their dark hair. The older brothers, Coleby and Julian, were dressed in their knightly finest while Cassian, the youngest son, had been brought home from fostering at Alnwick Castle for the event of his sister's wedding. He was dressed like a proper young master. In all, the entire family was lavishly dressed for the occasion, one that had particularly poignant meaning to Kellington because she and Jax had been married under very simple circumstances – a church, two priests, and no celebration. Kellington very much wanted a celebration for her daughter. After the events of the previous year, there was much to celebrate.

But there was also much to be irritated over. Every time Allaston moved, the train of the dress would move, and Kellington would start fussing over the big-buttocked cherubs and Addington and Effington would try to cower behind their sister, the bride. Jax, riding next to the carriage in his finest, spent the majority of the ride into town trying to soothe his wife.

The wedding for Lady Allaston de Velt and Bretton de Llion had brought allies and friends alike to St. Peter's Church and the town was full of families in their finery and knights of opposing houses. Christopher de Lohr was there with his brood, as was Keller de Poyer, Berwyn de Llion, Rod and Rod's entire family including his mother and father, as well as Yves de Vesci, Earl of Northumberland, and John Morgan, who was going by Morgan de Llion these days. It was this group that greeted the de Velt party as they rode into town, and the entire town of Coldstream had turned out for the spectacle. It wasn't often they saw finery, of great nobility, like this.

Christopher was outside of the church, watching his children play on the stoop, as Jax and his party drew near. He went out to greet Jax personally, and the man climbed off his horse to shake his friend's hand. Edward and Max had come also, moving forward to greet de Velt, as Bretton and Rod, on the other side of the street, moved forward to help the ladies from the carriage.

Bretton's heart was thumping loudly against his ribs at the sight of Allaston in her pink silk. She looked like an angel. Rather than helping her down to the road, which was muddy and filthy, he lifted her into his arms, train and all, and carried her into the church. That left Rod with seventeen year old Effington and fifteen year old Addington, who were gazing at the blue-eyed, black-haired knight as if he were Adonis himself.

Rod, usually quite outgoing and flirtatious, found himself swarmed upon by the two ladies as they latched onto his armored arms and vied for his attention. Jax, noting his daughters were going after Rod like two cats on a feeding frenzy, moved to call them off but Berwyn intervened. He liked see his grandson so uncomfortable. The sight brought him great laughter. Such moments with Rod were rare.

Once the bride and groom entered the church, the rest of the guests and family followed because this was to be a truly memorable occasion; the ceremony was actually two-fold. With his father, grandfather, and entire family watching, Bretton was granted what his terrible youth and circumstances had denied him. He was officially knighted by Christopher de Lohr and became Sir Bretton de Llion, much to the delight of his betrothed and everyone else in attendance.

Once the knighting ceremony was over, the priests stepped in, and Lady Allaston de Velt became Lady Allaston de Velt de Llion. After receiving a chaste kiss from her new husband, the entire wedding party was moved back over to Pelinom Castle where the celebration went well into the night.

It was well after sunset on the eve of the wedding as Christopher, Jax, Berwyn, and Morgan stood on the battlements of Pelinom, a cup of fine wine in hand, gazing up at the brilliant blanket of stars against the

May night and tossing trivial subjects around. The younger children seemed to be more interested in the bailey of Pelinom so the men ended up watching the gaggle of children below as they played and chased each other around.

Christopher's children were much younger than Jax's brood, but the de Velt children seemed to have taken a strong liking to the de Lohr children, so Effington and Addington carried around little Christin and Brielle de Lohr while young Cassian tagged along. Christopher's two youngest children weren't ready to be out of their mother's sight yet, so Dustin sat on the stoop of Pelinom's keep, watching her toddler boys as the older children chased them around and made them laugh.

"I never thought I would see the day when I would be standing with the great Christopher de Lohr, enjoying him as a guest to my home," Jax muttered over the rim of his cup as he watched the children play. "It all seems very strange still."

Christopher grinned at him. "Soon I will have you as a guest to my home," he said. "You have yet to meet my brother, David. When I told him of our adventures with de Llion, he was quite stunned. He does not believe you and I have become allies. He says that no one befriends Lucifer."

Jax gave him a half-grin. "Your brother sounds like a skeptic."

"He is."

"So was I, once."

They shared a laugh, watching as Rod emerged from the keep and Effington and Addington raced to him like moths to flame. Rod tried to run back into the keep but the girls stopped him, pulling him out into the bailey where the rest of the children were. Berwyn, standing behind Christopher and Jax, grunted.

"That one is going to be trouble," he muttered. "Rod has seen twenty-nine years and he still has not selected a wife. He is not even close."

Christopher laughed while Jax grinned. "Give him time," Christopher said. "I did not marry until I was well into my thirties."

Berwyn elbowed Morgan, standing next to him. "See how the de

Velt girls flutter around him?" he asked. "Mayhap you should approach Lord de Velt about a marriage contract. The elder daughter is quite lovely."

The smile vanished from Jax's face as he looked over at Berwyn and Morgan. "I will pretend I did not hear that."

Berwyn lifted his hands. "Why not?" he asked. "Your middle daughter is at least sixteen or seventeen years of age. That is a perfectly marriageable age. Besides, look at the way she handles Rod. She already has him under her thumb. That is what he needs, a wife with a strong hand to beat some sense into him!"

Jax rolled his eyes. "She does *not* have him under her thumb," he said. "I am not comfortable with this line of conversation. Speak on something else."

Christopher grunted as he watched the children play. "I have two young daughters," he said. "One of them would be perfect for your youngest, Cassian."

Jax pursed his lips at the lot on the battlements. "Why are you try-ing so hard to marry into my family?" he asked. "Mayhap I do not want the likes of you... present company excepted, Christopher. I am perfectly happy to have a de Lohr in the family, but another de Llion... I am not entirely sure. One is enough."

The men were all moderately drunk from a day of celebration and Berwyn gave Christopher an exaggerated wink. He was going to have some fun with Jax.

"Rod is a fine young knight, Lord de Velt," he insisted. "Well, ex-cept for his gambling habits. But other than that, he is quite acceptable. Well... that is, except for the fact that the man has the intelligence of a goat. But other than that, he would make a fine match for Effington. Think of the beautiful children they would have. Stupid if they take after their father, but beautiful nonetheless."

Jax threw up his hands and turned away as Berwyn scampered after him, extolling the virtues of his grandson in an offhanded manner while Morgan and Christopher watched, laughing when Jax put his hands over his ears and disappeared into a turret with Berwyn behind him, emerging at the bottom with his hands still over his ears. When his children saw him in the bailey, they ran to him, all except for Effington. She was still with Rod, strolling through the bailey beneath the moonlight with her hand on the knight's arm. But that changed when Rod saw Jax coming and he quickly removed Effington's hand and fled back into the hall.

But that didn't stop Effington. She followed Rod into the hall as well and, on a warm August night of the next year, after a serious adventure of their own, Rod and Effington celebrated their own marriage in Pelinom's keep the same day as Allaston gave birth to a big, healthy boy at Belford Castle.

Young Gareth de Llion brought the world of The Dark Lord and the dominion of the Devil together in a way none of them could have ever imagined.

Jax wept that day. And so did Bretton.

CS THE END SO

AUTHOR NOTES

DEVIL'S DOMINION was a very complex tale involving a hero with a lot of emotional baggage. Robbed of the life he knew, Bretton had to struggle to survive – literally. Allaston could have felt disgust towards him, but she really never did – she came to understand the man was a survivor and doing what he did was really all he ever knew. He'd forgotten that the world could be kind. But when he started to realize that there were nice people in the world, people – like Allaston – who were willing to help him and show him compassion, that's when things started to change for him even though he really bucked against it. As he told Allaston, he wasn't sure he could change from what he'd become. But she didn't give up on him.

Did he change over too dramatically in the end? Not really when you think about it. Things had been building towards that for 2/3rds of the book, and when John Morgan was presented to him, it was like all of his hatred and vengeance left him. There was no longer any reason to be angry at the world. Sure, he'd been screwed over when he was younger, but Allaston was more than willing to make up for that. She felt a lot of pity for the man, which made her very torn because the guy was out to kill her father.

Speaking of Allaston, how *could* she love a man who was sworn to kill her father? Maybe because she saw something in him others didn't. She saw hope. He'd given her little clues about it – not killing her right off the bat, showing her some kindness after he'd abducted her, things of that nature. She knew there was something in him that wasn't all killer.

And what about Jax and Christopher making major appearances in this novel? It was a lot of fun bringing Jax back in and, surprise! – he had been living a peaceful life as of late. No more brutal warlord! The discussions between Jax and Christopher were some of the best, in any Le Veque novel. As for Rod, now he has to get his own story with Effington de Velt as his lady-love. It's going to be a good one!

Finally, to be clear, there wasn't much mention of Grayton after he remained behind at Comen, mostly because he wasn't around at Cloryn Castle at the end. He kind of started the revolt against Bretton but Teague finished it. You can bet that, at some point, Bretton and Jax returned to Comen Castle and subdued Grayton. Same goes for Olivier at Rhayder Castle, although Olivier did not have a big role in this book.

As it has been mentioned before, this book was complex and it is hoped that you sincerely enjoyed it. Find all Kathryn's novels online.

Now, enjoy a few bonus chapters to follow!

The House of de Llion is connected to the House of de Titouan in Spectre of the Sword.

Spectre of the Sword

A major appearance of Jax de Velt from The Dark Lord, and Christopher de Lohr from Rise of the Defender is in this novel.

The Dark Lord

Rise of the Defender

For more information on other series and family groups, as well as a list of all of Kathryn's novels, please visit her website at www.kathrynleveque. com.

A bonus chapter from THE DARK LORD with Jax de Velt.

'Doomsman of Deeds and dreadful Lord,—Woe for that man who in harm and hatred hales his soul to fiery embraces'

-Beowulf, Chapter II

CHAPTER ONE

May, 1180 AD
Scots Borderlands, England

H E HAD HER by the hair; strands of spun gold clutched in the dirty mailed glove. Perhaps it was because she had tried to bite him and he did not want to chance another encounter with her sharp white teeth. Or perhaps it was because he was a brute of a man, sworn to Ajax de Velt and knowing little else but inflicting terror. Whatever the case, he had her tightly. She was trapped.

The woman and her father were on their knees in great hall of the keep that had once belonged to them. Now it was their prison as enemy soldiers overran the place. There were memories of warmth and laughter embedded in the old stone walls, now erased by the terror that filled the room.

Pelinom Castle had been breached before midnight when de Velt's army had tunneled under the northeast tower of the wall, causing it to collapse. The woman and her father had tried to escape, along with the populace of their castle, but de Velt's men had swarmed them like locusts. It was over before it began.

Around her, the woman could hear the cries of her people as de Velt's men ensnared them. She had been captured by an enormous knight with blood splashed on his plate armor and she had understandably panicked. Even now, trapped against the floor of the great hall, she was panicked and terrified. Tales of de Velt's atrocities were well known in the lawless north of England, for it was a dark and lawless time. She knew they were about to enter Hell.

From the corner of her eye, she could see her father on his knees. Sir Keats Coleby was a proud man and he had resisted the invasion gallantly. Why he hadn't been outright killed, as the garrison commander, was a mystery. But he was well-bloodied for his efforts. The woman couldn't see his face and she fixed her gaze back to the floor where the knight held her head. He very nearly had her nose pushed into the stone.

There was a great deal of activity around them. She could hear men shouting orders as the screams of her people eventually faded. Horror consumed her, knowing that de Velt's men were more than likely doing unspeakable things to her servants and soldiers. Tears stung her eyes but she fought them. She wondered what horrors de Velt had planned for her and her father.

She didn't have long to wait. With her face nearly pressed to the stone, she heard a deep, rumbling voice.

"Your name, knight."

The woman's father answered without hesitation. "Sir Keats Coleby."

"You are commander of Pelinom, are you not?"

"I am."

"And the girl?"

"My daughter, the Lady Kellington."

The silence that filled the air was full of anxiety. Kellington could hear boot falls all around her, though it was difficult to see just how many men were surrounding them. It felt like the entire army.

"Release her," she heard the voice say.

Immediately, the hand in her hair was removed and she stiffly lifted her head. Several unfriendly faces were glaring down at her, some from behind raised visors, some from helmless men. There were six in all, three knights and at least three soldiers. There could have been more standing behind her that she did not see, but for now, six was enough.

Kellington's heart was pounding loudly in her ears as she looked around, waiting for the coming confrontation. The knight to her right spoke.

"How old are you, girl?"

She swallowed; her mouth was so dry that there was nothing to swallow and she ended up choking. "I have seen eighteen years, my lord."

The knight shifted on his big legs and move d in front of her; Kellington's golden-brown eyes dared to gaze up at him, noting a rather youngish warrior with a few days growth of beard and close-shorn blond hair. He didn't look as frightening as she had imagined, but she knew if the man was sworn to de Velt, then he must be horrible indeed.

"Does your husband serve Pelinom?" he asked, his deep voice somewhat quieter.

"I am not married, my lord."

The knight glanced over at Keats, who met his gaze steadily. Then he turned his back on them both, leaving them to stew in fear. Kellington watched him closely, struggling to keep her composure. She wasn't a flighty woman by nature, but panic was the only option at the moment.

"Are there any others of the ruling house here?" the knight paused and turned to look at them. "Only the garrison commander and his daughter? No sons, no husband, no brothers?"

Keats shook his head. "Just my daughter and I."

He deliberately left out 'my lord'. If it bothered the knight, he did not show it. Instead, he turned his focus to the gallery above, the ceiling and the walls. Pelinom was a small but rich and strategically desirable castle and he was pleased that they had managed to capture her relatively intact. The chorus of screams that had been prevalent since the army breached the bailey suddenly picked up again, but the knight pretended not to notice. He returned his focus to Keats.

"If you are lying to me, know that it will only harm you in the end," he said in a low voice. "The only class spared at this time is the ruling house. All others are put to death, so you may as well confess before we kill someone who is important to you."

Keats didn't react but Kellington's eyes widened. She had never been a prisoner before and had no idea of the etiquette or behaviors involved. Living a rather isolated existence at Pelinom for most of her life, it had left her protected for the most part. This siege, this horror, was new and raw.

"What does that mean?" she demanded before she could stop her tongue. "It is only my father and I, but my father has knights who serve him and we have servants who live here and…"

The knight flicked his eyes in her direction. "You will no longer concern yourself over them."

She leapt to her feet. "My lord, please," she breathed, her lovely face etched with anguish. "My father's knight and friend is Sir Trevan. He was with us when you captured us, but now I do not see him. Please do not harm him. He has a new infant and.…"

"The weak and small are the first to be put to the blade. They are a waste of food and space within a military encampment."

Kellington's eyes grew wider, tears constricting her throat. Her hands flew to her mouth. "You cannot," she whispered. "Sir Trevan and his wife waited years for their son to be born. He is so small and helpless. Surely you cannot harm him. Please; I beseech you."

The knight lifted an eyebrow at her. Then he glanced at the other knights and soldiers standing around them; they were all de Velt men, born and bred to war. All they knew was death, destruction and greed. There was little room for compassion. He looked to Keats once more.

"Explain to your daughter the way of things," he turned away from them, seemingly pensive. "I will listen to what you tell her."

Keats sighed heavily, his gaze finding his only child. Though a woman grown she was, in fact, hardly taller than a child. But her short stature did nothing to detract from a deliciously womanly figure that had come upon her at an early age. Keats had seen man after man take a second look at his petite daughter, investigating the golden hair and face of an angel. He was frankly surprised that the de Velt men hadn't taken her for sport yet, for she was truly a gorgeous little thing. He was dreading it, knowing it was only a matter of time and there was nothing on earth he could do to stop them. The thought made him ill.

"Kelli," he said softly. "I know that you do not understand since you have never seen a battle, but this is war. There are no rules. The victor will do as he pleases and we, as his prisoners, must obey."

"He will kill a baby?" she fired back. "That is unthinkable; it's madness. Why must they kill the child? He's done nothing!"

"But he could grow up to do something," Keats tried to keep her calm. "Do you remember your Bible? Remember how the Pharaoh killed all of the first born males of Israel, afraid that one of them would grow up to be the man prophesized to overthrow him? 'Tis the same with war, lamb chop. The enemy does not see man, woman or child. He only sees a potential killer."

"You understand well the concept of destruction."

They all turned to the sound of the voice; a deep, booming tone that rattled the very walls. Keats had the first reaction all evening, his brown eyes widening for a split second before fading. Kellington stared at the man who had just entered the great hall as all of the other men around her seemed to straighten. Even the knight who had been doing the questioning moved forward quickly to greet the latest arrival.

"My lord," he said evenly. "This is Sir Keats Coleby, garrison commander of Pelinom, and his daughter the Lady Kellington. They claim that they are the only two members of the ruling house."

The man who stood in the entrance to the great hall was covered in mail, plate protection and gore. He still wore his helm, a massive thing with horns that jutted out of the crown. He was easily a head taller than even the tallest man in the room and his hands were as large as trenchers. The man's enormity was an understatement; he was colossal.

He radiated everything evil that had ever walked upon the earth. Kellington felt it from where she stood and her heart began to pound painfully. She resisted the urge to run to her father for protection, for she knew that no mortal could give protection against this. The very air of the great hall changed the moment the enormous man entered it. It pressed against her like a weight.

The great helmed head turned in the direction of the knight who had been doing the interrogation, now standing before him. Then he loosened a gauntlet enough to pull it off, raising his visor with an uncovered hand. The hand was dirty, the nails black with gore.

"I have been told the same," he replied, his voice bottomless. "We counted only four knights total, including Coleby, so this is the lot of them."

"Would you finish questioning the prisoners, my lord?"

For the first time, the helmed head turned in their direction. Kellington felt a physical impact as his eyes, the only thing visible through the helm, focused on her. Then she noticed the strangest thing; the left eye was muddy brown while the right eye, while mostly of the same muddy color, had a huge splash of bright green in it. The man had two different colored eyes. It unnerved her almost to the point of panic again.

"I heard some of what you were saying," the enormous knight said, still focused on Kellington. Then he looked at Keats. "Your explanation was true. You comprehend the rules of engagement and warfare so there will be no misunderstanding."

Keats didn't reply; he didn't have to. He knew who the man was without explanation and his heart sank. The knight continued into the room, scratching his forehead through the raised visor. Kellington followed him, noticing he passed closely next to her. She barely came up to his chest.

"I am de Velt," he said, returning his attention to both Kellington and Keats. "Pelinom Castle is now mine and you are my prisoners. If you think to plead for your lives, now would be the time."

"We must plead for our lives?" Kellington blurted. "But why?"

The massive knight looked at her but did not speak. The second knight, the one in charge of the interrogation, answered. "You are the enemy, my lady. What else are we to do with you?"

"You do not have to kill us," she insisted, looking between the men.

"Kelli," her father hissed sharply.

"Nay, Father," she waved him off, returning her golden-brown focus to de Velt. "Please, my lord, tell me why you would not spare our lives? If you were the commander of Pelinom, would you not have defended it also? That does not make us the enemy. It simply makes us the besieged. We were protecting ourselves as is our right."

De Velt's gaze lingered on her a moment. Then he flicked his eyes to the man at his side.

"Take Coleby."

"No!" Kellington screamed, throwing herself forward. She tripped on her own feet and ended up falling into de Velt. With small soft hands, she clutched his grisly mail. "Please, my lord, do not kill my father. I beg of you. I will do anything you ask, only do not kill my father. Please."

Jax gazed down at her impassively. When he spoke, it was to his men. "Do as I say. Remove the father."

The tears came, then. "Please, my lord," she begged softly. "I have heard that you are a man with no mercy and it would be easy to believe that were I to give credit to the rumors of your cruelty. But I believe there is mercy in every man, my lord, even you. Please show us your mercy. Do not do this horrible thing. My father is an honorable man. He was only defending his keep."

Jax wasn't looking at her; he was watching his men pull Keats to his feet. But the older knight's attention was on his distraught daughter.

"Kelli," he hissed at her. "Enough, lamb chop. I would have your brave face be the last thing I see as I leave this room."

Kellington ignored her father, her pleas focused on Jax. "If there is any punishment to be dealt, I will take it. If it will spare my father and

383

our vassals, I will gladly submit. Do what you will with me, but spare the others. I beseech you, my lord."

Jax's face remained like stone. Seeing that the enormous knight was ignoring her, Kellington broke free and raced to her father, throwing herself against him as de Velt's men pulled him from the room. Keats tried to dislodge her, but his hands were bound and men were pulling on him, making it difficult.

"No, Father," she wept, her arms around is left leg. "I will not see you face the blade alone. They will have to kill me, too."

"No," Keats commanded softly, hoping the knights dragging him out would at least give him a moment with his only daughter. He lifted his bound arms and looped them around her, pulling her into an awkward embrace. "It is not your time to die. You will live and you will be strong. Know that I love you very much, little lamb. You have made me proud."

Kellington wept uncontrollably. Her father kissed her as their brief time together was harshly ended. There were many men attempting to separate them and someone grabbed her around her tiny waist and pulled her free. It was de Velt.

"Lock the girl in the vault," he commanded. "Take the father to the bailey and wait for me there."

He handed her over to the blond knight, who heaved her up over his shoulder. As he turned around to follow the father and other knights from the room, Kellington's upside down head found de Velt.

Please spare him, my lord," she begged. "I will take all of his punishment if you wish, but do not harm him. He is all I have."

Jax watched his knight haul her away. She wasn't kicking and fighting as he had seen her do earlier when she had first been captured. She looked somewhat defeated. But the expression on her face was more powerful than any resistance. He gaze lingered on her a moment before pulling on the loose gauntlet.

He had no time to waste on mercy. He was, after all, Jax de Velt.

Read the rest of **THE DARK LORD** in eBook or in paperback.

A bonus chapter from RISE OF THE DEFENDER
with Christopher de Lohr.

CHAPTER ONE

Year of Our Lord 1192
The Month of September
Lioncross Abbey Castle
The Welsh Marches

L ADY DUSTIN BARRINGDON bit at her full lower lip in concentration. Climbing trees was no easy feat, but climbing trees in a skirt was near impossible.

Her target was the nest of baby birds high in the old oak tree. Her cat, Caesar, had killed the mama bird earlier that day and now Dustin was determined to take the babies back to Lioncross and raise them. Her mother, of course, thought she was mad, but she still had to try. After all, if she hadn't spoiled and pampered Caesar then this might never have happened. Caesar had no discipline whatsoever.

She pushed her blond hair back out of her way for the tenth time; her hands kept snagging on it as she clutched the branch. But as soon as she pushed it away, it was back again and hanging all over her. She usually loved her buttock-length hair, reveled in it, but not today. Long and thick and straight. It glistened and shimmered like a banner of gold silk.

Her big, almond-shaped eyes watched the nest intently. But not just any eyes, they were of the most amazing shade of gray, like sunlight behind storm clouds. Surrounded by thick dark-blond lashes, they were stunning. With her full rosy lips set in a heart-shaped face, she was an incredible beauty.

Not that Dustin had any shortage of suitors. The list was long of the young men waiting for a chance to speak with her father upon his return. She truly didn't care one way or the other; men were a nuisance and a bore and she got along very well without them. Nothing was worse that a starry-eyed suitor who mooned over her like a love-sick pup. She had punched many idiots right in the eye in answer to a wink or a suggestive look.

"Can you reach it yet?" her friend, Rebecca, stood at the base of the tree, apprehensively watching.

"Not yet," Dustin called back, irritated at the distraction. "Almost."

Just another couple of feet and she would have it. Carefully, carefully, she crept along the branch, hoping it wouldn't give way.

"Dustin?" Rebecca called urgently.

Dustin paused in her quest. "What now?"

"Riders," Rebecca said with some panic, "coming this way."

Dustin lay down on the branch, straining to see the object of her friend's fear. Indeed, up on the rise of the road that led directly under the tree she was on, were incoming riders. A lot of them, from what she could see.

Her puzzlement grew. Who would be coming to Lioncross this time of day, this lazy afternoon in a long succession of lazy afternoons? The riders passed through a bank of trees and she could see them better.

She began to catch some of her friend's fear. There were soldiers, hundreds of them.

"Rebecca," she hissed. "Climb the tree. Hurry up."

With a shriek, Rebecca clumsily climbed onto the trunk and began slowly making her way up.

"Who are they?" she gasped.

Dustin shook her head. "I do not know," she replied. "The only time I have ever seen that many soldiers was when my father…." She suddenly sat up on the branch. "My *father!* Rebecca, climb down!"

Rebecca didn't share Dustin's excitement. "Why?" she exclaimed.

Dustin was already scooting back down, crashing into her friend. "It is my father, you ninny. He has returned!"

Rebecca, reluctantly, began to back down the scratchy oak branch. "How do you know that? Are they flying a banner?"

Dustin hadn't even looked. She didn't have to. "Who else would it be?" She was so excited she was beginning to shake.

The army was quickly approaching the ladies' position. Thunder filled the air, blotting out everything else. Now, they were upon them. Rebecca was down from the tree but Dustin was still descending.

Dust from the road swirled about as several large destriers kicked up grit with their massive hooves. They had come up amazingly fast and Dustin found herself paying more attention to the chargers than to what she was doing. As the knights reined their animals to a halt several feet from Rebecca's terrified form, Dustin tried to get a better look at them.

She was trying very hard to single out her father but her distraction cost her as she lost her grip on the branch. With a scream, she plummeted from the tree about ten feet overhead and landed heavily on her right side.

Rebecca gasped and dropped to Dustin's aid. "Dustin! My God, are you all right?"

Dustin rolled to her back, now oblivious to the knights and men that were watching her. All she knew was that she could not catch her breath and her chest was so hot it would soon explode. As Rebecca tried to get a look at her, one of the knights dismounted his steed and knelt beside her.

"Breathe easy," came a deep, soothing voice. "Where do you hurt?"

Dustin could not talk. She could only manage to lay there and gasp for air. The knight removed his gauntlets and flipped up the faceplate on his helmet.

"Take deep breaths," he told her, putting his plate-sized hand on her abdomen, just below her ribs. "Slowly, slowly. Come now, slow down. That's right."

As Dustin's shock wore off, tears of pain and shock began to roll down her temples and, for the first time, she opened her eyes and focused on the man with the kind voice. She was shocked to see how big and frightening he was. He gazed back at her impassively.

"Are you hurt?" he asked.

She shook her head unsteadily. "I do not think so," she choked out. "I can breathe a little better."

He silently extended a hand, carefully pulling her up to sit. The first thing Dustin noticed was how big his hands were as they closed around her own.

The knight continued to crouch next to her, his gaze still unreadable. Shaking the leaves out of her hair, Dustin gave him the once-over.

"Who are you?" she demanded softly. "Where is my father?"

"Who is your father?" he returned, ignoring her first question.

Dustin had a bad habit of speaking first and thinking later. If these men were her father's vassals, then they would have known her on sight.

"Why, Lord Barringdon, of course," she said, grabbing the ends of her hair and shaking them hard. "Where is he?"

For the first time the man showed emotion. His sky-blue eyes widened for a brief second and he abruptly stood up. She tried to look up at him, but he was so tall she had to lay her head back completely and she could not do that because her head was killing her. So she cocked her head at an odd angle, still looking up at him, as she struggled to her feet.

The man didn't help her rise, although he probably should have. He just kept staring at her.

"Lady Dustin Barringdon, I presume?" he asked after a moment.

His voice sounded queer. Dustin managed to stand on her own, putting out a hand to steady herself as the earth beneath her rocked. The knight reached out to balance her.

"Aye," she replied, pulling her hand away cautiously and taking a step toward Rebecca, who clutched at her. She eyed the man warily. "Who are you?"

She had no idea why the man's eyes were twinkling. His face held no expression, but she swore his eyes were twinkling.

"I am a friend of you father's," he said. "My name is Christopher de Lohr."

"Where is my father?" Dustin demanded yet again, excited to hear this man was a friend.

The knight hesitated. "Is your mother home, my lady?" he asked. "I bring messages for her."

Dustin's excitement took a turn for the worse. She had asked the same question three times without an answer. She was coming to suspect why and her stomach lurched with anguish. *God, no!*

"*Where* is my father?"

"I will discuss that with your mother."

Dustin stared at him a long, long time. He gazed back at her, studying every inch of that beautiful, sensuous face. The gray orbs that met his blue suddenly went dark and stormy. She closed her eyes and turned away from him, beginning to walk back down the road. Rebecca, puzzled, yet not wanting to be left alone with a company of soldiers, ran after her.

Christopher watched her go, knowing she must suspect at least part of the reason why he had come. When he began to hear soft sobs, fading as she continued down the road, he knew that her fears were confirmed. She knew her father was dead.

He turned to his brother. "Get the men moving," he said, mounting his destrier, but his eyes were still on the lady.

Christ, but he was still reeling with surprise and pleasure at the discovery of Lady Dustin. She was beautiful. Damnation, he hadn't known what to expect. The entire trip home had been filled with dread and foreboding, but he could see his worries were for naught. Even if she was as stupid as a tree and as disagreeable as a mule, she was still beautiful. If he had to marry, she might as well be pleasant to look at.

Any other qualities were superfluous.

Slowly, the army followed several paces behind her. Dustin had never known grief before and discovered it to be the most painful thing she had ever experienced. The knight wouldn't tell her where her father was and that in and of itself was confirmation of the worst. She wasn't a fool. Sorrow overwhelmed her and she suddenly could not breathe again. Her sobs grew into raspy puffs of air and the ground began to sway again. Dustin was aware of a blissful, floating feeling as a strange blackness swallowed her up.

Christopher saw her go down on the side of the road and he spurred his destrier forward. The animal came to a halt in a cloud of dust and he dismounted, pulling Lady Dustin's hysterical friend away from the crumpled form in the grass.

"What's the matter with her?" her friend cried. "She's dying. The fall will kill her!"

Christopher knelt down, noting the even breathing, steady pulse, but pale color. Mayhap the fall did contribute to this. He suddenly felt strangely protective, knowing that the woman was to be his wife. Wasn't it right for a husband to feel protective? It was the most peculiar sensation he'd ever experienced.

"What's your name, lass?" he asked the panting redhead.

"Rebecca," she replied, "Rebecca Comlynn."

Christopher nodded, turning back to the woman in the grass. "You will take us back to Lioncross, Mistress Rebecca. I will take care of Lady Dustin."

Rebecca started to protest but David grabbed her and seated her on his destrier before she could put up a fight. Christopher scooped up Dustin and managed to mount his own steed with surprising ease. She was light, this one, and small, too. Standing her full height she barely met his chest. She was little more than a child in his arms.

He stole a glance at her as he gathered his reins. Her lips moistly parted, she looked to be sleeping in his arms. Her hair, so incredibly long and silken, hung all over them both and he had to pull it free from the joints in his armor a couple of times. He could feel lust warming his veins. Spurring his great warhorse, they proceeded on to Lioncross Abbey.

Lioncross Abbey was so named because it was built on the sight of an ancient Roman house of worship and actually incorporated portions of two walls and part of the foundation. Additionally, Arthur Barringdon had christened it Lioncross after Richard and the quest. Prior to Arthur inheriting the keep from his father, it had been named Barringdon Abbey. Some older people in the region still referred to it as such.

The fortress sat atop a ridge overlooking a large lake and the deep purple mountains that marked the Welsh border could be seen in the distance. Thick banks of trees surrounded the fortress and made the region appear lush and fertile, even in the dead of winter.

Christopher took a good look at what was to be his new home, verily pleased. It was a fine fortress, easy to defend, with a small village about a half mile to the north. He found himself growing more and more satisfied with each passing step of his horse. Aye, he was worthy to be lord of this. He already found himself making mental notes about the structure, what needed improvement and reminding himself to ask questions about the revenues. As fine a warrior as he was, he was an equally fine scholar and knew what it would take to make Lioncross a profitable keep.

Dustin stirred in his arms and he was reminded of his burden. He looked down at her just in time to see her lids opening, slowly, as if a curtain rising. Again, he was entranced with the bright gray eyes and noted the thick lashes as she blinked. She was staring up at the sky as if trying to remember where in the world she was when her gaze fell on him. She blinked once, focused on his pale blue eyes, and then sat up so fast he had to throw his arm down on her to keep her from pitching herself right off of his horse.

"Put me down!" she hollered.

"Steady, my lady," he said. "We're almost back to your keep."

Her head snapped to the horizon where Lioncross indeed loomed.

She began to struggle against him and he could not understand her panic, but he relented and let her slide to the ground.

She took off like a rabbit, her skirts up around her thighs as she pounded down the road. That incredible mane of hair waved behind her like a banner. Rebecca, not to be left behind, jumped from David's destrier and ran after her.

David reined his steed alongside his brother's, both of them watching the racing figures. "Now, what do you suppose that is all about?" David wondered aloud.

Christopher shook his head. "I have no idea," he replied, then grinned at his brother. "What think you of my new keep?"

David nodded his approval. "Exceptional. As is your new bride."

Christopher cocked a blond eyebrow. "I am surprised as well," he admitted. "Lady Dustin Barringdon looks nothing as I imagined."

"With a name like Dustin, I had no idea what to think," David snorted.

"Nor did I, little brother," Christopher agreed.

They entered the outskirts of the little village, passing an interested eye over the small buildings and tradesman's shacks. It smelled like sewage and livestock, and bits of dust kicked up in the occasional breeze. The road leading to Lioncross was a wide one and peasants scattered to stay clear of the approaching army. Christopher's horse accidentally crushed a chicken and sent a woman wailing, much to his displeasure.

Finally, the jewel of Lioncross loomed before them. The gates of the fortress yawned open before them and he halted the caravan with a raised arm.

"This will cease," he indicated the open gates. "With Wales so close, these people are fools to leave themselves vulnerable."

Beckoning David forward with him, he left the rest of his troops outside the gates. There was one bailey to Lioncross, a huge open thing used for a myriad of purposes. He studied it intently, already noting what needed changing as he and David rode for the massive double doors of the entry.

Sentries met them at the base of the front steps. Christopher announced himself and his purpose, and waited while one of the guards disappeared inside. He reappeared several minutes later followed by another man dressed in mail and portions of plate armor.

The knight studied Christopher with piercing dark eyes. He was not particularly tall, but Christopher could see the muscles on the man. He was a seasoned warrior. His face was severely angled with a sharp nose and a sharp mouth. Immediately, he sensed hostility.

"What is your business here?" the man demanded in a strong Germanic accent.

"I am Sir Christopher de Lohr," he repeated, matching the man's tone. "I bear a message for Lady Mary Barringdon from King Richard."

The man looked Christopher up and down, taking a step toward him. "Give it to me and I will see that it is delivered."

"I have been instructed by our king to deliver it personally," Christopher said evenly. "I would deliver it now."

The man didn't say anything but continued to glare until Christopher finally had enough of his animosity. Dismounting without permission, he removed two scrolls of parchment from his saddlebags and walked deliberately to the soldier, holding out one of the missives for him to see.

"Richard's seal," he stated in case the soldier was blind. "Twould be unwise of you to go against our king. Now move aside or escort me in; 'tis all the same to me."

The soldier stared at the seal, knowing it for what it was. He tore his eyes away and looked at Christopher again, but this time, with less hostility.

"You scared the devil out of Lady Dustin," he said in a low voice. "For that I should gut you right now, but because you bear the missives from our king, you shall be spared."

Christopher almost laughed. David, in fact, did, drawing the soldier's angry glare. The battle lines were already being drawn.

"What is your name?" Christopher demanded of the warrior.

"Sir Jeffrey Kessler," he replied. "I am captain of Lioncross while Lord Barringdon is away."

Arthur had made no mention of a captain but it was of no matter. Christopher would dismiss the man as soon as he wed the fair Lady Dustin and put David in charge of the men.

"Gain us entrance, Sir Jeffrey," Christopher requested, but it sounded suspiciously like an order.

Jeffrey's gaze lingered on Christopher before complying, just long enough to emphasize he could not be ordered around by a stranger. Christopher followed, somewhat hesitantly, wondering if he shouldn't bring a contingent of men to protect him against any trickery from the Germanic knight.

He kept his hand on the hilt of his sword just in case as he followed the man into the dark and musty keep beyond.

☙

DUSTIN STOOD IN her mother's drawing room, pacing endlessly by the oilcloth-covered windows. Lady Mary, unflappable as always, continued to calmly work on a piece of needlework, ignoring her daughter's sighs and grunts of worry.

"Why do not you change your dress, dear?" her mother said calmly. "We have visitors."

Dustin glanced down at her surcoat. It wasn't even really a surcoat, it was just a dress made from faded brown linen, and a darker brown girdle that would have emphasized the magnificence of her breasts had the white linen blouse not been so over-sized. Dustin never gave any thought to her clothes, mostly concerned with the other aspects of her busy life. As long as they were clean and functional, it was all that mattered.

"Why?" she asked, rather clueless.

Her mother put the sewing down. "Because you look like a peasant waif," she said patiently. "Look at your slippers – they are dirty, as are your hose. Please change into something more appropriate.

"Appropriate for what?" Dustin wanted to know. "Appropriate to hear of father's death?"

"Do not raise your voice, please," her mother said quietly. She was a pale woman with black hair hidden beneath a wimple. She'd never been particularly well and had spent the majority of her life reclining one way or the other. It was a great contrast to Dustin's vigor. "You shame your father dressed as you are. Please go and change."

Dustin grunted in frustration and turned to her mother to argue until she realized the woman's hands were shaking. Her heart sank with despair for her mother's feelings. She knew how much the woman had loved her father. She forgot her own feelings as she focused on what her mother was surely feeling.

"I am sorry, Mother," she said, forcing down her lofty pride as she went to kneel by her chair. "I did not mean it. The truth is that the knight never actually said father was dead. I really do not know why he is here."

Mary stroked her daughter's blond head. "I know," she smiled gently. "Now, please, go change your clothes. That would please me."

"Is there anything else I can do for you? Wine, perhaps?"

"Nay, my dear. Hurry along now and do as you are told."

With a reluctant nod, Dustin rose and moved for the door. She crossed the threshold and turned the corner only to run headlong into a broad, armored body.

It was a strong impact. Dustin shrieked, jumping back as if she'd been burned as her eyes flew up to face her accoster. The same sky-blue eyes that she had seen earlier smoldered back at her, now with something more than mere politeness. Now, there was something appraising there.

"My apologies," Christopher said.

Dustin nodded unsteadily as Jeffrey led Christopher into the drawing room, leaving Dustin standing in the corridor with her hand on her throat, wondering how a mere gaze could make her feel so vulnerable.

De Lohr's eyes were piercing and consuming, something she'd never experienced before. It was an odd sensation. Coming back to her senses, she rushed to her bedchamber to do her mother's bidding.

Ready or not, she wanted to hear what the man had to say.

Read the rest of **RISE OF THE DEFENDER** in eBook or in paperback.

ABOUT KATHRYN LE VEQUE

Medieval Just Got Real.

KATHRYN LE VEQUE is a USA TODAY Bestselling author, an Amazon All-Star author, and a #1 bestselling, award-winning, multi-published author in Medieval Historical Romance and Historical Fiction. She has been featured in the NEW YORK TIMES and on USA TODAY's HEA blog. In March 2015, Kathryn was the featured cover story for the March issue of InD'Tale Magazine, the premier Indie author magazine. She was also a quadruple nominee (a record!) for the prestigious RONE awards for 2015.

Kathryn's Medieval Romance novels have been called 'detailed', 'highly romantic', and 'character-rich'. She crafts great adventures of love, battles, passion, and romance in the High Middle Ages. More than that, she writes for both women AND men – an unusual crossover for a romance author – and Kathryn has many male readers who enjoy her stories because of the male perspective, the action, and the adventure.

On October 29, 2015, Amazon launched Kathryn's Kindle Worlds Fan Fiction site WORLD OF DE WOLFE PACK. Please visit Kindle Worlds for Kathryn Le Veque's World of de Wolfe Pack and find many action-packed adventures written by some of the top authors in their genre using Kathryn's characters from the de Wolfe Pack series. As Kindle World's FIRST Historical Romance fan fiction world, Kathryn Le Veque's World of de Wolfe Pack will contain all of the great story-telling you have come to expect.

Kathryn loves to hear from her readers. Please find Kathryn on Facebook at Kathryn Le Veque, Author, or join her on Twitter @kathrynleveque, and don't forget to visit her website at www. kathrynleveque.com.

Made in the USA
San Bernardino, CA
26 September 2016